6.98

H,NS

The
House of Fulfilment

Also by L. Adams Beck:

The Perfume of the Rainbow
Dreams and Delights
The Key of Dreams
The Ninth Vibration
The Splendor of Asia
The Treasure of Ho
The Way of Stars

The Library of Spiritual Adventure republishes classic novels of the quest for human growth, the evolution of consciousness, and the transformation of the spirit. Some of these works are well known; others have been previously neglected.

Other books in this series include:

Star Maker by Olaf Stapledon
Last and First Men by Olaf Stapledon
Jacob Atabet by Michael Murphy
Lady of the Lotus by William E. Barrett
The Philosopher's Stone by Colin Wilson

The House of Fulfilment

L. Adams Beck
(E. Barrington)

Foreword by Marion Zimmer Bradley

JEREMY P. TARCHER, INC.
Los Angeles

Library of Congress Cataloging in Publication Data

Beck, L. Adams (Lily Adams), d. 1931.
The house of fulfilment / by L. Adams Beck (E. Barrington); foreword by Marion Zimmer Bradley.
p. cm.
I. Title.
PS3503.E18H6 1989
813 '.52—dc20 89-5048
ISBN 0-87477-532-9 CIP

First published by Cosmopolitan Book Corporation 1927

Jeremy P. Tarcher, Inc.
9110 Sunset Blvd.
Los Angeles, CA 90069

Distributed by St. Martin's Press, New York

Manufactured in the United States of America
10 9 8 7 6 5 4 3 2 1

First Jeremy P. Tarcher Edition, 1989

THE supernormal happenings in this romance are true to and are founded upon the ancient Indian philosophy of the Upanishads. The sculptures I have been permitted to describe as those of Brynhild Ingmar are by Katherine Maltwood of London, a sculptor more deeply imbued with the spirit of Asia than any other known to me.

To her I dedicate this book.

Canada

L. Adams Beck
(E. Barrington)

Foreword

I first read *The House of Fulfilment* when I was eighteen years old. At that time I knew very little about what would afterward become a major interest, and a minor specialty within the general field of fantasy fiction wherein I was to find both vocation and avocation: the occult novel.

This kind of fiction has major overlaps with fantasy fiction, occasional science fiction (can anyone doubt that Olaf Stapledon's *Odd John*, dealing as it does with the ethics and probability of the superman, is a truly occult novel?), and even, occasionally, with horror fiction. Vivian Warner's *Sea Change*, which deals with a most unpleasant witch, and Whitley Streiber's *Cat Magic*, which contains, among other things, a most penetrating analysis of the country past death, were both marketed as horror fiction, as were all my own occult novels, most notably *The Inheritor*. Occult fiction, as distinguished from horror fiction (though there may be some overlap), has a series of events I once briefly characterized as follows: "Someone whose life is stalled or at loose ends encounters a practitioner of occultism, and his life is thereby greatly enriched." This falls within the general paradigm of fiction as "a worthwhile character tries to live and do well against the slings and arrows of outrageous fortune," which in generic or popular fiction is usually described as "a likable character fights almost overwhelming odds to win a worthwhile goal." There are exceptions, but in most major fiction, the exceptions are few and far between, and by and large the genre-fiction paradigm assumes overwhelming importance to most book marketers, not to speak of those who want to tell stories for a living. (As opposed, perhaps, to those who simply want to write and don't particularly care if they get published or not—which presupposes that they are either independently wealthy or somehow don't have to earn their living.) Leaving these lucky people out of the reckoning, most occult writers have a purpose that somehow goes beyond the desire of the ordinary writer to entertain; they have a purpose that can be called didactic, which is to say they wish to tell, or better, to show their fellow beings how to live and prosper.

I read L. Adams Beck's *The House of Fulfilment* when I first went to college, in the winter of 1948–1949. At that time I was a particularly immature teenager, eighteen in age, more like twelve or thirteen in maturity. Rereading it after a hiatus of forty years, I am astonished at how well it stands up. A good many of the books I was reading then are virtually forgotten; many of the best-sellers of that time have virtually disappeared. The major best-seller of that day, *Gone With the Wind*, now strikes the more enlightened reader as racist and unenlightened, to say the least; and who today reads *Anthony Adverse*? An even more deplorable fate has come to writers such as Kathleen Winsor, whose *Forever Amber* was a *succes de scandale* in its day, and now has vanished from all public libraries that try to stay current, though a few copies may be languishing in small-town libraries where people do not read very much and therefore never notice what's there and what isn't. Best-selling authors like Edgar Rice Burroughs have an even sadder fate; a few copies of *Tarzan* or *John Carter of Mars* may survive—in the children's section, while the fate of the enormously popular Sax Rohmer is limited to a few bad movies about Fu Manchu. Talbot Mundy, too, survives only in the boy's adventure section, and even Conan Doyle remains alive only in the hands of a few enthusiasts.

By and large the fate of occult writers is somewhat better; could it be because they have something to say? Madame Blavatsky's major works can always be obtained in specialty bookshops; and the novels of Dion Fortune have been continuously in print for more than fifty years—although they read, in the eighties, almost as quaintly as those of Mary Roberts Rinehart.

Still, those of us who read addictively each cherish the memory of the best books, and the most meaningful, of a lifetime's reading. I am convinced that this is why occult fiction survives, because when it was first published it changed someone's life, and that person cherished a tattered copy, a Christmas gift, or a library discard, and passed it on to his or her children and grandchildren. This is the only kind of bestsellerdom that is worth anything; and I say this as a writer of at least one best-seller that has reached its popularity, I am convinced, because the readers each bought copies for their sisters and their cousins and their aunts.

Outside the occult life-changing field, I do not think much of bestsellerdom. When someone asked me if I were proud to have my books on a best-seller list, I replied, "What's on the best-seller list most of the time? The latest diet book and the confessions of some movie star." Not, in short, very edifying or important writing; simply the lowest common denominator, on a level with the scandal-sheet tabloids sold at checkout counters in the supermarkets. It is of such books as these—and the endless soppy romances that provide soft-core pornography for dreaming housewives—which inspired some philosopher to say, "It is better to be able neither to read nor write than to be able to do nothing else." If one's reading stops at the *National Enquirer*, it begs the question of the value of literacy. These people supposedly can read street signs and fill out their tax forms, but one could hardly call them literate in the sense of improving their lives with books.

Ever since universal literacy became desirable, if only to enable people to fill out tax forms, there has been a more or less constant argument about novel reading on the lips of some people—often simply illiterate Bible-thumpers who dismiss all novels as "lies." These people are prone to say, "If it's in the Bible, it's unnecessary; if it isn't, we shouldn't read it anyhow." This, of course, is analogous to the fanatical Moslems who burned the world's great libraries on the grounds that the only book needed was the Koran, other books being either sinful—if they disagreed—or superfluous if they agreed.

A deeper view of the unsuitability of novel reading, especially for women, was found on the lips of various Victorian educators. By and large they went along with the questionable arguments of those who argued against the education of women on the grounds (I do *not* exaggerate) that studying and learning in "masculine" fields of endeavor would destroy a woman's fertility and value as a mother. Yet if reading Latin and texts on science would damage her mind, it was also felt that novel reading would impair her morality. (Reading some French novels, one can understand if not sympathize with this point of view. I tend to agree with Judge Augustus Woolsey, the High Chief Justice who refused to find Joyce's *Ulysses* immoral. "Emetic, perhaps; not aphrodisiac," he commented, agreeing that the book might produce nausea but no desire to emulate the dislikable characters therein. And standards of immorality change; the major book for "secret" reading when I was a child, *Lady Chatterley's Lover*, is now considered so inoffensive that it is required reading in college literature classes—which may do more than censorship to keep it out of the hands of the young. Norman Mailer, James Jones, and other writers have contributed to reveal the commonest obscenities to be repetitive and boring rather than shocking; and kindergarten children now use as common invective the names of perversions that I did not understand until my second marriage.

Does all this debase the coin of literary language? Probably. Not long ago, in Greeneville, Tennessee, a concerned mother wanted to ban the children's book *The Wizard of Oz* from required reading in school because it spoke of a "good witch" and depicted "courage, intelligence, and compassion as personally developed" rather than being gifts of the Christian God. One wonders what poor old Frank Baum, a Bible-reader and Sunday-school teacher, would have thought. This lady is not alone; no less a person than the author of *Alice in Wonderland*, Lewis Carroll, was pained by the children's performance of "H.M.S. Pinafore" and the "pure young lips" proclaiming "a big, big D" with "Damme, it's too bad."

This mother was quoted in our local paper as saying "Our children's imagination has to be curbed." As a writer of novels and of fantasy, as a mother, and even as a writer of some children's books, I take grave issue with this mother; for I have always felt that if anything proclaims us as God-stuff and differentiates us from the beast-kind, it has to be our imagination.

And this, in short—our imagination, and the fact that

we can conceive of something more than hard facts—is what keeps us all from the horrors of what some Fundamentalists like to call "Secular Humanism" and speak of as a danger to pious humanity.

Without the powers of imagination, how could we conceive of, or believe, any of the wonders that surround us? I dare say a child who cannot imagine a witch, or a unicorn, could not imagine an angel. He could believe in one—because he was told about it, as I believe in the Fiji islands or Australia. But to know about angels and their wonders demands God's greatest gift to man: the imagination. And, if you like, the imagination stimulated by fantasy—even fantasy fiction.

I will come right out and say it, then: Fantasy nourishes the imagination and thus is a necessary food for the mind.

Even psychology has come round on this point. When I was in school, psychologists were deploring fantasy and "magical thinking," but the wheel has come full circle on this; no less an authority on child-rearing than Bruno Bettelheim has come out in favor of fantasy and fairy tales for children as a way of distancing psychological concepts that he considers universal.

A world without fantasy is a bleak one. I dare say it is the use of fantasy that prevents such monsters as Ted Bundy from their strings of crime; a child who has imagination and empathy—nourished by good fiction—is not likely to grow up a psychopath. In fact we could say that the definition of criminal psychopathy is a lack of empathy—a lack of the imagination to see oneself in the other's place. The Charles Mansons, the Ted Bundys, the Ian Bradys of this world come from the ranks of those without empathy or imagination, those who cannot follow that simplest of rules, as valid for the Secular Humanist as for the Buddhist or Christian: Do unto others as you would that they should do to you. Every society contains some version of this in its precepts of behavior. But it cannot be taught without imagination—the ability to put oneself in the other fellow's shoes.

But above and beyond this highly self-serving reason why society should stimulate rather than suppress the imagination of the young—to save ourselves, perhaps, any more Ted Bundys and Charles Mansons—there is the knowledge that good fiction has always served a major social purpose: that of teaching us by precept and example *how to live*.

And so we come back again to Elizabeth Barrington/ L. Adams Beck's *The House of Fulfilment*.

Now the hero of this book—Hew Cardonald—is not, when we first meet him, a man anyone would choose to admire, far less to emulate. He has multiple faults, and in the light of what we now know about life, he is busy, or so we find out rather quickly, busy destroying his own health and self-esteem. He has a crime on his conscience, which after some time we learn to be that he has committed adultery with the wife of his best friend. This does not strike the modern feminist as a very serious sin; one must read books in the context of the society in which they were written, and in the society in which Ms. Barrington wrote her book, the world of Europe between the two world wars, it was a fairly serious social offense, if not a sin before God and man. It would, by the parameters of that society, seriously disrupt social relationships, not to mention destroying the social bonds between individuals by which we survive, as well as putting a severe strain on friendship. Hew Cardonald's major regret comes to be the way in which he destroyed the relationship with his friend.

I find it somewhat significant that the person who leads Hew to the first step toward his new life is the woman with whom he later seeks love. Buddhism has a rather bad reputation among those who seek fullness of life in the modern world because some of the narrower Buddhist groups speak of chastity, by which they seem to mean only total abstinence from sex, as the first requirement for following the Noble Eightfold Path. At least in the Western world, when it comes to the path of Brahmacharya (the path of the monk or nun), the total abstainer from sex, one could say that many are called but few are chosen; and I find one of the most reassuring things about this book for a widespread Western readership is that it does not come out and say that one must practice total chastity before all else. This—the concept of chastity before all else—has been a widespread stumbling block for Western seekers of Truth, and when they come up against any book that advocates this wholly unrealistic ideal, they drop off disgusted. I still remember with astonishment one of the Theosophical books of the late Max Heindel, which advocated that, even for married persons, "each person owns his or her body" and one was justified in denying even a marriage partner unless a child was desired by both, and that a rational healthy person should perhaps perform "the sex act" maybe three or four times in a lifetime. With this sort of advice, it is no wonder that such writers attract few disciples.

After his introduction to meditation—which is now known to be an effective discipline for simple mental development—our hero is introduced to a Buddhist lama and later to his Master, and from there he is led to a confrontation with his major source of guilt and self-contempt: the husband and friend he has betrayed.

The denouement of this novel, coming as it does after an exciting journey into the mountains of Tibet—a paradigm for the hero's own "unknown country" of self-discovery, makes this book uncommonly good reading, even on its surface as a good adventure novel. But it wears well. I have always said that a book a young person will "outgrow" is nine times out of ten a book on which he should not waste his time in the first place.

It was a distinct pleasure to read this again; it is not a book one can outgrow. Like many of my favorite books, I found something new in it when I reread it, even after forty years and God only knows how many books in between. I remember it as one of the first books I ever read of this kind; and it is just as good to read—both for enjoyment and for its deeper meaning—as it has ever been. One of the touchstones of genius is inexhaustibility. The music of J. S. Bach keeps its newness and freshness; every time I hear it I discover something new in it. Compare this with some cheap piece of "pop" music; by the time you learn it you are deathly sick of it and never want to hear it again.

At the very last I should say something about the claim of how this work was written. I do not take a claim that a given book was "channeled" too seriously. As a writer, I know that our best books sometimes flow directly from some place in our subconscious to which we have no conscious access; that the book exists in itself on some level to which the surface personality has only indirect access, and one does not so much *invent* the book as *listen* for it.

One need not imagine oneself a medium for that; but it isn't any crime either. About these claims, frankly, I am hardly qualified to speak. What remains is the book itself; and, on any level, it's a good one.

MARION ZIMMER BRADLEY
August 1989

The
House of Fulfilment

The House of Fulfilment

THE ROMANCE OF A SOUL

CHAPTER I

IT WAS IN THE MOST UNLIKELY PLACE IN THE WORLD that I heard of the Dunbars. When you were in Simla you might go to the Mainguys every day for a month and hear no other subject mentioned but the scandal of the place, which at Simla looms large, various and engrossing. Indeed the aggregated scandal of India—meaning of course all that concerns the governing race—rises like the smoke of an especially black and acrid nature to the Simla heights, and hangs thick in the pines on Jakko. It not infrequently gets into your throat and chokes you. But the Mainguys.

Their bungalow, perched on the steepest cliff that a house could cling to, teeth and claws, without sliding down the abyss into bottomless depths beneath, was where all the gup (gossip) centered. People sat in the veranda looking out level with a blue sky cloudless as ocean itself, over measureless leagues of country far away below, fading into phantasmal beauty where it mingled with the horizon edge, and there, drinking pegs and smoking myriad cigarettes, they hacked reputations to bits, devouring them with relish and flinging the mangled remnants down the gorge. A cannibal feast at best and seasoned with much sniggering and chuckling.

But one went there even if it bored one stiff, for really Mainguy and his wife were good fellows in their way, and had no prudish scruples either about the deeds or personalities of the victims they served up—rather liked them than otherwise for the run they gave them. And besides, those two had more knowledge of India in its byways, its short cuts and incidentally its prices than any other two in the Peninsula. So that if you were planning a trip, shikari or otherwise, anywhere from Cape Comorin to Kashmir, you went to the Garden of Allah (as they humorously called their diggings) and got enough knowledge to start a guide-book.

That was my errand on this particular day. I found Mrs. Mainguy on the veranda embowered in creepers thrusting magnificent orange trumpets like a blare of sound in at every crevice of the trellis. I don't know what it was but to this day when I smell a scent heavy as yellow honey and as sweet, a blaze of orange breaks and I see Blanche Mainguy attired in a violent trousered negligée of orange and purple, lying in her long chair, propped upon orange cushions to match, an iced "peg" in the receptive wicker hollow beside her, smoking cigarette after cigarette and sending a reputation to flutter down the gulf with each one.

That veranda was a difficult place for weak heads to stand. There was but a plank between you and perdition, so to speak, and the railing so rotten that a kick would have sent it flying in flinders down the abyss. But for the Mainguys, who had ridden six-inch paths in the Himalayas with a blank precipice up on the one hand and down on the other, it was nothing to hang poised in mid-heaven. They slept there in hot weather.

"And I walk in my sleep. Bad conscience and too many cigarettes, you know!" she said that day. "And some night Lyle will wake up and find me hovering on the railing, and then—"

"What? A push?"

"That depends on how I've been behaving. But listen, Car. You're talking about a painting trip up to the back of beyond in Little Tibet— Well, I've got the very person here to give you all the tips. She's having tea with her Excellency and—"

"She?" I ejaculated. "A woman? Never. Not where *I* want to go!"

She tossed the butt of her cigarette over a foam of orange trumpets, and I saw it eddy like a white butterfly down—down—down—and disappear.

"She knows more than that! My good man, have you never heard of the Dunbars? Lucia Dunbar? They go everywhere in Asia! Come now, you *must!*"

"Never, on my soul! And why on earth should I? And why do they go everywhere in Asia?"

"Well, considering that she and Lance Dunbar are rolling in riches, and could have everything the world offers and yet go off and live in a temple in China and a sort of log house up in the mountains in Kashmir, one would think you *might* know something about two such March hares!"

"And still I don't know!" I retorted. "You'd better

give me the points so that I can place her before she bursts upon me."

"Bursts! God pity the daft! She's the most gently flowing, harmonious thing in all the world, like the gray evening moths that float about these flowers. She's—"

"But *who* is she?" I almost shouted.

"Gowk! Did you never hear of Lord Rostellan—the last earl, a stony broke Irish peer with an unspeakable reputation with women? She was his only daughter, and her wicked old aunt Lady Polesden married her at eighteen to a man as bad as her father—Hubert Sellenger. She endured it for ten years and then divorced him. Her friends insisted. Come, you must have heard of him?"

Yes, I had heard of him. Most men had. I remembered very well how his wife had divorced him after indescribable miseries, and he had died and she had married—whom?

"Lance Dunbar. He came in for his cousin's money—that delightful other Lance Dunbar who wrote a book called 'Sundering Seas'—a queer highbrow thing I never could read. Anyhow he went west in the war, and the other Lance got his money and turned Buddhist—"

"Good Lord, why?" I interjected. To me it gave much the same impression as hearing he had turned Mormon. I hadn't the faintest notion of what was implied. Nor for the matter of that had she.

"Ask me another! How do I know! Anyhow he married Lucia Sellenger and they live in a Chinese temple and a log house in Kashmir."

"He in one and she in the other? Well, that's quite the fashionable modern marriage."

She went off in one of her shrill mirthless chuckles.

"Gosh, no! They're the pattern pair of the universe. She'd seen quite enough of that sort of thing with Rostellan and Sellenger to give her a violent liking for propriety. Their life in the wilds is the queerest romance you ever heard of—all magic and mystery and extraordinary natives and spooky people. But the loveliest house you ever saw, and she's like—a dream."

She didn't say this in the conventional way that calls a new hat, a new cocktail, a dream. Her voice dropped on the word as if she meant it. Then she chuckled again.

"Don't I just know— You're thinking, 'Isn't it absolutely creamy that a woman like that should be putting up with little Blanchie?' So it is—and I don't suppose she'd ever have absolutely rummaged creation for me, but she's a kind of cousin. Rostellan was my father's first cousin, and I used to stay there long ago. She's younger than I am. A little over thirty now. By the way, she's a cousin of her Ex's too. The Rostellans were related to everybody."

"Still, she sounds a little out of drawing in Simla," I said cautiously. "What's she here for?"

"To meet some Canadian girl that is going up with her to Kashmir. Now if you really are going up that way yourself, though I should have thought there was enough in India to keep you in water-colors for the rest of your life, why not—"

A soft movement in the drawing-room, and the gaudy striped palampores dividing it from the veranda parted. A woman stood between them, worthy of a better frame.

She was all in gray, wearing a long chain of gray moonstones, with faint blue and golden lights swimming in them. Her hair, turned back winglike from the pale oval of her face, was feathered with silver though she looked a young woman. This, with features clear-cut as a gem, gave her a most arresting air of distinction emphasized by a sensitive mouth and gray eyes in a deep shadowy setting of black lashes. Shadowy—that was the word that expressed her—twilight, dusk, quiet as a dream. She brought that atmosphere with her. It was a new note in the gonging of the red and blue palampores and Blanche Mainguy's orange cushions and vociferating costume of orange and violet trousers and coat.

"Come on, Lucia!" she shrilled. "Here's a case for first aid. This is Hew Cardonald—Lady Lucia Dunbar—and—oh, but do sit down and be chummy. He wants to get up somewhere beyond Ladakh into the mountains for shooting and painting. He's simply landscape-mad and has made a success already. I've told him you know every inch of the place. Now don't you? Doesn't Lance? Start away by calling him 'Car' as I do. Let's be friends."

Her voice—voices interest me—was twilight too, like the running of a very little stream in darkening woods. After Blanche Mainguy's it sounded like a low song and inspired inward delight that can never be spoken. She settled into a chair at the edge of the veranda, laying an arm on the railing, and immediately the mountains and azure distance of earth and sky became a noble background for her slender throat and finely poised head and the grace of her long folded limbs. It reminded me of a picture in the Uffizi Gallery—St. Catherine—she of Siena—dreaming on the red city wall with nothing above or around but deep measureless blue—the formless infinity of her vision. I had done some portraits in water-color and pastel, not wholly bad, and at that moment my whole being resolved itself into a wish to paint her after my own fashion—as I saw her. The very name of the portrait—for all my pictures had names that came with them—flashed on me. But I will tell that later.

Why dwell on these things? I want to get on to what matters—to where this extraordinary story really begins. But there are preliminaries not to be passed over.

She was kind and interested at once, offered me her husband's help, invited me to break the long trek at their house in the pine woods above the Sind River where the track goes up from Srinagar to the heart of Asia. Clearly and concisely she gave me the information I wanted, and turning to my art talked of the landscape work of the great Chinese and Japanese artists and of her collection until I forgot time and place in the fascination of the subject and her own. And Blanche Mainguy smoked and smoked, her vivid, ugly face twinkling into mischief as she saw me caught in the strong toil of graciousness which, to people more in the world than I, had been irresistible from the beginning.

"Lucia, you humbug!" she interposed with a grin. "When you know you hate shooting beasties as much as you love painting, and think every man a butcher that kills so much as a bird! Why are you helping him in his iniquities?"

She beamed into the bright tranquillity of a smile.

"People do what they must at the point where they stand. You know I never preach, Blanche. And I'm sure when Mr. Cardonald gets up among the mountains he'll give nothing else a thought."

She stopped, the smile deepening in her eyes—how shall I describe it?—like one holding back a secret of enchantment that must not be loosed lest misunderstanding should brush the butterfly's dust off its feathers. And I began to understand a little. After all, I am an artist first and the rest nowhere, and this woman had the key of the fields as well as I. If we could only get rid of Blanche Mainguy, who cared for none of these things! Providence was good to me.

A grave servant appeared between the palampores with all the dignified melancholy of the best Indian manners.

"My tailor!" And off went Blanche Mainguy to the conference. I wondered what on earth the man would think of Englishwomen when those trousers dazzled his view. Lady Lucia looked after her and caught my thought, laughing audibly.

"Do you know how kind she is? I wonder how many people do! I could tell you lovely things about her. But to return—Satshang is the place for you. The mountains and mountain valleys there are beyond all description, and in Ladakh the rainbow colors of the lower mountains are incredible. Nothing I have ever seen does them the least justice, and Alam Khan is the ruler. We were up camping there and saw a great deal of him, and afterwards when he fell ill he came down to our guest-house to be nursed."

This was heaven's own luck. I questioned eagerly.

"About twenty-eight, and you'll like him. He lives in the queerest old castle-fortress perched in mountains jagged like a lion's teeth. Pure romance. Our guest-house? Oh, we have two. One for Hindus. One for Mohammedans. All sorts of people come and go, and each guest-house has servants of its own faith. Europeans stay in the house with us. Yes. We have a little hospital too. I trained as a nurse, and I have a woman who helps. You can't think what a blessing it is among these people far away from all doctors. They come right down to us from all sorts of places. I think it will amuse you to see it."

I thought so too. There was something so new about the notion, the remoteness, and yet people of all nationalities coming and going—an unrivaled opportunity for seeing below the surface. The curse of Asia is that a European man travels, gets civility, sees the outside of the picture, and there is halted. "Thus far and no farther" is on every Asiatic face about you. Unless—yes, indeed, unless— Suppose one had this soft graciousness, this exquisiteness of manner, which would appeal to the inherent Asiatic law of stately behavior—why, then, one might get through the barred door and into wonderland. Fool I might be, and no one admitted it more cheerfully than myself, but I knew what I was—and that's not a bad step-off into the depths. To be sure that Asia is a sealed book is an excellent check to hasty opinions and definite conclusions. But I did not yet know that no man can paint Asia who does not know her soul as well as her face and love the two in one.

Every minute I watched her more keenly. She had a certain air of strangeness as of thoughts and goals very different from any I had met before.

I wanted to understand—they stirred the deep-down something in me which had always been more or less in the way of my work, something weary and discontented, touched it with a faint promise of some dim life stirring in roots that had never grown. Again I say the strangest thing in the world to meet at the Mainguys' house in Simla. So I listened but watched as she talked of the wild woods and rushing mountain rivers, talked like the very soul of them—a few words only, but to my mind perfect ones. Her cool sweetness embodied all that the mind of man has dreamed in sky-cold heights and forests—Dryads, Oreads; and I did not know why, for neither then nor at an infinitely wiser moment did I know that she was beautiful as men reckon beauty. But she was what beauty means—she had the same effect on the something below and beyond feeling. I can answer for that. One remembered, longed—but not for her.

In my heart I was desperately searching for courage to ask if I might paint her; but what found its way into speech was a banal supposition that she was in Simla for a change—to see life again. She shook her head laughing.

"Life! You little know the life we have at Baltar! We have every sort of change up there. I have come to meet a girl, Canadian, but of Danish birth. Her name is Ingmar. She is coming in along the Simla-Tibet Road from somewhere near the Shipki Pass."

"A nurse?" I ventured.

"Oh, no! She has been studying"—she stopped as if she had been about to say more than was allowed, and went on smoothly—"studying with some people near the Tashigong Mònastery. She arrives tomorrow."

Again I fail in description, but everything she said was like moonlight hovering on a dark forest. Even the deep clanging name of the monastery suggested the mysteries within; let us say—lovely, grotesque, terrible creatures moving in the dark with eyes intent on things we can never know. It enthralled me—secret as a nest of nightingales, a hidden song.

I summoned up a gleam of courage and ventured a step further.

"Lady Lucia, you interest me enormously. May I ask *what* you are working at, at Baltar?"

She looked at me with perfect simplicity.

"For one thing we work at the science of mental concentration. Did you happen to read Keyserling's 'Travel Diary of a Philosopher'? No? It was really interesting. Well, he was very much struck with the mastery of concentration in India and said it should be taught in all the schools of the West. It has wonderful consequences. It—"

Suddenly I had a sense of repulsion as from something pretentious and insincere. Not in her, Heaven knows. Not the most egregious ass could look into those limpid eyes and doubt. Her expression was transparent—clear unwavering truth itself. But one knows the jungles of charlatanry that attend the modern occult, and she might be a dupe and the young Canadian a fraud. I saw her in her beautiful house at Baltar the prey of greedy charlatans hastening from East and West to make their market of the rich gullible woman. Suddenly she smiled, answering my doubt. Did she know—could she?

"No—it really is not that kind of thing at all. Come and see. You'll like it."

A hurried entry, Blanche Mainguy, red with anger.

"That brute—that Wali Mohammed! He's cut my green and gold satin so tight that I can't sit down. Could you think men would be such fools? Lucia, if you sit there looking so calm, I shall scrag you. I smacked him hard in the face! And serve him right!"

There was no smile then; she spoke as eagerly as a hurt child.

"Blanche, you *shouldn't!* His people live near us and they are delightful. You would love them. The father brought me a brick of Tibetan tea the other day —and his mother is the loveliest old woman. A great Chinese painter who is with us is painting her. Oh, Blanche!"

I can see her grieved eyes now, but can never describe the oddity of the incident. She made the people human at once, brimming with interest and attraction, and Mrs. Mainguy atrocious but instantly disarmed. The worst of European life in India—in Asia—is that it reduces native life to a cipher—a mere background, let us say. Now it became terrible that Blanche Mainguy should have smacked the man in the face. Rather an incredible sort of happening. She felt it herself, and groaned with despairing rage.

"Lucia, you're a damned nuisance. If you get all Asia on our conscience like that, life will be a pest. What's one to do with all the fools and worse about us? And just now when they don't respect us a bit as they did and would be at our throats if they dared! Lyle says we *have* to assert ourselves."

"They're perfectly charming to me—one and all—the most beautiful manners in the world. Never mind, Blanche dear. If it's spoiled I have a wonderful pheran of Bokhariot silk, deep-sea blue and colors playing on it like a peacock's breast. You shall have that. It came over the passes a few months ago from one of the little chiefs beyond Leh."

"You goose! One can't help loving you, and yet you're the greatest idiot in the universe, and all these natives play upon you like—I don't know what."

She threw her arms about her cousin and gave her a resounding kiss—Lady Lucia like a sweet child half laughing, half startled in the rough embrace.

"They know I love them!" she said when she could speak.

I got up to go—ashamed to find how long I had stayed.

"Brynhild Ingmar and I leave the day after tomorrow," she said. "And we shall be so glad if you will come to Baltar. No need to write beforehand. There's always room and I promise that you'll find wonderful things to paint."

I remember Blanche Mainguy escorted me to the door. "Isn't she a dear? There never was anyone who didn't adore her. But I always think anyone could take her in, and I have it in my bones that this Ingmar woman is coming to fatten on them. I never like these foreign adventurers."

To Blanche Mainguy Canada and India were alike foreign. Indeed you must be English—and a Londoner, for choice—to be recognized as human. I laughed, and went slowly along the steep road pondering. That visit had given me much to think of. It had made things easier for my plans—yes. But it had also been something entirely fresh, had touched dusty unused chords which at present gave out a confused jangle of uncomfortable sound—opened a glimpse into worlds not realized. It was quite clear that I must see more of the Dunbars. Men said he was a good fellow, never thrust his queer views upon you, and if I had not been afraid of being a little at sea in such unusual company I should have felt nothing but pleasure in the encounter. Well—they could not freeze me to the bone if I only stayed a week or so, and the whole thing would be a queer experience.

I dined that night at the Viceregal Lodge, and she was there also. It was a great occasion—a royal visitor and so forth—and Lady Lucia wore her diamonds, her hair in a Greek knot bound with a starry fillet. Her profile against a gold brocade curtain was so exquisite that hiding in shadow I made a note on my shirt-cuff and prayed for memory when I got back. She looked a being of another race among the crowd of pretty bobbed, shingled, marceled women, and a line of poetry came and went in my head as I watched unweariedly: "She moved a goddess and she smiled a queen." Yet with it all, the simplest and happiest of anyone there.

She had known the prince in London, which was perhaps why he divided his attentions between her and his hostess. But I thought his taste excellent. Graciously at home with Royal Highnesses she was equally at home with their Excellencies' governess, who slipped timidly into the ballroom afterwards with the pretty flapper of the house—a golden-haired Lady Lettice. I was quick to notice that she dispatched a would-be partner of her own to dance with Miss Lyon, and it set me on dancing with the girl myself and leading the talk in the direction that interested me most. I had my reward.

"Lady Lucia Dunbar? Oh, no one in the world like her. She had me up at Baltar and nursed me when I was down and out with malaria—nursed me herself. But not a dull kind of a saint—no, not a bit. A great lady all the time. She can freeze the wrong kind of people stiff—you should see her!—but as simple, as natural— Isn't she lovely? And yet I suppose not a bit beautiful—except her hair and eyes. Asked you there, has she? Then I advise you to go. You'll see things—hear things— No, I won't attempt to describe it. It changed my life. The most beautiful place. Her Ex. loves Lady Lucia but she doesn't quite understand her. I don't know who does."

She did not dance yet was the center of a laughing group nearly all the time. I might have thought her one of them, if I had known no more, but that once a young Indian prince came up to her, and they moved together to one of the wide flower-filled windows, and stood talking for a few moments. He raised his hand and pointed to the far-away hills, and her eyes followed with an expression—how can I define it?—a homing dove near the end of a long journey—the content of absolute certainty. They understood each other, and his face, darkly beautiful, for a moment reflected her expression. They were in the same vibration; I, outside. If it be said I watched her all the evening, I admit the truth. I did.

CHAPTER II

TWO DAYS AFTERWARDS I MET BLANCHE MAINGUY and her husband riding in Annandale and, seeing talk in her eye, I dismounted under the deodars. She was a beautiful horsewoman and looked very much better in coat and breeches than in her appalling lounging kit. Her vivacious ugliness was really attractive under the shifting lights and shades of those glorious trees. Mainguy and his horse were one also. . . . They looked a steady-going English pair in those surroundings.

"And when are *you* off?" she hailed me. "And where?"

"Tomorrow. Kashmir."

"To the Dunbars?"

"Of course. Didn't you settle it yourself?"

She made a grimace. "Didn't I warn you? Don't I warn you now? Lucia Dunbar and her *entourage* —not to mention Lance—get hold of people in the most amazing way. Nobody's the same after they've known them. They cease to be good fellows and become—"

She halted for the right word, and I suggested, "Prigs." She meditated.

"Not exactly. Worse—and better! I'll diagnose more clearly when I see you after you've undergone the process. I only hope they don't get hold of the prince. I heard him saying he would dearly like to run up to Baltar. It gave me the creeps. Imagine if he returned a yogi!"

Mainguy burst into one of his sudden guffaws, making his horse start and sidle. "He might! That woman can do anything with anybody. Did you ever see the pretty Canadian, Cardonald?"

Mrs. Mainguy sniffed. "Pretty indeed! *That's* not the word. She's like a cold-storage marble bust of a young Greek empress."

"They hadn't empresses!" Mainguy interjected.

"Never mind. That's what she looks like. They lunched with us before starting, and then we all went up to Observatory Hill to say good-by to her Ex. I give you my word Miss Ingmar never uttered a word all the time except to refuse the cutlets. I said to Lucia, 'My goodness, you *have* got hold of a lemon this time! Don't ask me to Baltar while that young lady's around!' "

"Did she agree with you?" I asked curiously.

"She laughed and asked me to come up in the summer. She never says anything but just what she pleases, and does the same. If she wants you to marry the Canadian you'll do it as sure as you stand there."

It was my turn to laugh then. I knew too much of life to contemplate marriage with any interest, and except in the anatomical sense was conscious of a vacuum where the heart should be. A man whose nearest relations are a bunch of cousins and not attractive ones at that hasn't had the right drill for heart development. I told her so and she nodded with a grimace.

"That's all right! People all say the same sort of thing, but it invariably ends in the same way—they do what Lucia wants. I tell you there's something uncanny up at Baltar. That's all right too, but it would have been better for you if you'd been inoculated at eighteen. Dine with us before you go? So sorry! Well, at all events write and tell us what you think."

I promised vaguely and stood watching while they cantered off laughing and talking loudly. My next visitors beneath the deodars were their Excellencies, riding alone and enjoying the cool sunshine, shading into deep green light like sea water under the innermost boughs. They also pulled up, and their talk also was of Baltar. It seemed to me that all the world was thinking of Lucia Dunbar, and naturally the talk would be as different as the talkers. Her Excellency, fair, wholesome, a little unimaginative, but "good bread" all through as the French say, had a different angle from Blanche Mainguy's.

"Happy person! So you are going to Baltar! I want to go of all things. Colonel Hutchinson was there the other day and he says it is the most extraordinary thing he ever saw in his life. The most wonderful quiet."

"Considering who is the guiding spirit that's scarcely surprising," his Excellency put in. "I have known Lady Lucia since she was two and—well, she doesn't grow on every bush. Do you go on up into Little Tibet afterwards?"

I told him yes, and that I had a permit for the Hunza country, and we talked awhile of that and other things; and then they too went off, she leaning down and saying earnestly, "My love to her. My dear love," as the horses put on speed.

Well, these are the preliminaries! My story really begins when after reaching the Happy Valley of Kashmir and to my mind the loveliest spot of the world, surrounded by its snow peaks, I began camping up from Gunderbal at the mouth of the Sind Valley. One talks of valleys there, but the Happy Valley itself is over five thousand feet above sea-level, and the mountain valleys with their tumbling rivers are a climb into the higher heights through pine woods to the lonely and sparkling snows.

I had hired the usual ponies and their men, and my personal servants led the van with me; and so, in due patriarchal order, we went up by the river, camping the first night at Kangan and beyond that in two marches to Gund and Gagangair. There next day we left the Sind route for Baltar.

It is scarcely possible to describe that four days' march, the stedfast beauty of pines climbing the heights to the stars, the exultant joy of rushing rivers. An extraordinary exhilaration swept over me as we mounted higher and higher and the clean strong air filled my lungs like some strange wine of the gods. At higher heights it overpowers poor humanity and leaves it sick and stunned. Here it was divine, shot through with golden sunshine and flavored with the pure aroma of pines in their ranked marching myriads. Through every glade was a glimpse of awful peaks guarding a mystery wonderful beyond even their own wonders. And still we climbed, gradually but surely, beside the river rushing from the cold heart of a far-away glacier.

The track was lonely but not solitary. We met a few loaded ponies with black-browed traders beside them, men who know the dangerous heart of Central Asia and the hard secret ways that lead to and fro, men to whom all life is danger and adventure, who scorn the life of ease and look to meet their last hour in some brawl in a wayside caravanserai or in the vast solitudes of the eternal snow.

They shot their keen black gaze at me as I passed, gaging the English sahib to a hair and wondering if money was to be made out of the Feringhi. Many of such men I came to know afterwards and liked them well—excellent company, hardy, good-tempered fellows, and if a little unscrupulous, better the direct thrust you are prepared for than the sly honey-tipped dart of civilized exploitation.

And then there were the pilgrims, holy men making their way to the ruined temple of Shiva placed on a crag above the river. It was out of my way to Baltar, but I would not miss it, and we followed the narrow way through pines and rocks and great slumbrous ferns until we came to a crag above the thundering river, madly plunging for freedom among the rocks. There, set in deep glades of trees, was one of the most beautiful things I have ever seen in my life or shall see, a temple, relic of the great old days of Kashmir when mighty kings ruled her and scholars traveled from China and India that they might kneel at her feet and implore the crumbs of her unearthly wisdom.

In every crevice and niche of broken stone irises and ferns had rooted, and the blue of the iris was better than jewels. It was as though the long dream, water-lulled, of ancient stones had broken forth into loveliness of blossom. I looked through the ancient doorway into a sunk quadrangle with carved niches about it, where once devotees had sat tranced in meditation, looking down into the water at their feet, and marveled once more at the hidden beauties of this divine world.

While I sketched it the man at my elbow told me it had first been a temple to the wise and half-divine Snake-people of legend, who dwelt in Kashmir and loved to mirror their beauty in calm water; and when the day of their worship passed it became sacred to the Great God who meditates upon the starriest heights of the mountains with the crescent moon for a jewel in his hair. And now it has fallen into ruin and no priest does service at the broken lingam of the little shrine, though still the faithful pilgrims come to mutter prayers and finger rosaries and pour libations from a small stream that sings through the quadrangle before it slips into the thundering glee of the river below.

I turned reluctantly away. It seemed to me that nothing at Baltar could be so lovely, and I would willingly have camped there for days in the sun-shot shade. But we went on steadily, doing about twelve miles daily, and after four days the woods grew denser and the river louder and the way among moss-grown fern-plumed rocks narrower. The ponies had to be checked and encouraged with many shouts of *"Khabar dar"*—"Take care!"—to look to their footing with wary instinct, and Faz-ul-din striding beside my pony said with emphasis:

"We now draw near to the residence of Dumba Sahib, the great English lord who beautifies the mountains with his countenance. And since the Presence is his friend I desire to remit the customary present which is made in addition to the contracted charge for ponies and men."

Here I own myself to have been almost too staggered for utterance. Not for nothing had a relation of my own, impelled into poetry by extortion, proclaimed:

> "If you gave a Kashmiri both heaven and hell,
> He would ask for another five annas as well."

And this renunciation was the strongest tribute to the Dunbars which had yet assailed my senses. I received it in silence, uncertain how to meet it.

My first impression was quiet and deep green shade, and the sound of running waters which intensifies quiet itself—the heart of a great forest diversified into glades where flitting shadows of wild creatures might pass at their ease. High up the side of a mighty hill—a mountain in lesser lands—was a glorious spring pouring down in cascades half hidden in maidenhair, and this, known as the Peri's or Fairy's Spring, they told me fed the house with water and electricity. One drinks wild water with caution in India, but there was no need for caution here. It broke pure as crystal from the strong heart of the hills.

And the deodars with tilted boughs upon which woodland spirits might lie and swing were magnificent in height and sweep, and where the glades opened were tall rhododendrons mingling masses of fiery blossom with the velvet background of the deodars—and below them beds of golden and white violets embedded in moss and fern—the small things as lovely as the great.

My God, what beauty; what a home! I thought, and how far from "roaring London, raving Paris," and how blessed in its remoteness! Would one ever weary of it?

"Down that way is a little village of people all in the service of the great sahib, and the water is piped to their houses as to his own so that there shall be no sickness, and the children here grow up straight and tall like the children of the sahibs." So spoke Faz-ul-din, willing to overwhelm me with marvels, but I, rapt on the unknown, returned no answer.

The forest was opening its arms and beyond soared the awful peak of one of the mightiest mountains of the Himalayan range—not golden nor white, but some miraculous blending of both into a color unnamable and glorious. It stood alone—a divine presence between earth and heaven, dominating all the world about it or rather gathering it up as an offering to something far and high, to be felt but never spoken.

And now we were slightly descending the rocky path, and the river which we had almost lost in the wild woods was nearing again, and before me I saw half hidden in deodar and rhododendron an immensely long house built of hewn logs, brown-roofed, widely windowed, with a great rustic portico, and a garden that opened my eyes wide with delight and astonishment—lawns, smooth as green velvet, and flowers I had never seen grouping with those that spoke of home in happy companionship. To right and left, farther back among the trees were two more houses of the same build, but a little smaller, and high up on the vast hillside a fourth house, long, brown-roofed, with what I should have guessed was a detached chapel on ground a little higher.

"That great long palace-house is the house of the sahibs!" said Faz-ul-din with showman's pride, pointing a grimy finger. "Within are rugs and noble chairs and divans worthy of the Maharaja of Kashmir himself. Have not these eyes seen it? And beds formed of rare woods and brass and other shining metals. And lights are furnished by the river even as in the city of Srinagar, and it is said—but this may or may not be truth—that even the cooking is done by the river's light, which if it be so is a marvel of the jinn. To the right is a house equally splendid for those guests of Dumba Sahib who are followers of the Prophet and the true faith. To the left is a noble house for Hindu guests to whom the eating of the cow is abomination—a craze which is not to be understood. But it is a thing to be remarked that here no meat is given for food, yet no person can desire slain meats, so glorious is the table spread for all. And I speak from knowledge for the sahib has provided a caravanserai for me and my ponies and those like me, and here we rest for the night as his guests and receive noble treatment and such food as is served to true believers in Paradise, and the very ponies have a stable worthy of king's horses and their food is princely."

He had halted me that I might have the full benefit of this oration and it flowed like the river itself from his lips.

"Truly the law of guest-right is in this man's open hand!" I said gravely, and indeed needed to feign no astonishment, so wonderful was the picture, so amazing the setting. Men were passing to and fro between the houses on various errands, in white with scarlet *cummerbunds* after the manner of Indian servants; but here and there was a stranger sight—two or three men bare-headed, shaven, with robes of a dull yellow. One, unmistakably a Chinese, stood not far off, watching my arrival with interest; another, as evidently English, was coming up from the river, book in hand; a third—but why continue? It was an astonishing place—the threshold of a new world.

Faz-ul-din resumed his discourse.

"And here, when the ponies have delivered the honorable baggage to the servants of the house, I desire permission of the sahib to depart to the caravanserai, hoping that he will sign this chit attesting my good behavior in men and ponies on the road."

I rode slowly along the approach to the great portico of rough-hewn logs with the bark left on—a palace for Pan, and with what unknown recesses within!

A tall, fair-haired Englishman with two delightful Scotch terriers at his heels came forward; he was light and strongly built, with the air of woods and large spaces upon him, and a quick sensitive way with him that won me. He wore coat and breeches of the rough Kashmiri puttoo which seems as much a part of the surroundings as heather on a Scotch moor, and looked to the manner born—even in the clear ring of his voice.

"Welcome to Baltar. You're Cardonald, aren't you? My wife and Miss Ingmar rode up the valley and haven't got back yet. No—don't bother—the men will see to your stuff. Yes—you want to settle with Faz-ul-din? He's a very decent fellow."

I settled with Faz-ul-din, and as I hope to be believed he refused any sort of tip; stoutly, steadily refused it. He accepted, on pressure, a box of cigarettes, but immediately tendered a pouch of leather ornamented with brass, a tinder-box with flint and steel which he had had from a Yarkhandi trader above the pass. I had to take it and so with salaams we parted, and the train of ponies wound off among the trees.

"But how can I get hold of him again when I start? Is it worth while for a few days—"

The other man laughed.

"We can always get him by wire to Gunderbal. I have my own line. But as to a few days—everyone who comes here stays just as long as he is inclined to give us the pleasure of his company. We are in wonderful country here, wonderful in many ways, and most people find something to interest them. Do feel at home. Will you come in now, or stroll about and see the place?"

I elected for the stroll and lighted up, and we went slowly about the lawns, and by the stream that not only watered the garden but filled it with woodland singing. We approached the little cascade where the Chinese I had noticed before stood in a position of silent abstraction by a cascade falling from a beautiful rock in threads of silver among the maidenhair. He looked up smiling as we drew near, and Dunbar made the introduction.

"Shan-tao, this is my friend Mr. Cardonald. He also is a painter and hopes to do some work here. I'm sure you will allow him to see some of your landscapes."

To my amazement the reply after a deep Chinese

salute was in good enough English with little more than a foreign inflection.

"That will be honor for me. I am most glad. I hope also to see."

It was promised and we passed on.

"But why, who, what?" I demanded in bewilderment. "What on earth is a Chinese doing here, and an English-speaking one at that! And why the yellow robe?"

"Didn't you hear at Simla?" Dunbar said good-humoredly. "No—you probably wouldn't. There's a monastery in China, some days' journey north of Peking, and I do a lot of work for them at old manuscripts, translating and editing them with the more learned monks. They come out into the world to spread the teachings of pure Buddhism and are men of different races, but all English-speaking, because English goes further in Asia than other foreign tongues. Well—we are at work on some wonderful manuscripts now which have been buried for over sixteen hundred years in a Chinese monastery in the mountains, and Shan-tao is here for that reason, and another monk named Haridas whom I think you will like. But there are others as well, all of the same community. We have made a rest house for them, and they come here when they crock up or need rest. We have two Burmese there now, and one from Ceylon, and a Tibetan lama—and that last is interesting for a reason I'll tell you later."

But it was all interesting—so much so that I scarcely knew on what to focus my thoughts.

"And are they all Buddhists?"

"All. But don't be frightened. They won't force it

on you, and they're all men who have seen a good deal of the world, and a queer world. I believe it will interest you."

I reflected. "I say—I do hope you won't think it rude, but the Mainguys said at Simla that you were a Buddhist yourself. Is it true?"

"Quite true. Several of us are, but don't bother your head about that. What does it matter? We have about ten different brands of religion here, and for all I know you may add an eleventh. But all the same we are quite like other people."

If there was one thing of which I was convinced it was that the Dunbars were extremely unlike other people, but it was not the moment to press the point; and we wandered on from one beauty to another stopping at last by the glade commanding the mighty presence of the mountain solemnly fronting the sunset.

It was an entranced silence—the ecstasy of a blessed spirit in serenest heights of exaltation. Gold flushed slowly into a diviner rose as if from the glow of an enkindling spirit within. It deepened sublimely into an adoration of surging hues that made the mountain one with the skies swimming in splendors about the peak —chorded colors, unutterable in any words and inspiring belief in hues incredible until the eyes open on eternity. How long we stood I did not know. Beside us was the Chinese monk with an Indian beside him, caught up into the same ecstasy.

So, uplifted into the glory of the heavens, seeing things not lawful because impossible to be uttered, we stood and watched it fade slowly into the gray mystery of twilight and the past; and when a young crescent moon hung like a faint lamp in the pines, we turned slowly toward the beautiful dim house, lighted now like a magic lantern with strange shadowgrams of human life reflected on the blinds.

The two brothers were slowly ascending the hill to their dwelling, shadows among the trees.

"My wife must have come back long since. Let us go in," said Dunbar, quickening his steps, and for a moment I envied the man who owned so much, round whom so many interests clustered and crowded.

I said as much and he smiled with kindly eyes.

"And you an artist? If I had your gift I should ask no more of earth or heaven. It includes both."

We returned as no strangers. That communion with beauty had built a bridge between us, and thought went to and fro in happy certainty of welcome.

CHAPTER III

I WENT UP TO MY ROOM STRANGELY PERTURBED AND tranquillized, and stood looking about me. A beautiful room, paneled with Himalayan cedar carved in a frieze, low-beamed, long and the very heart of home with ruddy firelight sending jewel-lights and shades about it. A room of quiet and simplicity though before the eastern window the pomps of dawn would be glorious on the mountains, and the southern ones gave on the garden and the stedfast beauty of marching battalions of pine forest. I filled my lungs with their strange pure odor to which the garden is as sensualism to asceticism. Yes, I was glad I had come, for a new world lay before me both in the outer and innermost; and which would capture me how could I guess?

So, going down the broad, shallow staircase, I found Dunbar alone in the beautiful hall with a solitary lamp and firelight flooding the low ceiling and distant corners. A London paper was in his hand—one from New York on the little table beside him. He rose to meet me.

"One reads and marvels. How that city civilization gets men and breaks them into bits until they are content to be a mere mosaic, flat and lifeless—atoms in a pattern and an ugly one. But they call it life and are content."

"It's a good life enough for the average man who has no resources in himself," I said. "After all very few men *have* any resources in themselves, and what is there but the passing show to keep up their spirits? They would go mad amongst all this solitary listening beauty up here. No, we have left all this a long way behind us."

"Listening beauty. That's the right phrase," he said, looking at me with more interest. "Yes—Nature in an ecstasy, too engrossed to take any notice of us, unless indeed—"

He halted for there was a sound of voices nearing the landing above, whence the wide, shallow stairs ran down into the hall, and presently two women appeared hand in hand. Dunbar pressed a button and soft lights sprang up revealing them. A woman coming down such a stair can hardly fail of grace, and I thought the picture worthy of the setting about it.

I have described the one. Lady Lucia glimmered in gray like a twilight moth, pale and large-eyed in firelight and shadow; but as I looked up my eyes fixed on her companion.

Shall I describe Brynhild Ingmar? I must, for she is the soul of my story, and if the soul makes the body as I have learned, the hieroglyphic is worth study though that knowledge is slow in coming and the gradations may sometimes be startling. I own it astonishes me to compare my first reading with the later.

She appeared to be a handsome modern girl of the boy type, long-limbed, slight and lissom. Her hair which I thought must have been magnificent in growth was cut short and lay in massive waves like bronze about her low, wide brow and water-gray eyes. The features were clear and composed. One could not imagine that she would ever fear anything, with such assurance did she move. Assurance, let me say, is a very different quality from self-assertion, and as a matter of fact she walked with the careless grace and strength of a goddess who wastes no thought on the outward because the innermost is a citadel inviolate. I remember I thought at once she was no subject for my art. She demanded the sculptor and one in the grand manner, capable of indicating repose and strength in their confident prime.

We were introduced and she smiled, remote but kindly, with a touch of that modern air which scrutinizes but guards its own entries. Thinking Lady Lucia by far the more interesting and sympathetic—a woman to welcome all the world home—I felt a subtle thrill of pleasure as I slipped into the chair beside her and felt the gentle warmth of her presence.

"Miss Ingmar and I have been making plans for your getting a foretaste of the mountains before you go up and on to Satshang. That is all so tremendous that it's better to begin on a lower level—the foot-hills. So we think you may want to do some painting here first."

"Yes, landscape, but you have other noble subjects—that Chinese monk today! If I could do a portrait of him against the pines—just that! But portraits!—I have never satisfied myself yet."

We were called to dinner, and still the talk went on in the brown room glimmering here and there with gold, curtained with copper-orange and green dragon brocade from China. Brynhild and Dunbar were speaking of the extraordinary endurance and sagacity of the mountain ponies. I caught a word here and there through Lady Lucia's talk of my work, her gray eyes shining with as much interest as if it really could matter a straw to her. I said something to that effect, touched by her kindness.

"But it *does* matter!" she protested with gentle surprise. "Every attempt is a word of the language that will be universal when we begin to understand things as they are. And Blanche Mainguy told me she had seen beautiful work of yours. She spoke of a silver birch in snow—"

"She!" I said, stupefied. "Do forgive me—but I should never have dreamed that Mrs. Mainguy was a woman who would understand anything of that sort. I never heard her say a word, and surely—"

She laughed, more with eyes than lips.

"Ah, you're thinking of the palampores and the smoking-suit? I scarcely blame you. But, believe me, Blanche takes a very great deal of knowing. The oddest creature! Do you recognize her in this story? When we were in Switzerland—girls together—she went out for a climb alone one day from a mountain village and found a child of about eight who had slipped down into an awful place on the edge of a frightful precipice. My head swam giddily when I stood at a safe distance from it next day. She went straight down and rescued the child. Her own story to me was this: 'And when I got the little devil up I gave it the soundest hiding it had ever had in its life until it simply *roared*. The mother came running up furious and nearly knocked me down, and I told her she was a damned brute and we were barging each other like mad when the rest of the village arrived and brought me back in a chair for I found something had gone wrong with my ribs, probably from laying in on the child.' "

"Yes—I can believe that. I am sure she has endless courage; and don't you remember Wali Mohammed and how she corrected the misfit?"

"Ah, but hear the end! Of course she had injured herself crawling up with the child. We were in that village six weeks and the mother grew to adore her. She came back to England and was her maid until she died, and the child is in her house now."

I reflected. No—that was not my Blanche Mainguy. That had a touch of beauty and I had seen no beauty in her—a jarring, noisy self-conscious woman with a relish for gossip. I think that was about the first instant in my life when I felt a conclusion of my own totter under me. Suppose one has to own one does not see true in the world one lives in—what then? A guide?

She read my silence.

"People are very different with different people, and I own I don't like her Simla set. Taken apart each is attractive in his own way—but together! Haven't you noticed that a circle or set has a sort of composite spirit of its own?"

Again I reflected. Yes, I had often adjusted myself to that circle on the perilous veranda, as noisy a fool as the best of them. But I knew the relief of coming out under low stars into the breathless purity of night even when sodden with smoke and cocktails. Did they? Or did I soar superior? I had the usual belief in my unlikeness to others.

But the subject died into a general talk of the country and people and left me with the germ of an idea—no more. When I decently could I watched the girl and wondered about her tranquillity and poise, reminding me of a bird balancing on a wind, engrossed in watching and without a thought for its own action. I had never believed it possible for a woman to be washed clean of self-consciousness, yet these two beside me had no trace of that subtle flattery in women which preens and burnishes itself for the delight of man. They went their own way companionably and gave what you could take.

I know well my account of that first evening at Baltar is fragmentary and disjointed. My mind was the same. Something in the atmosphere stimulated and irritated. I felt myself an outsider among people who had aims I could not understand and of which from the inbred courtesy that concedes and is silent they would not speak. Something in my mind would have implored, "Tell me!" if it had dared, but it was resentfully silent, and the talk was only what one expects from charming well-bred people who have seen pretty well all there is to see of the world and use it as a colored background on which to embroider all of themselves that they can spare to their guests. But this was not what I had hoped from Baltar—not only from the light drift of comment at Simla, but from Lady Lucia's own eager sweetness—a queer phrase but it expresses her.

Then into our midst dropped the unusual—that, also, irritating at first, because so strange.

I asked Dunbar a question about his literary work.

"It's interesting just now," he said. "Some months ago in an ancient monastery near Hankow one of the brothers of the Kan-lu-ssu Monastery for which I work found a most wonderful and unhoped for treasure. Have you ever heard of a Chinese monk in our year 629 whose name was Hiuen Tsang? He made a tremendous pilgrimage from Chang'an to India through the great desert and mountains where 'he advanced guided by the bones that marked the way,' and came down into India by Kashmir. Well, he stayed in India some twenty years and returned with priceless manuscripts and images to write an account of his stay there, and a wonderful account it is. However, I fancy it made most people wish for more, for it is very incomplete in parts, and now we have found the more and are at work doing it in English. Would you like to see the manuscript? It is in our guest-house for the monks just up the hill."

Would I? I fancy there are few that would not thrill at the thought of a treasure so recovered, with the dust of centuries upon it. I said so and asked if it were a dry monkish chronicle or something more human. He meditated for a moment.

"I should describe it as an astonishing religious fairy-tale, brimming with color and romance. The man was a poet as a Chinese gentleman of the time was bound to be, and a writer of great imagination, so you may imagine we are a bit exalted about the find. It will give an unsurpassed picture of long-ago India that will delight people who care nothing for the religious side of the adventure, though that is fascinating too. India at that time held the Holy Grail of Buddhism for China, and the Chinese monks were always pouring out on the terrible adventure. But I must not bore you. Though there is a point connected with it which might interest you because it has to do with Satshang, where you are aiming."

"Let me get the letter, Lance!" Lady Lucia interposed. "Brynhild hasn't heard it either—of course he will be interested. It is all the most amazing beautiful thing you ever heard of."

He smiled at her. I grew to watch and like that meeting smile of theirs with its perfect understanding. She went off with her swift gliding grace, and Brynhild drew up her chair to Dunbar's, eyes fixed on him like entreaties for delight.

"Have you done much of the manuscript yet?"

"About half, and we thought we were going smoothly on to the end, Shan-tao and Haridas and I—"

"Who is Haridas?" I interrupted, too eager to wait.

"A very learned Indian Buddhist monk of great wisdom. He is here at the guest-house and we three work together like one man, each contributing what he knows. You will see him tomorrow and I think—you will like him."

He had intended to end the sentence differently, I could see. Now he switched back to his story and pulled a note-book out of his pocket as Lady Lucia returned with a leather case.

"Well, as I said, we were getting along, when suddenly came another bombshell. Our pilgrim, Hiuen Tsang referred to a Tibetan monk named 'The Diamond Scepter' who had studied with him in the monastery of Nalanda in India. 'This man,' he writes, 'had arts and powers of marvel unsurpassed but all conformable to the precepts of the Buddha, and none can fully comprehend my writing nor those of any religion unless they feed their minds on the wisdom of this Master of the Law. But he retired to his own country, having worked almost to the extinction of his health, and from there sent me a message, by means which it is not lawful I should describe, to tell me that he had placed his writings in safety and that death would not touch him until after the coming of the Buddha of Love whom in all reverence we expect.' "

I was startled into abruptness. "But you don't mean to say you believe that?"

He hesitated a moment as if reflecting upon his answer.

"Well—if you ask me that—perhaps it is best to say I probably accept many things you might think impossible. But since I do it on grounds you have not examined we are scarcely in a fair position for debate. And on this particular point I hold my opinion in balance for the moment. It is certain the Hiuen Tsang manuscript is authentic, for on that we have had the best opinions in China and the world. For the rest it must wait until I make the journey it involves. Would you care to hear the letter? Say if you're bored."

I protested eagerly. I knew enough of India to know that a record of royal and monastic life there in the seventh century would leave all fiction miles behind for strangeness and beauty, and would doubtless revolutionize much history. I was as keenly interested as man could be, and Dunbar saw it. He smiled and

I have seldom seen a face I liked better. It had the frank enjoyment of a boy's.

"The letter now, Lance!" his wife threw in, almost breathless with excitement. She had opened the case and pushed it into his hand. We were warming up to it now—the barrier was down and I was no longer an outsider. I looked at my fellow listener. She was still as marble, her whole aspect fixed on Dunbar. I was soon to understand the reason. Dunbar unfolded a silk wrapper.

"Well, of course the obvious thing was to make inquiry in all the available Tibetan lamaseries, and we had some hope, for their continuity has been wonderful considering the lapse of time, so Haridas and Shantao were chosen to go up over the great Himalayan pass about this and reconnoiter. They went, and disappeared. For a year we heard nothing, and I was just about to follow up with a big caravan when this letter came. See how strange."

He put before me, Brynhild leaning over my shoulder so close that I could feel the perfume of her hair, the strangest letter I had ever seen, engrossed, or rather painted, on an old vellum in an unknown character, and headed with the roughly painted miniature picture of a dignified person with a strange pointed hood falling in lappets down his cheeks, and disclosing Mongolian features, touched with the pride and subtlety which are marks of the priest all the world over. If I add that the letter did not look perfectly clean I do it no injury. But Dunbar handled it like diamonds.

"I can do a little Tibetan and have been through this with one of our monks. Here goes!

"FROM THE ABBOT OF THE MONASTERY OF THE MANIS, ABOVE SATSHANG.

"HONORABLE BROTHER OF THE PEN:

"We have heard from our brother (and yours) Haridas, the very wise and instructed Master of the Law, that the Monastery of Sweet Dew in China, the great and ancient kingdom, has need of certain manuscripts to make clear the teaching of the Blessed Buddha as given through the mighty pilgrim Hiuen Tsang. Be it known to you that in the library of this Lamasery are manuscripts of an antiquity so vast that the wisest are awestricken in seeing their glory. Now our brother (and yours) Haridas has gone down into Kashmir with these tidings, and it is his thought (and ours) if you will travel here in late spring, when the tracks begin to be free of snow, that great light may be cast upon dark places and great marvels seen. And for the lady your wife, who is known beyond the bounds of Empires for a white lotus in the hand of that Divine One who looks down forever upon the sound of prayer, place shall be found for her close at hand to the Monastery of the Manis in a convent where dwell the nuns of the Divine Tara, and her safety and comfort shall be more to us than our own. True it is that our reading of the teachings of the Perfect One is not yours, but wisdom is one and knowledge is its servant. Therefore come, glad and making glad.

"It ends with a formula. 'I worship the Enlightened One. I worship the Law. I worship the Assembly.' "

I own I was delighted. What man is not when a new and astounding treasure dazzles in his eyes? I know my first thought was the question as to whether I could make any interest to be of the party if one were going upon such an adventure. It was hovering on my lips when Lady Lucia intervened:

"So you see, when Haridas returns we have decided,

unless he has any reason against it, to go up beyond Satshang to the Lamasery of the Manis, and with Shan-tao and Haridas search through all their treasures and perhaps go on to other Lamaseries if we fail there. If you liked we could leave you with Alam Khan at Satshang. I should feel safer about you if you were not wandering in the terrible mountains without us."

Dunbar was as kind and earnest about it as she. Brynhild Ingmar alone was silent; was she not certain she herself was to be included, or jealous of a stranger's good luck? Her stillness and silence were remarkable. Suddenly she spoke and with an eagerness that for the first time troubled her face, and opened the gates of expression.

"But I must come too, Lucia. You know I must. I could not leave you and—you know!"

Lady Lucia caught her hand. "I know—I know! Of course you will come. We never thought of anything else. And you shall see the mountain goddess, sitting alone and dreaming on those fearful peaks. No one could do it like you—when you have seen!"

Do it? How and what? What did they mean? Another mystery in this strange Baltar! It opened out on me in surprise after surprise; and again the feeling of irritation and suspicion revived in me.

"Is Miss Ingmar an artist?" I asked cautiously, preparing myself for the usual pale feminine attempts in water-color, and getting up a little bored resentment into the bargain.

Lady Lucia holding Brynhild's hand lifted it up and showed it to me laughing. "No, this is no hand for a brush. Guess again."

I shook my head, perhaps with a rather too visible impatience, and Dunbar looking on laughed quietly to himself.

"Well, you could never guess, so you shall be told. Miss Ingmar is Narendra."

I started as if I had been shot; the blood ran up my face in my utter astonishment. Narendra! That was the signature to a certain sculptor's work which had come from India during the last two years to the great exhibitions of the West and those who knew had, seeing it, said, "A master." It was known, of course, that the signature was a *nom de guerre,* but none doubted the Indian manhood of the artist and all whose opinion was worth a rush had hailed him as a new and brilliant star dawning in the darkened heaven of Indian art for though only three of his works had been shown in London and Paris each was an achievement. It was allowed that Narendra had recaptured the inspiration of the ancient great frescoes and sculptures of early Buddhist art in the net of a masterly modern technique; and his imposing novelty and originality had carried the forts of instructed criticism by storm, though for the general public he was an artist more to be wondered at than loved.

His work had a pull over me which I could not explain to myself otherwise than as I felt it to be the very voice of Asia, which was no explanation at all, as at the time I had no rights in Asia and knew little enough of it. Still there it was. I felt it.

But Narendra! I stood stupefied, looking across at the girl who looked calmly back at me, her hand still in Lady Lucia's—she watching me with a kind of mild triumph.

At last I found my voice—fragmentary and unbelieving.

"Of course Lady Lucia's joking. That 'Ecstasy'—the Buddhist Angel—I can never believe you did that. It's a great work. It has all the dream of Asia—the face of Asia. No, impossible! That's a man's work if ever I saw it."

"But I did it!" she answered, her lip trembling with what I thought might be suppressed laughter. "Why don't you call it by its Indian name—'Samadhi'? I like that best."

And still I stared at her—all manners forgotten in that amazing moment. "It's a man's work. Not a woman's," I insisted doggedly. "A mood a woman never could understand or attain. Women do charming things, but they don't do that."

"You have the true English idea of the inferiority of women in matters of art. They don't say it, but they think and imply it in every look. Well—leave it at that. I am not Narendra."

She said it haughtily, drawing back a little.

The Dunbars were watching us with amusement. We had certainly come together with a clash. Her dark brows drew together with a kind of hurt dignity, and I felt myself an ass and went on:

"But all the world *knew* that Narendra was some connection of the Tagores who had studied in Paris. Am I dreaming or are you?"

"I am no connection of the Tagores and I never studied in Paris. My teacher was a monk of the Monastery of Tashigong—and really—but what does it matter? Nothing but experience rids a man of his disbelief in women as artists. If I prove Narendra's work is mine you'll take refuge in saying it is worthless because it is a woman's. No, keep your own opinion. A man convinced against his will—"

She broke down into the loveliest laugh I have ever heard in my life, but with more than a touch of scorn in it; and it transfigured her into such brilliant, courageous youth that if I had been told she could scale the very heavens I should have doubted no more. I held out a hand for peace-making.

"Narendra is too big a man to bear any malice for incredulity!" I said with my best grace. "After all, my stupefaction is the best tribute, for a little artist such as I am could never suppose his luck would bring him face to face with a great one in such a happy chance."

But she turned coldly from me.

"Great?" she said, her face sobering. "I have not said that, and the world shall not. On the day when it does I shall go up into the mountains and—"

She checked herself. "You know, Lucia. You always know," she said. "Ask Mr. Cardonald to keep my secret, for there is more behind it than he can guess yet, much more. Make him promise!"

I promised it in a surge of astonishment that beat down my reasoning powers, but still she held away from me; and as we stood face to face with the Dunbars looking on, the curtains parted and a Japanese servant came noiselessly in with a folded paper. Dunbar opened it.

"By George! Haridas has returned! I must go up at once to the rest house and see him. Pray manage to look a little less unbelieving, Cardonald. I know you haven't digested Narendra yet. Pray look a little more forgiving, Brynhild. After all you can show him the studio tomorrow and shatter unbelief with your mallet!"

"Do I care?" she said proudly, and turned away for a moment, while Dunbar whistled the Aberdeens and went off into the starry night.

"Perhaps I shouldn't have told you," Lady Lucia said anxiously. "But it's so natural to me that I think all the world must feel it when it comes near her. I see it in the very way she holds her head; to me her hand tell its own story."

The way she held her head at that moment scarcely promised peace. Narendra or no, I inclined to think her a vixen. The breach was not really mended when she said good night and went off up the stairs with the long sweeping step of careless youth and health.

When I got up to my own room and looked from its firelit security into the low and gloriously starred sky I thought I had fallen by chance into the most amazing house in the world. Something unforeseen must come of it. But what?

I heard Dunbar's voice below the window with another man's before sleep took me, however, and caught one phrase:

"A man must train himself to love without coveting. Relinquishment is the only road to great art."

That point of view certainly was new to me. I fell asleep with manuscripts and sculptures and low-browed angry eyes whirling in a sort of devil's dance in my bewildered brain.

CHAPTER IV

WAKING AT SIX O'CLOCK NEXT DAY I LEANED MY ARMS on the wide window-sill and looked out eastward into a glorious dawn, for the sun was standing on the mountain peak looking radiantly down upon the adoring world, dews and vapors rising like a steam of incense mingled with splendor before him. Can I ever forget the glitter of light on myriad pine-fronds, their wild pure odor, the sense of the spirit of the bridal earth prostrate in worship before the Bridegroom? And in a quick reaction rose before my mind a dull dawn breaking on rainy London, trapped in a squalor from which there is no escape, with soot-blackened trees, dumb birds and the chilling absence of happy animal life which is death to all that unites us with nature. In the cities we are rebels that have broken out of the fold; and what shall open that gate to us again? Here, I knew that the infinite woods were full of living creatures rejoicing in the life that touches ours at so many points and yet is so far. Understanding it we shall learn the secret speech of Nature, but not otherwise. They hold it still; we have lost it.

Thankfulness that I was climbing the ascending heights of Asia, and could be a looker-on at this keen vibration of beauty, filled my heart and soul like the welling of a crystal spring. I was no part of it yet, but I saw and was content. I heard voices drawing nearer and nearer from the woods. They did not break the harmony but enhanced it and made the tranquillity more tranquil. One was Brynhild Ingmar's, the other I did not know, but presently the speakers wound along the mossy way from the little waterfall and were in full sight.

A man in the yellow robe with keen dark features subdued by inner forces into a noble calm. I recognized that instantly as one recognizes it in great sculpture—power, self-domination, unity. His head was shaven and in his hand he carried a large palm-leaf fan to shade his eyes from the dazzle of the low rays shooting through the trees. The dull ocher-yellow of his garment became splendid as they fell upon him, and I saw him as it were blazing in gold. She walked beside him in white, bareheaded, talking most earnestly, her face all eagerness, and expression playing on it like the ripples of a sea in sunlight. It was then I first recognized and did justice to her singular beauty, realizing also that it could scarcely be beauty except for the one who knew the secret and compelled the unfolding of the rose. To others she would be what she had been to me, cold, unalluring, even a little repellent.

They were on the lawn under my window now.

"What shall we find up there?" she was saying. "Is it true that the man really is still alive and holds the secrets we all desire to know? For you remember in my dream . . ."

"Daughter, I remember—and the gift you received. Yes, for I have seen him, but it is not possible I should say much, or that you should understand until the light comes to you in the high mountains. Only last night I stood before him when the moon rose in these gardens. . . ."

"Last night? But you were here; he there," she interrupted. "Is it possible?"

"You know," he said, and halting fixed his eyes on her. I knew I had no right to listen, and pushed the window up noisily. They heard and went slowly forward.

But for me I remained astonished. Were they talking of the Diamond Scepter, the man who fourteen centuries ago had vanished into the mysteries of Northern India and Tibet, and if so was the monk trying to impose a lie on the belief of a girl? Since no one looking at her could imagine her such a plotter as Mrs. Mainguy had suggested, I now transferred my doubt to the priest who certainly from what I had gleaned already held a kind of dominion over the heads of the house. This was undoubtedly the Indian, Haridas, and I own that the beauty and dignity of his bearing affected me unpleasantly because I chose to imagine it a pose and therefore a weapon.

I dressed quickly and went out into the golden morning. It was no day to endure a roof over one's head little or great, and I went bareheaded.

It was an early household and the servants were all astir, hurrying to and fro on their errands between the houses. Two of the monks were coming down the little hill from their abode in shine and shadow of the trees. What a scene; what a picture! I had my sketch-book under my arm and leaning against a black trunk began to take notes with what speed I could.

The Chinese as he passed me halted on his foot for a moment, smiled, and with a courteous salutation said, pointing to the left:

"Go up there, and draw the Lady of Mercy as she stands with her birds about her in the dawn."

He paced onward and the two went down the mossy track. I closed my book and went upward through the pines.

Where shall I find words to describe what followed . . . a sight so strange and lovely that I could almost swear no other eyes than mine have seen it in all the modern world? A sight like a faun's dream of a nature goddess or fair elemental spirit of the dawn at one with nature. Let me try, and fail.

As I went quietly through the trees the pines fell back from a little open space of ferns, but dappled them with pure sunshine, clear as the running water of the small mountain stream singing its way to the garden. Leaning against a trunk was Brynhild Ingmar, and at her feet and perched on the branches above her a cloud of birds of many sorts and hues. One, a wild pigeon, lovely in gray and mauve, stood on her shoulder, pressing against her cheek, . . . a smaller bird in the hollow of her hand, with bright uplifted eyes. Beautiful, but the strangeness overwhelmed the artistry. Do ordinary women win the wild hearts of the woods like this? A small gray squirrel, sensing my nearness as I supposed, sprang from her arm up the rugged bark and disappeared. A young deer, exquisite to behold, pressing against her knee, quivered and looked with frightened eyes toward my hiding-place, and so darted into the shade over the pine-needles which had heaped themselves for centuries, dumbing the footfall.

But she had heard mine or known it through the going of her creatures, and without moving, spoke clear and low as a bird's note in twilight: "If you wish to see them, don't move and they will come again."

I was silent, almost holding my breath to see the wonder. Presently the little deer stole back, drawn by a call his heart could not resist; the squirrel ran down the bark, a slipping streak of gray, and ran up her arm to her shoulder, pushing his nose with little quick movements against her throat. I expected to see her crumble food for them—that was surely the charm!—but no.

Standing in profound stillness she began to sing in a very low murmur, scarcely above a whisper of music, and I saw all draw closer. There was a rustling in the woods behind her as though something large and clumsy were pushing its way in haste, and a big bear cub came rolling into the open and to her knees, without disturbing the others held in the spell which had called him. They crowded a little closer to her and that was all. Can I describe what I felt on seeing the innocent magic? Impossible. As to sketching . . . I forgot it, and what need of it? That scene will live in my being forever. Strange associations and possibilities unnamable and urgent came floating through me. Was this the meaning of the woods? Could it be possible that ancient stories were true and that men beholding a sight like this had returned babbling of Oreads and Dryads and mysterious spiritual presences in the solitudes? Could it . . .

Her voice continued like an unbroken rune but strengthening into more audible sweetness. One might see that the creatures fed on it, drew some strange inspiration from her, clung to her. What did it mean? I could not understand. To me, only a sweet voice in the quiet. To them, some bread of life unspeakable.

In my eagerness to see more I made some movement—a twig snapped, and in an instant the picture dissolved. The squirrel vanished up the tree, a gray streak of fear. The bear cub shambled off through crashing undergrowth. There was a wild flutter of wings. She stood alone looking steadily at me.

"That was a pity! They will remember it next time and be on the watch."

"But how, how do you do it, and what do they want? I never thought such a thing possible. Is it a kind of snake fascination?"

The look of scorn on her lip!

"If you don't know the difference between terror and love how can I make you understand?" She half turned away; then, softening: "After all . . . it is strange to you and I have always been used to it. No . . . they love me and the singing is a kind of speech they understand."

She walked slowly beside me under the trees.

"But how did it begin? Did you tame them with food?"

"Never. They can get that for themselves unless things go very badly. My father taught me. He had a wonderful power and was in the closest touch with all life. You would not believe— But I am sure you don't care for such things."

Her tone wounded me into protest.

"I do care—anyone must be interested. I saw the kind of beckoning gesture you made. Is that it?"

"That would be nothing without what is behind. But why should I tell you? You spoke last night . . ."

"I meant no harm. It was only that I was so profoundly astonished."

"Yes. Astonished because you think there is no place for women in real art. I know most people think it, but you are in the midst now of most wonderful things and if you are able you will see. This house, these people . . . they *know* where others grope."

She spoke almost with passion, but no pride. It was not that she thought herself a part of the marvels, though to me she seemed the most mysterious of all, with her extraordinary powers and simplicity of bearing. I stopped, obliging her to stop also.

"Forgive me for last night . . . it was sheer amazement. I could not believe you're Narendra. But I will say now that in the atmosphere of this strange place many things begin to seem possible that I never dreamed of before. I have been here only one night. . . . I don't know my way about, yet even now I have a strange home-feeling as if friendly eyes were looking over my barriers. You would forgive me if you knew what a very straitened life mine has been. I have not had much chance; I have neither mother nor sisters."

"Nor I!" she said with the ghost of a smile. "Well, if you hurt me it is over. As to my birds—have you ever heard of the Ninth Vibration? That is only a meaningless name, but I call it that for reasons. It is a plane on which one meets other sorts of life in perfect understanding. Watch now! Sandy and Jock are lying by the fire in the hall . . . but I can bring them."

She stopped and resting one hand against a tree threw the other up, looking steadily towards the house. I could hear a noise of barking, a servant ran from the garden to open the door, and in a moment a storm of two little grizzled Scotch terriers broke madly yelping over the lawn and up the hill to us, leaping elbow-high about her as she caressed them. I was mute with astonishment, watching until the turmoil lapsed into more tranquil joy.

"That power must have very strange things behind it," I said as we went down to the house. "It is no chance or individual thing."

That pleased her. She looked up smiling with her water-clear eyes. "Right! It's a law and a very far-reaching one. I learn more of it every day, and Haridas tells me I shall use it in ways I can't even guess yet. It has done a great deal for my work."

The smile gave me courage at last. "Then if you think me not quite unworthy, may I see your studio?"

A second's hesitation and she smiled again. "Certainly. Come after breakfast. Perhaps Haridas will be there. He comes sometimes while I work."

"Who and what is he? I wish you would prepare me a little for some of the people I am to meet here. You are free of it all. I'm a stranger."

"You need not be . . . you won't be long. Ask Lance Dunbar anything you want to know. He will tell you better than I. Come, dogs! Run!"

She ran herself like a deer down the slope with the dogs after her. I followed slowly with a more wistful sense of loneliness than I had ever known before. Again I felt myself a clumsy outsider among people who moved happily on their own sunlit orbit . . . much like a man hearing others fluent in a language of which he knows nothing. The place was alive now with people going to and fro on their occasions. The golden solitude of the dawn was ended.

After breakfast, seeing Lady Lucia making for the garden, I joined her and asked for guidance to the studio. She pointed to a high-pitched building on the left of the house.

"We had it built the first time she came here. She had done nothing then—but dream."

"And in this enchanted place do dreams always come true?"

"Always . . . if you dream true. That's the secret."

I reflected a moment.

"I remember in Du Maurier's 'Peter Ibbetson'—rather a beautiful book in its way—that the secret of dreaming true was to lie on your back and cross your feet and then you got into a kind of fairy-land where you dined at the best restaurants and heard the best music—in fact became a dream-millionaire. But that subject has often been played with in literature."

"Oh, yes. 'Peter Ibbetson' is one of the books that set people guessing at unknown powers. But Du Maurier didn't see the real point. We know now."

"And what is it?"

She looked at me clear-eyed. "You really want to know? I'm most terribly afraid of being a bore."

"I want to know most sincerely. I can feel that here you are all trying to make a practical life of some philosophy instead of drifting as we all do more or less in the West. Well—I have drifted. I'm tired of it both from the point of view of art and life. If there were anything practical for me . . ."

"You are an artist. Let us talk for a moment of art," she said.

I suppose I had expected some high religious statements for that surprised me; but pacing up and down under the pines, she did what she called her "very poor best" to enlighten me.

"You see, Brynhild Ingmar takes the Indian view of art. She came over to India from Canada with her mother who is now dead, simply on a pleasure trip and to foster a taste for painting in water-color—not very strong but rather charming in its way. To make a long story short, after a while she began to dream . . . not after the Du Maurier fashion . . . but dreams which set her free, as she believes, to come in touch with influences of power that are really one's own, but buried under the daily happenings of the surface self, which is no real self at all. Am I very involved?"

"No, not a bit. You mean she began to realize her subconscious self? We all know something about that nowadays."

"In a way, yes. She began to realize the eternal self hidden beneath the daily self, and that realization brought her in touch with other people in sleep. You see it must be so, for the eternal self is part of the

One Self and therefore of all that exists. But I have no authority to tell you her sleep-life. I will only say that one night she woke with a sentence on her lips which she says determined her life. It sounds very simple. Just this: 'I have learned concentration from the Maker of arrows.' She had never heard it before."

"I don't understand. But what happened?"

"Haridas was there at the time and she told him. He answered that the words were from a very ancient Indian book she had never read, and that it referred to *Yoga,* which is the Indian name for the science of concentration. Everyone knows that word and associates it with magic, but it really only means a discipline to produce perfect control of the mind and thought and so to switch on to the sources of power. It certainly should be taught in every school . . . East or West."

"Yoga? But surely that is the practice of the wildest self-torturing fanatics in India. No European . . ."

"Many Europeans!" she said smiling. "Do my husband and I look very wild fanatics? or Brynhild? We certainly know nothing of torture."

I was all but stupefied. "Do you really mean . . ."

"Yes, of course I really mean! Let me tell you what happened. Under the advice of Haridas she told her mother she wished to study the science of the mind as a kind of preparation for art . . . if she should prove to have that in her; and the mother agreed and went home to Canada. Haridas put Brynhild into the hands of a friend who lives with his sister in a most beautiful solitude near the Shipki Pass into Tibet . . . not very far from the Tashigong Monastery. They are Indian people of the highest type and he a great thinker and writer. For two years she underwent that discipline of mind and body, and I can truly say it is not easy to learn to concentrate and steady the mind on one thought instead of letting it skip about like a monkey from branch to branch. It wants study."

Suddenly and irrelevantly I said:

"I hate hypnotism and all those tricks by which a man gets control over other people's minds, and for women it is revolting. . . . Who can tell what use may be made of it? These masters and teachers!"

She looked at me calmly. "I am so glad to hear you say that. Indeed I agree entirely. But yoga is a form of discipline which strengthens the mind to bar its doors even against its own intruders. People who know it may well feel very strong among the people who are open to every wind of influence and suggestion. One sees that going on most dangerously every day, especially in the sort of society you and we lived in."

That was true enough and I disliked it for that reason. I could not gainsay it, but I tried.

"Surely we get along very well," I said jealously.

"That depends on how much you want. Brynhild Ingmar wanted a good deal. However, in learning the discipline she learned much more. She learned the secret of art."

She said this in the most ordinary way as we paced up and down in measured rhythm, she stooping now and then to touch a flower . . . not to pick it. But something in the assumption of her last words irritated me, and I may have shown this a little in my tone.

"Rather a large order, surely! The secret of art!

That means the secret of life and death and all that lies between and beyond."

She went on as quietly as if I had not spoken.

"Perhaps I can put it better than I did. She learned that art is yoga . . . that concentration gives you the power, within very wide limits, to choose what you will take out of the treasure-house of the universe. Her powers of visualizing developed every day, and at last her very thought of them had power to throw them out from herself into what we call actuality. Does it sound very high-flown if I say that in these states of perception the human self grasps all it can perceive of absolute beauty? That may not be very much but it is the highest point our senses will allow us to reach here and now. She had then only to externalize what she saw."

I was vanquished. In spite of myself I began to understand, to grasp the amazing interest and possibilities of what she was trying so patiently to tell me. I knew that there had been moments in my own life . . . hints, shadowings, blind gropings, when I had guessed and failed for want of knowledge. But this girl had had courage to follow the star of knowledge, to fight, endure and control; and I began to wonder whether there might not be some truth in this system of mind-training—something true, not only for her but for all.

"Do you mean to say that she could do that Narendra work on the strength of a vision?" I asked slowly.

"She suddenly found she could model in clay and, as I think, gloriously. For the technique—the dealing with marble, alabaster and bronze she naturally had to be shown the mechanics of her art. But she learned that like lightning. The curious thing was that at first she could not tell whether the images she saw were to be expressed in music, writing or painting. It appeared to her that all were one, and it was merely a sort of divine chance how the power would manifest."

"Perhaps that is conditioned deeper down still," I returned.

"Perhaps. But isn't it wonderful to think that instead of a divinity rough-hewing our ends of life, the divinity in ourselves enables us to shape them as we will? And that is the simple daily-proved truth. But it leads one far."

Her tone moved me by its mingled simplicity and confidence. I ventured a step further, for people like that never misunderstand but always take you at your best.

"And you, Lady Lucia. Did you choose too?"

A moment's hesitation in lifting the veil, and then she answered:

"Yes . . . but nothing grand, nothing wonderful like Brynhild. There's a lot of work to be done, help needed, and I have concentrated on that. This place is my yoga. My husband's is the wonderful language work he does for the monastery. You cannot imagine his mastery of tongues and you would never believe it unless you knew."

I stopped and looked about me at her yoga. Wonderful indeed in beauty and method and warm generous welcome . . . surely the friend of all the world. Yet I knew only the fringe of it now and was to learn much more later and to think her achievement perhaps the most sensitively beautiful of any. Not on the moral plane—art has no use for morality as morality, but the result may have an unearthly loveliness merging into that Beauty which includes the esthetic of deed and thought as it does all else. One could certainly say that of hers.

We stopped by the little waterfall, and she touched the ferns that hung above it with a finger gentle as a breath.

"Shall I take you to the studio? She is there now."

CHAPTER V

WHEN WE ENTERED, THE PLACE SEEMED TO ME almost as high-pitched as a church, bare, austere, but beautiful, for from the roof hung curtains of some thin yellow stuff controlling the light and dividing the great length into what I felt to be antechapels leading up to some inner shrine—these themselves peopled with dreams made visible, but yet a highway to the supreme expression of some one perception . . . something that would be neither marble nor alabaster nor any medium, but nearer and farther than they.

And now face to face at last with the work of Narendra speculation ceased; surprise and the artist and critic in me woke in this temple in which I too could call myself an acolyte, having swung my incense in however poor a thurible. We met on common ground here, and I forgot yogas and superstitions and prepared to take what I saw at what it was worth according to my standards, which I believed to be educated and innate.

I was alertly and keenly interested, and especially so on seeing in the first room, if I may so call the division made by the curtains, the extraordinary group which had brought me again and again to the exhibition room in London. It was stranger than strange to meet it here among the pines and rivers of Kashmir, and as I stood before it she came through the dividing curtains and without a word pulled up a blind so that a strong shaft of sunshine fell across the supple bronze.

I saw a camel and his rider—the man, an Arab in haik and burnoose—entangled in the snares of the desert. One or two rocks were indicated, standing gauntly above the flowing sea of sand. And as I looked the walls of the room lifted and exhaled, and I saw the desert before me, golden, illimitable, terrible as eternity. There was its inhuman vastness alive with warnings and sinister meanings. And one might see how the spell overpowered both beast and rider; the man swaying aside on the saddle, staring down, down into the golden depths as though they had become translucent, and his eyes beheld beautiful and terrible submerged creatures moving towards him, waving, calling, as doom overtook him. The knees of the camel were loosening; a moment more and he also would sink relaxed upon the sands into a fatal dream, out of which he and his rider would never rise again. What drew them? What force implacable and dreadful held them and made escape impossible?

I saw faintly outlined on the sand a huge, dim encircling Presence, so vague that one rather felt than saw it—a dim outline traced in sand . . . a fluent hand raised to grasp, to draw—but nothing beyond an indication that death and despair were beneath, hidden in beauty and awaiting the slow absorption of their prey.

I stood a very long time in silence whilst her dream filled my brain and overpowered my thoughts, startled as I had always been by the conception and the power of its presentation, for every time I saw it, it became a fresh revelation alive with new meanings So it must surely be with all great works which awaken response in the heart. She standing beside me was silent also, her own eyes fixed on her work, Lady Lucia's arm about her.

At last she moved slightly and I spoke:

"The first time I saw this I thought it an absolutely pagan thing—I believed you were on the side of the desert. I thought it was another phase of the Indian delight in the power of the Destroyer. After all what is a man's life in the eternal flux of things? But now I see much more. It reminds and recalls all the experiences of illusion. Mirage—no more. The man who is hypnotized sinks to his ruin; the man who for the moment is clear-eyed sees and laughs at the other's folly, as we do in looking on. It's a bitter sort of thing for a girl to have done. Solomon might have taken it for a text of the worthlessness of life. And you called it 'Mirage' !"

She looked up at me thoughtfully.

"I never thought it bitter. I don't now. It seems inevitable that the world should capture men for a while, but the prison is not so strongly barred but what you may fly out of the window whenever you want to. I always knew that Tannhäuser must leave the Venusberg, and the man and the camel come triumphing home at last. But his life would be more beautiful and full of meaning because he had lain in the arms of the hot sand, and seen the stars come out over the desert."

A strange speech for a girl of her age, but the truth of it went home. It recalled experiences of my own, of every man's, that vouched for its truth. Galahad is well for the world, but Lancelot is better. He knows and every scar is a symbol of victory.

She flashed a look of understanding at me keen as a blade of steel.

"That's it. Now shut your eyes to the other things as we pass and let me show you the last thing I have done. It completes the 'Mirage.' "

I followed through the divisions, looking at nothing but feeling the golden air about us quivering with vibrations of beauty. It seemed to me that I would choose to be alone in the great silent room at night, with a high moon looking in at the top lights and revealing so much of them as would make mystery their mother. A true work of art is always a bird fled hither from the heart of things, the land that is very far off.

I looked up when we reached the last division with pale veils hanging about it, and my eyes fell on beauty inexpressible. I saw the Buddha after his enlightenment, looking out over the world in a deep dream of peace. He sat uplifted on a rock which might have been the starriest peak of Gaurisankar. It gave me the feeling of immense and remote height, and so looking downward he beheld the earth in all its griefs and crimes with the serenity of perfect comprehension. I never saw, I never have since seen anything that went so deep and soared so high in all the secret places of the soul. It was the answer to the riddle of the Sphinx and itself unanswerable.

When I could realize anything but the beauty before me she pointed silently to the base. . . .

> Having like an elephant broken through the creeper I have attained Reality.

"You see," she said, "the first was Mirage. This is the Truth."

We stood awhile and then she led the way silently from the shrine—for so it seemed—to where Lady Lucia still waited, looking at the man swaying from the camel to his fall. And not a word had I said.

But after that we became friends. I go ahead of my story to write that here, but it is true. There were no explanations, it simply was so . . . an accepted fact, and I was so far made free of the studio that I could go in and out and watch her modeling, chiseling—almost see the winged thoughts flying to their home. The most wonderful of all my experiences in that place of wonders, as I thought at first; not later. It was not surprising that the Buddhist monks came down each day from the house on the hill to meditate beside that Peace; and that Haridas when I learned to know him compared it for pure spiritual feeling to the most famous work of the Buddhist primitives at Sanchi and Amaravati, so deeply had she drunk of the water of life as it wells from the rock in Asia.

When I learned to know him. That came in no flash like the revelation of her art, but quietly, gradually, like a rising dawn. That very evening after dinner Dunbar took me up to the house on the hill, winding by starlight through the dewy lawns and trees with the dogs at our heels. I felt the strangeness of the occasion in every fiber of my brain even while I rejoiced in the contacts which were opening such new worlds to me. I said as much and he answered kindly.

"I felt from what my wife told me that you would soon be at home with us, and when you are you can help immensely if you will. Every fresh person who recognizes the vital need of disciplining and training the mind and soul along the ways of concentration, known and taught so long in India, becomes a light-dispenser. But it's early days yet! Wait until you see more and then form your judgment. I know from experience that there is a kind of charm that assails one, but the assent must be intellectual too."

I felt the good sense of this as opposed to my own impulse, and asked him to give me some understanding of the monks and their relation to the life of the place, as we went.

"They are constantly changing, all but the ones who work with me, for this is a rest house to fit them for further work and to bring them into touch with new people. None come into my house—not even Haridas—that would be against their rule. And my wife and Brynhild never come up here though they talk with the men they know in the gardens when they meet. One monk is dying slowly in the little hospital. He escaped with a broken body from an avalanche in the passes and has been brought here to die. I wish it could have been in China. Their monastery there is tranquillity in its most spiritual form. But we do the best we can, and my wife and Brynhild are constantly with him."

I wondered. The monastic ideal has never appealed to me, and I said so.

"But after all, Cardonald, men band together for every purpose that needs group-work. How else can it be done? These men's aim is to act as intermediaries between men—especially in the West—and a great truth which they believe is vital to them. They must coordinate and play into each other's hands. And remember that in the Buddhist rule a man may return to the world at any instant. He breaks no vow in doing so. And surely there must be a kind of asceticism in any concerted work. There is an asceticism of the soldier on duty and so on. These men are always on duty. Think it out and I believe you will assent."

More was said on both sides, but prejudice was strong on me when we entered the unlocked door of the House on the Hill and found ourselves in a long low room, cedar-paneled and beamed, with a long narrow table and a great log fire to center the talk and relaxation. Eight men were sitting there, one with a book, two with the Chinese chess-board, the rest talking among themselves. All bore the badge of shaven head and yellow robe. All rose and bowed with joined hands when we entered, and I imitated Dunbar by returning the salute with especial courtesy as he introduced me to one after another, giving the English equivalents of their Asian names in religion . . . of all but Haridas. Him he spoke of and to in that fashion and no other.

This done, the two returned to their chess and the eldest to his book, and the rest gathered about us and the fire.

"For I have come," said Dunbar, "to ask your friendship for my guest and to tell you, Haridas, that he will join our expedition to Satshang. We shall very likely be passing through places where another man's help will be useful, and Mr. Cardonald has his own reasons for visiting the heights."

"It is well," Haridas answered, "and since he is an artist it will delight him to see the pictures in the Monastery of the Manis. There is a series of events from the life of the Buddha bright as jewels and perfect as pearls. It is just possible that the abbot might permit copies to be made of some. Most of the Red Order will have no dealings with other orders, but these are above division."

His English had scarcely a foreign inflection—and I might say almost the same of the rest. No man was permitted to join the order until he was letter-perfect in our tongue. But I did not learn this at once for there was much decorum and sparing gravity in its use. The younger men in particular sat in listening silence unless specially called to speak.

"Do you really think there's a chance of that?" I asked. "One has heard that no foreigners are wanted in the Tibetan lamaseries."

"Much more than a chance. The abbot is keenly interested in our translation of the manuscript of Hiuen Tsang and anyone who comes with Mr. Dunbar will have a welcome. Besides this is a very educated *gompa.* They are learned men in their way, and one or two would be called learned anywhere. You will perhaps find it different from anything you have imagined for I own many of the *gompas* are both ignorant and slothful. Bring all your materials; they will not be wasted."

He turned to Dunbar.

"But let us remember that there can be no certainty

whatever that the manuscript we need is there. They have begun now to take out and survey vast hoards of manuscript, the accumulation of more than a thousand years. It seems that centuries ago smaller *gompas* placed their manuscripts there for safety and never reclaimed them. So that even if we cannot find the treasure of treasures we may find what will be a light and wonder."

Dunbar thrilled responsive. I saw him flush like a girl with delight.

"Amazing! But, if I had to choose, sooner than all I would find the Diamond Scepter himself. Imagine hearing a man who had worked side by side with Hiuen Tsang fourteen hundred years ago. Is it possible, Haridas, is it possible! Are all the dreams to come true?"

For answer the monk turned to a man who had sat listening silently; a Chinese, his face singularly sweet and calm—a sunset look upon it, like an Alp illuminated by a sinking sun. I started when Haridas spoke to him, for the name fell in with my thought.

"Speak, High Illumination," he said, "and, if you will, relate the story of the man you beheld in the Monastery of the Height of Heaven in Shansi."

He rose and stood leaning with his hand on the back of a chair. His English, though fine and carefully chosen, was not so fluent as that of Haridas. I thought how natural it was that beauty should be a possession of the highest and lowest in a land where a man of the people could so look, think and speak as he. It was a painter's chance for a great portrait as he stood with firelight flickering on the yellow robe and worn

Chinese face and thin hands in an attitude of perfect poise and self-control.

"This inferior person is honored in laying his hoard of knowledge, small as a squirrel's nut, before the wise. When this ignorant one became a monk of a monastery in the holy island of Puto he was sent on a mission to another in the north of Shansi, and there being welcomed he was made free of the holy places. Of that he will not speak except to say that there he heard talk, as of men assured of the truth, of the existence of the Diamond Scepter in a Tibetan monastery. And he was made known to a monk who had seen this great saint and showed a word of wisdom written by him."

"How was he described?" asked Dunbar.

"As most still and tranquil of spirit, a very lamp of wisdom, dwelling in patience until the coming of the Lord Buddha. And as for the letter it said these words:

> "If the consciousness is withdrawn from death, death does not exist. Why then should spiritual men be amazed that I live whose hour is eternity?"

"That is both beautiful and true," Haridas said slowly. "The wise have always known that nothing in this world of form exists except in opinion, and death can be no exception."

But the practical side of the question was what interested me at the moment, and I asked eagerly enough if the letter had given any clue to the whereabouts of the writer.

High Illumination replied gently:

"It is said that the abbot of the Manis Monastery in

company with one other great ruler had power to reveal where this wonderful saint awaits the coming of the Lord. But for this inferior person, he has since had no doubt of his existence, especially as it is known to all who live the spiritual life that when a man has attained enlightenment many barriers are removed, and actions appear simple to him that are impossible to others."

He sat down, with hands folded across his yellow robe—the thin pathetic hands of the peasant whose living they have been; but the serenity of his expression was celestial. It is a part of my trade to watch faces and I wished to see him smile. . . . I knew instinctively that it would have been a gladness to more than himself. My atmosphere was changing. I began to find it strangely tranquilizing to sit amongst these men whose chosen life was so strange, so incomprehensible to me. I felt that for hours I might sit watching them and guessing, guessing at the riddle of what determined their thoughts and actions.

Dunbar spoke suddenly.

"High Illumination, you have the clear sight. If it were his wish could you tell this gentleman why he is here and what it will bring him? Would that interest you, Cardonald? I have a special reason for suggesting it which I will tell you afterwards. Don't do it unless you like, though."

I caught at the notion. The experimental side of it interested my incredulity immensely.

"Nothing I should like better. Though there's little to tell of the past there may be more of the future. Does the operator see the victim in private?"

"No—that's not the Eastern manner. Only look at him and clear your mind of other thoughts. Fix it on him."

I turned and fixed my eyes on the Chinese, he looking at me steadily in return.

"Do we begin with past or future?" I asked.

"Past and future are but names to those who have the sight. There is nothing but Now. But since it is true that sight is given to this inferior person shall it be told here and now, or alone?"

"Here!" I said with bravado, firm in the certainty that memory and mind are strongholds into which none can break unless the guard is pierced by hypnotic suggestion or some such false magic. The chess-players continued their chess, the reader his reading, the rest sat silent but with attention courteously withdrawn among themselves. Only Haridas fixed me for a moment with penetrating eyes, then turned to Dunbar and began a low conversation with him.

Shall I describe my sensations in that singular moment as I heard my own story briefly told by a man who could have known nothing on the plane which the world calls knowledge?

He spoke clearly and even dramatically as one who has seen, giving me higher impulses and hopes than had ever been known to myself, and later . . . the records of a wasted youth. It was too late to stop him then for I had become forgetful of all hearers. He and I sat, as it were, on a lonely seashore, the waves beating drearily on a desolate sand as he told my drab story. It dulled my senses into a kind of acquiescence as I heard. It was a thing done, fixed forever without any possibility of escape, its claws in my heart until it ceased to beat.

For very drab it seemed to me; pleasures immeasurably little, pain without dignity, irking, nagging worries and disappointments. Not that he went into details, but they rose up to confront me like ghosts at the word of power. I blushed, not at the wickedness, but the insignificance, of the pleasures which had seemed so desperate in their daring long, long ago. Very long ago it seemed as his passionless voice recounted them. I winced as he laid a finger on the poisoned sore of memory.

"And but for that woman, the wife of your friend, you would have met the man whose breath must have kindled your art into a flame leaping to the sky. A heavy cost, for though they will meet you face to face in the mountains you have thrown away ten years that only eternity can restore again from the clenched hand where they are held."

A miserable story of might-have-beens and great opportunities trodden down in the mud of the sensual sty. I listened in stunned silence and without a plea. Then suddenly realization broke with a revulsion on me. How could this Chinese monk have known, how could any know the secrets of the human heart? I had not known myself—had never understood the implications; how could he pry into what was mine so deeply that it had never been mine? I put up my hand furiously. . . .

"Stop. How dare you drag me into the dissecting room? How dare you . . ."

Instantly he ceased, withdrawing into silence as into

a distant chamber. I could not have said another word to save my life and was bitterly ashamed of my outbreak and equally unable to make any apology. It terrified and shocked me to the very roots of my being that I should be read like an open book and by so simple a reader before a roomful of men. With what zest they must have listened and seen my emotion! Horrible thought! For the moment it paralyzed my tongue and I looked about me in sickening shame. At last I found my voice and spoke to Dunbar.

"You must forgive me for having obtruded my very uninteresting affairs. I had no notion such a thing was possible or I would never have allowed it, and . . ."

"No apology is needed. I heard nothing, nor did anyone else," he answered with a smile. "When such men see they think their sight to you—or rather perhaps awaken your own. Haridas and I have been discussing the details of our expedition to Tibet in a silent room, and as for you . . . you sat apparently in deep thought. But it is an interesting experience, I think. Don't you?"

"Interesting? Yes . . . no. Terrible. Never again! But how is it possible such things can be?"

"Ask Haridas! Ask High Illumination. But anyhow you can't suppose it possible that he would speak of things belonging to yourself in public. That is not the way these men work."

I looked at the perfect simplicity and sweetness of the old man's face and knew it to be impossible, yet I asked him:

"You did not speak aloud?"

"Very certainly, no. The sight is not thus. Your honorable memory set free beheld the now which men call past and future."

"But you saw, you knew also."

"While you saw only. Now it is forgotten."

I could say no more. I was haunted for the rest of the evening by my own past and the miracle of its resurrection. Haridas brought out and showed me with all reverence the marvelous manuscript of the pilgrim Hiuen Tsang written in beautiful Chinese characters unused now among his own people—a miracle to see and touch, reposing in its scented box of cedar like a queen's jewel. Dunbar and he translated a morsel from it lovely as an Indian night's delight, the description of some palace whose "richly adorned towers and fairy turrets like pointed hilltops are congregated together. The observatories are lost in the morning mists and tower above the clouds. And on deep crystalline pools grows the blue lotus, and the trees exhale their dragon-brain scent, delicious to the nostrils."

But how could I listen? For then and later as we walked back under the faint light of a rising moon I trembled within myself, feeling that the past is the ever-present and that I was recaptured by a force I thought long since left behind. I did not know that I had tasted the pangs of the first stirring of knowledge. It is at least something to have realized one is a prisoner. The possibility of escape comes much later.

But that night I did not sleep. The moon and the great quiet looked in through the windows and beheld my room filled with presences. A woman wept beside me with imploring hands, appealing to a love I neither felt nor understood. A man who had trusted my friendship stood beside her with cold averted face. Little things and great, terrible and pitiable, filled the air, and lost amongst them the cry that filled my heart found words I had long since forgotten:

I will go down to self-annihilation, and eternal death,
Lest the Last Judgment find me unannihilate,
And I be seized and given into the hands of my own selfhood.

And before dawn, unable to bear enclosing walls any longer, I went down and out through the ever-open door, and strode along the track by which I had come to this beautiful, merciless place where my past had tracked and followed me.

I returned exhausted, pleaded illness, and saw no one that day. On the next I asked for an interview with Haridas. It appeared to me that his cool, ironic nature shot with gleams of wisdom, for so I now conceived it, might be the antidote to my feverish imaginings.

CHAPTER VI

It was a week later when I had my audience, for I took time to consider my request and for two days Haridas was engaged with matters of more importance than my questions. I must own my doubts of the wisdom of discussing my affairs with him were reviving when at last we met by the waterfall, he, to my surprise, dressed like a Kashmiri mountaineer for the climb and shod with the native *chaplis,* or leather sandals, which certainly gave a better grip on the slippery grass than my nailed boots. Somehow the figure he presented, divested of the yellow robe, full of strength and agility, encouraged me. The man was on a nearer plane than the monk, and I felt assured that the interchange would be more human.

He greeted me cordially and we struck straight up the side of the hill through the woods in a deep and glorious solitude. Even the breeze was still, breathing gently as a sleeping child through the boughs above us. They seemed to float entranced upon a sea of azure.

"What is there in this place that charms one so powerfully?" I asked. "I suppose I have seen places as beautiful but never one so lovely."

"A good distinction," he answered, breasting the hill

steadily. "Yes, it comes home to one. There is not a man in our monastery in China that does not come here gladly, and the sick long for it. If you wish to see 'the joy of departing' as we call it, you should visit our brother High Gladness in the hospital. And I think that peculiar radiance is caused by the presence of the lady"—so Haridas always called Lady Lucia—"whose own name signifies light and whose own yoga is to help others."

"She aimed at that," I said slowly.

"Certainly, and therefore has attained as she could have attained any other thing she had chosen. The things she does with the people about her are purest magic. It would make a story of wonders. Of course in the West also are people who succeed in the same way, entirely individually and unconsciously. They scarcely understand how much help is given by deliberate intention and training of the mind. As she did."

"Do you mean that she could have had worldly success and . . . power if she had chosen those instead?"

"Certainly. That is there for the taking. . . . Concentration is not necessarily concerned with what is called spirituality in its ends, but it is always power. Take for example Mr. Dunbar and Miss Ingmar. In both these is a very deep and experienced consciousness, and on that they have deliberately grafted power. His skill in languages is only of a few years' growth. Her marvelous art is a thing of yesterday if you count as mortals count time. So . . . you see!"

"But then, if this discipline of concentration became general it might be the cause of hideous wrong in the hands of people who grind their own axes."

"It has been often enough already and will be again, but the person who acts in accordance with law and spirituality is always the stronger eventually because he is swinging round with the universe; and the end is sure though not perhaps as we conceive it, for it sits above what we call good or evil. Besides, attainment needs such faith and patience that it is not often the low type of consciousness attempts or carries it through. By the way, if you can climb so far there is a glorious view of the Sind Valley from a crag above us."

If I could climb! I was the younger by ten years, and no man likes a doubt of his physical powers, though I must own he swung on and up before me, leading the way like a runner, every muscle smooth and braced. But I was panting a little and he was breathing evenly.

"You do it better than I. Why?" I asked at length, halting for a breather by a little spring bubbling in solitude from under a rock in perfect and lonely beauty. From far heights above, the shrill scream of a marmot came faintly. "Is your muscular power also yoga?" I added with some irony.

"Certainly it controls the body almost absolutely. You can for example transfer your nerve consciousness from one part to another, and that is not to be despised when there is pain. But for my part I have had the luck to be brought up without any of the poisons of civilization, and no doubt that counts. Could you, for instance, guess my age?"

Standing a little above me he looked down at me, laughing, and I surveyed him closely as I had never done yet. The golden-olive of his face was unlined, the eyes in their setting of heavy black Asian lashes were bright and clear, his hands smooth and expressive. Of his active figure I have spoken already. But all the same, determined to thwart any triumph, I resolved to overshoot the mark.

"Possibly forty," I said coolly. He laughed outright.

"A good guess, even a brilliant one, for that is the age I keep in mind while I am at work. Not too young to expect attention, nor too old for use. But I was sixty on my last birthday."

Silence.

"I don't believe it!" I said doggedly. He took that as a joke, laughing again.

"Don't be so incredulous! Have you ever met anyone before who has never tasted the flesh of any creature, nor any alcohol, nor the drugs in tea, coffee ana the other drinks of the kind—who lives entirely on fruit, milk and cheese with a little cereal . . . very little . . . now and again, and vegetables? Remember too I had the luck to be descended from generations who lived in the same way. But it is not only myself. The level of health in our monastery is amazing."

"You people would be perhaps easier to live with if you had a few vices. The superior man is alarming company," I retorted, beginning to climb again.

"Yet surely, though I lay no claim to representing him, it is the aim of every civilization to produce him as far as possible, and if it does not succeed it drops out."

It is difficult to argue on an almost perpendicular

climb, and in more ways than one he had the best of it; so I followed in silence, digesting what I had heard and still further inclining to the belief that Haridas, as a man whose aims were evidently comprehensible whatever his methods might be (for all the world understands the craving for health and success), would be the counselor I needed among the beliefs and attainments of Baltar. He could at least understand my point of view in a way which I was certain no one else would attempt. By his own account he had the experience which comes with years, and I appreciated the tact with which he left me to introduce the subject of my questions.

"Shall we sit here a bit?" I asked at last, my heart pumping in my ears. "I was seedy not long ago and perhaps I haven't quite pulled up yet!"

"By all means!" He sat down quietly among the ferns and leaned against a jut of rock, looking up into the serene above us. I huddled up with my arms clasped about my knees, and the pines drawing back a little whispered their own secrets among themselves in a soft monotonous undertone.

No balking now. I plunged straight into my subject, recalling his far-away eyes and thoughts.

"You did not hear what the Chinese monk told me the other night."

"Certainly not . . . not a word."

"And you never guessed or felt any of it yourself? The life here is so astonishing from many points of view that in spite of the perfect normal surface I feel as if I were living in a dream. It may be that you see through all my defenses as the Chinese did . . .

watching my little antics like those of a goldfish swimming in a glass globe. Is that so?"

He straightened himself, sat up, and gave me his whole attention instantly. His face changed, becoming grave and concentrated.

"I cannot deny that I see things. It has been a part of my training. I see for instance that you are not happy . . . and why."

"Not happy?" I said angrily. "I am one of those fellows who enjoy everything and . . ."

"No, no. You are not happy. If you wish to consult the doctor, why hide the symptoms? If I can be of any use command me. If not—shall we make our way up to the crag?"

That brought me to reason. I gripped my hands in each other about my knees and began:

"No, I am not happy. I want more and less than I have. Why do I remember things that other men forget and make nothing of? It's true the Chinese brought them to the surface a week ago, but he could never have done that if they had not been lying there. Most men bury them, grass and flowers grow above them, and so an end. They can divide themselves into water-tight compartments. My life is like the links of a chain. I can't let one drop. I want to forget."

His look was so fixed and remote that for a moment I doubted if he had heard me. It seemed to be fixed on some inward thought of his own. But he looked down at me and I knew myself mistaken.

"The reason is that you are in a more advanced stage of perception than the men of whom you speak, though it is very difficult to judge them. You begin to connect cause and effect. If you could not sleep that night it was because you felt that every deed casts its shadow, and that you lie in the dark of your own life. If a man puts out the sun can he arraign any but himself for the darkness?"

"If you knew what I felt, do you know more? Tell me if you will before I leave Baltar. I am so bitterly out of place here. I shall go up into the mountains alone."

"You cannot do that. The time is not ripe for it yet. You would be sent back. And you are not out of place here. You are only suffering the pangs of adjustment to a new conception of the universe . . . but you will conquer and outgrow them. Am I to speak freely or no?"

"I wish it if you will."

"What has chiefly gone wrong with you (difficult enough to avoid in your environment!) is your relations with women. There has been no harmony there . . . destruction and the pain that is the following shadow of very brief enjoyment. Was it worth it?"

"Ah . . . you are a monk. You can't understand. But—yes, . . . it was worth it a hundred times. It was life, and life is not one color but all, and the man is nothing without the woman or the woman without the man."

He smiled unexpectedly.

"You are perfectly right. That was why I asked you. You know it taught you certain things well worth the cost. So it does. But what did it teach you?"

Now I collected my thoughts. That was a hard

question. It was some minutes before I could answer.

"I won't belie love and for love itself I have no penitence. It's the complications that make the ruin . . . the people that stand in one's way and that one must trample underfoot to get to the goal; the petty deceits. All that I can't deal with, and it leaves a bitter sour taste in the mouth . . . but for love itself and what it taught me . . . It's the only thing in the world that ever made me believe in an existence outside my own. I forgot myself for good and all while it lasted. We were each both. I was swept along on a great rolling current that carried me to a kind of terrible heaven where only she existed. How could that leave me the same man? It didn't . . . it was then I began to paint. She sat for my first portrait. But it seems to have fizzled out completely now."

"So you too had your yoga!" he said, smiling with perfect comprehension. "That was yoga in its truth though not in its height. You were swept out of your prison-house of egoism while it lasted and saw the world as it is, transfigured into a kind of wild glory. And it bore its inevitable fruit in beauty. Love is a mighty kind of yoga. In its higher forms the only one. Well . . . be thankful you have known it though the prison doors have closed about you again!"

Astonishment seized me. A monk and this was his verdict! But I would not have it on false pretenses.

"You don't understand. She was another man's wife and he was my friend. As to other women, they were before and after, but they never counted."

"Do I say it should have been? That neither I nor

any other can judge," he answered steadily. "I am considering it only as a part of your development. Can you say you are the worse man for it? Was she the worse woman?"

I sat reflecting. A very hard question to answer—both for myself and another. At last I replied:

"Upon my word I don't know. I can't even say the end justified the means. It was during the war. She went back to her husband—as a matter of fact he never knew. Love blew over me and then away like a typhoon, leaving my life smashed up, myself utterly at sea, but with all my old illusions scattered, and . . . a bit of a painter. I have drifted since in body and mind. How do you diagnose the case?"

"Then you have no regard for her now?"

"In that sense, none. She is a bitter memory. I have—I think I always had—more true regard for her husband. But I want to go my way and forget. They say you are a wise man. Then show me how . . . and how to make something or other of my life!"

"And how can I or anyone do that until you understand what life is? Here at Baltar people are working on definitely proved knowledge to a certain end. No man can save another. He may throw the life-belt but no more. I can only say—be a lamp to yourself. You have done a certain deed. Take the use of what you did. Begin with small beginnings."

"For heaven's sake utter no platitudes about being good, and climbing up somehow to a heaven that would bore me to tears. Tell me something practical that will hammer a little common sense and resolution into me."

He smiled.

"One does not begin infants on the mathematics of infinite magnitudes. I suggest that you learn to control your thoughts and concentrate them with passion on the thing you really wish to have. You did that once unconsciously and gained the prize, and as to religion, you tasted it then; religion (so called) is a timeless ecstasy of union. Was it good enough for you to desire to possess it again with the added power of directing it to what ends you will? I do not speak to a man ignorant of yoga. You have had the experience without understanding its meaning. You are in a position to judge. What you felt is the highest symbol we know of religion."

His attitude and words filled me with such astonishment as drove me into silence. I sat, staring out over the trees below us. No censure, no sense of sin could I detect in any one of his words. But they conveyed a view to me; something he had not said overtook me, a sense of my ignorance as of a child playing with matches in a magazine with the certainty of thunderous explosions about him. I had had an earth-shaking experience and missed its meaning entirely— That was all, and enough, but I put it to the touch.

"Why have you not said a word of condemnation of a rather flagrant adultery? You are a monk, a man of religious life. Why don't you say straight out it was a crime? I should think the more of you."

Then indeed he turned on me with power.

"Who can communicate the truth to ignorance? And who can say what is good or evil? Those who are instructed know that truth sits above both, and that there is no dualism in the world at all. This I can say. You committed an antisocial act. Of that there can be no question. But a deed is judged in eternity by motive and consequences, and you can still make the consequence to yourself what you will. She also, if she has understanding and patience. Never doubt that you will pay the uttermost farthing that is due, but the deed is of earth, the thought behind it eternity."

Did I understand? Not wholly. But a glimpse of something high, august, watching implacable but friendly, shot across me like a sun-ray through tempest—something that drew the heart like a yearning for an instant, and was veiled in darkness again. We sat a moment in silence, and then Haridas continued in his usual tone.

"If you choose I will give you the rules of the yoga discipline for concentration. You will not find them easy, but they lead quite definitely to self-control if you have patience."

I accepted with some eagerness.

"And now for the crag."

He led the way onward and upward, talking, I remember, of the rock sculptures of Ellora and the inward meanings of Indian art. He knew his subject and as I toiled up after him its fascination was so powerful that for the moment I thought of nothing else. That man had intellectual mastery as well as spiritual, and I thought the former the stronger of the two and to me the more attractive. The notion of experimenting with yoga appealed to me however on that side only . . . a new and stimulating process of improving my work. Had I not Narendra as an example of its triumph in art? And something Western and arrogant in the back of my mind was half inclined to pooh-pooh the whole thing.

An hour later the crag loomed above us, and crashing through underbrush, with hands as well as feet we conquered it, even Haridas panting a little; I almost done. And there we lay, recovering. But it was worth it and more.

Rocks and giant trees, impenetrable woods about and below us, snow peaks closing the horizon north, south, east and west,—dreaming in sunshine as though, all terrors laid aside, they shared the truce of God. A bird sang from a tree and I heard a cuckoo's call drop into the valley like pearls. About us floated a flicker of butterflies haunting the myriads of flowers jeweling the turf between the crags. A sight divine and wonderful, to be remembered when age darkens down and memory burns dim like a lamp in the coming night.

It was wonderful past all whooping. We sat and gazed, drawing deep draughts of beauty, and said no word, absorbed into the breathing dream of Nature until it became the one living, salient reality and we ourselves a part of it, small as the blue-winged butterfly that alighted at my feet . . . a mote and no more in the ocean of sunshine and joy. What Haridas felt was beyond me. His face was fixed and calm as the Egyptian sphinx gazing out over the immensities. Nor can I tell how long we sat there amongst the sea of green pine tops. I saw a little blue curl of smoke and pointed silently. He smiled.

"Yes—the hearth. The home." And was silent. At last still silently we rose and leaving the august presences of the height made our way down to the level of humanity, speaking only of the way and its sights until we reached the waterfall and parted, the dusk rising through the trees like smoke.

That evening was brought a little paper of directions, so simple, I thought, as to be almost puerile, ordaining the posture in which I should sit, the manner in which I should breathe as the means of steadying wandering thoughts. I put it into the drawer of my writing-table and went down to dinner by no means decided to try my luck.

As a matter of fact it was driven out of my head by the arrival of another letter from the Monastery of the Manis brought down by two Ladakhi traders, with their yaks, who had been intercepted at some distance from the monastery and used as post-runners. They stood at the door in the light of electric lamps, so full of pride and importance at having acquitted themselves of a trust so honorable as coming from the abbot of the Manis that they refused stedfastly to accept any reward.

Brynhild was among them, stroking the great heavy beasts with steaming nostrils and heavy flanks, and wherever she moved their eyes followed her and could not be satisfied. The Ladakhis, with kindly grinning Mongolian faces, remarked upon it to Dunbar, as he told me afterwards.

"It is the power of the Buddhas . . . the Incarnations!" they said with delight. "See that yak—he is one that walks alone and hates all beings, man and brute, but when she comes he pushes his nose into her hand! So would it be with the snow-leopards up yonder. Possibly she is herself an incarnation."

They went off triumphant to the rest house, forcibly hauling the yak after them. We went into the hall, and Dunbar untied the silk securing the little flat parcel.

> BROTHER OF THE PEN:
>
> Many hundreds of manuscripts have been read and laid in order and great is their wisdom, the work of many lifetimes. But among them is one that fills our minds with amazement and our hearts with joy. And what we say to you is this: Come, making no delay when the snows melt even a little on the Zoji La. Surely those coming on such an errand will come in the power of the Buddhas; and what is snow that it should hurt them? We have learned from Those Who Know that this year the Pass opens early. Come, therefore, giving and receiving joy.

"They know what they are talking of," said Dunbar after dinner, "and I see no reason why we should not start in a month. Haridas has wished it all along. It will be a most wonderful experience, and as for the manuscript . . . I have a belief that it will be the one."

"I too!" said Lady Lucia. "And certainly I have no fear of the Pass. Nor has Brynhild."

"I long for it. I had the strangest dream of it last night, and of the monastery. Wonderful snow and mighty mountains and the monastery on the side of a precipice, high, high up . . . so much a part of the rock and mountain that it seemed our hosts would be the very spirits of the hills, and their talk the roaring of the wind down wild ravines."

"Trolls and kobolds?" I suggested, watching the illumination of her face.

"No . . . no. Something vast and kindly yet most

utterly strange and far from us. But we shall win them. We shall understand."

That I well believed, looking at the two women who were to be our companions. It would be a troll or kobold indeed who would hold away from Lady Lucia's radiance. It would be an adventure of adventures—a memory to center a life.

"Was there any date fixed for return?" I asked Dunbar.

"No—that's not our way. We wander while the spirit moves us and never turn back until we must. My faithful Japanese Tazaki comes with us and while we are away his brother rules all here. A Japanese is a fine fellow in a tight place, and there are tight places pretty often up yonder. Now I must take this letter up to Haridas."

Lady Lucia turned to cloak herself for a visit to the dying monk in the hospital, and Brynhild and I to her studio that I might see what I had not seen when "Mirage" captured me.

I had never really been alone with her before for longer than a few minutes, and like a jewel held where it can pick up light and reflect it she shone in her studio. A clear shining, not a restless one however, and with no flaw of pride in her achievement.

It must have been the talk with Haridas which had opened my eyes to new values for I saw it on an entirely different plane now. It offered a new relation to life and its deepest meanings. Can I explain with any hope of success?

She showed me the naked figure of a woman flung back violently almost prone on the air as she grasped upwards at something out of sight. In the hand two eagle feathers—the eagle uncapturable, far out of reach in the blue, but the remembrance, the token, left that would wing life henceforward to follow the flight. She had called it "Aspiration"—a word which has many different meanings for different minds. Here, with the words, and still more, the implications of the life about me, I felt it to be Attainment—as much at least as could be hoped in the purblind, crippled state of consciousness which most of us are content to call living. I said as much and she looked at me strangely.

We sat for some time talking more intimately than we had ever done yet, but little of her work. She avoided that and I had the feeling that it touched the very innermost strongholds of her being and that the singularity of the manner of its coming was inexplicable in part even to herself. She told me much, however, of her stay with the Indian friends of Haridas, and the terrible beauty of the mountains and wild ways leading into perilous places.

"It helped the discipline they put me through," she said simply. "One should choose one's place. Don't undertake that lightly if you ever think of doing it. It needs—many things. Be careful."

I would have asked her more. That subject was uppermost in my mind amongst the silent witnesses in her studio, but Lady Lucia came in from the hospital, still rapt in the peace of the dying monk, and we went slowly back to the house through flooding moonlight.

I knew then that I would not leave Baltar. That mood had passed. And so the days went by, slipping smoothly into weeks, and each day brought its harvest.

CHAPTER VII

IN MY SOLITARY HOURS THOUGHTS CROWDED IN UPON me now so new to me that I trembled before them as might a man landed in a new planet. I could not see Haridas often. The Dunbars and Brynhild were engaged with their own work, and though we met for rides, walks, talks, I knew that was but the surface play upon very profound deeps. Therefore I observed and commented in my own mind upon what was passing around me.

My painting I had laid entirely aside for the moment for it appeared to me—as it does often, I believe, to a man writing a book—that I had seen it from the wrong angle and the approach must be reconstituted. Haridas had sent me a fine translation of the books of the Vedanta with his own book, "The Norm," on Buddhist teaching, and was always at my service to elucidate a meaning, but very briefly before he plunged into his own work again. Amongst other things he said:

"A man's life is never truly his own; his courage is never aflame with the cosmic fire until he ceases to believe in evil and knows himself one and indivisible from the One that is the Universe and so much more as we cannot conceive except in moments of illumination."

"They will certainly never come my way!" I said, fluttering over the leaves of the books with discontent.

He smiled and went off with the one last word . . . "Read!" And I read.

Now as I read I saw why certain things which bewildered me must be. I saw why there was no proselytizing at Baltar, for instance; why they spoke so little and argued not at all on what they held for the mainspring of life. It was there, at the heart of every deed, but the lesser truths evaporate in words, and the greater truths transcend them; therefore the attempt at exactness of statement is not only unwise but dangerous, for it means the crystallization of living truth into dead dogma and petrifaction. But sometimes, book in hand, meeting Brynhild in the studio or coming and going under the sunny trees, I would open it and say, "Tell me—" that I might see her eyes soften into insight more beautiful than any words. Once it was a lovely passage from the Upanishads:

> Two birds, inseparable friends, alight on the selfsame tree. One eats of the sweet fruit: the other, eating not, watches without ceasing.

"You eat and are at home," I said. "I shall never be anything but a hungry looker-on."

"You are more already, but the watching bird means the Universal Soul watching while the hungry earth-bird feeds. Not that any winged thing is really earthy. The bird is always a great symbol in India and China like the dove in Christianity. And will you laugh if I say that knowing this has given me my power with birds? The Self is at home in them as it is in animals, also, for those who take the trouble to understand their true consciousness and not to intrude our own on them. Would you like them to come to you as they do to me? But you must be very quiet."

She read my face and as we stood under the trees whistled a note like a fairy flute, laying her finger-tips on my shoulder.

A moment and there was a soft whirring of wings above us, and two wild pigeons hovered down through the boughs circling slowly to the ground. She stretched out her hand and one settled in the palm, the other on her arm, looking up at her and me with human understanding and pleasure and little soft movements and expanding feathers, a lovely ruffle of life. She raised her hand slowly to the level of my shoulder, still keeping her finger-tips on the other, and one alighted there, the other on my hand.

For the moment it seemed to me that I had never had a pleasure so pure and selfless as that perfect trust of a wild thing. I have said so often, "I cannot explain it"—of the happenings of Baltar, nor can I this, but it was the great wild woods coming in to find a refuge in my heart. I was an exile no longer. The gates of Eden had opened and within was:

"The Golden Age, the Golden Age come back."

Does it seem much to spring from a small cause? How can I tell? I knew in that moment that I would break truce no more. Those wild-bright eyes looked up into mine, and my shooting days were done. It is better to hold the hand of Nature and look into her eyes than to alienate and slaughter her. One climbing up nestled in my throat—the warm pulsing life touched mine and how long we stood in that enchantment I do not know. She whistled again very softly and they fluttered to my feet, at home and content. Then gradually their own affairs claimed them and they flew off. She lifted her hand from my shoulder.

"Do you know what you have done?" I asked, turning on her. "You have given me one of the loveliest moments of my life—a moment of revelation. I have done with *shikar* now and henceforth."

She laughed a little.

"I knew you'd say that. No one gives up a great happiness for a worthless thing. And you'll be amazed when you find what can be done with practice. Some of the wise men in India have no fear of tigers or snakes. They never hurt them. I suppose it's because the thought of fear on either side never passes between them. Fear cuts off all the currents—it's a horrible low-down skulking thing."

There I could agree, but it is easier to condemn than avoid, and again I had my lesson in sterner fashion. We rode up one day to the glacier of Wardrang—a day of sunny and delicious peace irradiating the mighty crags and the smallest flower rejoicing beneath them—Lady Lucia, Brynhild and I with two guides.

I shall never forget the crystal running of the mountain streams as our ponies splashed through them, the universe of illimitable breadth and crystalline purity in which we breathed and moved, the sense of perfect health and freedom. We were truly enough friends by this time to talk or be silent as we chose, and often, as the track rose into the heights, were silent and yet the nearer for it.

No sign of life—not even the hut of a Gujar tending his flocks in the mountain meadows—did we see. Excepting indeed the hawk and eagle hovering above us and the piercing shriek of the marmot thrilling through still air, with his quaint brown body vanishing as we turned. It was Giant-Land, the immensities of huge mountains crowding round the track, storming the sky, even the courageous pines lagging behind us in the valleys.

It was when we reached the moraine of the glacier and saw the cave high above like a wound, whence the icy, crystal life-blood of the mountains welled eternally from its heart, that a black cloud rising in wrath suddenly dimmed the harebell blue of the sky. So one must not intrude unasked on the solitude of the gods! I noticed that Lady Lucia looked up quickly, and putting her hands to her mouth, hallooed to Brynhild, who had dismounted and wandered off upward:

"Come back. No time to lose!"

"We must get back instantly!" she said, turning to me. "Those sudden storms always mean danger here. No—we can't delay for lunch. We must ride hard."

And literally before the sentence was done we were lashed with stinging, whipping rain, and the deluge was upon us from clouds thickening and blackening until the blue was lost in tragedy. We mounted and rode at the quickest pace that the guides could keep up, for it was their experience which must guide us along the now lost ways and above all across the rivers.

"Rivers?" I said in the utmost astonishment. "But there were no rivers. A child could scramble across."

"You don't know the mountains!" Brynhild said

laughing. "Those brooks will be raging torrents in half an hour of this rain, and we've got to cross them, for the storms up here last for days sometimes."

"And there's nowhere to shelter!" Lady Lucia added, urging her pony on. "It's always touch and go when one gets caught up here. The mountains are quick-change artists."

They were both laughing, gay and cheerful as at a summer picnic, the rain streaming off them (for it turned out that the coolies had forgotten the mackintoshes) pouring in spouts from their riding hats, themselves as ready and fearless as if to risk one's life in the mountains were part of a day's enjoyment.

The coolies alone looked set and anxious as they strode on, heavy with responsibility to the sahib for his wife and guests. Crashes of thunder, flashes of lightning. That track, that day, will always stand for a symbol of desolation in my mind, with the frightful roar of thunder volleying from crag to crag about us, the gloom torn by lightning flashes.

I remember a dead ewe and her new-born lamb lay pitifully beside the track, done with the struggle, drenched with rain. It centered the terror in helpless dumb protest. But still the women rode on laughing, though even the ponies, rain-lashed and storm-beaten, would have gladly turned for shelter under any crag.

And it was then we came to the last brook we had crossed that morning—a crystal runnel then, it was now a great torrent plunging down the hill like a lion roaring for its prey, carrying fallen logs and branches lost in a tatter of destruction.

"We can't do it. You shall not attempt it!" I said

resolutely. "I'll ride through with one of the men to try it, and you stay here and get what shelter you can with the horses until I come back. I beg you to listen to me . . ." For I saw refusal in Lady Lucia's face before she spoke.

"I must go first for I know the fords best. There are three more of these torrents to cross before we get to the neck of our own valley, and the last is the worst of all. If we get so far I'm sure they will meet us and try to run a Kashmiri bridge across if it's too bad to ford. Don't be afraid for us. Brynhild doesn't mind."

And certainly I can answer for it that she did not. There she was in dripping coat and breeches, her hat long since reduced to pulp and flung away, the rain pouring off her hair, rosy with exertion, as glad and gay as any girl in Christendom or out of it.

"I'm going first!" she shouted against the wind. "No, Mr. Cardonald, I know the ropes. You stay with Lady Lucia. Come on, Subhana."

I had to catch her bridle, restrain her by force and thrust myself in for the first try, though I believe now the safest way for them might have been to send them first. They agreed instantly, seeing my meaning and time precious, while the two men closed up on either side of my pony to steady him in the desperate thrust of water. In a moment more we were battling for our lives. I had one glimpse of Brynhild's face as we went in and saw it calm, assured and steady, watching with clear understanding of danger and chances, and secure either way. She waved her hand to me. After all, when death grapples with a man it is something to have such eyes on duty.

The weight of water sent us staggering down-stream, and I thought we were gone; but the courage and skill of the men steadied the pony, and he was himself chock-a-block with wary wisdom and intelligence. In the thick spuming brown water neither he nor we could see an instant's footing. We trusted and tried and balanced and crept, dashed with flying foam above our necks, and in a wild dazzle of wind and water and rain somehow we got into shallow water and ashore. I tethered him to a forlorn juniper bush and staggered back with the men to fetch the two. It could be done, they decided.

Lady Lucia insisted that Brynhild should be next and there was no time for argument. She came. A terrible rush of water swept her from the saddle into my arms as I waded beside her, nearly breast-deep, and a man stumbled and I thought all was over. It would have been, but for her activity as she scrambled upright again and crouched forward to ease the pony. Even before we reached the other shore she was down and off, wading and leading him, calling to us to go back—she was all right.

The third trip was the worst. I need not describe it. The pony fell, and we dragged Lady Lucia from under him and got him on his feet and made the passage somehow with my arm about her and the certainty in my mind that if the other three fords were to be like this the thing was impossible. Her wrist was cut, the temple bruised, and if those ponies had not been the hardiest little stout-hearts on earth there would not have been a chance for our lives. I can see Brynhild now stroking and gentling them in the storm, and their eyes on hers with reassuring and comfort passing between them. She walked and Lady Lucia also whenever it was possible to spare them.

Have I made a long story of it? My excuse must be that I learned so much of the two who had played and were to play so large a part in giving me what I may call the Key of the Fields . . . in other words, the knowledge that means liberation. From that day I loved them both with the love which I suppose must always follow understanding of any such humanity.

After the second ford, which I shall not linger to describe, we heard shouts and knew our difficulties were done. It was Dunbar with a party of men, ponies and tents. A Gujar who had seen us pass had come in with news of a storm over Wardrang, and instantly guessing the danger, he had set out with eager volunteers, crossing the streams below without danger to set up a night's home in the wilderness. The unemotional English meeting amidst the excitement of the Kashmiris was as characteristic as the Japanese stoicism of the excellent Tazaki, Dunbar's servant, a man as true as steel and apparently as cold; but I saw his eyes on his mistress and understood his reserve.

It was a strange night. The comfort of the tents was what Indian servants provide as a matter of course in the most impossible circumstances, and it was weird enough to hear the wild saga of the rain driving outside in the frightful desolation and the roar of rivers frantically dashing down the gullies. Yet it was home; a brazier flickered firelight over the tent-walls, and after hot baths and dinner the adventure might never have been but for Lady Lucia's bound wrist.

She had thanked me where no thanks were due, with her lovely graciousness, for my dash through the torrent—Brynhild more slightly and with a reserved little smile. She alternately drew and repelled me in the strangest way. One day I could swear our friendship was ripening into sunniest warmth; the next, she was again at a distance, was coolly kind; no more. Was she afraid of me? Or of herself? It was enough to pique any man, and the more so because I loved the courage and gallantry in her, the look in her fearless eyes, the buried glow of strength which she covered with silence in daily life, allowing it to escape only in the sinister beauty of "Mirage," the loveliness perfect and divine of the "Enlightened Buddha." No man could afford to lose such a friendship and I least of all, whose footsteps were stumbling on the borders of the undiscovered country to which Baltar was the gateway. I half resolved to summon up courage and find out where I stood, making it perfectly clear that she had no demand to fear more urgent than that small share of friendship which she had already promised me in looks if not in words.

I sat studying her by stealth and wondering how she would take my question, when Dunbar gave me a letter he had brought up for me. It was from Mrs. Mainguy. I read it with interest whilst the others were busy with theirs. It was extremely characteristic and recalled her vivid, ugly face in every word and dash.

Dear Car,

And how is the angelic choir using you? You promised to let me know but not a scratch of your pen has reached this child, and all Simla that's Simla (though very few

> folk are here yet) is jumping to know how the black sheep is faring. Baltar's a queer place, and I can imagine it giving one a chill on the liver if one didn't fit in, though Lucia's always Lucia. And how's the Canadian lemon? I heard an extraordinary yarn about her the other day. Did you ever know Halmar Olesen from Ranipur? He's here and says she was desperately in love two years ago with John Ormond, a friend of his. They met in a rest house on the Simla-Tibet Road, and the end of it was she said she could have nothing to do with him until he had worked up all kinds of occult things which it appears she prides herself on. And the misguided man went up into Tibet Mahatma-hunting and has never been heard of from that day to this! What do you know about *that!* Ask her about John O. and see what she says. Olesen tells me she practically considers herself a widow. Didn't I know there was something queer under all that silence? It would make a good dish for my next bridge-tea if you could find out what really happened to Ormond. Didn't I know she would be unbearable the minute I saw her, and did *you* ever know me out in my reckoning?

She diverged then to other topics with enthusiastic messages to Lady Lucia and an enclosure to her which I duly handed over.

It is not too much to say that my nicely balanced emotions as regarded Mrs. Mainguy toppled over into distaste pronounced enough to be classed as detestation when I crumpled the letter and tossed it into the brazier. Brynhild sat opposite reading a letter of her own which called up the wistful beauty of expression that to my mind transfigured her for the moment into human, approachable loveliness. Was it from John Ormond? And was her reserve the common "Don't touch me, I'm another's," which some women flaunt in a man's face?

We had all seemed somehow to belong to each other at Baltar—a perfect square, apart, yet belonging, and to have an intruder, a fifth, thrust in was revolting.

I could not even imagine how Lady Lucia could endure such a woman as Mrs. Mainguy, but that never had been clear to me except on the principle of loving the enemies whom one could never like. Yet she read her own letter with enthusiasm.

"Blanche is a perfect wonder—what do you think she is doing, Lance? Having that poor governess of Mrs. Coryat's up to stay with her—the girl we had here. She has been ill again. And Blanche says—isn't it just like her?—'And I mean to find her a husband that'll turn all the spins green with jealousy.' And she will! And the absolutely wrong one!"

"She had better let it alone!" I said so sourly that the incident dissolved in laughter.

But not from my mind. John Ormond invaded my peace. Not with the jealousy of a lover, but with a teasing persistence coloring all my thoughts of Brynhild. Could it be true? Was that the secret at the back of her apartness? Was her heart wandering through the Himalayan snow wastes in search of lost love, and did that explain her cry to Lady Lucia: "You know why I want to get to the mountains! You know!" Despise Mrs. Mainguy's gossip as I would she had damaged my peace and I detested her, even with the assurance that supposing I broke my leg she would nurse me like a mother.

We were held on the mountain waste for two nights, for though next day dawned divinely the torrents were still too dangerous. Brynhild and I hunted for garnets along the edge of the swirling stream that might have drowned us. They are plentiful in many of the hill places, and Dunbar told us that some of the border tribesmen used them for bullets, imbedded in lead which is far more precious.

All the time I watched her face and words for revelations, and none came, and I dared not venture an inch further, though the old urge of leaving Baltar recurred for the moment. For I felt so cut loose and disjointed by that cursed letter that I wanted to be alone and think things over. I had the feeling that I was being captured and I must get my bearings clearly before I submitted. But I led the talk as subtly as I could to the journey before us beyond the pass that climbs to the upper country.

"It seems rather a dangerous undertaking for you and Lady Lucia, and since yesterday when danger was on us in a flash I've been wondering that Dunbar risks you. Of course he must go but it can't be urgent for you."

She smiled, fingering the little rough stones.

"Neither she nor I would stay behind for the world. We shall see the most wonderful pictures and images in the lamaseries. I expect them to give me quite a new angle on my work. . . . And imagine waiting tamely down here while you are all hunting for the manuscript and perhaps coming face to face with the Diamond Scepter!"

"But do you really believe that story? Surely no more impossible yarn ever came down from the mountains."

We were sitting on a rock with sheep cropping the

short herbage about us, their master black-browed and black-turbaned leaning on his staff a short way off and watching the sahibs and their doings with fixed interest. An astonishing change from yesterday.

"Why not? I've known things as strange though not so dramatic, and the same cause at the back of all. In what they call Raja Yoga, which is what Haridas has suggested to you, there are powers that one can lay hold of according to one's strength and knowledge. Hasn't he told you?"

I caught at the opening.

"Scarcely a word. He gave me a few rules but I put them away and— Well, I have had a lot to think of and I waited for another talk with him. Do tell me what you know."

She sat for a moment, looking at the dangerous rush of water, then said slowly: "I couldn't tell you much and I'm not sure you really care to know. If one does care one thinks it worth a lot of trouble. You should ask Haridas. But I can tell you a very little if you really like."

I made my protest. She went on, her hands folded in her lap— That was one thing I had noticed—the extraordinary stillness of all her poses. She would sit without moving an eyelash even when she talked. At first it had the effect of monotony. Gradually I understood it as control.

"Those rules and a few more train one's mind-stuff to the point where it can identify itself with the *real* meaning of the things one sees about one. That's very different from the surface meaning. But, when you *know,* you are in the same vibration—you have realized your oneness with them. You can see the oneness of past and future and lose the earthly idea of time. You can have the knowledge of what is far off. You can have control of your body and do what seem strange things with it. And there are certainly a few who have been able to see there is no reality in death and to go on indefinitely re-creating their bodies as we all do daily in health and youth."

I listened in amazement. "Do you repeat this like a parrot? Or can you really mean you know anything practically about it?"

Her eyes were bright and clear, and she fixed them steadily on mine.

"I know a little. How do you suppose I call my birds and beasts? I understand every sound they make because we are in the same vibration. How do you think my work came? But I have a lot to learn yet. So have we all. If you think into it, you'll see all this only means achieving freedom, and that, after all, is our right. We are such prisoners of our senses."

My mind was retracking her words. "Do you mean that yesterday either of you could have done anything superhuman to get us out of danger?"

"No—not that. There's no such thing as superhuman. It's all law, and those who know can of course still the winds and waves, as you remember. But even if one could one wouldn't unless there were some great divine reason. One shouldn't interfere unless one knows. When one is free what meaning has death? What I think and am is very much more important than whether I die before night, and far more interesting."

There was a long silence—if it can be called silence where the myriad voices of the water shouted about us.

"Can you understand that?" I said suddenly, pointing to the rushing river.

She laughed aloud. "I should think so! And you? Listen."

She gathered herself together—I can use no other expression—and laid her hand on mine. Instantly the miracle happened. I was caught up—a breathless instrument—into a thundering orchestra of joy. Joy broke about me. The sky rained bliss, the mountains shouted it one to another, the rivers roared their triumph—but not theirs alone for all was one. A mighty pæan, the unstruck music of the universe, drowned all hearing. Was it sound or the innermost of silence? I shall never know. I forgot her existence and my own. All was a part of the atom, the atom held the whole in its circumference. Utterance failed. Had I died of the agony of joy? Was it death? Was it life? . . . Something in me exulted in waves of confused delight—the spray heaven-high—the billows in and outside of time.

She lifted her hand and once more I heard with my ears and saw with my eyes. But I hid my face with my hand and was speechless.

Long afterwards—as we walked slowly back to the tents in the sunset—I asked if she had made me dream awake or what. She detected the undertone in my voice and answered quickly and kindly:

"Oh, no. For a moment you saw through me. Perhaps I did wrong, but I thought it would be beautiful if you could be one with the world up here for the moment and dip your feet in the ocean of joy splashing and tumbling about us, though sometimes it lies as calm and shining as the Indian Ocean at night. You would have to learn to see for yourself. It's never right to lean on other people. Does it make you want to learn?" she added wistfully.

"It makes me realize that it is the one thing worth learning," I said, and for the first time meant it.

After a pause, I put one more question.

"Do you see and feel this always?"

"No—I couldn't live my daily life on that plane. Only a perfected soul could do that. I don't know enough yet. But I can have it when I wish and need it—and always before I work." Her voice trembled a little—for the first time I saw her composure broken, though so slightly.

She pushed aside the curtain of her tent and went in.

That night I made a brief creed, if so I may call it, from the book which Haridas had given me. I had read a little daily of his summary of the highest thought of India in matters spiritual. My reason had acquiesced but my heart had not as yet spoken. Now there was a dim stirring, a drawing toward things unseen as if they might be of avail in all the problems of life. Late into the night I sat, reading over what I had written.

> I believe that in all the world is no duality, but only the One of which we are a part. I believe that what we call "good" is undeveloped perfection, and that what we call "evil" is undeveloped good. I believe that every form of life from the lowest forms of what we call mat-

ter is on its upward way of evolution and will inevitably attain perfection, enlightenment, and union with the Source. I believe that with our fallible senses and brain we cannot attain to the knowledge of absolute truth but only to the knowledge of relative truth; and that therefore we live in a delusive world created by the false perception of our senses, but that around and about us lies the true universe of things as they are, which has been beheld by some highly enlightened or perfected souls in flashes of higher consciousness, and that it should be the aim of all to attain to this true perception. I believe that the road to this perception is indicated in differing degrees of truth in all the faiths of the world, and that they should be regarded as the same statement in different languages, each suited to the environment and stage of evolution of varying souls. I believe in the evolution of the soul as well as of the body, and that the former is accomplished by the return to the stage of earthly experience which in the Orient is known as the process of reincarnation, though it may well be that this bald statement is to be regarded only as the symbol of a truth we cannot apprehend in its true verity. I believe that love, human and divine, is the great prison-breaker of that prison of the selfhood in which each of us lives barred and guarded until, like the flower within the buried bulb, he breaks his way to sunlight and the knowledge of the universe as it really is, thus attaining the crown of the processes of evolution and release from the need of what we term further earthly experience. And I believe that, for those who have attained true enlightenment, supernormal powers are available, but that in all the universe there is no possibility of the breaking of natural law, but only of understanding and using its supernormal possibilities. I believe that grief is ignorance. I believe our sole prayer should be:

"From the unreal lead us to the Real.
From our blindness lead us to light.
From evolution lead us to perfection.

Break down in us the prison of our false individuality and selfhood,
And unite us with the One who is in us and of whom we are a part.
Teach us to rejoice in our own nobility and to recognize our divinity that, in blindness, we may never sin against our true self.
Give us therefore to see death and life as dreams vanishing in the dawn of the soul."

That is only my own rendering and faulty enough, but it was a step upward for me at that time. I sat reading in the silence of the sleeping house and the greater silence of the night at my window, and some dim apprehension of great Presences about me stirred in my heart. For the first time in my life I listened for them in awe.

CHAPTER VIII

THE SUN WAS STRENGTHENING DAILY, AND THE GARdens were in a flame of wild beauty when the time drew near for the start of our expedition to Tibet, but the life at Baltar had grown to be so much a part of my inmost self that I dreaded anything which must break up the routine of daily life. And who could tell to what this upheaval might lead? I took all change as a menace, for it was impossible for me to think forward to any time when Baltar would belong to me no more, and the world outside would have recaptured its prisoner.

I knew now that I had made an escape from the land of bondage, from the tame and commonplace, the monotonous and unastonishing, the ugly and moral into the kingdom of the beautiful and amazing, the instinctive and spontaneous, the new and amoral. Nobody at Baltar talked of whether a deed was good or bad. (I use antithesis in describing, but they never did.) They thought and spoke in terms only of happiness and beauty and if a subject held less interest than that it was dropped out as one drops an ugly color.

Does it sound dull? It never was. Mrs. Mainguy's letter, apart from its gossip, recalled to me with painful intensity the boredom of her bridge and cocktail parties with the scandals sandwiched hotly between. God knows they were dull! There was not one of us but could have predicted to a letter what would be said, eaten, drunk, smoked at the next assemblage, and at what point the ghastly monotony would become intolerable and we would file out, talking and laughing loudly and keeping our hearts up to the last, pretending we had enjoyed ourselves. I never was able to imagine why any adult of higher mental rank than a prize rabbit should go there at all and came to the conclusion that the only answer was—he didn't. We were idiots, men and women alike, but no one had ever told or shown us a better way of amusing ourselves, and human nature must have some attempt at distraction however it gets it. That fundamental was fully recognized at Baltar, with the sole difference that the amusement was—amusing. The days fled like swift-winged birds, and the nights were fulfilled with sleep.

An extraordinary realization of health grew in me—a sort of inward sunshine. I had never before known the magnificence of bodily well-being, and could only suppose it the result of the purest air in the world, the healthy living and complete enjoyment of it. At Baltar it was good to be alive. I remember I said this one day to Lady Lucia, adding that I wanted never to leave it again—it had grown to be home to a homeless man. She asked with her childlike earnestness:

"And why should you leave it? I can see no reason on earth unless you get tired of us. But what about the mountains? Don't you want to come?"

"Of course. Baltar would not be Baltar unless you

were all here. You three make it home. You are goodness itself and I must not trade on that."

"Friends never trade!" she said laughing. "They are part of oneself, and this place belongs to us all." Then more gravely: "Brynhild and I have seen our dying monk this morning, and he told me that he had spent the night in a land as much more beautiful than Baltar as Baltar is lovelier than a grimy city." I listened enchanted. It was like a song. "He saw the trees loaded with flowers whose scent can be heard in music and the music is speech. Thought is speech also, and the now is always the past and future as well, and time and space are no longer fetters and divisions." She stopped as if words were useless, then said slowly:

"It's as if all the senses were resolved into one clear perception. I think that's what he tries to make clear. I know it myself—but one sees the hopelessness of speech—one wants a new language to express such things, or rather to think them to each other—a kind of silent music."

"But it's the land of the fourth dimension!" I had read most of what is said on that very high and difficult subject, and the inference flashed into my brain. "If that's true and it interpenetrates our world as the mathematicians say, then heaven is here and now, and things are happening about us which would strike us dumb if we understood."

"Exactly what he said. 'I step out from you and yet am amongst you who remain in the land of shadows though I walk in sunshine. You will know, you will see me sometimes in dream and vision until I go my appointed way; then no more for a while.' "

"His appointed way?"

"He means reincarnation, though that word expresses only little of its mysteries and that too is beyond words. But such as it is, it must be undergone until the last stain is gone and the heights are reached. For him they cannot be very far away. Would you like to see him before he dies?"

"He would not like a stranger," I said with hesitation, "otherwise . . . And then I could not understand him."

"He always speaks English with us. No, he would not mind if you wish it. Ask Haridas to take you. I think you would be glad to have gone. I see Haridas coming down the path now."

I took her at her word, more by impulse than thought, and caught him as he turned to the little hospital about ten minutes away, fronting east, with a glazed veranda facing due south and flooded with sunshine where several patients were often to be seen sunning themselves like winter flies on a wall.

"Come with me!" he said as we met. "You are used to seeing men die in war. Have you seen it in peace?"

"Strangely enough—never. But is it so near?"

"He will die this morning. We always know, and he told me this yesterday. So I am going to bid him good speed on the journey. The others will follow soon."

I turned back. "Then you will wish to be alone with him and I wouldn't push myself in for all the world. I'll go off now."

He laid a hand on my arm. "He wishes it and you

will not find it painful. You asked my advice some time ago on the way to escape sorrowful remembrance. You did not take it. Now I tell you that this death will be a part of your experience. You will come."

It was an assertion, not a question, and I fell in beside him. No word was said until we were in the room looking to the east.

That was its name, painted above the door, and I noticed others as we went along the wide passage: "The Room of Sleep"; "The Room of Joy"; "The Room of Quiet." It would be good to rest in any, if they resembled the one we entered now.

It was large and the broad window gazed towards the mountains, seen in wide vistas through the solemn green of the pines. They tossed against the sky—blue in the shadowed ravines bathed in morning gold, most ethereally fair and far. They seemed an aspiration—the vision of a soul at peace rather than a reality, so fair and faint they floated between heaven and earth. The doorlike sashes were flung wide, and the room was flooded with the perfumed breathing of the outdoor world. It was not unlike a flower itself—white with white draperies—and full in sight of the bed a most noble Chinese picture, one of the jewels of Dunbar's collection which I had seen in the hall a few days before. "Mountains and Pines in Mist." Nature, one might say, submerged in a gray trance of exquisite dream. It must have whispered "home" to the man who lay there, his face worn to transparent delicacy, his eyes closed in some white mood of bliss. Instinctively I halted on the threshold, but Haridas drew me on and silently closed the door.

Yet he heard and, as it were, came out from the innermost to meet us, for his eyelids opened and he smiled with a slight movement of the lips, raising a thin hand in welcome.

"It is well, brother?" Haridas asked in English.

"Brother, it is better than well," came the faint answer.

"I have brought a friend who will be more than a friend."

"He is welcome."

What could I say who felt myself nothing in spite of the prophecy of Haridas—I, who had not even taken the first step, lost and bewildered as I was in dying doubts and dreams? I stood like an image near the window, feeling myself most utterly a stranger and out of place. I would have gone if I had dared, but that seemed as impossible as staying, so I effaced myself and waited. The quiet voices went on.

"You had no pain in the night, for we all waked and upheld you with certainty."

"Brother, none. It was a night of bliss. I knew you were with me, and now freedom draws near. By what thoughts or deeds have I won this joy?"

"Remember and understand." I saw Haridas stoop and lay his hand on the dying man's brow. "Open the inward sight. Awake the hidden memory."

There was a long silence. I saw the men winding down from the House on the Hill and knew that death filled the room with his slowly rising tide. I could not have moved then. I waited breathless as though the whole world had paused to listen and yet with not a thought of death as I had hitherto understood it.

I could not measure time, but after a while Haridas withdrew his hand and the other opened his eyes with a smile of joy and wonder and spoke slowly:

"It is good. I shall remember in lives to be."

Haridas turned to me. "He has a word for you. Come." And as it seemed without will of my own I stood beside the bed trembling inwardly. What word could be possible between a Chinese monk and a man whose life had led him through such a world as mine? The atmosphere was charged with dread. He raised his hand feebly and laid it thin and transparent on mine. I could feel the dying life flickering and pulsing brokenly in it. He spoke:

"Nothing is forgotten—how should you forget? You will meet him again and with him your peace."

He looked at me with love and pity—the new dawn in his eyes, the body fainting under the strength of the expanding soul it could hold no longer. I would have answered as the meaning rushed on me—I would have asked for another word—but the door opened and the yellow-robed brothers entered and gathered about the bed. How could I break that peace with the tumult awakened in my mind by such words, they calm and recollected, I tossed on the waves of memory and dread? So I left them to their quiet.

In the garden below I met Lady Lucia and answered the question in her face. "It is the end." And so went on alone into the woods.

Thus the ghosts we have thought to lay rise and confront us, and whether they are beautiful or terrible we cannot tell. In that first moment terror was all I felt—that and the impulse to flight. But gradually the strong and steady beating of the heart of Nature reassured me. The sunshine was power, and the gentle lulling of the wind in the boughs peace . . . and with my nerves steadied to resolution I went back to the house. In the hall I met Dunbar. He stood by the window, the dogs at his feet. He looked up. "He is gone."

"I know. . . . Dunbar, I want to ask you something. Is it possible when a man has made a fool of himself—or say a knave—as men do—is it possible for him to attain the calm and understanding of these people? I cannot wholly get at them—they move on a far orbit. But you are a man of my own people. You know what our life is. Well—I have lived it. Can I get into this knowledge naturally and normally and without utterly sinking my own individuality? Where will it take me? And what must I give up?"

He understood. I can see him now, leaning over the back of his chair and looking at me with that direct look of his—a man who said little and did much. It was perhaps something of an effort to him to speak now of things that went deep with him.

"I'm not much of a hand at explanation. Haridas or any of the men up there would do it better, but I see what you mean. It's natural. Where will it take you? That comes first, I think. Well, you'll believe there is only one thing in the universe—the Power that rules it—no, not rules—*is* it. Nothing outside it at at all. That you yourself are part of it. That there's no evil in the world, only different stages of evolution. That soul evolves as the body does. That Law is inflexible—no punishment, no pardon, only the working out of unalterable processes."

He stopped a moment—looking out into the gathering twilight. The brothers walking slowly and led by Haridas were carrying a bier upward to the House on the Hill. A yellow robe, now discarded, covered it with long folds. They disappeared into the darkness of the trees.

"And that too is one of the processes of life—the endless beginning," he said, when they were gone. He continued more slowly: "As to individuality—the whole aim of knowledge is to get rid of the ego and realize one's union with the whole. In other words—to switch on to the Power-House of the Universe—to hitch one's wagon to more than a star. The ego can do nothing. The Whole can do All."

Again there was silence filled by the little dropping noises of the fire—always lighted and lovely in the dusk. I said suddenly:

"But what about the so-called sins? Do they bar one's way to this knowledge?"

"Not if one has the longing for it. They have to be worked out and the sharpest pain is to see the goal pushed farther and farther into the distance by one's unnecessary lapses. I know that—we all do. But it's in one's own hands to go ahead or play the fool, remembering that there is one thing which knowing we know everything."

"And practically—what must one do?"

"I should study yoga."

I interrupted him there. "The truth is I hate the sound of those native words. It gives it all a false kind of affectation to me, like the half-fraudulent kind of stuff detestable men and women talk who have picked up a smattering and find their account and make their shabby power over others by what one feels and knows is charlatanism. I believe that's what has put me off so long."

"I can understand that perfectly. I had the same feeling myself at one time. Well, take it as a drill. What do names matter? Though yoga happens to be a useful portmanteau word conveying union, concentration, and several other ideas to those who have tried it. But for actual yoga itself you need no more faith or belief than you do for taking daily exercise. . . . It need not be a spiritual matter at all. It's a fine discipline in physical and mental self-control. None better. Teaches you to say no to yourself. Strengthens the body—and certainly keeps the mind from slopping over when you want to concentrate. Simple living's a part of it too, and as all the doctors are coming round to that, I suppose even the man in the street will soon be admitting its value. Don't call it yoga if it rattles you. Call it concentration, and then no prejudice can object to it."

"You did it yourself? I apologize for asking."

"No need to apologize. Certainly. I had to be good at languages and am not naturally apt. Well—it enabled me to be useful. Why not try the posture and breathing just for a bit?" He paused and switched off elsewhere: "I wish after dinner you'd come out with me to see the head *sais* at the stables. He has got together a splendid lot of ponies for the trek next week. He's looking them over and feeding them carefully now."

The upshot was that that very night I flung open

my windows to every delicious air that breathed over garden and pines and, profoundly influenced by the events of the day, set myself to my first real consideration of concentration—the immemorial science of India.

The first step is to lay aside certain hindrances—in other words, accept some elementary rules of morality; and it was in considering these that I began to feel how curiously all experiences lead up to them.

Truthfulness, honesty, continence, avoidance of luxury—certainly as far as I had got, life had pretty well convinced me that there is not much to be gained in contravening any of those elementary laws and a good deal to be lost. I fancy most healthy-minded and healthy-bodied men would go so far as that admission even if only theoretically. The prohibition of taking life for food or pleasure would be a stumbling-block to many. It would have been to myself, but for the experiences of Brynhild's strange power with birds and beasts, and my growing sense of the delight it gave her and the singular way in which it reacted on her work. That was an influence which I could not resist. The whole brutal, bloody business stood naked before me, and I was glad to be rid of it. Yes—even as far as food goes. At Baltar I had really forgotten that death did not serve the table. One ate excellent food and was satisfied and there an end. And it might be that a part of my increased health and endurance came from that source also. At all events I had no objection to offer there.

And I may as well own that the lives lived about me drew me upward and on with a kind of urge of aspiration to reach their point of view. My three house-mates—none of them cast discredit on their beliefs. Each would have been noticeable in any society for power and that simplicity which is really the highest point of good breeding. In that point Lady Lucia was exquisite, and Brynhild's reserve covered, as I began to guess, wells of sweetness and light. Nor could I deny that the lives of the men in the House on the Hill moved me to marvel. I knew there were depths there beyond my sounding at present—things I would not let escape me willingly. That scene in the morning had left me with a sense of expectation—almost of fear, for my conscience told me the meaning of the dying man's last words to me: "You will meet him again and with him your peace."

The stranger because such a meeting would shake my life to its very foundations. I had loved the man as my best friend; I had wounded him as his worst enemy. If I had known he was in one town I would have fled to another to avoid him. And yet his forgiveness and understanding seemed at moments to be the only possible gate to any peace of mind. Baltar had lulled no memories. It had awakened them into sharp-toothed life, and through this as in all else fitted me for the beginning of the experiment I was about to undertake.

"There is no such thing as my body or yours, in any sense of reality," Haridas had said a few days earlier. "There is the seething vortex of constantly changing forms which may whirl what you call yourself into many whirlpools of change. Meditate first on flux and reflux, going and coming; the perpetually interchanging of what we call matter."

Recalling this I sat erect holding the chest, neck and head in a straight line, the chest expanded. This calls you to attention in a way that slouching does not and is so far understandable. Next came the breathing. There I remembered hearing a well-known London doctor say that rhythmic breathing was a powerful soother of the nerves and should be used medicinally daily. According to my instructions I closed the right nostril with my thumb, and breathed in through the left to the full of my lung capacity, then expelled it through the right, closing the left. Then, I reversed the order of in-and-out breathing. Simple enough—too simple, I thought for a moment, and yet not so easy as it sounds, until it becomes rhythmic and instinctive. That gives it ease. I did it first for ten minutes, and left off where I began—no different.

But naturally I expected no more at first. This breathing is called the purifying of the nerves and must be done four times a day. After thorough mastery of this breathing exercise comes a very different business which I will describe later. It is enough to say now that I saw the breathing through, steadily increasing the time by a little every day until it became as natural to me to breathe rhythmically as it is to the average man to breathe carelessly and only just below the throat. Fine training! I went on gradually, gaining sure foothold before I took the next stage; and I may have done it the more easily because so far the business commended itself to my reason and I saw that whatever else it might be it was a sensible health counsel. The mere sitting erect instead of lounging was a bracing discipline, and the deep breathing gave me an amazing control of the abdominal and chest muscles.

So well did I succeed with this that I gained breathing-power and control which it pleased me very well to test sharply up the steep hills; and it is simple truth to say it put me into condition, and I began to understand the untroubled breathing of Haridas on the almost perpendicular climb to what I called the Crag of Great Views. Incidentally, Dunbar told me that even the high passes in the Karakorum were much more accessible to men who had used this training, and I longed to measure myself against the heights.

I find it difficult to express the strength and lightness this exercise once mastered gave me. I would have gladly run instead of walking. Drowsiness was banished until I laid my head on the pillow at night, and then I slept instantly and dreamlessly. Every function of my body was tuned to concert pitch; and I use that phrase deliberately because I gained a kind of realization that I was "tuning in"—and putting myself in the right attitude for receiving—what? Ah, that I could not know yet.

I antedate my story here a little to tell the next step, though that came after our start for the Zoji La.

I was taught through breathing to control the nerve system of the body. Instead of counting my breaths as I had been doing mechanically, I was now to use certain words instead of numbers, and the first was that one sacred through Asia, the word AUM, which represents the trinity of Power in its perfect unity. I was to use this, flowing evenly in and out with the breathing, considering as I did so the word and its meaning. And this discipline was to be done at night and early in the morning.

My difficulty all along had lain in controlling my thoughts. I literally could not meditate. I started one train of thought, and another would instantly dash its spray over the edge and mingle itself irretrievably with the first. My thoughts leaped to and fro, backward and forward, like monkeys in the boughs, until at last ashamed and furious at my lack of mental control I used to jump up and take a composing tramp with a sense of defeat that I was not going to stand for long. And then I would return to my drill. Gradually—very gradually I made one or two interesting discoveries. I mastered the nerves which control the breathing centers and was amazed to find that this gave me momentary control over the others. And not only so but I began to understand the secret of rest.

Everyone knows that you may sleep all night and yet wake entirely unrefreshed, perhaps indeed more weary than when you began. My discovery was that when the body falls into rhythm a wonderful state of physical serenity is attained—shall I call it a Sabbath of the nerves?—to which the rest even of good sleep is as much less as moonlight is less than sunlight.

It is difficult to express with what delight this affected me. One may read of things for a month of Sundays, but to feel them, to have struck out in the dark for oneself and found a treasure is the most exhilarating thing I know. I tried it out to the full. I conscientiously exhausted myself, then sitting alone put myself into rhythm, and rest followed, complete and perfect, running along the nerve currents of the body like an ethereally gliding sleep, which left no fiber unpermeated by its healing. One night I held myself awake, sitting rigidly until dawn flushed the mountains, and then with word and breathing putting myself in touch, I climbed to the plane of exquisite repose and there immersed myself in the fountains of healing.

"I am gaining power!" I told Haridas. "I could even fancy sometimes that I can control the heart-beat."

"Go on steadily and quietly," he answered. "You will control more than the heart-beat. Never hurry. Attain complete physical control and then it will be time to talk of the next step. You need no encouragement from me now that you see the uses of discipline."

That was true. I needed no encouragement but had by no means outsoared the need of sympathy.

Therefore I told every advance I made, every hope it encouraged, to Brynhild. I realize now that I must have seemed like a child counting its tottering steps in infantile pride, but she took it much as a young mother might—with beaming eyes and gladdening lips.

"That's beautiful!" she would say. "That utter serenity of the body. I know. One is scarcely conscious of its existence. After a while one begins to feel—but no, I won't tell you. It might color your mind. One's mind should be transparent . . . clear, without hopes or wishes—ready to take, to reflect—"

"What will it reflect?" I asked eagerly.

"Ah, who can say? You see—the mind is the next stage; you haven't come to that yet. This is a thing you can't jump. Will you come and see my 'Evolution'? That was a reflection!"

We stood by the lovely thing—the cosmic millstones grinding chaos into order and beauty. At the bottom, gripped in their revolving, rough unshaped stuff, hopeless, one would think, for use and beauty. Above, the shaping forms still indeterminate and rough-hewn, and at the summit, emerging from the torment of the grinding, figures of the most delicate and powerful beauty, fit rulers of the world which had travailed in such cruel pangs to fling them upward to the sky. I never knew which of her realized dreams or, more truly, her realized knowledge, was most poignant to me. Each was a world in itself, developing the utmost spiritual meaning latent in matter and so presenting it to the seeing eye, the hearing ear in a language of beauty all her own. Her aerials were tuned to catch every murmur from the seeming void. I began now to understand how and why, and the sympathy of understanding strengthened between us daily.

When I had told her how it affected me, the meanings which it revealed, she said slowly:

"There was a man once who quoted to me those lines about the Mills of God which all the world knows, but he said—and I thought—that they are forever grinding the stubborn rocks into the plastic stuff that can be dreamed into beauty—lovely form and color. The rocks are the bulwarks of the eternal city—even more—they become its very dwellers."

But the beauty of her speech was blurred instantly in my mind by the certainty that the man was John Ormond and that he had understood and guided her along the highways with a sympathy she admitted from him only. Was it jealousy—the pang that followed? I scarcely knew, but that night I could not settle to my drill until an hour had gone by and the moon had risen like a golden world orbing into splendor above the black banks of trees. Then I seized control and that thought with all others lapsed into quiet.

Next day we left Baltar for the heights.

CHAPTER IX

THAT WAS A GREAT START THE DAY WE LEFT BALTAR, the ponies collected before the door, loaded with tents, provisions and everything necessary for ourselves and the men with us. Lady Lucia, looking like a tall, slender boy in her riding kit, stood with Dunbar and beside them Tazaki, consulting and deciding for himself, his keen Japanese eyes quick as a sword-flash. To such men as he it is best to leave everything in entire trust. A fine honorable man of this world, samurai and gentleman, as good a Far Eastern type as man need wish to have beside him in the tightest place between this and death, such as we might well meet in the passes. He spoke English and Kashmiri.

"How well he manages them!" I said to her.

"Yes. A sahib's a sahib all the world over. That's why he'll get the best out of the coolies—they know a sahib and that he means what he says. Look how they fall in when he speaks so quietly."

Certainly, if you have to deal with a shrieking, gesticulating crowd of Kashmiris instead of a smiling, bowing Japanese one, that was the way to do it. They were falling into line now, every man in place and the two tiffin coolies ahead with their baskets.

"Banzai!" said Tazaki at last with his Far Eastern bow and smile.

Just then Dunbar halloed me up to the House on the Hill for a farewell to those remaining behind, and I ran up eager to see them. Haridas and Shan-tao were among them taking their farewell, Haridas holding in his hand a letter from the abbot of their monastery at Kan-lu-ssu.

"I wanted you to hear this—he's just going to read it," said Dunbar. "It will interest you. The first part was a few general directions to the brothers."

Haridas, saluting me, resumed his reading:

"And I would say more. In the North and especially in the Gompa of the Manis are wise lamas skilled in that science which enables men to see, hear, and apprehend beyond the senses and limits of the body. They make themselves one with that underlying self which is transmitted from life to life, bearing secretly the accumulated treasure of experience and knowledge in all as an uncut jewel hides its fire. But be wary. Even in Asia sense-cheaters are abroad, and we know that Europe is throwing itself greedily upon fragments of this knowledge, unaware of its vastness or dangers, and so plunging blindly into the illusions of magic and shape-changing. Therefore, let Haridas our brother bring back what it is well to learn of the wisdom of the lamas and study it that we may consider what is valuable for our teaching when our brothers go out into the world, for evil must be met with power. But on one and all we enjoin caution. It is told us by a brother newly returned from England that he was bidden to what they call a séance, and going with open eyes and understanding he beheld about these people such forces that if they had understood they would have fled shrieking from the place. But they lamented that the results that day were small, the truth being that the true knowledge in our brother held the Dark and its illusions at bay."

"Most true," said a young Chinese, "and a man can but see what he is fitted for and nothing beyond the stage to which his karma has brought him. If in a terrible enlightenment he could see more it would be his death."

An old monk in the corner warming thin amber-colored hands over the fire put in his word, sighing:

"It is true. I knew a brother who, being sent to Europe, was beset by an ignorant crowd who tempted him that they might hear of wonders, and thus he threw himself on the power of illusion and sense-cheating, and made men and women see as he willed the vain and terrible imaginings of his own ruined soul, and so died, flung violently back from the goal. Therefore, as my Lord says, beware."

All this was in English, the daily language of those men of many nationalities, and again what impressed me like the drive of a die upon the coin was the virility of life at the House on the Hill. There was no seclusion there and no suppression of opinion; they went and came throughout the wide and narrow ways of the world and because they knew were strong.

On the shelves about us rested precious books and manuscripts, the harvest of the soul of Asia. From one shelf the eldest of the monks took a little cylindrical shrine of carved wood, which opening into two wings disclosed a small golden figure of almost miraculous beauty—the Buddha of Love—who is to come: seated, the hands in a mystic gesture, a smile of infinite sweetness upon the face, dreaming a celestial future in timeless peace. The doors were enriched inside with tiny miniature paintings and emblems.

"Take this," he said, tendering it to Dunbar, "with our greetings to the abbot of the Manis Lamasery and say we give our best in token of brotherhood, for this image was made thirteen hundred years ago in China, and the eyes of saints and emperors have dwelt upon it in longing and devotion. It was the possession of the great Tibetan monk whose manuscript the abbot aids us to recover, and is a symbol of the world's desire and ours. And in gratitude and love this is sent to him from our monastery of the Sweet Dew in China."

He shut the door of the shrine and raised it in both hands to his forehead, and Shan-tao taking it with reverence enclosed it in an outer box of sandalwood and ivory. When Dunbar received it he laid it in the hands of Haridas and all bowing bid us farewell.

"And a safe return with treasures unspeakable. We shall hear of you in ways that do not wait for ink and paper. Between friends are no distances. Therefore if I say we joyfully desire your departure you will understand our true hearts."

With that we parted—the men crowding out to see our going. I looked back and saw them, golden figures against the pines. They waved their hands and stood until the road winding downward hid them.

After leaving Baltar our third camp was at Sonamarg, high above the Sind Valley and to me, unaccustomed to camping, and new to the wilder beauties of Kashmir, it seemed that no Paradise could exceed its wonders. We entered this uplifted meadow, climbing through a narrow gateway in fierce crags, where the river tore like a thing mad for escape to the lower levels and again, as had happened more than once already, I rejoiced in the sure-footedness of the ponies, for it is no easy trek and especially at that time through those slippery tracks by the river. But when we emerged in the mountain-high Golden Valley—for that is the meaning of the name Sonamarg, and found the spring again at this higher level showering the grass with golden crocuses so thick, so radiant, that it was indeed a Field of the Cloth of Gold, the intoxication of the high air and bewildering loveliness so possessed me that I could have shouted for joy if I had been alone and with no English dignity to keep up before beholders.

The silent sunshine dazzling on the gold, turning a mighty cliff into an evanescence of dove-gray, tender in the shadows dwelling on the surrounding mountains like a benediction, was strong wine to me. The crag where our tents were pitched beneath the pines with a wild rushing river beneath was more than any home, for it was a house where the great heights were good to us and adopted us silently into their enormous being. With such friends familiarity breeds content.

"I want to go no farther," I said to Brynhild as she rode beside me. She slid off her horse and stood, slim and strong, surveying the scene with delight.

"It's freedom!" she said. "We've cast off the last fetter now. We are nomads like so many of the people who make their living up here by trekking up and down the long trails and passes with their queer merchandise. I want to go on and on and never stop—up to the Pamirs, into Chinese Turkestan—anywhere, anyhow!"

"And what shall we find at the end of it all? I know what I want. Do you?"

"Very well indeed. And we shall all find our heart's desire up there."

She flung a hand toward the mountains far and near, and there was triumph in her face. Indeed I myself began to know that joy of attainment—I had not relaxed my discipline on the way up. I could not now if I would for the thing had got hold of me. It was good to slip away from the rest and find a niche above the boiling river, there to breathe and control and fix my imagination on the unfolding lotus of vision and rise refreshed in body and soul. I could get no further as yet . . . but that was an earnest of better things, and though I could not travel the road now I could see it rising white and far into the mountains of the World's Desire.

We watched the wonderful coolies, overseen by Tazaki, building a hut which should serve as a sitting-room and meeting-place for the sahibs—pine boughs cut, trimmed, fitted and roofed with strong matting—even a window contrived and a swinging drape of matting for a door. Next day it would be rolled up and the place abandoned to the next comer. But meanwhile they built with the swift care and cunning of animals or insects, to whom in their affinity with nature they are nearer than we.

Even in the companionship of traveling Haridas lived alone with his books and work, joining us only for walks and climbs on the upward way. He sought me out now.

"Come for a walk, Mr. Cardonald, if you will. We have had no talk for a long time."

That was true and I had felt the lack of it. I flung

my bridle to a *sais,* and joined him as he struck up the high slope leading to the Valley of Glaciers.

"If we cross the Zoji La tomorrow—and the weather looks more than hopeful—we shall be among the Mongolian peoples, and from that our way lies straight on into the heart of things. I have been thinking— Will you tell me how far you have got in your quest?"

I told him and he listened with attention, then said simply:

"That is a good advance. You will soon enter another stage, and if you could do that before we reach the Monastery of the Manis there is a teacher there who is much looked up to and revered as one who holds the Keys of the Way."

"I want none but you!" I said hastily, for the thought of being turned over for ghostly counsel to some unknown Tibetan was very far from what I had hoped.

"But I have done nothing for you. I have been so busy and now am busier still. And what you are about to attempt needs very careful explanation. Do not be headstrong. You would regret it. You will see your teacher in a dream tonight. Tell me tomorrow what you have felt."

That was an easy promise for I scarcely thought I should be called upon to fulfil it.

"You must not be disappointed if his teachings seem very strange to you. They will not when you have attained his point of view. Remember that what seems folly to the ignorant may be a high wisdom. Let me tell you a saying of the Lord Buddha's: 'How should

Jayasena, born and bred in the pursuit of worldly and sensuous desires, know and realize that which can only be realized by coming out of these? The case resembles that of two friends walking hand in hand until coming to a crag one climbed it. The other called from below, "What can you see?" He answered, "A garden of loveliness, a glorious landscape, a lake and wood of exquisite beauty." "That is impossible!" said the first. "I see nothing." But the other dragged him up and he saw and marveled.' So it will be with you. You will not believe all that is told you, and one day you will climb the last crag and see the world spread beneath you wholly fair. Could you turn back now if you would?"

I searched my heart for the truth before replying:

"If I were suddenly flung out from among you all, perhaps I might forget. Amongst you, never. Already I have had some wonderful moments as when Miss Ingmar laid her hand on mine and I heard—what I cannot describe. Do you hear it now?"

"Try!" he said, and laid his fingers lightly on mine.

An extraordinary thing followed—his aerials caught different sounds from Brynhild's, or Nature was in a different mood today. The scene before us rolled away from my eyes like a dissolving view fading into mist, and for a moment there was nothingness like the vastness of a gray sky meeting a gray sea and nothing between, not a sound—dead terrifying silence as if in the innermost heart of a grave, and I was alone as a dead man is with grass growing above him. Then suddenly I saw great snow mountains with sky-piercing peaks, white and aloof, and the silence was broken by the distant muffled roar of an avalanche. I saw a little shelter contrived behind a rock that might stem the bitter torrent of icy wind, and before it a man standing with a dog at his feet, looking up toward the heights. He seemed but a black speck in a waste of white desolation—until swiftly the whole picture moved toward my eyes, rushing at me as a train does in a cinema picture; and as it loomed large and almost threatening above me, I knew my friend most unmistakably, and even as I recognized him and lost him he had fled past the place where I was standing as if on the wings of the wind. I heard the thunder of another avalanche and saw great vibrations of violent joy running over the snow in forms that I cannot describe—the elemental spirits of some enormous triumph that moved the very mountains to their foundations—gladness beyond human sharing, terrible to see and feel; and shaken to my very soul at its nearness to my littleness I turned to escape and saw Haridas and the Golden Valley before me and all was gone. Was it a dream? He had lifted his hand from mine, and was speaking in his usual tone.

"You have advanced indeed. With Miss Ingmar you could only hear. Now you can hear and see. Presently you will do more. You will touch and speak. In other words, instead of seeing through my sight or hers, you will be able to project your own essential being where you would wish to have it."

"Did I see true?" I asked, too bewildered to hear what he was saying. . . . "I saw a man—a friend. You know. You made me see."

"Certainly you saw true. That place is on the great

mountains beyond the Monastery of the Manis. You should consider how you will meet him, for that meeting will come. There is much to come to you in this wonderful journey we have begun."

"Can you see? Can you tell the future? Shall we meet and be friends again? Can you tell what he will say—what I should do?" I asked, tortured with anxiety.

"I am no magician. I see some things. Others I do not see. But it is true that I can see when it is needful for me or anyone with whom I have to do. Have you in your turn considered how the ancient Indian knowledge which gives me this power is linked with science as the world understands it today?"

I said no—I had not. It had all seemed to me a marvelous ancientry like the lost wisdom of the Egyptians, but as to science—

"Consider this. Science teaches that there are three forms of consciousness, all blending at their edges so that it is hard to say where one ceases and the next begins. There is the consciousness of what we call inanimate things, stones, plants and so forth, which are truly as living as we. Next the consciousness of animals, then the 'I am I' consciousness of men. But above that is the higher consciousness, the cosmic consciousness which is attained by our teaching and reaches unimaginable heights. That is the consciousness of 'I am All. All is I.' The world has found the mathematical approach and calls this the fourth dimension, recognizing that in that consciousness things must be very different from what they appear to be—and are not—in our own dimension. In a word, science is beginning to explain by the mathematical approach what the Buddha, the Christ, Saint Paul, and others saw when suddenly the world-walls fell down in ruin about them and they saw the reality that lay beyond."

"But the world of the fourth dimension surely is quite incomprehensible to the average man," I said in great astonishment. "It is the highest problem of our time. Even its existence is not admitted, and there is no language to express its qualities. Are you not playing with a dream?"

"Such as the fourth dimensional world is you have had a glimpse of it today. You were in a place at least four hundred miles from here. You saw sights impossible for human eye, you heard sounds impossible for human ears. You did this by means not to be explained in any human category. You were in a world where the word 'solid' has a very different meaning from any you have ever heard, where the part may contain the whole and tomorrow is yesterday and now. No, you cannot understand it stated in words, and men have no language to fit it. It can only be told in parable and symbol. But along the road you are traveling you will soon taste it, at first with fear and bewilderment, afterwards with joy. Is it worth while? I repeat: Such as the fourth dimensional world is you have had a glimpse of it today."

But indeed I could not answer. Like other men I had heard talk of the fourth dimension and its impossible paradoxes. They left me cold—the thing was only an academic curiosity. Now, under the mountains, with the Himalayan pass before us, it took on a very new complexion. It became menacing, terrible yet drawing—if I may use the word—a thing I longed to understand, conquer, attain, and yet dreaded because it brought the cold aura of other worlds than ours and when the mortal flesh saw it, "it began to tremble right hard," as when the light of the Holy Grail struck swordlike upon the Knights of the Round Table. I put out a hand as if to ward it off.

"I must go slowly—slowly. A man might go mad who felt the immensity and his own powerlessness. I beg you show me no more until . . ."

"Until you learn that its immensity is your immensity and its power your own. That is all that concerns one. No—I will show you no more now. Next time you will see under very different conditions, but it was necessary that you should know with certainty that he is waiting for you up there."

"Does he know?"

"Yes—he does. Ask me no more now, but consider it in your heart. Let us come down to the tents. Look at the glory of the crocuses before the sun drops behind those mighty hills and consider what the real world must be if even its shadows are so beautiful."

He lifted his hand towards the hills as we turned and went down to the tents over the triumphing river.

That evening a fire was kindled under the trees, and we sat round it with wonderful lights flung on the trees and black rushing water and above us the listening starry night drawing closer, closer—listening, guarding its mysteries well. And Haridas told us a strange, wild story of the great hills above the Monastery of the Sweet Dew in China and the vision of the great

T'ang Emperor who died for three days and, returning, gave his journey in the unseen world to the awed and silent court.

Then a Kashmiri boy sang a song of the mountains and the trooping of cattle to the uplands in spring and the splendor of flowers jeweling the high pastures, and his voice in the wild solitude had the pure beauty of something disembodied and alone floating on air to a goal unknown. A strange and enthralling night, with the firelight glittering on faces seen pale and wistful in its rosy flame.

But not so strange as my dream when the fire was flickering down, and night resumed her ancient, solitary reign, and all our little life was locked away in sleep. For then I found myself standing in a room the like of which I had never seen or imagined. A room high up in some building of which not only the height was immense in itself but which soared from some mighty mountain. For I stood by the window, looking down upon a dizzy drop to a land of rocks and rivers with mountains about it like waves upon a lonely shore.

And before me was a man in a pointed hood that fell in lappets upon his shoulders, and upon his breast an amulet set with red and blue stones—a man haughty and angry, or so it seemed to me, and I heard him say as if speaking close beside me:

"How is it possible that you should learn from any but the man who was your friend? He loved you. In his hand is the Key."

And at that a great alarm seized me, which weakened all my body, and I woke in such a panic that I heard my heart-beats like hammer-strokes, and in the silence the far-off howling of a dog.

I said nothing of this next day to Haridas though I was sure he knew I felt that dangers were gathering round my way and that I myself must face the specters of the mind with what courage I could. That part of my life was never to be forgotten. It was to be the test by which I must stand or fall.

After that I noticed Haridas avoided me. The same instinct was upon him also—my battle was to myself. But I noticed also that Brynhild drew nearer to me; we rode, walked and talked together; and of the goodness of Lady Lucia and Dunbar I cannot speak. It was as though they came as far with me as they could and then stood to see me go onward with kindly anxious faces. Nothing definite was said—it might have been my own imagination, yet I felt sure it was not. I carried on my discipline of yoga steadily—an easy enough matter in the solitudes.

And so we went on our way.

CHAPTER X

TWO DAYS LATER WE CLIMBED THE GREAT HIMALAYAN pass on the hard-frozen snow, and leaving behind and far below the loveliness of Kashmir, entered on the wild upper country of Little Tibet and the Mongolian peoples, and were at last steadily on our way to the Monastery of the Manis amongst its own believers. A waste-land of stony and illimitable plains and many-colored mountains, cold and terrible with sweeping winds, and the one trail marked with little whitewashed rest houses at the intervals of a day's march—places where travelers might shelter for a night from the piercing cold and desolation. No comforts but a shelter and a fireplace and a caravanserai where men and beasts could troop together for warmth.

At Matayan, under a ridge of mountains pinnacled with what looked colossal figures or the images of saints on some rock-rough cathedral, messengers from the Monastery of the Manis were waiting for us with a letter and deeply interested tail of followers.

"Greeting and welcome from the upper country to our brothers Haridas and Shan-tao and our Brother of the Pen. Yaks for your journey await you at Matayan. We expect your coming in joy. Precious manuscripts await you also and a brother skilled in the ancient learning to give help. Therefore come onward, fearing nothing, for the storms shall blow behind you and the avalanches fall when you are past and all be well."

It was signed again with the threefold formula, and sure enough, outside stood six great yaks, powerful, draped in long hair—Nature's protection from the cold—great monumental sluggish beasts. They stood heavily making surly grunts and movements belying their great oxlike eyes, and one carried gifts of dried apricots and bricks of tea and curious flat cakes sprinkled with seed and, as the crowning splendor of the gift, two Chinese robes of splendid furs for Lady Lucia and Brynhild. Swathed in them up to the ears and with a light drift of snow blowing about them, they looked like two cat-princesses of a Central Asian fairy-tale. Three experienced mountain guides were a part of the welcoming procession.

It was weird beyond description that, when darkness fell on the lonely rest house and the tents sheltering those who could not find other room, the wind rose higher, and strange cries and shouts echoed from the wild mountain above us.

"The men say the rock figures come alive!" said Brynhild, her eyes distended in firelight. "They are the troops of a king on his way to Yarkand hundreds and hundreds of years ago, and because they would force their way up that sacred mountain, they were frozen with stone and never got there."

Lady Lucia stood looking out at the little glass window into the dark and drifting snow showers. She turned.

"Yes, and the men say they come awake every Saturday—and this is Saturday—and rattle their swords and say, 'Tomorrow we will go to Yarkand!' For they don't know that time has done with them. And then they cry and lament most pitifully. Listen to that!"

A wailing shriek, frightfully human, broke from the heights above, followed by a tumult of cries.

"It must be human!" Brynhild said paling. "Lance, they're men. What can we do?"

For he entered, stamping the snow from his boots after having seen the ponies cared for.

"Come and listen!" he said, and we trooped after him to the door.

In the unstarred dark it was so real, so near and terrible, that I felt cold running down my back like water. Tazaki emerged unconcernedly from some door.

"Yes, *danna sama,* it is the ghost-men on the mountain. What else? We have such in the mountain in Nippon. When men die without that they can do what they want their ghosts cry on the wind. It is their *ingwa* (karma)."

"And no way to help them, Tazaki?" Dunbar said laughing. "No—no men this time. Great holes in the rocks like pipes, and the wind screams through them. Are the men frightened?"

"Terrible frightened, *danna sama.* But they eat good supper—they forget."

I mention this because it was a bad beginning and made the men nervy at the start. We were to feel the effect of it later.

And certainly that journey was no picnic. It was and will be one of the great enduring joys of my life for many reasons, but I shall never deny that it was hard going and that the mind was kept in a kind of painful suspense most of the time. It is true that we had no falling snow to fear, nothing but drifting snow showers, and that what had fallen was frozen and therefore comparatively easy, but the ways were dangerous in spite of our guides' inside knowledge, and the fact that we had women in the party kept us all more or less on the stretch.

I should explain that we quitted the track, which is politely called a road, at Dras and struck up to the right into the mountains where the lamasery was situated, and this being a comparatively unfrequented way made our work more anxious. It is amazing the love these lamas have for setting themselves in the wildest, most inaccessible places possible. Even in this desolate land are little oases of green where one might think they would choose to be at peace. But, no! They must be gripped in the teeth of a great mountain with, for choice, a mighty precipice dropping plumb from their windows, and if there is a wild river, hard and cold as crinkled metal, dashing from the heights, and a six-inch way leading to the place with death below, all their aspirations are satisfied. I speak of what I know, for we passed no less than four lamaseries on the way to the greatest of them, and in every case the scene was as near the perfection I have sketched above as it could be. And the hearts of our Kashmiri coolies were like water.

At each and all we received a kindly welcome, and

Haridas and Shan-tao were at home; but we could not delay. We pushed on steadily day after day and with such care that we lost only one man and one pony and left two sick at one of the lamaseries—a very small butcher's bill in such a place and in spring.

Finally, for two days we climbed a steep ascending gorge with a mad river fleeing from the eternal snows to its meeting with the Indus. It had a look of terror in its haste, the pallor of its foaming eddies and the rending rocks barring the way and breaking and shattering it before the plunge. Precipices towered on the right, terrible, untrodden by the foot of man, and I think the awful magnificence drove us one and all into our own thoughts for laughter and talk died and we climbed in silence.

During those two days we met only two men: one a runner from the lamasery, whose cheerful *"juli"* we heard as he went by; the other was gathering *burtsa* plant, the cheerless fuel which grows in this wild place and can be burned green for economy of the more precious cattle and horse dung.

We had reached a point of the gorge where terrific mountains and precipices appeared to bar the way to any but winged creatures, when the eldest guide raised his hand to point before us and all looked about them in hope and then in amazement, for there was nothing to be seen but roaring river and towering mountains and still he pointed. We looked higher, higher still, and, behold! far above any spot where one could suppose a human habitation might rest was an enormous building fitted into the living rock like a tooth into its socket, soaring upward with it, gaunt, many-windowed, of enormous height, more like a colony than a house—a barrack of human life huge beyond any expectation.

"But," said Lady Lucia, shading her eyes from the snow dazzle, "hundreds and hundreds of people could live there!"

"Four thousand lamas live there, and in the lower one are nuns," Haridas answered, pointing to another building on a shelf below, looking as if with a touch it might slip off into the river and be dashed to atoms.

"It's an awful place!" said Brynhild very low. And indeed awe was the atmosphere of the gorge and the lonely lamasery above, staring down its precipice into the escaping river. Dunbar came up.

"What about the ponies? They can never do that!"

"There is a way round that shoulder of rock," Haridas answered. "It is a miserable track, but it serves the need of the lamasery and will ours. It is no worse than some we have done already, and the lamas keep it in traveling order—such as it is."

There was no more to be said. We addressed ourselves to the climb along a way as narrow and rugged as the way of righteousness, where a false step would have had even more immediately fatal effect. It was strange to look back and see the men and yaks winding up after us, the ponies having been left below among the huts of the dependents and servants of the monastery where it would be possible to feed and rest them.

Haridas led the way, walking with ease, the drop to the river troubling him no more than as if he had been winged like the birds hovering disturbed about us. Shan-tao followed him, then two guides with a rope binding them to Dunbar and Lady Lucia, two more bringing up the rear. Then Brynhild and myself, harnessed in the same way for safety. And I may as well own that I preferred to look steadily on and up and to forget as far as possible the downward prospect on the left. Yet we were told the lamas and even the women went up and down daily in perfect ease and comfort.

The path widened and wound aside among some upward rocks after about an hour's climb, and we were then released and went on in safety. And I may note here that the breathing drill had produced in all who practiced it strength and endurance which did not surprise me even in the two women. Moreover it fulfilled another promise. Counting the level of Kashmir above the sea, our ascent at the Zoji La and the climbing we had done since, we were now fourteen thousand feet above sea-level, and yet not one of us made a difficulty of the rarefied air. That was very far from being the case with Tazaki and the Kashmiris, who suffered to disablement with mountain-sickness on this last lap of ascent.

I began to feel my body adjusting itself to new and higher conditions, obeying as a boat obeys the rudder, and I cannot express the sort of awed astonishment this brought me—a new desire discovered in the most unexpected place.

Suddenly a roar of great conch shells from above set the echoes flying like wild birds unloosed all over the mountains. Each flung it to the other, and it was tossed back and forward and reverberated down the great gorge in dizzying confusions of sound, renewed again and again until the waves broke at one's ears and deafened them.

"It is a welcome!" said Haridas, turning and trying to make himself heard. As he spoke it ceased, and the cry of trumpets and pipes broke out, and rounding a rocky corner we came upon a group of red-robed lamas with pipes, trumpets and conch shells, prayer-flags with sacred inscriptions fluttering above them, and on either side of the widening way to the entrance the *manis* from which the lamasery takes its name. Two walls of praying-stones higher than a tall man's height, the top sloped, and on this eaving deeply sculptured images of the Buddha and the sacred words, "Aum mani padme Aum"—"Hail to the Jewel in the Lotus"—the prayer repeated by millions of men, praying-wheels, sacred stones, river-wheels, and many other mechanical devices, all over Asia.

At each side stood also a *chorten*—a great receptacle for relics—standing on a huge pedestal.

It should be possible to describe the effect of this bright coloring and the amazing view as we left the rocks behind us—and yet I despair. Such air at such a height and the effects it has on view and distance must be seen before they can be understood. The immaculate purity of the air shot through and through with sunshine, keen and cold, destroyed all sense of distance. Far might have been near and near far, and the mountains in their vast heights and distances were painted, as it were, upon a sheet of crystal, flat, bright, against a hard, pure sky of palest blue and with little perspective. Each and all challenged and baffled the eye alike.

In a group the lamas moved forward to greet us—a pool of red against the snowy background. Their

Mongolian faces had the gentle melancholy which comes of long solitary meditation.

> The sleep that is among the lonely hills—

And their voices were cool and remote as the very far-off music of a bell.

A group of women hooded and robed stood there, waiting to take possession of Lady Lucia and Brynhild and lead them downward to the right and across a bridge swung over a terrible ravine going down to the river depth itself. This led to what I may call the convent, blocked in a scoop of the mountain. But by a special grace they were to be permitted to visit us daily in the lamasery above.

Little scarfs, the visiting-cards of these regions, were offered and accepted on both sides, and then turning, our lamas led the way to the great door into the lamasery, surrounding Haridas and Shan-tao as they went and questioning them eagerly about the journey. At the entrance they stopped and welcomed us. The impossible—as it had sometimes seemed to me—was accomplished. We were inside the long-desired lamasery.

We stood in a passage with more doorways opening into more rooms than a rabbit-warren has burrows. An army might have been tucked away among them. Stone steps led up in so many directions as to dizzy a man, and still our group of lamas led on, gradually dropping one here and there until only two were left. They guided us through a long corridor where we were quartered, each with his own room looking over the vast landscape of mountain and river. It was all as high and giddy as though swinging in the branches of a mighty tree, but from that moment I understood the love of the lamas for their heights, for nothing of the lower world was left to recall the mind, and only the aspiration of the peaks and purity of the icy rivers parted it from the solitude of the heavens. A place indeed for meditation.

We took possession and were then summoned to our audience with the abbot. It almost appeared to be the visioning of a dream when, after climbing many more stairs and traversing endless corridors, we found ourselves before a singular door of dark wood, hinged and bound with metal like the famous chests of Korea. It was swung open immediately by an attendant lama, and we stood in a huge room and in the presence of his Holiness the Incarnation of the Eternal Compassion, represented in Tibetan art as a divine being, young, beautiful and merciful, with ears ever open to the sound of prayer and hands ever urgent in help.

The Abbot of the Manis was neither young nor beautiful, but to me as a portrait painter, his was one of the most interesting faces I have ever seen, dark with thin hair graying about the temples, Mongolian-featured with full lips locked in an expression of immutable quiet steadied on a great resolution—the look of a man accustomed to rule—and narrow kindly eyes, sunk in the thick eyelids of the Chinese-featured peoples, but bright as searchlights when they woke into watchfulness. A face full of character in which not even humor was lacking. His dress was white, and the only other difference between him and the lamas was his pointed hood with lappets falling over the shoulders. Even to the magnificence of some of his surroundings I could not give a thought at the moment —so did his Holiness capture me.

We were presented singly, Haridas and Shan-tao, whom he already knew, introducing us and standing each on one side of him.

To Dunbar he said graciously in his own tongue:

"Brother of the Pen, welcome and again welcome. In all this *gompa* there is not one man who is not at your service, one thing which is not yours to aid it. And for all your goodness and that of the lady, your noble wife, to our traveling brothers how shall we thank you? To your heart and hers to be sick, solitary and poor is to be welcomed like a king. May all the Buddhas reward you and her for your hearts of mercy in this incarnation and reward you also in those to follow. And this will certainly be, for you build yourselves a mighty karma. Let no thought of differences of doctrine disturb your spirits, for in the great wisdom of Haridas and your own high charity are all union."

To me he said through Haridas:

"Welcome also to the friend of all nobilities whose feet walk in the beginning of the Eightfold Path and will most surely attain. Be free of the *gompa* and all that is in it as though you were yourself a brother of the Peace. And what you ask is yours for the taking."

It moved me because it was not only graciously said, but with a look of much kindliness.

Then first I became aware that behind the abbot, at his shoulder but in shadow, stood a man of middle age, as I should guess, robed and hooded in yellow and therefore differing from all the rest. His robe was also worn differently. One shoulder was bare and from that it fell in noble drapery to his feet. In his hand he carried a thing strange to see in this cold country—a palm-leaf fan, used in Ceylon and Burma to shield the face from the intolerable sun.

He was so motionless, so stiff, in the cold repose of his attitude that it gave me rather the impression of a statue than of a living man; and why I cannot tell, but I had the belief that his eyes were on me with an unwavering gaze all the time. Suddenly the abbot added, with a gesture toward his hidden face: "This is the teacher you have chosen—the Illuminated Pearl."

That I had chosen? No. Who had chosen me. For then I recalled my dream in the Golden Valley, and again the cold air heralding supernormal vision breathed on me from heights higher than the surrounding peaks. He never moved, when turning to me the abbot continued: "Two hours are appointed daily for your study. The pictures of the *gompa* shall be brought out for your pleasure."

It flashed into my mind that I might dare beyond daring and might there and then make my request.

Bowing deeply I replied, again through Haridas:

"Holiness, I am grateful. And if it be true that I who deserve so little may ask and have, I request that I may paint a portrait of yourself for the pleasure and good of the faithful."

If it had been sternly refused I could not have been astonished, but the abbot smiling agreed that if he had time at his disposal he would grant that request.

"But," he added, "it is the Illuminated Pearl whose portrait should be given to the faithful, and this they know and have hitherto asked in vain. Though there is one—" He paused suddenly.

But the Illuminated Pearl had withdrawn into the shadows, and of his face I had seen nothing but the steady, unflickering eyes. I dreaded but dared not refuse those hours of instruction.

Our meals were served in a little room set apart for us in a wing, if I may so call it, of the vast building. There we met Lady Lucia and Brynhild, safe and happy among the good homely women, but with a kind of awe upon them at the strangeness of the place—which could scarcely have been greater had we climbed the bean-stalk into another planet, though of course Dunbar and his wife and even Brynhild were more at home amongst the people than I.

Our own servants did what was possible towards providing food so there was little to complain of; and Brynhild had already discovered that there were many walks and climbs over the rocks and mountain of the monastery which were safe enough if one kept to carefully indicated tracks. They too were to be allowed to see the monastery treasures and make what drawings and notes they would. As for me, a messenger brought word that the Gelung (a title of honor) the Illuminated Pearl would see me next day when dusk fell, and that the room where Dunbar would work among the manuscripts was now ready and could be seen next day also at his pleasure.

So the remainder of the day went by, and night came and faint light-points glimmered all over the lamasery until, swinging lighted lanterns, we and the servants took Lady Lucia and Brynhild down the hard snowy track to where the railed bridge hung over soundless deeps, and so returned, silenced by the awe of night glittering with frosty splendors of her ancient constellations. But my new teacher was a trouble in my dreams.

When we entered the working-room next day it was with almost a shock of pleasure and wonder. Outside was the mighty aerial view common to all on that side of the buildings, but as the sun sank in the west the dying light fell through a ravine on the royal roar of the river and turned the sad-colored water into a jewel full of flying lights dancing through the ravine on its happy way to the sea. The mountains hovered opalescent with unnamable hues, transparent as bubbles blown on a child's breath—the strength of the hills forgotten in a sunset dream. Why is it that in beholding such unattainable perfection the first sensation is pain? Is it humanity bruising its heart against the prison wall that bars it from Beauty, or the pain of loss—the divine homesickness? We stood and looked in silence, as though ourselves floating winged above it.

But what a place in which to work—on what a subject! Shelves were about the room with precious manuscripts wrapped in faded silks, some, after the Chinese manner, enclosed in narrow boxes. Dishes of Chinese ink stood ready with delicate brushes laid across them for writing—our ponies having brought the English material needed by Dunbar. Chairs curiously carved were set in readiness for the four workers, each with a brazier beside it for warmth. Piles of Chinese and Japanese books lay in waiting; it seemed that nothing had been forgotten. And on the four walls of the room hung four great unrolled pictures—brilliant as precious gems in color, noble in conception, lighting the place as with lamps from their intrinsic glory.

One was a death of the Buddha, dying beneath the flowered trees, surrounded by disciples stern in calm and comprehension. Another, the renunciation, when laying aside his magnificence he leaves his palace for solitude in the forest. The third, a great portrait by a Chinese artist, of the Tashi Lama, one of the high spiritual Popes of Asia. Splendid in jewels and miter it must have dominated the room but for another illuminated to glory by the direct rays of the sinking sun.

This was a man in the yellow robe seated in a curious high-armed and carved Tibetan chair, on either hand a divine being—haloed and robed in gold. Not a Buddha—not a glorified saint—a man, but with power and knowledge stamped upon his features if ever I saw them—a face royally commanding by right of the strength it revealed and concealed.

"That's the most wonderful thing in the room and the greatest picture!" Brynhild said as if to herself, standing before it with locked hands. Dunbar had joined her with Haridas. "Strange that they should have a yellow-robed monk here."

"The Diamond Scepter!" said Haridas, and turning walked to the window.

I could at that moment have believed any mad story which connected that man with power and miracle, so complete was his attainment, so invulnerable his stedfast pride. Solitary also in inexpressible solitude.

> . . . a silent face
> The marble index of a mind forever
> Voyaging through strange seas of thought alone.

I stood and stared, wishing I had the secret of those old Chinese painters who saw the truth in a man, his summing up of life and its molding of his own being, and set it down that generations of men yet unborn might read and marvel. And as I looked the sun dropped behind mountains grown suddenly black and mysterious, and dusk had come, as yet unstarred.

With it came soft feet along the corridor outside and a figure at the door:

"The Gelung the Illuminated Pearl is prepared for his pupil."

I followed, and for the first time in my life felt what I must call a ray of memory, clear, sharp as a searchlight, flung across night's dark—the certainty that somewhere, somehow, this had happened before. In a strange narrow way, with new sights and sounds about me, I had walked quailing to an interview with some man in whose hand was the shaping of my destiny. That memory walked beside me like a presence until I reached his.

CHAPTER XI

NOW WHEN I ENTERED THAT ROOM IT WAS LIKE SINKing in a sea of shadow, for darkness sat there, relieved only by a faint point of light at the farther end seeming to intensify its mystery. As I stood uncertain an unseen drapery was drawn back and made visible two chairs and a table. A man was in one of them, his face almost hidden by the lama hood, and though he rose and turned toward me I could see nothing but a robed figure and had only the consciousness that he was looking steadily at me as I made my way up the room. It seemed I was not permitted to see his face.

Arrived there, the chair was pushed silently forward, and having no wish to sit I laid my hand on it and waited. He seated himself by the table and spoke, to my astonishment, in excellent English.

"It is your wish to study the Raja Yoga under my direction?"

I answered mechanically, "It is my wish," though something in me protested against the statement. He must have been conscious of a disturbance in our atmosphere for he went on imperturbably as though I had spoken.

"Yet though you may not desire it now the time is near in which you will rejoice. This is certain, and the matter is important because you will soon be face to face with a mental crisis which will determine your destiny. Do you wish to meet it with courage and understanding?"

"Can any man desire less?" I answered, but my voice sounded lost and weak in the dimness and size of the room. It seemed that the guidance of my life had passed out of my own hands. I felt ineffectual, adrift on a torrent that plunged to its goal careless of what was torn from its old moorings.

"That is good!" His voice was one of cold approval. "Then will you tell me what point you have reached in your studies?"

I seemed a schoolboy rehearsing an infantile and ill-learned lesson as I gave the account of my efforts to grasp the skirts of a truth too great for me. To my surprise he unbent for the first time, and there was even a human note in his next words.

"That was well done and brings its reward as sincere effort must. You have attained the power of perceiving through others which is denied to many who have studied for years. In other words, you have demonstrated that you are a recipient of truth at second hand. But that is a position in which one may not linger, because truth is imperious and will have all or none. I should like to make a test."

He paused, reflected, and continued:

"Fix your mind intently on some person or subject of interest to yourself. Sit, that no discomfort may distract you."

I sat, and laid my hands on my knees uncertain of what or whom I could make use in the test and whether

I could focus at all in this strange room, this man before me whose influence was so strange that I could not at all disentangle its effect. And because I was determined to let nothing escape my mind which could give him any clue or hold over me, I would not think of the subject which had preoccupied me during those later days at Baltar.

I threw myself into the first fleeting thought that crossed my mind: Blanche Mainguy and her veranda at Simla, the first meeting with Lady Lucia—an idle looping chain of thought where one link led on to another and so—

He interrupted.

"Is the woman of the loud tongue worth a moment's memory? No. *Fix* your mind, breathing as you did in your room at Baltar."

I started awake from the idle reverie and obeyed. I concentrated on a portrait I had painted—not to my satisfaction—of a literary man well known in London, putting it before my eyes, studying it, correcting. Suddenly it all blurred away; I could not hold it, and in its place rose the man whom I had injured—kindly, frank and quick to laughter, the swell of a heathy down behind him and a bright wind blowing swift white clouds over the sky. The old days—the beloved days when we tramped the hills together, and never a moment seemed long and never a day but he completed it—came back for a moment of content. He stretched out his hand laughing, with a photograph in it of the girl he was to marry. The brief bliss vanished.

"You'll like her! You'll like her!" he said. "This won't be a marriage that invalidates friendship. No!

Two lives can enclose nothing. The third makes the perfect triangle and shuts us three in!"

Ill-omened words! I shuddered as I heard them, with a sickening prevision of evil to come. It was he I always thought of with remorse—never of her. For what did I owe her but the one atrocious memory of deceit and betrayal in my life? She had ruined my peace. And I despised her the more because she had returned to him and was living her lie day and night in the sunshine of his trust.

Now that he was in the mountains she would be living her trivial life in London, gay, dancing, setting her beauty off to the best advantage, one of the childless wantons who are the luxury and curse of the modern world; and we two had to thresh out the ruin of our lives caused by a thing so worthless that I would not have stopped to pick her up in the streets, given the chance. She had made her own fate and mine. Let her take the consequences! But he—this tragic friend—it seemed that if I fled to the uttermost ends of the earth he would meet me face to face.

"You see!" said the quiet voice beside me, shattering the vision. "You see you can never outrun your treachery, nor concentrate rightly on vision until you and he have adjusted your honor. You should seek him high and low and learn to understand your deed and its consequences. How otherwise? These things are rocks in the way. It is a cancer in you."

I could not even stop to marvel that he had shared my vision. I answered as if I had laid my life willingly before him.

"Do you mean that I should tell him and perhaps break his heart with a grief he never knew?"

"I mean that when you meet and the truth is laid before you you must act and speak according to the nobility that is in you."

"Do you mean that I am to take his hand in friendship—as I did long ago when all the time I knew—what he never knew?"

"That too might be a necessary part of your suffering, but neither I nor anyone can say what you should do at that moment. I repeat: Act according to the nobility that is in you and the conquering years will justify you to yourself and to *that*. But of this you must rid yourself."

"Nobility!" I said the word with bitterness that half broke my own heart.

He reiterated, "Nobility. Did not the Greeks say, 'Know yourself'? All you have known is the non-self in you, greedy, perilous and foul—whilst the eternal you, beneath it all, is eternal, great and happy. A wonderful self, if you did but know it! Consider its powers. Very soon you will be able to get in touch with anyone, anywhere, and work with them without hindrance of distance and time, your body no obstacle. You will use your nervous system or disuse it as you please. You will realize that you draw nourishment from the sun by assimilating his energy through plants and animals, but that there are quite other means of assimilating the energy besides eating, and that the very essence of the body may be so changed by this knowledge that birth and death lose all meaning, and death as the ordinary world understands it does not overtake you. The last enemy to be destroyed is death. Your body in so far as it contains you may be the House of Fulfilment . . . Learn that and go forward with no thought to bind you to the common beliefs and fears. Cease to be an automaton. Learn to live."

He had risen and stood almost threateningly over me, his eyes darting somber fires. I rose also and stood holding by the table between us. All fear had dropped from me.

"You are my master. I have the right to question you!" I said. "Have *you* done this? Have you gained such complete mastery of the body that you can lay it aside and act without it? Because if not, how dare you hold out hopes that must break one's heart if they fail?"

"Right! That is courageous; that is how you should speak. You shall learn my right to teach by experience and then you shall know what I have achieved and how. The way to the goal is experience through many so-called lives, and experience, which teaches the swan to seek the water by what we call instinct, and the eagle the air, will shape you for the sphere that is your right. And none holds you back but yourself. Break the rotting bond and come!"

I think I stretched my hands to him for his voice was a trumpet-cry. Suddenly, the sense of expansion. He was throwing out influences of power and cleansing so strong that the air between us was charged with vibrations, pungent and piercing, invading me by every channel of sense and nerve. Things beyond reason, for reason is mortal, were loosed upon me, assailed and beat me down and conquered. I was trampled by conviction. Nothing in my life had been like this. It was a powerless creature invaded by a mighty, becoming receptive, responsive, being tuned into a key. No.

Words fail me but I knew then, and not by timid experiment and arid reason, that it is but to will and the way is clear, the end sure.

They say that when the face of Wisdom is unveiled terrible is the love she inspires. I knew it—I knew it then. What can I use but similes to express the inexpressible? I stood as long as I could endure, and then my body failed under the ordeal. I dropped into the chair and hid my face in my arms, feeling the assailing forces ebbing from me like a receding tide, having accomplished their work of pure lustration and carried on their tide—what? I did not know, but was the lighter for its loss.

Silence—for how long I cannot tell, while they were reabsorbed whence they came. Then in the dim lamplight a voice said:

"You have had your first lesson. Return tomorrow." And somehow I got myself stumbling out of the room and to my own, and for an hour felt as if every strength in me were broken forever.

Strange! At the end of that hour the physical strength in me that had been ousted for a while returned mysteriously reinforced. I sprang from the bed where I had thrown myself, strong and full of courage. Not a word, not a word would I say to anyone. Haridas might know, the others might guess, but no speech should dilute the secret I held like a hidden diamond in my heart. It was inevitable now that I should work, toil, struggle until I regained the lost kingdom of my rights. As a wise man showing to another who has believed himself a peasant that he is truly born a king—so was I.

The time between this tremendous intuition and the next appeared a desert to be traversed. How mix with others, how forget for an instant that flooding, uplifting power? If even for a flash only, diluted to meet the weakness of inexperienced humanity, the cosmic energy has once sent its spark through a man, what can he do but cease to be a hindrance and dead, and become a conductor and alive that the cosmic joy may flash through him to others? For I know, were all humanity to feel for a breathless instant what I had felt, earth would be Heaven and immortal bliss open about us like the flowering of the Mystic Rose. So vast would be the direction and discharge of energy that all illusion would be shattered into reality, as when a lightning flash rends the night and discloses a world livid with listening.

But I steadied myself somehow. The immediate inspiration dwindled, I tried to smother flame with the ashes of custom, and after a while went down to the room where we met, with the vast starred night bare to its deepest profundities looking in at the windows, and earth so far below that it had become a memory.

The others had supped. I could not eat, for amazement was still upon me. Brynhild, quick-eyed, saw, smiled and said nothing. For the first time it occurred to me how deep her sympathy might be if I needed it. She too had had her lessons and had been trained in the stern discipline that beats down the outer defenses, and opens the citadel of the soul to beauty and wonder besieging it for so long in vain. Though I had never dared to ask—had not indeed known enough to ask—I could imagine now how in the strange loneliness of mountain and forest by the far-off monastery of Tashigong, alone with people not of her own race, she had borne her ordeal, and I began to estimate the valor and constancy which had carried her through to victory.

I came up to her, drawn by the invisible bond of sympathy, as she sat by the window, while Dunbar at the table sorted papers with his wife's help, and I stood looking out beside Brynhild at the vision of the rising moon floating steadily upward between the spires of mighty mountains seeming to bar her way. When she emerged above them in golden serenity Brynhild turned to me and spoke:

"You had your first lesson this evening."

I said yes and hesitated. Was it possible I should answer truly?

"I know. Don't speak of it if you don't wish. After mine I felt broken with strength and delight. But tomorrow you'll understand better what it has done for you."

Then I found voice; the bond of human sympathy in one who also knew was stronger than my will to silence, but it was only possible to speak haltingly; the thing itself I could not attempt to analyze or describe.

"But will every lesson be like this? An inrush stronger every time? I almost dread the thought."

"Oh, no! That's only to clear the way for beginning. It must be all your own work. The experience you had today would all pass away if you yourself did not work on. But isn't it wonderful? It brought me the knowledge that I could be—Narendra. What will it bring you?"

"If it brings me peace I shall not ask more of it than that."

She quoted:

> "Peace subsisting at the heart
> of endless agitation—"

and went on:

"I suppose peace includes knowledge for it certainly brings that with it. Gradually, of course, and as one becomes more and more receptive. It certainly connects with scientific knowledge. Haven't you realized that it conquers time and space, and makes one know that they are only forms of our own picturing, so that as knowledge widens we can get past them into something that can't be told in any words we possess but where we know absolutely without words?"

As she spoke in lamp-light that was dimmed, almost extinguished, by moonlight flooding in at the window, she had the air of a strong young goddess climbing from strength to strength on her supernal way—yet building steps behind her that others might follow. But what are words to picture the swift instant grasp of the mind upon the reality of human power when even a glimpse of it is given? I saw what I saw—that is all I can make of it.

"You have reached great knowledge. I envy you," I said slowly.

She laughed with real amusement. "I? I know almost nothing. Enough to begin to see how much there is waiting to be known and to cheer me on. It doesn't follow that one is free of the treasury because one has seen a few of the jewels."

I considered a moment. "You mean one has to

realize one knows nothing and make that the starting point?"

"What else? Isn't that the beginning of all the faiths—to become as a little child? We have to learn we have never seen the world as it is, but only through the five blind feelers of our senses, just as a semi-blind man gropes, and that there is a treatment which gives clear sight. That is what they call 'yoga' out here."

There I interrupted with my objection. "No—not our senses only. We have the microscope, wireless, the telephone. How do you get over that? They are revealers."

She shook her head laughing.

"Even with those extensions we still have to use our senses. We still have to use the microscope with our poor little eyes and hear the wireless with our ears. That means we use our blind feelers to grope a little farther, but we don't really know or see. We can only feel our way in the dark."

For a moment that silenced me. True. Intuition outruns—outflies sight and reason, and all the faiths have had the intuition of a Consciousness exceeding our own more vastly than ours exceeds the worm's. Hearing her speak, seeing her face, seeing before me the huge and silent strength of the mountains bathed, drowned, in the silent glory of moonlight, I felt for the moment the walls of the seen and material broken down, disclosing through the gap undiscovered lands, uncharted oceans, and horizons where new suns rise and set.

I had no wish to speak, nor had she, and yet I can most truly say there was communion between us better than any words. I began—at this time my life was a series of beginnings—to comprehend that speech is a very faulty instrument even in the hand of a master, a broken light on the depths of the unspoken.

> —Even your loved words
> Float in the larger meaning of your thought
> As something dimmer.

And further, that what I had believed hitherto to be inanimate things—mountains, oceans, plants, and the rest—can communicate with us sometimes more intimately and nearly than any human voice. That was what Wordsworth meant by his spirit in the woods, what the Greeks meant by their Oreads, the mountain-haunting nymphs; their Dryads, the tree-dwellers; and beyond them the universal Pan, the collective being of them all. Beliefs which I had half loved, half gently derided as myths, turned another face on me now, revealing their exquisite truth beyond all groping words. They are myths only because they attempt to reveal in impossible words what can only be known by disciplined intuition. I cannot express how in that strange moment things hitherto unallied rushed together and fell into shape, combining into lovely geometrical designs, not as yet understandable to me any more than the colored designs of a kaleidoscope, yet revealing immutable law in every change as surely as the crystal in six-sided growth.

"But is this world which we begin to perceive a distant world?" I said aloud, yet following my own thoughts. I do not know at this moment whether Brynhild or my questing thought answered the question.

"No. It is not a distant world. This world we see is the real world, only we see it wrong. The *illuminated* are those who either steadily or in flashes of higher consciousness see it as it really is. For it goes its way independently of us, secure in its own being, and we see it in a glass darkly, but the wise—face to face."

I know now it was the leaven of what Brynhild had called my "first lesson" working in me which at her touch wakened this clearer perception, but I know also that this could not have been if Haridas and the Baltar life had not sown the seed, and I with my poor attempts at concentration had not paved the way to the base of the Mount of Vision.

Dunbar called from the table where they were at work:

"We have had a most wonderful time in the manuscript room. They have treasures there that would take years to examine, and very little has been done beyond sorting out those likely to be useful in our particular search. I foresee great times!"

I pulled up a chair beside him. "Have you found anything yet?"

"A good start. You must come in and see tomorrow morning. Some of the manuscripts are magnificent in their way—the Tibetan ones written horizontally and from left to right, written with tiny sticks of bamboo cut like a pen, and the paper sized with milk and water to prevent blots. Of course there are Mongolian manuscripts too and beautifully brush-written Chinese ones among them, and the one we are hunting will be Chinese. Even today we found some delightful bits—anecdotes, illustrations—I'm tremendously bucked about it all."

"And isn't the place wonderful in itself?" said Lady Lucia, propping her chin on her hands and looking at me with eyes like two mild suns, beaming with kindness. "The strange life all round us— Doesn't it give you a very curious feeling to hear the endless, almost noiseless feet passing along the endless passages? And the weird whispering—almost mute talks they hold with one another. That's a ghostly thing in its way. They really have no curiosity about us—their own life absorbs them, and we just have to hover on the edge of it. I hope we shall get inside."

"You will, if anyone can. Yes—it's a marvelous experience. And to think that all the rest of the world is going on its daily way. Astonishing! Listen!"

For far below, rising in a dulled volume of sound came the strong chanting of men from the temple—for so I called it—where they celebrated their services. We had not yet seen it, but were welcome to when we would. We all made for the door instinctively and threw it open. Not a creature outside. All had assembled in the heart of the vast buildings.

"Come down—now, this minute, and let us listen!" Lady Lucia said, throwing a fur about her; and guided by the great ebbing and flowing waves of sound we made our way down endless stairs and through bewildering passages, until we came to heavy dragon-wrought curtains showing lights within and emitting the peculiar odor given by the butter-fed lamps of a Tibetan monastery. A strong voice, resonant and powerful, chanted inside in Sanskrit:

"So said the Blessed One. The man who desires

riches is as a child eating honey with a sharp knife. Before he can taste the sweetness there remains to him nothing but the bleeding of his lips."

And a great chorus answered, thundering after him:

"So passes the glory of this world into nothingness. But the True, the unchangeable, abides forever."

I have these words written before me as Dunbar translated them. Coming after the events of the day they had the profundity of a great Amen—the experience of humanity affirming from the mountains the laboriously attained knowledge of the sum of mankind.

Again the voice resumed, and again and thunderously the men responded. Then there was silence, broken only by the metallic tinkling of sacred vessels—I could not tell what. And again the voice spoke, this time like a parting benediction bestowed in uttermost tranquillity and quietude.

Silence. And then the great curtains were drawn aside, and the lamas poured out in what seemed a never-ending current of red-robed humanity. Haridas and Shan-tao were among them, and very kindly they extricated us and showed us a near stairway leading to our own heights.

I went to my own sleeping place, possessed by such influences as never before had crossed my mind. In such glimpses one may very well assent to the proposition that this world is in truth far other than it seems. I did not even realize the marvel of our admission and that of Haridas among men regarding Buddhism from so different an angle, nor how all—all had opened the way for the revelation which was to be.

CHAPTER XII

As the days went by some things became familiar while many remained unapproachably strange. We learned our way about the buildings so far as they concerned ourselves; many of the lamas gave us friendly greetings and some would halt for a few words, giving me a lesson in colloquial Tibetan and laughing with huge enjoyment at my stumblings. They were for the most part a good-humored simple crowd who took their faith as they found it and did not look below the surface—the same in that way as most of the professionally religious people I have met all the world over.

Brynhild achieved a feat which made a deep impression on the minds of all the red-robed brethren. With a word and a touch she tamed the huge Tibetan mastiffs which in every monastery live their chained lives in a state of ceaseless fury, bounding to the length of their tethers with bared daggers of teeth, ready to fly murderously at the throat of any unwary being who may venture within reach. I shall never forget the faces of a group of silently watching lamas and my own momentary terror when one morning we entered a courtyard where four were chained, baying to wake the dead, choking themselves with frantic plunges at us. She walked straight up and (strictly against rules, though we did not know it) uncollared the first; it was a beautiful sight in its way to see the huge fellow rear up against her, pushing his yellow muzzle into her face and her hands in a very delirium of devotion. One by one she unchained the four.

"I shall take them for a walk over the rocks every day I'm here," she said confidently to me, the lamas watching mutely.

Word was sent to the abbot, and to the consternation of all he put his head out of his sacred window and coming into an overhanging gallery viewed the scene without any comment but evident interest, as she led the way out to the snowy rocks, the four sacred creatures leaping about her in ecstasies of freedom. And stranger still—what will not be believed, but is true—I have seen the ibex, which came about the monastery fearlessly at all times owing to the Buddhist respect for life, halt as she came with her guard of dogs and stand while she stroked them, holding the dogs behind her quiet as marble, held by one look and word. The windows were crowded with heads when this occurred, as it often did, and her reputation for miracles grew great. The event became a commonplace, for she freed them daily and earned the reputation of untold acts of compassion in former lives.

"They say she is either an incarnation of pity now, or has stored up the merit of countless pitiful deeds in other lives," Haridas told me. "Which for all I know may be true. Of course the foundation of it is that she has no fear. An animal feels the fear in you almost before you feel it yourself. She thinks love to them, and they leap to meet it. An instinct we have forgotten."

Apparently she and Lady Lucia "thought love" to others besides animals, for it is not too much to say that the women adored them. I can recall nothing stranger and more touching than the way in which they made a home of that queer place and among those ignorant women. For ignorant they were. They had grasped the formulas of their faith, and the rest left them behind. I have always been sure that they considered the two superhuman, faintly alarming and approachable only through their compassion. That was one of the things that did not grow commonplace; it was always a new wonder.

So too was the Illuminated Pearl known to the others as the Kitat or Chinese Lama. I could not fathom the reason for this, for though I had never seen his face in full daylight but always hooded and shadowed in dusk, I knew very well there was nothing of the unmistakable Chinese type about it. More than once I asked Haridas why they called him the Kitat Lama; I never had a clear answer. That his learning was Chinese was once given as a reason, but they might as well have called him the Indian Lama or anything else, for his learning appeared to be universal. I noticed that he never mingled with the others as we watched them coming and going, never ate with them nor joined in the mighty teas which gave the *gompa* an oddly familiar touch while they lasted, breaking as they did through the vigilant discipline of the life. I never wearied of watching these simple feasts—only taking place when some benefactor provided the wherewithal—when tongues were loosed for a while from the grave silence which was normal.

They would sit in companies in the great courtyard, while the young monks went off to the kitchens, returning with heavy jars of milk-tinged tea. Each lama sat with his wooden bowl before him, patiently holding it up to be filled from the bounteous jars. They made the journey round twice, and while we were in the monastery Dunbar as a gift added oatmeal cakes and a slice of fresh butter for each lama. It may be guessed how this added to our popularity. A little psalm of gratitude always ended the function.

Meanwhile the work of sorting the manuscripts went on steadily, and special treasures were set aside for examination. Brynhild made another curious success in that art of modeling in butter which is one of the most amazing features of some of the great Tibetan lamaseries.

We were invited one day to see the preparations for the immense Festival of Flowers, as they call it, which would draw all the countryside on pilgrimage to the Lamasery of the Manis, and great was our astonishment to find a group of artist lamas sitting in a row with buckets of snow beside them in which they chilled their hands from time to time as they modeled bas-reliefs in butter stiffened with some substance that gave it proper consistence. It was a fascinating sight to watch the work grow under their hands in great panels illustrating scenes from the life of the Buddha. Their dexterity was amazing, and some of the scenes really beautiful in their way.

"But I can do that too!" said Brynhild; and every

hooded head turned to her though none understood her words. They very well understood what followed, for she seized upon a great lump of butter and sitting apart from the others began modeling swiftly and silently.

"Delightful stuff to use!" she said, working away without looking up. "Much better than clay or plasticine, if it could stand the sun. I wonder what they put in it?"

For a moment I was afraid, for who could tell how Asiatics might resent the sight of a mere woman modeling their sacred histories? She did not give them the chance. Boldly and skilfully she modeled her medium into a rocky precipice rising from rough river-banks at the base. I saw the row of eyes fixed upon her in silent expectation, work suspended. I heard the almost inaudible whisper pass from mouth to mouth. Working more rapidly now she indicated high up the precipice a great and many-windowed building clinging precariously to it. As this came into being a light of comprehending pleasure broke on every face, and they struck their hands together in vociferous applause.

"Wonderful, and most wonderful! This woman is indeed an incarnation of knowledge. There is not a man among us who could better that likeness of the Gompa of the Manis!"

Haridas, standing behind us, leaned forward to her.

"Would you make them an image of the Lord Buddha? It would give them great pleasure, and it might possibly be allowed to appear at the festival, if the abbot approved."

It was a surprising sight. Their own work was

laid aside and one fetched a great lump of butter two feet high. A bucket of snow was pushed to her feet by another, and then all stood expectant. I watched eagerly with the rest, but with certainty, for I knew not only her self-possession but her skill. It was beautiful to watch the speed and certainty of her fingers.

First the background of a boat-shaped halo, or glory, very richly worked in small designs of winged figures with garlands between them, some with joined hands. In front at the base, a large lotus the many petals opening into a flat throne on which the sacred figure would be installed.

The news had spread, and many lamas came hurrying to see the strange woman at work upon a subject so entirely their own, but she never raised her head from the empty lotus throne before her, working swiftly with touches from her finger-tips and from a little slender stick she had picked up. Now, shaping into separate form in her hands, came the seated figure, about a foot in height, and I own it was miraculous to me to see the molding of the folded feet, hands resting in the lap, head lightly poised, leaning a little backward with the weight of the dream. Light touches indicated the hair, the characteristic prominence on the head, and slower and more delicate ones the ears and curves of lips unsmiling and calm above the lifted chin. It took time but she worked on steadily, never failing and scarcely correcting, until the figure was complete, and she set it on the lotus throne, curling a few petals upward about it.

"Good stuff to work in! Who can ever have thought of such a thing?" she said, dipping her hands into the snow. "If only it would last! Imagine exhibiting a butter sculpture in London!"

Then indeed admiration and wonder broke out unstinted.

"It is the Holy Buddha—the Perfect One," they cried. "See his hands! He is in ecstasy. Is not this a wonder? And for a woman!"

The men crowded about her, more friendly and at home than ever we had yet known them, for here was a touch upon what they valued most in the world. A messenger carrying the achievement seated on a little board was sent off with it to the abbot and it was more than hinted that with his approval it might figure among the Flowers of the year.

"Did we not say she was a divine Incarnation?" said one to Haridas, with the others consenting. "There is no mistaking their gifts when this occurs. Animals recognize it instantly—they have the true instinct for a saint. Pity indeed that karma compelled her to be born in the form of a woman. There must have been some sin to be atoned for in a past life!"

"But it is easy to see that she acquires merit every day!" chuckled another. "This work alone will wash out any wrong-doing. And though a woman and born in a strange land she has the root of the matter in her. Reverence should be paid to such persons. They walk in the favor of Heaven."

Haridas smiled assenting, knowing better than they the root and blossom. After that odd episode she was exalted in their eyes even above the great learning of the Brother of the Pen.

I may say here that every day the friendship between

us developed. I have said I loved her—and that is proof that a man may love a woman—no, not as he loves a man friend, for there are subtle differences to be felt, not told—but yet without any fever of coveting or passion of possession. I thought and still think that this is the surest gate by which to enter marriage, if that is to be the goal. And I have some right to speak for the situation was certainly tested later. For one thing, we were thrown upon each other's company by the necessity of things, for the others were all engrossed in work, Lady Lucia helping, as she always did, in copying what they Englished. The tap of her typewriter must have been the first ever heard in the Monastery of the Manis, and from the abbot downward it was a source of wonder and delight and made her name also great in the land, though after a different fashion. Haridas was undoubtedly regarded as a great magician by the simpler brothers.

Indeed we all grew in favor. It may seem incredible that we could have fallen in with such a life and have been regarded with such friendly eyes, but so it was, no doubt very largely because Haridas and Shan-tao served as a connecting link between the lamas and ourselves. But, below the differences of surface, are not humanity and purpose the same everywhere? The question of the likes and repulsions of men is, I am convinced, a matter to be measured only by the different stages of soul-evolution at which each has arrived, and there love and tolerance must be on the side of the one who has climbed highest on the ascending spiral. The lower will not understand—and miscomprehension is always repulsion.

Of my own progress in education it is not easy to speak, but it must be done since it is a part of my strange story.

Day by day, in dusk that grew later as spring advanced, I went to the room where my teacher always met me hooded, with face more than half hidden and personality hidden still more deeply in reserve. Since that first evening there had been no other—explosion, shall I call it?—of the great forces underlying life as we know it, but every day I learned to understand a little and yet a little more of their terror and beauty.

Using parable, symbols, and the sights about us, he taught with unfaltering skill the meanings of the spirit of nature and also of the soul of man. For in man also are vast solitudes, mountains and plains, the strong splendor of the sun unleashing the avalanche upon its work of destruction, the thunder of rivers breaking rejoicing from locked glaciers. In man are the bitter snow-blasts, the passionless fall of snow, blotting out life. In him the peace of the growing moon dwelling like a thought of Heaven upon the topmost peak. And in him, latent but present, Godhead the Many-named, Maker and Destroyer of Illusion—and to upbear it the strength of more than the hills. How could it be otherwise when he too shares the Universal Spirit?

So I learned my lesson of the Divinity in Man from a mighty teacher and tasted at moments in my own nature an elemental joy foreshadowing meeting of earth and Heaven.

I still feared him, for fear is the beginning of wisdom, though only the beginning, but his company was more to me than any other in the world. When the dusk began to drop its veil over the receding castles of the mountains where one might fancy such strange cold-eyed elementals might dwell, I put aside whatever I might be doing and my heart began to beat faster; the cold air of the unknown stole about me like a ghostly breath. As I climbed the stair to his eyrie I repeated to myself always, and each time with fuller realization:

> "He who sees about him the manifold goes from death to death. See therefore the One and be free."

Sentences of his clung about me like hands that hold.

> "The energies we perceive as manifold are in truth like the rain falling on a mountain-top and running down in many streams, but in their Source they are One."
>
> "They who in this world of illusion find Him the Changeless; they who know Him as the Soul of their souls; unto them is peace eternal—unto none else; unto none else!"
>
> "He is the eternal Banyan Tree, rooted in the Unseen beyond our senses, and throwing out his branches to make the Universe. One with Him are all the leaves and sprays and branches. He is the Root. He is the Root."

How shall I describe the mighty organ music rolling in majesty through a soul prepared? What fiber of inmost psychic being did it leave unthrilled? At last I set foot step by step on the stair he wrought and climbed—with halts, but never a doubt now. For I had learned that this earth is greater than any dreamed-of Heaven, for in no Heaven anywhere can we learn, as in this life and within the soul, to understand Reality.

Reality. That was the quest: to know the world as it is, to attain the Kingdom of Heaven that is within the soul. And I was learning. What I may call the physical drill of breathing, posture and fixation of the mind of the system they followed became daily easier. I had hope that one day, however distant, I might attain the quiescent state in which the being like an ocean at rest reflects the beams of the Divine in a great stillness.

One evening later on, I climbed the Stair of Shadows, as I called it, to the Room of Great Light. Not material light—far from it—but a light that must shine through my eternity until lost in the Light of Lights. My teacher stood by the window, watching the mountains recede through violet mist into the night. He heard me and spoke without turning:

"You come in hope and joy—the air before you is glad. That is well. Today you have realized: 'My miseries are of my own making, I can undo them. What I made I can unmake. I only am responsible. I am a Master Builder. Let me build in strength.'"

That was true. For hours of the day I had sat on a crag overlooking the river thundering downward with the weight of melted snows to the Indus and the ocean, to lose itself in a greater until it should reach the Uttermost. And so meditating while time was forgotten I had been myself as the river, my teacher as the mighty Indus sweeping my waters on to the immeasurable, unsounded ocean. And as I dwelt on that thought realizing it in analogy and truth, suddenly a new sense dawned in me; my eyes were opened and my ears heard.

If I say I saw the spirit of the river it connotes a form human or semi-human and that is pure nonsense. I saw its essential and know no words to describe my own sight. But it went with the thundering water, one with it, expressing, centering it, and resuming all its joy and freedom into a being so great, so glad, as to be utterly beyond my comprehension. It was alien to me and therefore inspired the fear a giant would inspire if one met him drowsing enormous on some mountain in vast sunshine and sky. But that was because I had not reached the stage of unity which gives the freehold of the Kingdom, though even at that moment I knew fear lay only on the threshold. It could not penetrate the House with me when I entered. I can say no more than that it was color, sublime and unknown, the very passion of bliss, the very liberation of power, complete and perfect in harmony. Harmony—for as I saw I heard—but louder, more instant, the mighty music I had realized in the valley of the mountain of Wardrang, while I touched the hand of Brynhild.

It passed; or how could I have endured it? And the river was glorious water rushing to its triumphant union again. But I had its secret, grasped in my hold as a diver grasps his pearl.

This my teacher knew, and no words were needed. He sat down and motioned me to my place. His talk was of evolution and devolution, of the ascending scale and of the descending, in which a man may hideously involve himself in temporary death and ruin. He concluded with the Vedantic prayer, which is in truth an assertion and the only one possible in truth to the man who has broken so much as one fetter of the many imposed by misconception of life.

> Death and fear I have not, nor caste, nor creed. Father and mother I have not, nor birth nor death, nor friend, nor foe, for I am Existence, Knowledge and Joy. I am the Blissful One—the Blissful One! I am not bound by happiness or misery. No book nor pilgrimage nor ceremony can bind me. The body is not mine or mine its decay, for I am Existence, Knowledge and Joy. I am the Blissful One—the Blissful One.

"There was One, there is One, and but One," he said ending.

The room was dark now with only one faint glimmer near the distant door, and outside was visible only the wide-swept sky glittering with stars—no moon—stars, stars in a glorious infinitude to the very limits of space. I sat looking out and revolving his words and it did not seem long until he spoke again. They startled me instantly aware and awake.

"If you consider you will see that the destiny you had made for yourself involved your coming to the House of Fulfilment—to Baltar. Not that that was the beginning of your development, but it is known to you how and where it opened the prison door. The time has come when the next great step, or fall—whichever you may choose it to be—is necessary in your experience. You have had many foreshadowings of it—"

For the first time I interrupted him:

"Not up into the mountains—not to meet him! I am not ready. There is much more I must know before I am able to bear it. If you knew—"

"I know, but if the right time had not come he would not be where he is. He has journeyed from Chinese Turkestan to that meeting, and if you avoided it you would be a coward. What hope is there for the coward in this world as you now know it?"

But what could I say? Every strength I thought I had grasped fell away from me and left me most miserably alone.

"I cannot do it. I'll go down into Kashmir. I'll go back to the West. Not only for myself. . . . It would be a cruelty to him."

Silence. My battle was to be to myself, and most literally it was a battle, for, fallen from my perception of unity, I was torn violently into two fighting personalities, each struggling to conquer the other and reign alone. Illusion fell about me once more, thick as snowflakes in storm, blotting out all behind it. What I had gained seemed not only lost but nothing. I had been a fool wasting my time in these solitudes, with these dreamers, while I might have been a man among men, strengthening my art in prosperity, winning the prizes, forgetting the past. I forgot my master's presence, for every temptation is in the wilderness, and in the wilderness of my own soul I sat and was afraid.

"You cannot send me," I said at last, more to myself than to him.

"Certainly not. You are a free man unless you fetter yourself."

"Does he know the truth?" I asked at last, debating whether knowledge or ignorance would be the easier for me.

"I cannot tell. Nor does it matter."

"I beg your pardon. It matters very much to *me!*" I said bitterly.

"Nothing matters to you but your own attitude."

The silence was like gulfs of darkness between us. Now I knew I only feared him. How could any man love an austerity like a black pine tree dumb with snow against a gray sky? I got to my feet and said loudly:

"If you had waited a little longer I might have been able to face this. You have not understood me, and therefore I shall learn no more. What is the use if I am to be broken like this?"

He rose also and stood tall above me—a part of the darkness.

"Remember the nobility that is in you, and the jewel in your soul. Think now before you choose."

Outside, the night was a listening quiet as though attentive to my poor decision, and the glory of the stars was terrible—life heaped on life, the golden grains of the eternal harvest shed abroad over space. When he ceased they took up the tale and spoke. The universal life I had shared that day flowed into me, strengthened me, pointed me to resolution. I stared at them for a long time, listening, guessing a spheral music, deafened by the crash of warring instincts in me. But I cannot describe the processes at work within me—how should I? They were as mysterious and as simple as the growth of a plant. I can only set down the outside commonplaces of speech and action.

At long last I said sullenly:

"I will go, but how? It sounds like a madman's chase. Where is he? How do I know?"

"Two mountain guides are provided. It is not far from here. He is on his way from the Hindu-Kush to Skardo and he will diverge to meet you in the mountains. It is not very far; about a ten days' march—but that depends on the state of the river, for you will cross the Indus."

"And when am I to go? And how?"

"There will be men and provisions and tents. You should start the day after tomorrow."

"And why is all this trouble taken about me? What does it matter to you or anyone else?" I asked suspiciously. But his patience was inexhaustible.

"You could answer that first question yourself if you chose. If men are indeed one with the One, they also are one with each other. There is nothing you need which would be refused."

A new suspicion woke in me like a darting snake.

"Do my friends, the Dunbars and Miss Ingmar, know anything of this? And if not how am I to explain my leaving the place?"

"They know nothing. Will it not be possible to say you are going to sketch? I can assure you, you will do such work there as you have not done yet."

Even that did not move me, though at times it had alarmed me that no impulse to work had stirred in me since I had been swept into the life of Baltar.

"After all—why should I go?" I said to myself, but aloud.

"You are free to choose," he repeated. "That cannot be said of everyone—but you are free."

Shame seized me. If one agrees with necessity, and something deep down in me recognized it as necessity, it should at all events be nobly, not churlishly done. I used a very different tone.

"Sir, I apologize for my ill manners. I will go and I thank you for opening the way. What will happen I cannot tell, but whether good or ill I shall thank you for the intention, and when I come back I shall be most grateful if you will still be my teacher."

"Very gladly—if it is still needed. There are teachers of more sorts than one, however. Now . . ."

His gesture was dismissal—but kindly. I asked if I should see him next day and the answer was yes. Then I got away, but how tossed about, how confused and fearful, I cannot describe. It was a terrible ordeal to which I had pledged myself—and I was torn with doubt. Indeed I thought it a senseless, useless business at best. It would only torture the man if he knew the truth and if not—what friendship could there be between deceiver and deceived?

I could not face the others. Dunbar would be bending happily over his manuscripts, lost to the world, his beautiful wife beside him as whole-hearted in the pursuit as himself; Brynhild by the window watching the wheeling of the stars with her strange brimming quiet and content. No—no room for me in the company of hearts afloat on the ocean of peace.

I got my coat and went out bareheaded into the night, along tramped snowy ways and zigzagged along the face of the mountain behind the monastery, trying in the vast silence of the solitude to face the matter with reason and common sense and consider the course I should take. But it was impossible. Jarring impulses of long affection mingled with the traitor's fear, until I almost cursed the day I had been born.

I tramped about for an hour or two, almost within sight of the dim glimmering lights from myriad windows, then went back and climbed the stairs to my room. I slept that night, but my friend troubled my dreams with hauntings and vanishings that wrung my soul. Next day I told Dunbar I had planned a sketching trip toward the Indus. He received the news with surprise.

"I'm glad to hear it. I know this is a confining life for anyone who isn't in my work. When are you going to begin your own? There's no lack of subjects here."

When the news reached Brynhild there was not a flicker of anything beyond kindly interest.

"Then that was why the old Mongol monk who lives by the entrance gate told me the mountain guides were getting ready. I envy you—that's a great thing to do. Lucia, did you hear? Mr. Cardonald will be up near the Skardo country? That wouldn't be many marches from Alam Khan."

Lady Lucia was full of interest.

"Oh, but you must have a chit to him! If you could go and stay at his queer old feudal castle it would be an amazing experience. Of course you must have a chit. He'd take it from us as the most fortunate introduction."

Even in my disturbed mind some sparks of gratitude were left, and I showed them. I realized also that there would be a pang in leaving friends so kind and true, and how many stars had shone for me in Brynhild's brave eyes—far from being "lights that do mislead the morn," rather, beacons to welcome a man from stormy seas to the haven of home!

When we parted after the ordinary lesson of my course which held no reference to my errand, my master stood a moment in thought, then said as it were at parting:

"I wish you much happiness in your meeting with your friend. To meet a friend anywhere in the world is well. Here in the heights it is better. May high certainty go with you and lead you back in joy."

In the early morning of a glorious day in summer, with the sun showering wide light and warmth from a cloudless sky, I took my careful way with guides and servants down the face of the precipice to the hamlet beneath, where the ponies would meet us. To the arrangements on which my life might depend I paid no attention. They did not interest me. My thoughts all burned toward the goal of that mysterious meeting.

When I had reached the river I turned and looked up at the flat great buildings staring stedfastly across the river to the mighty snows and the mightier river which I must cross. It all seemed near and dear to me—a home in the wilderness with Brynhild's faithful eyes along the wastes sending friendly beams to light the way. I loved her for her lovingness, so free from sentiment that it had the tang of a brave boy's hidden regard.

I stood a moment looking steadily upward to the window where she commonly sat like a bird in her nest ready to launch into the wing-ways of the air, then mounted my pony and began the long trek.

CHAPTER XIII

I PASS OVER THE FIRST FOUR DAYS OF THE JOURNEY and stand in one of the great gorges of the Indus in dumb amaze at the glory of the hurrying water and with serious question of the chances of crossing the terrible rapids. I said as much to the guides in the sufficing colloquial I had picked up for daily use in the Lamasery of the Manis, and was reassured by their cheerful grins.

"No difficulty, none. Here the river is so wide that there are shoals and sands. The ponies can do it well, and for the deeper channels are goatskin rafts. Very good traveling, as will be seen."

Good, but risky as even my inexperience knew. The Indus is no child's toy. But the heat was great on the rocks and beaches, and the sand blew in whirls that wearied the eyes, and it may be that a kind of fatalism had seized me, for in those days the spiritual aids on which I had begun to count as my own had broken under me and left me mere human and with a dryness of the soul more painful than any physical thirst. Best leave it untold.

I sat on the bank and watched them swim the ponies across the first rapids—half swimming, half leading, in difficulties which recalled the unforgotten day at the Wardrang. For myself there waited a raft of framework supported on many goatskins inflated by the simple expedient of blowing air in through the legs and then securing them tight, and on this my baggage was placed by two men who sat ready to pole and row me across.

We started, using the poles as oars and very insufficient ones, and so shoved along into the first shallows where the men got out and waded whilst I remained in solitary grandeur on the raft. On the next lap we poled through the rapids, sweeping down-stream in spite of all our efforts—and I took a hand myself, recalling old days on sluggish Thames, tame as a domestic rabbit compared with this wild volume of water that held us in its cold clutch, for cold it was beyond any endurance but that of the hardy mountain men.

Again they walked in the shallow water, towing, and again scrambled on for the next plunge with busy oars into the rapids, the goatskins leaking air plentifully and at times, I thought, rather alarmingly, if I had cared one way or the other. But the men blew them up like flattening tires, and still we held on, drenched with spray in the rapids, half choked with blowing sand in the shallows and islets, and so after a long and tedious struggle reached the other bank. A wonderful river indeed.

But its gorges and their magnificence! Can I ever forget their wild glory—buttresses of gray precipice through which the river cut its age-long way? Here the forces of nature were sublime and terrible, filling the soul with awe. It suited my mood—the vastness calmed me like a cold hand laid on aching temples.

After all what did my pigmy worries matter in the presence of this mighty life moving on its own vast orbit where man and his concerns were nothing? Above me spired untrodden peaks resumed into the sky, fit companions of the stars; and I crawled along my upward way, dreading their avalanches, watching the sky for storm omens, out of place, out of memory, a poor jest on the unveiled splendors of awful whiteness lying about and beyond me.

They uttered their great peace in the majesty of silence: "In all the changing manifolds of the universe, he who beholds the One, the Unchanging, knowing that he is THAT, has alone reached the goal." And, as I heard, the hallucinations of fear and shame fled away at times like dreams at dawn. Only at times. Not for one moment must I pretend that the days were a triumph of wisdom. Often I was sad, bewildered, fearful, but not wholly swept away by tormenting seas of illusion.

So we climbed along the mountain ways to a cluster of mountain huts at the almost incredible height of sixteen thousand feet, having climbed two thousand since leaving the Monastery of the Manis. Villages are high indeed in this land of wonders, and the people so habituated to breathing the pure air that they die in the grosser air of comparatively low levels—such, for instance, as the Happy Valley of Kashmir, itself 5,000 feet above sea-level. My men apparently made nothing of the pass-sickness, and I, strengthened by the science of right breathing, made a better show than most Europeans would have done.

Ibex, markhor, many snow-dwellers we saw, watching and leaping away to their fastnesses from our slow approach. It would have driven me mad in the old days with blood-lust, but that lay behind me now. They also were a part of the peace, and beautiful exceedingly.

The avalanches, loosened by summer, were the greatest danger, and we had one or two narrow shaves not worth recording. But it was a tense excitement like drinking strong wine to watch them on their thunderous way, starting the echoes with wild laughter volleyed back from peak to peak in aerial heights. There were moments when I felt it would be good to live there forever, lost in meditation like an Indian forest-dweller, apart from all the complexities and ruin of life as the world lives it. To become a part of the Great Silence with only the hovering eagles for friends and the vast solitudes for refuge—how it drew me! But that dream too was mirage—*maya*—and I knew it and pressed on and up.

The end came sooner than I expected, when the huts were still some hundreds of feet above us and, the guides calculated, at least four hours' work. It was a glorious dawn as we reached a little dish-shaped valley in a crevice of the mountains, so crowded with flowers that it seemed a casket of jewels spilt about in lovely thriftlessness. There were Christmas roses, great ranunculuses, acres of blue forget-me-nots, masses of a small orange wallflower and many others, unnamed and beautiful, their hearts of rapture drawn out in strong perfume by the glowing sun shining down as into a hollow. Such beauty—such wonder! How could the whole round earth contain its gladness and vivid living?

There was no trace of snow in the valley itself. Some cattle were feeding peacefully and in a smaller nook opening from it there was a little cultivation of grain. I wondered idly if the bread made from its scanty gold might not have some vital quality differing very greatly from that grown in the lowlands. Winter might have been forgotten in this little happy place if it had not been for the bluffs and precipices and spires above and around it mantled in dazzling glittering purity.

I threw myself on the warm grass and we ate, and for drink had the mountain water, clear as light flowing from the sun. After that I fell asleep, and waking rested and refreshed, climbed a bluff for a wider view, and saw what I saw.

My very heart seemed to stop beating, and the blood rushed to my face.

On a snow-slope above me was a little shelter built behind a rock for protection from the sweeping razor-edged blasts that wake into fierce life in a flash. Before it stood a man with a great dog at his feet, both looking up to the peaks sailing like white swans in the blue. Before waking eyes I saw the vision of the Golden Valley of Sonamarg.

There are moments when to fling oneself forward is the only refuge from the madness of flight. I did not think—I knit my whole being into resolve, and leaping down the other side of the bluff climbed on and up steadily. Indeed I could not think—all that was left was a dull hope that something would befriend me in the hour of need and give me some word to say not utterly despicable. The dog rushed downward baying, the man turned and saw, and in an instant more was hurrying and slipping down to meet me. He shouted aloud:

"Don't come up, dear old boy. Stick to the valley. I'll be down in two twos. Hold on!"

I found myself among the flowers again, scarcely conscious I had moved and with ten minutes in which to collect my half-stunned senses. It was more than that when the dog bounded down and stood wagging a friendly tail—more still, when Maitland dropped the last fall with a leap and seized my hand, looking into my face with eyes shining with the old remembered kindness. And still I was as one who dreams.

No—of the first moments of that meeting I cannot write. It is locked in the innermost.

After a while we were sitting on the grass, and he was telling me how word had been passed along to him in the almost miraculous way in which it travels these lands to say I was in the upper country and could meet him hereabouts.

"And it seemed unbelievable at first, for what could have brought you here in these wild places? You—a fashionable artist, but so much more as well!—you, full of success and prosperity—why, in God's name, have you thrown it all up? Tell me, old chap. I'm at sea!"

"You too!" I said to gain time. "And what are you doing? I haven't heard of you for ages. I'm very easily explained, but what about you?"

"I?" He still held me with those peculiarly clear gray eyes, which I had always thought the truest, most candid in the wide world. "But I've written—more than once. You never got the letters?"

"Never. Not one."

"Well, perhaps one shouldn't be surprised when places like this are the post town—but I did my best. Let me see!" He reckoned on his fingers. "Yes—four times I wrote. And then I thought you might be away shooting somewhere and I gave up trying. Things lapse outwardly, but never inwardly. Isn't that it?"

He sat with his back against a rock and the dog at his feet looking up at him with more than human adoration. To me his face had always been beautiful because of what it meant to me, whatever it might have been to others—from boyhood the gladdest sight I could see. I still thought the same, though it could mean gladness to me no more. He had not aged; the mouth was still firm and fine, untouched by a war scar on the cheek; the smile a warmth of the soul; the good strong shoulders unstooped. The years had done nothing at all to harm the citadel of the man. I remembered the darting thought was: Why in God's name had she preferred a creature like me to such a man and her own?

"But tell me!" he urged. "What brought you here? I heard you were with those wonderful people at Baltar—the Dunbars. They're a godsend to all the country for a hundred miles about them. Is it true?"

"Quite true. I met her at Simla and they took me in there. He's at the Monastery of the Manis now, manuscript-hunting for his friends in China, and Lady Lucia with him. We came up together."

"Ah, you wanted to study the mountains?"

"Yes."

It was coming, coming. I felt confession nearer, nearer to my lips. It was choking my throat, beating in my temples, throbbing in my eyes. Yet, oh, the misery of meeting such a friend for such an ending! Suddenly he spoke—still holding my eyes.

"You never got my letters. Then you did not know that Helen died and I sold Footways and came out to India?"

How could I answer? Mountains, sky, valleys all whirled into one bright confusion that dazzled and stunned me. Not joy, not sorrow, confusion only. It seemed long before I stammered:

"I knew nothing. That must have been when I was in South America."

"Yes."

Silence. Then very slowly he said, still looking steadily into my wavering eyes:

"Soon after I came back from the war and we could be together again she became a Catholic. I saw it was from the need of some inner support she could not get from me, but when she began to be ill she was more and more drawn to me, and we grew nearer and nearer to each other as life darkened down for her."

There I interrupted—whether with false or true courage I cannot tell even now.

"Maitland, if she had been living I could have had no right to speak without her consent. But now it's different. The living come first—you and I."

"I honor her memory," he said, very low. "But speak. There is nothing earthly that could deface it, for I love her and that means understanding."

How had I the heart? I went on, impelled I

suppose by my own great need and inspired with yet bitterer contempt for the woman who had tried "to make her soul" so cheaply at the end. I know now the cur and coward I was then, in spite of all I had learned.

"That you should remember her with honor and meet me as a friend is intolerable. I can't stand it. You must know us both for what we were. We deceived and betrayed you; we wronged you in every thought and deed. Your love and trust were wasted on us both."

I choked there. It was done and what would come next was beyond all my imagining. The flowers swayed in a gentle breeze; the little rivulet from the spring beside us murmured its peace. The sun shone on just and unjust alike in a benediction. I could not stand it—I threw myself along in the grass and hid my face from it all and wished for death.

It seemed a long time before he spoke:

"Did you think I did not know this?"

Think—how could I think? I lay still and hidden, waiting.

"I knew it when she came to me after the war. It was known to others who told me, but I never told her."

Long pauses, as though he were looking back into the grievous past and painfully recalling what he wished to say.

"But I took her in. She was so young and dear. I thought it all out. There are crueler things than that, and I saw . . ."

"Crueler?"

"You forget— You also had meant much to me."

"Which made it the more damnable cruelty in us. There is no forgiveness for such devil's work."

"Forgiveness? No, none. But that is not the word. There is understanding. I learned to understand. She was so lamed with grief—wings broken. It was like the last rush of blood from a wound when she told me. It left her drained."

"And you could endure to take my hand? To sit here beside me? I tell you I have climbed up into the mountains to meet you and throw myself down the next precipice if you bid me. My life is yours."

"I had rather you climbed up!" I felt the waving of a hand toward the peaks storming the blue.

Another silence. He spoke again.

"All those angers are wisps of cloud blown about the eternal summits. They come and go and are illusions. I had my moments of doubt, but they passed. My old uncle died—just after Helen, and made me his heir on condition I took his—my mother's—name. That helped also to break up the old life which had broken under me, and I sold Footways and came out to India. There I learned the meaning of life—and that dispelled my last doubt as to the meanings of what had struck me down. I see it now as a thing with tremendous issues for us all, but nothing to storm at. I understand. We shall none of us escape the shadow of it in this life, but in others we shall see it all as a part of experience, and it will wound neither her, nor you, nor me, any more at all."

"But, good God, you see the horror of it? If you had done that to me what would you think of yourself?"

"Exactly what you think, because in this matter you start from a lower level than I. Therefore you see it from below and I from above and with a clearer viewpoint. Have you learned since last we met? I have learned several things which have forced me to take life not from the common angle but from quite another. And there's another thing to be said. You have thought harshly and contemptuously of my wife. Well—she was never yours—always mine, for I knew the beauty in her and you never did. She never said a hard word of you—not one—when she told me; she spoke of you with true tenderness. . . . She made the way straight for our meeting today."

Something in me cried out in agony when he said those words. What had I done—what broken, so far above myself? She had caught fire at his glow and both were eternally above me. It was as though some strong divinity caught my soul and plunged it in baths of purifying fire—anguish and self-loathing and scathing remorse. I had no word—nor he. The breeze had its way in the blissful upper world, but we were silent. The revulsion was too violent.

At last I said: "There is no forgiveness—none."

"But you can turn it into beauty and strength. Who wants forgiveness?" he answered. "That was child's talk. The other is men's work."

After a long while he added: "Tell me of yourself now. I ask it in all sincerity."

In this strangest of interviews nothing had happened of any one of the possibilities which had tormented me. His presence, his voice shed quiet even upon the huge uplifted quiet of our meeting-place.

I collected myself, and facing him still with difficulty and with sickening self-repulsion, told him the story of Baltar as well as I could with my own want of understanding. I spoke of Haridas, of the new teaching, of my efforts in discipline and the study of Raja Yoga, of the sense of powers about me, incomprehensible as yet but destined to mold my life as a sculptor chisels his marble. A sculptor! . . . Brynhild . . . I had not yet spoken of her though I had told my story as I would have told it in the happy days when life had not parted our friendship. I would have spoken of her then but he interrupted.

"That's good. Now I can tell you a bit of my own story. I came to India pretty well done in—at sea with no harbor in sight. And a friend sent me up to a little house in the woods beyond Simla to pick up. Neither to him nor to anyone had I said a word of what I suffered. Yes, I did suffer. I don't now. And up there I met a girl—no, not a love story. Something above and beyond that—indescribable—I won't attempt it. But she opened the door into another world for me—the real world—though at the time she rather felt than knew the way herself. She has wonderful natural gifts, she—"

I had listened with a growing chill of intuition.

"Maitland—what is your name now?"

Something in my voice halted him in great amazement.

"Ormond. My mother's name. But why?"

I turned my face from him.

"Go on," I said. "A wonderful story and not unlike my own experiences at Baltar."

But what he said I only remembered and pieced together afterwards, for the grip I held on myself was like a strangle-hold that binds and deafens. Brynhild. Did he love her? Did I? What was the meaning of the interweaving threads of destiny in his life and mine? However that might be, the only hope was to give no sign of feeling about her but what might be common to all the world who loved her. There at least my way was clear. He went on:

"And springing strangely from our friendship came the decision that I would come up into the mountains to study the science—not of what goes by the name of psychology—but of the soul, and I have learned so much that I own it has turned the world I once lived in to a shadow-show, one I could never be part and lot of any more."

Then I said with more courage:

"Our experiences have run parallel, but mine not nearly so far as yours. But before we can enter freely into all that, tell me—is it possible that we could still be friends?"

We were sitting opposite each other—both with hands locked about our knees. He looked straight at me.

"I think it impossible we should be otherwise. Distrust and betrayal are earth-bubbles when one knows them for what they really are. Love endures —even this. But why do I say 'even'?"

He had laid his hand on the noble head of the great dog couched across his feet. Then held it out to me. For a moment I hesitated.

He went on:

"While I hold it—let me say one thing. You never knew my wife—or the real loveliness of her. Now you have understood it. Don't you think there may also be something to understand about yourself? Self-contempt is almost more bitter, rotting work than despising other people."

"I?" I said, half stunned with self-contempt. "I have a right to despise myself if any man ever had."

"Then speaking as a friend I say, 'Despise yourself no more.' Is one fall to blacken the whole of life? I should say: Learn from it. Climb higher."

"Haridas said that too."

"He was right. Haridas is always right. He has the far sight. Who is your teacher?"

I told him, with some attempt to describe the effect he had upon my mind—no, more than my mind: my inmost being.

"He must be a great man," Ormond said slowly. "There are not many like that. When I was in the Monastery of Tashigong, studying day and night, there was one like that to whom I am indebted for—all. I believed him to be from Tibet. They called him the Illuminated Pearl, but not a creature there really understood him. He stood like a mountain among them and if I know anything he had a history of great things."

"That's he!" I said eagerly. "Come back with me to the Lamasery of the Manis and see him. I see now that he knew you. He foresaw . . . ."

And even as I spoke I remembered Brynhild and the hateful letter of Mrs. Mainguy, and it rushed upon me with certainty that if he came a friendship with such dear deep sources would grow and strengthen, and I be left in outermost cold alone, deprived of both the friendships that had shaped my life. . . . What should two such people want of me if they had each other?

"I should like to come but I cannot!" he said thoughtfully. "Will you take a message from me?"

"A thousand."

A mean little shoot of pleasure ran through me—with a sense of security. He would not come—then all might be as it was. I do not extenuate my littleness. I confess it.

"I think he would know—for he knows strange things—where I could see that girl. I want to talk with her if possible. Her name was Brynhild Ingmar. Will you ask him? I trust it all to you. It is of great importance to me."

That roused me into common honesty. Who had the first claim on her friendship if not he? And for me, subsisting by his mercy, what claim had I? I told him where she was. I told him all she had done for me. I made it all as clear as it was to myself, which was not luminous—all said and done—for I had never analyzed my feeling about her and could not.

He listened with a kind of grave pleasure as one does listen to the praise of one beloved, making no comment, and it was impossible to decipher his thoughts. But when I spoke of her work as Narendra then indeed he listened with joy.

"So it was that—it was that!" he said, more to himself than me. "I knew something wonderful was bound to come of her own personality and that tremendous training. She has found her yoga indeed. Will you forgive me if I say I should like to think this over a bit? You'll understand, old boy, I know. Meanwhile I suggest we camp here in this place for a couple of nights. I have lots of stuff and our men can get what they need from the huts. I'll be back in an hour or so."

He looked at me with his old smile, and climbed the bluffs to his shelter, the dog at his heels.

CHAPTER XIV

I SAT ALONE EXHAUSTED AS IF A GREAT STORM HAD passed over me, yet with release, relief sinking into me like a happy opiate. Brynhild? But that was utterly at his decision. I must take what crumbs fell to me and be thankful—thankful too if none came my way. I gave the order for camping, and mechanically watched Ormond's men and mine setting up the little huts on the confines of the meadow of flowers.

At the end of two hours he came back from some secret retreat above, plunging downward through snow, blue under gentian sky, his strides sending it before him in blue diamond-dust. We shared our meal, to me sacramental for it was as though all clouds darkening our old friendship had dissolved in azure serenity. Not that I could forget while an atom remained that made me man, but that I began to understand the need of translating my superconsciousness into daily life unburdened by the hindrance of grief or remorse. I had thought my own thoughts in his absence, and realized something of his great surety and wisdom. Oh, for an inner history of him during the years he had lived among the mountain peoples! Nearer than Dunbar, more human than Haridas and my mysterious teacher and my friend. What might I not learn from it! But there I halted. I dared not ask a syllable more than he volunteered.

Afterwards, after much good talk of men and things, leaning against a sun-warmed rock with the glorious company of flowers about us and Michael the dog at our feet, he began:

"I have decided that I can't come down to the Monastery of the Manis. I have two years' work before I should be among my own people again. If I broke into it now it would be difficult to reknit. And if you'll take a letter for me to Miss Ingmar she will understand. She knows I'm a worker at foundations. Drudgery—but worth while."

It was not until long after that I realized he was setting me a test—shall I call it a test of trust?—by his withholding, withdrawing himself and leaving me to my own devices in a matter which might mean much to him and to me. I took it as simply as he said, but it was a nucleus of resolution that was then and after healing to my self-inflicted bruises. Then the talk diverged into one of our old and delightful discursions, but with what changed values to us both, what new hopes! They made the distance between past and present immeasurable. I remember asking him why he thought it of such consequence that in spiritual matters the West should accept Eastern teaching. Would the Oriental garment fit it?

I said:

"Individually I have no fears. It has captured you, Dunbar, myself, and through Haridas I hear of a rising wave of belief in Western lands. But nationally?"

"I see that as an absolute necessity for many reasons. Look at the avalanche of modern scientific discovery which has flooded the West and swept it away into materialism. They can learn from India that the thought of the Vedanta assimilates all science with perfect ease into the religious consciousness, because it was foreseen, and its aspirations and delimitations marked out, with the perfect understanding of psychology and the relation of knowledge to the Divine which is India's own. What one works at now is to interchange and consolidate the ideals of East and West, and at the present moment I see nothing else worth giving one's life to. All that may seem to be upon the lower plane of superconsciousness, but it is most surely its basis."

There I could agree, though I knew that for me at all events there must be a long interval of self-preparation before I could take my stand in the ranks. I said this and he answered quickly:

"Very true. But you'll go ahead. You're not conscious yet how many fetters you have dropped, but that's very clear to me who haven't seen you for so long. Freedom—perfect freedom and the serenity that it brings, with the resolution to cram nothing down people's throats because we find it good for ourselves. That was the mistake of the Christian Churches. They were always bumping people into the paths of peace, and never seeing that a soul can only take what it can at any given moment. So many are the stages of its evolution! It gets enough anyhow to crawl upward by, as bulbs push to the light."

"I wish you hadn't got so far ahead of me," I

said after digesting this awhile. "There are times when I feel pretty well left. Tell me—if you were I would you chuck painting? Will it be a hindrance?"

The cordiality in his voice was heart-warming.

"Bless you, no. A help! What? Give up those ripping things you used to do and will do a million times better? Isn't art spiritual expression? What about Narendra? By George, what wouldn't I give to see what you've told me! Art and spirituality are one. No, no! Nothing fanatic or desperate. Keep on, keeping on. You have a great teacher, and he will lead you to the point where you want only what is worth having. 'When a man comes to that place where he dreads Heaven as much as Hell' he is free. Oh, those dreadful heavens of our youth when we trod on golden floors hedged in with pearls and diamonds, and the dogs sat outside and howled for their lost masters! But you wouldn't want to get into that metallic splendor, Michael, and I'd sooner be outside with you than where all was petrified and dead from everlasting to everlasting. Think of that, and look at this! Life, life, welling from the source!"

He waved his hand to the illimitable glory of mountain and sky and space, and laughed for joy.

"Sometimes I wonder it didn't crumple and break us altogether. No—India is right. There may be heavens, but thank God, not eternal. One lives through them, if endure them one must, and comes out above and beyond. See how the Buddha puts all joys of the heavens below the experiences of man: 'Him the Gods envy from their lower seats.' "

I broke the silence after a while.

"And what's the summing up of all the great Eastern teaching in your mind?"

"What else but love?" he asked in surprise. "Love breaks down the walls of individual personality and restores one to unity with men and THAT. The great prison-breaker! I know no other. That's why the greatest of these is always charity. Indeed it is one and all. 'Though I have all knowledge and have not love it profiteth me nothing,' you remember? Now watch the sun dropping behind the mountains. And get your thick coat. It's jolly cold up here after sunset. You should do some sketching here."

So we walked up and down the marge among uncounted flowers, beholding the wonder in silence. Who could speak in a presence so majestic—the sky a vast ocean of billowing splendor without name, the mighty mountains intercessors between earth and heaven—a celestial confluence of beauty. The gradations of dimming and dissolving light were divine, as twilight softly overpowered peak after peak withdrawing it into a mystery of peace—the nightly ecstasy of communion with beauty above human knowledge. They forgot us. They were gone, and the stars set their watch and it was night.

As we turned to the fire the men had kindled Ormond quoted the Freemasons' questions and answers:

> "Whence come you? From the East.
> Whence go you? To the West.
> For what? To find that which is lost.
> Where do you hope to find it? In the Center."

"That sums up our work," he said. "Come along, Michael. Supper!"

The next morning dawned bright and beautiful, our last day together and one of such blue and golden glories of drowsing skies as no man can believe until he has known. We both needed a rest after hard climbing and took it—I may say a rest of mind and body. He spoke as naturally and simply as a boy, but every word revealed the heights he had climbed, and I treasured them. I took some notes for sketches, he watching me.

So we sat there in welling sunshine, laughing sometimes, at others talking of the world we had both known and left, partly on the surface and sometimes of deeper thoughts it suggested. I set down a few of his sayings.

"It all seems such child's stuff down in the world yonder: the fuss about nothings, senseless amusements, mad competition, cheap would-be cleverness, and the howl of party politics above and around it all. And to think the puppet-show once took one in, and one jigged away with the rest! I'm not trying to be superior, God knows, and every one of those people matters profoundly; only one mustn't let them take one in—one mustn't join the Dance of Death with them! Ever see the bridge at Lucerne with the pictures of Death as the partner always—with the bride, the lover, the rich man? Horrible! . . . skull and cross-bones . . . the diseased imagination of the Middle Ages at its worst, when what they call faith dominated the world. But it's horribly true until one understands."

"It's a stage of growth. One mustn't despise it," I said.

"One must despise it, but not despise them; they're divinity if they realized it. Apollo toiling at tending the sheep of Admetus. I suppose they would think this life of ours—escape from the House of Bondage—deathly dull. But they don't know . . . they don't know! All this means such wonderful things in the life of the world itself too. A new form of civic duty. Yes—Wisdom has builded her house. We touch the luminous threshold. When shall we go into the Palace?"

His face kindled in speaking to brightness beyond the sunshine. If ever I knew a man drunk with beauty—with the God-Idea—it was Ormond. I could not wholly understand it then; it bewildered me with a kind of awe. I understand it better now. Again:

"I know most people would think me a madman to have come up into the wilds here and chucked everything to do it; but how can a man know himself in the market-place, and what can he do if he doesn't? They live as they breathe—only from the throat upwards—never stirring the deeper centers of life. The Japanese talk of 'the mirror of the passing show.' What else can any man see if he is never alone—never communes with the Divine through nature? Some do. Wordsworth was a true Sannyasin—wonderful! Read him, old boy. Live much in the solitudes and with animals. What I have learned from Michael! And then, when you know a little worth telling—go back and tell it."

"Are those your plans?" I asked, deeply interested.

"Plans? I have none. I go on the current that carries one to the Center. The opportunity comes when one is fitted to take it. One's part is to fit oneself."

He entered with the warmth of true friendship into my life and its developments and, I remember, counseled me to ask my master to make a study of my subconscious self that he might advise me with more certain knowledge.

"Nothing that means any subjection to his influence any more than you feel now as his disciple. Diagnosis, that's all. Did you ever know a man who could describe his own condition scientifically? I never did. But these men *know*, by heredity and training. Yes, I should certainly ask him. He is a great psychologist. Knows how to cut out the bullet."

I agreed, seeing his counsel good in all he touched, and then he diverged to another subject.

"I was told up yonder that the Dunbars think of coming up to Alam Khan's country. If so and you have the chance I would come up with them. He's a fine young fellow and stanch Mohammedan. You should see that side of things too. Don't miss your luck, old boy."

I promised. The dream of that trek had been what led me to Baltar. I wanted it anyhow—I was fixed on it now.

"But I thought you might be going. Take me along, Ormond."

"Can't do that—but I tell you what. If things pan out that way I'll give you a meeting there! Good stuff, eh?"

Very good stuff, I said—almost beyond hoping.

So the day grew through all its gradations—a fugue

of many themes of beauty uniting in the largo of twilight and the consummation of peace. There was no moon, but the stars throbbed with glory, divinely near and bright. When I turned into my little shelter I saw Ormond standing in thought, a black figure against the stars.

We were up early next morning, and the parting came too soon—his way lying up over the great Pass, mine downwards at first and so to the Monastery of the Manis. He put the unsealed letter in my hand as we stood out of reach of the busy men already taking their diverging trails—and then came a moment's silence. He had long passed beyond the zone of emotion, for the higher training teaches a self-control which at moments may seem inhuman, but his eyes were full of the old kindliness as we grasped hands.

"All good go with you. We may never meet again, for who knows the next turn of the road? But anyhow, anywhere, we can never part."

He would have turned away then but I held him, though the words stumbled in my throat when I tried to speak and at first could not.

"If I could tell you what you have done for me in this meeting. I despaired—you have given me myself again—and to think I feared you!"

I could say no more. He looked me calmly in the face, still holding my hand.

"You and I both hold the belief that we are more than friends. We are One. That is the Teaching which is the breath of our lives. What have you to thank me for? Still, I ask a gift for your own sake and therefore mine. When you think of my wife—and I hope you often will do that—give her the same love that you give me."

He dropped my hand and turning away began the ascent, resumed into the solitude of his life, though never man was less alone. Michael went with him step by step, the blue air was full of presences to be felt in the depths and heights of aspiration. I stood fixed until he had passed out of sight behind a great jut of rock above. The last was when I heard his cheery voice shouting to one of his men ahead. Then I stooped and gathered a few blades of grass from the place where he had stood—I have them now—and began the dangerous downward trek; and of all the places I have known or, I think, shall ever know on earth, that mountain valley is to me the most sacred, for there in its sunshine love met me face to face. There is not a day when it does not rise before me with its undying gifts and memories. My wound was healed. As he and Haridas had warned me, I must now take the good of it.

I must not dwell on the journey back to the Monastery of the Manis, memorable for a storm in which we lost our way and very nearly our lives; but that too hangs in my picture gallery of things most beautiful, for at the time earth itself was transfigured in my thoughts into a divine spirit as glorious in moods of terror as lovely in repose. Oh, the joy of terrible glooms shrouding the precipices and hiding the mountains in darkness rent only by the daggers of lightning! To share that wild elemental glee was a right. The wide-sweeping rains washed my very soul in their cleansing; the thundering winds were wings; the roar of the Indus a shout of freedom. Never had I known such gladness. I realized the enormous joys of solitude. Nature had a new face for me—I was the son at home in the house of a mother. She shouted for joy in the crash of avalanches, and I laughed with her.

"He is made one with Nature."

That alone is a bliss to fill the body and soul with the wine of immortality and its divine intoxication of joy. It cannot last at that pressure, or the drink would shatter the mortal cup to madness or death, but its flavor abides, and the man who has tasted may taste again.

I thought it not without meaning that before we entered the ravine of the lamasery a Ladakhi man, grinning with pleasure, came down it, carrying in his arms a splendid pup, strong enough to use his queer little legs to some purpose, and coming up offered the small chap to me with a laughing salute of "juli."

"Have and keep," he said, and pushed the dog into my arms, standing off with glee to see how I took the gift. The dog looked up at me with comprehending eyes. A beautiful creature with keen, upstanding ears and noble mask.

"He will grow big," said the Ladakhi, "but his heart will be bigger always than his body. Have and keep, I say."

I offered him a much lesser gift than his own, but he would not have it and nodding good-humoredly to the dog went his way. I held the little fellow in my arms for the sake of his companionable warmth, until they ached, and then we made a nest for him among the tent-stuff loaded on one of the ponies. So I brought back with me yet another gift from the snows, a great gift also. He lies at my feet now as I write, loved as a bit of myself and more. Had Ormond willed it, remembering his Michael and what lessons a dog may read his master? Such thoughts cannot seem wild or strained after such an experience as mine. I called him Michael.

When we had made the big climb to the Manis dusk was falling and the great place glimmering with lights. That house, which had seemed at first sight strange as the dwelling of things inhuman, gnomes and kobolds, was now like home, and friendly faces looked out to welcome me and speed the news of my coming to the people whom it concerned most.

Haridas was first with the faithful Shan-tao at his shoulder.

"And the vision was fulfilled," he said, "the vision of peace. You have seen a man great because he has found the Precious Pearl, and lives to share its light with others."

"I have seen, and the very face of the world is changed," I said.

So we entered the house side by side, and there Dunbar and his beautiful wife met me, full of eager questions of the way and its adventures, but never a word of personal questions until and unless I chose to speak of myself. I am convinced that good breeding is a noble shoot of the highest in thought and deed. The world will have climbed a mountain-step upward when every man is a gentleman, far otherwise than in the debased symbol of that long-suffering word.

But Brynhild? I met her at our evening meal and had her cordial welcome. She too was full of friendly questions of my experiences. She wore a white dress and looked more than usually slender, strong and erect; and for the first time I could imagine there were moods in which she might be feared. After the meal we took possession of the sky-window as she called it, while the others got out their work. I laid little Michael in her lap, and with her own wizardry she won him instantly, her hands going to and fro about him like a charm. Sometimes she lifted him in her arms and held him to her bosom, head in her neck—the picture of loving content. She was at her most beautiful at such moments.

I leaned against the window watching, but very ill at ease, doubting in every fiber of me how I could best lead up to the subject of Ormond, for Mrs. Mainguy's letter hung like a fog in the back of my thoughts, and Ormond had said nothing to enlighten me as to Brynhild's feeling. And I had my own too, but on that I need not dwell. Nothing was clear except the certainty that I must not thrust the letter into her hand without preparation.

"So you never went up into Alam Khan's country?" she said with interest. "I thought from what Lucia told me that you were thinking of that. But of course it would have taken much longer. How far did you actually get?"

I explained as well as I could, and then said guardedly:

"I really went to meet a friend—a man I had not seen for years—Maitland. A wonderful chance for me."

"Most wonderful! To think of meeting in a place like this." She waved her hand to the peaks lost in stars. "And was it all right? Did you find him?"

"Yes. We had two great days together."

"Will he come down this way and strike into the road to Kashmir? It really is the best."

"No. He has work somewhere else. But he said that if we could get up to Alam Khan's castle he would meet us there."

"He must be a very unusual man if he has any work up here but shooting or trading," she said without a grain of suspicion.

I shook my head. "Neither. But I know he wouldn't exchange it for London or New York."

"I can easily believe that. Do you know I can tell you one thing. Michael means to be a perfect beauty, with a heart of gold. I know it."

"If he is like his godfather, Maitland's dog, I ask no better!"

"He had a dog?" she asked with quick pleasure. "Tell me about him. And Mr. Maitland—what *does* he do up here?"

"He has been living here for two years, studying and working. He came up here along the Simla-Tibet Road."

I saw the quick blood flush into her face.

"Maitland? The Simla-Tibet Road? How strange!"

I would not look at her face. I lifted Michael from her arms and put him on a chair beside her, where he curled up and fell into a blissful sleep. Then having given her time to steady herself I began again:

"I knew him a good many years ago. We were old friends. But since I knew him he had changed his name. He is Ormond now."

Not a sound. Not a breath. Still looking away from her, I added:

"He said he had known you two years ago. He gave me a letter to give you. Here it is, and now Michael must be off to bed. Not good for little dogs to be up so late."

Not a word from her.

I gathered him and went off. When I came back she had disappeared, and I settled down to manuscripts with the Dunbars.

"The most wonderful luck you ever heard in your life. This is a blessed place!" said Dunbar, propping his chin on his hands. "It's such luck you'll hardly believe it!"

"*The* manuscript?"

"No, not yet, but one to open your eyes. An account by a disciple of the return of the pilgrim Hiuen Tsang to China after his twenty years in India, and this, mind you, in our year 645! What do you think of that?" His eyes beamed triumph and it was good to see Lady Lucia's blissful content. "Heavens! the riches he brought with him from India. No, not gold and stuff like that. Listen! 'A sandalwood figure of the Perfect One, the Buddha, with a shining pedestal three feet, three inches high, after the model of the sandalwood figure made according to the likeness drawn by the desire of Udyana the King. A silver figure of the Buddha with a translucent pedestal—it must have been crystal—three feet, five inches high, after the model of the Lord delivering his scriptures on the Vulture mountain.' And many more, including one hundred and twenty-four scriptures. *Now* what do you say?

"But to my mind the most interesting part is the account of his reception by the great T'ang Emperor of China. 'The Emperor was then residing at his palace at Lo-yang, and learning that Hiuen Tsang was approaching, he sent forth the Duke of Liang to meet and conduct him. And the news spreading fast, the people crowded in vast numbers to see and pay their homage to the master. The streets were so crowded that when he wished to disembark he could not for the crush, and so passed the night on the canal.' Ah, the Chinese knew how to honor great men thirteen hundred years ago, and the faith was the faith!"

"But think of that wonderful old Chinese city and the crowding people and the sacred images carried in procession, and the pilgrim with his face calm as the images he brought," said Lady Lucia. "What a picture! Can't you see them carried high above the crowd and the people kotowing? I see it in my dreams since we found it. The emperor rained honors on him!"

"And well he might, when one thinks of that journey through desert and mountains—often alone, mostly penniless— Well, let us praise famous men. And still more wonderful, the account of the man's life in his own temple afterwards, collating and connoting his precious manuscripts until at last he fell asleep in peace, praying that in Heaven he might be made one of those who await the coming of the Buddha of Love that they may help him in his ministry. A story like a white lotus and written by a man who loved him."

"Oh, Lance, tell what work he did! Mr. Cardonald wants to know."

"The translation of seventy-four different works. Painted numberless pictures illustrating his travels, and copied many scriptures with his own hands. He knew his death couldn't be far off, and worked until he dropped. 'Then, lying perfectly still as one content' —for they read beside him the list of his works—'he closed his eyes and folded his hands as one who surrenders the world, and having repeated some verses in honor of the Buddha of Love he so lay until death like a rising tide floated him from them to the Paradise of Peace.' Isn't it exactly the death of the Venerable Bede in England? And this was in the year 664. The wise men are the same everywhere. But you can see what a treasure. It gives us China as he saw it."

I caught fire—who could help it? "And if you find *the* one that will give you India! I congratulate you with all my heart. It was a good day when we came here."

"Yes—and the blessed kindness of the abbot and his people! Debts never to be repaid. And you, Cardonald—and the master? Haridas has told us some things of him since you went which have made me envious of you there. But I fancy he prefers to remain a mystery. None of us have seen him since that night we came. Do you get any nearer to him?"

A difficult question. I felt much might turn on our

meeting, now nearly due. I was about to answer when Haridas, stirred from his stately calm, rushed into the room with a case in his hand, breathless with haste, crying aloud, "The manuscript—the manuscript!" as if his whole being shouted for joy.

I know we all sprang to our feet—Lady Lucia white as paper, for he and the change in him startled us. Dunbar stood with a shaking hand on the table.

"It was this box—this box with great brass and silver hasps and hinges—the chest from the Lamasery of Extended Happiness in the mountains near Lharche—"

"But we turned it all out. We searched, you and I. Shan-tao—"

"I know—I know!" cried Haridas interrupting in his turn, a thing I never knew him to do before or since.

I turned and lo! the door was wide and the abbot and his chief *gelungs* crowding in with awestricken faces. Such a sense of the solemnity and greatness of the occasion crowded in upon me that I was all but overpowered myself.

The abbot ranged himself beside Haridas, grave and silent, with eyes intent on the long cylindrical wood case just lifted from the box. His presence steadied Haridas, and with an effort he collected his dignity, though I could see the tremble in his hand as he tried to undo the tiny hooks that held it shut.

"True. But the box was dropped by a careless monk. It had a false bottom—the fall started it, and then I saw there some treasure hidden. This"—he held it up solemnly for us all to see—"is the manuscript of the friend of Hiuen Tsang—the Tibetan monk of Janthang, the man who is said to have survived to this very day."

"If this is true," said the abbot in a tone of deep emotion, "blessed is this *gompa* and blessed the strangers who have brought discovery of a gem so precious. Open it that we may see."

We made way for him, controlling our impatience, and it was unrolled, he and the *gelungs* bent over it discussing it in low earnest tones with one and another. They had the first right, but it seemed an hour before the discussion was ended and each raised the manuscript to his forehead, kissing it devoutly, and retired, the abbot giving orders that two lamas should sit up with it all night.

"And let this be done until it is conveyed with all honor and care to the Monastery of Sweet Dew in China. For of a great man of Tibet it tells the story, and since it is now the possession of our friends let us treasure it like the deposit of a king."

This guard was indeed observed every night it remained in the monastery though in all the country round there was not one man who would not have given his life to protect it.

With joy and thankfulness for this success tossed on an undercurrent of thoughts and fears for Brynhild, I climbed the long steps to my sleeping place; next day might bring me some knowledge. It would certainly bring my half-dreaded, half-desired meeting with my master.

But I was not alone. Michael slept at my feet, and his companionship and quiet breathing made a little island in the sea of solitude. There I moored my boat and slept dreamless.

CHAPTER XV

NEXT DAY WHEN I MET HER I SAW NO CHANGE whether of joy or grief. She was with the Dunbars and as eager about the marvelous find as they, heart and soul in it with us all.

"Wasn't it a terrible thing that I wasn't there when Haridas rushed in? I'm like the old woman who watched for years to see Chichester steeple fall. She looked away for one minute to thread her needle and when she looked back it was gone! And did the abbot and the *gelungs* really come!"

"I should think so!" said Dunbar, radiating pride and triumph. "And this morning before you two came up they sent a magnificent gift to me in honor of the event. The goodness of those men! No greed for their own monastery, and yet they must know the money value of that manuscript if no more. Look here!"

He opened a straight narrow box such as holds the pictures of China and Japan, and drew one out rolled in silk. The ivory pendants chinked as he lifted and unrolled it.

A great gift and worthy of generous souls. A portrait of some long ago Tashi Lama, an Incarnation of the Divine Compassion, sitting in state, with the boat-shaped halo of divinity behind him outlining his head and person against a glory composed of small and brilliant holy persons, worshiping and giving thanks in a heaven of their own joy. And the robes and miter of the Tashi Lama were the least part of his beauty, for the Chinese artist had beheld the dignity, wisdom and serenity of his face with delight and love, and had made a noble portrait indeed of a man, not inhuman but lifted above ordinary humanity by tranquil certitude and realization of life as it really is. Lady Lucia saw my pleasure and could restrain herself no longer. I had seldom seen her so stirred.

"That's the Tashi Lama who visited the great Ming Emperor of China—Chien-Lung—as equal to equal. The emperor even came out to meet him. He died in Peking, and his beautiful marble tomb is there. I think this is going to be the jewel of Baltar though we have some lovely things. Lance says he must leave it to the British Museum. Indeed I doubt whether we should accept it at all, but it would have wounded them otherwise."

"Ah, but I have a plan!" Dunbar said, laughing with delight. "Two, in fact! First, I've sent word already, by the runner who went down this morning, to tell Tazaki's brother to pack and send up the sacred paten, holy-water jug and bell which came from Kunboum. You haven't seen them, Cardonald. Gold set with little garnets and turquoises, which go well with the barbaric beauty of their shapes. That's going to be Lucia's and my parting gift."

"They'll be a sort of rich jeweling on the great altar," Lady Lucia said. "And whenever they sing those wonderful chants at night—the time I like best—they'll have to think of us. It was an inspiration of Lance's."

"The other was as great in its way and on a larger scale," he said rubbing his hands with glee. "It's the fashion in Tibetan lamasery circles that a friendly soul should give a kind of ceremonial tea to as many of the lamas as he can run to. They don't often have a treat, and this lamasery has no cash flying about in spite of its splendid treasures. Wait till you see! It's going to be the largest—the most gorgeous tea-fight that ever befell the Monastery of the Manis, and will follow the Festival of Flowers. What do you think of that, eh?"

I said it was a second inspiration direct from the Tibetan Goddess of Good Deeds, and added, for the thought had just flashed into my head that I would do my best with the abbot's portrait, and that should be my offering. For I realized my share of joy in the discovery and generous gift of the manuscript and this noble picture. These men had given me also gifts not to be stated in words. The beauty, the atmosphere, the wonderful strange life about me would color my thoughts forever and ever—one of the unexpected and beautiful relationships into which life throws us as it were carelessly, leaving us changed men, and with the certainty that no chance exists in the universe.

Brynhild, who stood stedfastly regarding the picture, turned at once:

"They'll love that. It's curious to think how your picture will live in this beautiful place when we are gone and be a part of its inheritance. I shall envy it when I think of that (she waved her hand towards the sky-window) and of so many other things. And what shall *I* give? I too should like something of mine to stay here forever and ever!"

"I know—I know!" cried Lady Lucia, clapping her hands like a joyful child. "The little bas-relief of the three disciples of the Buddha after his death—Ananda, sad and disturbed by grief, the other two, further on the way, calm and self-possessed; I always loved that and they would too."

"Yes, and not too heavy for a yak-load. If you think it good enough I should like that enormously. Lance, will you order it to be brought? Tazaki junior knows where to find it."

So it was settled and Dunbar spoke again:

"I've been discussing matters with Haridas this morning, and he thinks we should have a man to work with us at the translation who couldn't come here. A great authority on many matters in it. He advises that the manuscript should go down to Baltar in his care and Shan-tao's while we pay our visit to Alam Khan and then follow by the Kanlang Pass—a most wonderful route down to Kashmir. I should like you two to see it."

I confess the notion of leaving gave me a twinge. I am a man who digs into a place where he is happy, and this high uplifted land and the lamasery itself filled some emptiness in me, awakened some passion for things I had never known I cared for. How could I care when I had not even recognized their existence until the gate of Baltar opened to me? And now Baltar lay far away and below, and Ormond had got up into the heights, and in this place there seemed more chance of my following—not overtaking him either inwardly or outwardly, but—it was nearer somehow. I can get no more of it than that into words. Dunbar interpreted my silence after his own fashion.

"The only thing is, what about your master, Cardonald? Could you come or would you rather stay on here and come down later? The preliminary work on the manuscript will take about a fortnight or three weeks, and then we could start for Alam Khan's country along the route you took the other day. All the same it will cost me a pang to leave this place and people!"

"Me too!" I said. "One gets to be at home here. Don't go anyhow until after the Festival of Flowers, and then let me choose what to do. You both understand, I know. I didn't speak of it before, but I met a friend up yonder—Ormond—you know about him—and he said he might be at Alam Khan's castle when we went up. But he didn't expect us to be there so soon."

"Ormond!" Dunbar said in great astonishment. "A man I'd give a lot to meet. Did you hear that, Lucia? If we had wanted a reason for trekking to Alam Khan's country there it is. We must let him know somehow when we're to be there. I hadn't the least idea that you knew him."

"Nor had I. His name was Maitland in the long-ago days, and I had lost sight of him for years. It was a great surprise to find they were one and the same."

I carefully avoided looking at Brynhild as I spoke.

I felt it would have been an intrusion, but she joined in:

"I knew him very well two years ago—he should have got far by now."

"He has—he has!" I said eagerly. "If he's at Alam Khan's castle—"

There I stopped for I knew there would be pain for me in their meeting. Does one think of pain in the higher regions of the soul? I think not. I think it is an inhabitant of the lower regions and dies in pure air. But I myself was a dweller of those regions as yet. I thought inwardly that I must lay my case before my master, taking Ormond's advice, and clear my head of the uncertainty and doubt that possessed me now. Brynhild turned to me.

"Will you walk up the hills with me after breakfast? I should like so much to hear about him," she said.

That would be a very difficult story for me to tell, entangled as it was with my own. There was more dread than pleasure in my mind as we went out into the wonderful purity of the air shot with sunshine that turned the upper snows into blinding brilliance. Summer had come and nowhere so beautiful as in this strange, austere spiritual country. In the little valley to which we wound down by the bridge gentians were a blaze of deep-sea blue, the masses of forget-me-nots were Heaven fallen upon the happy earth. They reminded me of the valley where the shadow of a crime lost in light had left me forever.

Brynhild stood looking at them in a kind of rapture and indeed no lowland flowers can equal the glory of those of the upper world. Is it because they are so many stages nearer to Heaven and so are stained and dyed with its azure, or because their life on earth is so brief, that they distil such shining joy? The sunshine was at home among them. The mountains had borrowed their celestial blue and wore it like the cloud garments of revelation.

I found her a seat where she could lean against a rock starred with white saxifrage, each blossom with a ruby in its heart. She wore a large hat, for the sun beat down with strength, and I hardly saw her face. Michael in perfect happiness rustled his way through the flowers or drowsed in warmth and perfume.

"Sit down too," she said. "You'll be patient if I ask you several things. Isn't it heavenly here where the height drops away to the river? Shall we ever care for the low-country summer after this? Now, you're comfortable. First, will you tell me if John Ormond was well and strong?"

"Both. One of the many impressions he left was health and strength that half the world might envy."

She folded her hands quietly in her lap like one at rest, and went on:

"And did he seem happy?"

"Radiant." Did I catch a suppressed sigh? "No, radiant is hardly the word. Contented, calm, self-possessed. Does that recall him?"

I found, perhaps a little to my own wonder, that I had no temptation to do him less than the fullest justice. I had wronged myself for once. Take it how she would it was joy to me to speak words that set him before her in the gracious beauty of his thought and ways. She said nothing and I went on:

"When he came springing down the rocks to meet me I thought he seemed a part of all the power of the upper world. Am I fanciful if I say it had made its home in him as much as he in it? Does that mean anything to you?"

"Very much." Her voice was low and restrained as if she kept a steadying hand on it. Then slowly: "But when I knew him he was only beginning the search for—for what he has found. I think—I think he had gone through some great trouble then—" She broke off, and again said slowly, "I think the world had tricked him somehow. It always does sooner or later—"

Never had I seen her so moved, so womanly, and it touched me deeply in more ways than one. In many more. To a sense of self-horror that bit into the bone. It silenced me—I say no more than that—and for a time that seemed long the flowers drowsed in sunshine undisturbed by any voice or movement from us.

I had the temptation to confess that it was I who had caused his grief, but I resisted it and I still think rightly. Why to ease my own miserable conscience was I to open his wound before her even by a hint, whether my hint—for it could be no more—set her guesses right or wrong? I could only harm a silence better left in his own hands. If he chose—but he never would—to speak I could accept it as perfect justice and good.

"He spoke of me?" she said at last.

"More than once. You would not like me to tell you now, for any other words would spoil it. He said, however, that he would have given very much to come down here."

The talk was full of pauses. At last she asked:

"And did he really mean to come to Alam Khan's castle? I want to see him—I want it. You could not understand, but we were very strangely brought together. Do you think he will be there? Would his work hinder him?"

"He said so little about that—how can I judge? Certainly he said it would keep him in this country for another two years, but I gathered that he goes to and fro a good deal."

"I want him to see my work," she said suddenly.

"I told him of it. He said he longed to see it. Also that he knew you had great powers, but he could not have guessed what form they would take."

I began to hope that she would tell me her trouble and that I might help her more directly, if it was in my scope. I knew now that I honestly would. And still I could not analyze the love I had for her. I would have died for her—that is the simple truth; but, longing for her love in return, I still knew I could live without her, at least until I had gained more knowledge of what would help us both to the full of all within us. Something beautiful in the austerity of going our several ways, rapt in our own work, meeting perhaps years later, each bringing our sheaves with us, appealed to me more than a dream of any present joy. But after all who was I to ask anything now or at any time? Better slip into the background and be forgotten by a woman who would see me with horror if she knew the facts.

I have begun now to know that even in love must be a certain austerity for those who wish to taste its perfection. Those who desire all in an orgy of passion will never know its spiritual significance. It was in that moment I began my training for comprehension of the force "that moves the world and the other stars," for I sat only at her feet then, not even her eyes fell upon me, but none the less she gave and I took, and my reward followed. For I said at last:

"It is very easy to understand how you must wish to see such a friend as that. I never knew anyone like him. All words would fail me if I tried to tell you what he has done for me and from what a height above me. Now listen. If you feel you need to see him I'll go after him."

She looked at me with dilated eyes but said nothing, fixed in listening.

"He said he would stop for some weeks at a village six marches beyond where we parted. He was to meet some man there. Say the word and I'll go tomorrow."

She stretched out her hands to me, and suddenly and without the least concealment great tears brimmed in her eyes and spilled down her cheeks. That was my reward: her trust and the opening of the doors of confidence.

"I know you would. You are a true friend. That's why I cry—it moves me so. But no. He couldn't come—and how could I hinder him by a day in his work? . . . Perhaps at Alam Khan's castle . . . No —don't think I am sad. How could I be who know what I do? I was only moved by your friendship and thank you with all my heart. Let us sit now awhile and watch the light changing on the mountains. That sight flows like a rising tide into every dry crevice of one's heart."

She was right. No weariness of the spirit could survive the ecstatic quiet of the mountains floating in an ocean of sunlight. At last, seeing her thoughts completely absorbed, I rose and went to and fro along the trails with Michael, keeping a sort of guard upon her solitude, thinking thoughts of my own. She came to join me after a while, and we went back to the house together. On the way she said:

"I know how much I have to thank you for. I want to tell you that last night I had a word with your master. I am sure it was he. It was night, and the passages were dimly lit, and I was going up the steep steps to the sky-window room when a lama with cloak and hood came along the passage above, and I stood aside to make room for him. He stopped and said very kindly: 'What bar are the mountains or the skies and earth itself to those who desire to meet? Sleep is an open door, and yours is the yoga of the Beautiful. Grasp your power and see!' Just when I was feeling so strengthless! Then he went on. Last night I could not sleep."

"But tonight you will. What that man says is truth. Concentrate on the vision you desire. You made me hear. See yourself."

She turned away without a word, and I went on into the room where Haridas and Dunbar were at work with their three helpers, the table heaped with books brought up for reference, the precious manuscript spread between them with some transparence fine as glass laid over it that no hand might touch. They were so completely absorbed that no one looked up as I came in, though Dunbar said a friendly word. But a lama followed me and spoke aloud. Then indeed Haridas laid his pen aside and listened, afterwards translating for me the words I could not understand though I had grasped more than a bit of the ordinary talk.

"His Holiness the Abbot, the Sacred Incarnation, declares that today, an hour from now, he will sit for his picture if it is still desired."

Judge of my pleasure! I had talked of beginning my work again, but something, perhaps the quest itself, had seemed to dry the springs in me. Now interest and hope leaped like a fountain. What was there in this wonderful place that divined and supplied every want? For myself I would have called it the House of Dreams-Come-True. Dunbar laughed and congratulated me with all his heart. Haridas smiled and the others viewed me with awe and surprise.

"If I fail—" I said, and yet thought I could not.

"Nothing can fail here!" Dunbar said confidently. He called after me, "Tell my wife," as he settled to work again.

An hour later I was in the room where the abbot gave audiences—the very background I wanted for my picture. Heavens, what a chance!

There were Tibetan carpets, the like of which I had never seen before, queer flowers ramping over a dark blue ground threaded with gold, very gorgeous. On a raised dais, in a splendid chair carved in wide-scrolled tarnished gold sat the abbot, behind a lacquer desk, the color black with embossed gold designs about the edges; and to complete the magnificence he wore his robe and miter-shaped hood of the monastic red with gold enhancements. On the dais and visible beneath the desk were his red-clothed feet and a pair of slippers curled upwards at the toes placed neatly beside them. A very splendid figure with a golden image on either side of him, raised to his own height on pedestals. And before these sacred images were two golden incense-burners with aromatic smoke ascending and two butter candles in golden candlesticks, burning steadily and filling the room with their peculiar aroma. On his desk stood the gift of the Monastery of Kan-lu-ssu—the Kwannon in her open-door shrine.

And so, seated before him I began my sketch, much to the disappointment of the two attendant lamas who had expected a blaze of color at once. The abbot, undisturbed by either hope or disappointment, sat serenely telling the beads of his gold and turquoise rosary all the while, with a face like an ivory mask of serenity—a most exemplary sitter, lost in his prayers with complete absence of any self-consciousness. I felt instinctively that with this help I might hope to achieve something not wholly unworthy, and so thinking began with more force and certainty than I had ever known before.

After an hour he rose and courteously dismissed me and before I left the room graciously gave me with his own hands a curious and beautiful little box of gilded leather decorated with turquoises sunk in a very ancient design and containing the famous prayer, "Hail to the Jewel in the Lotus," written on Chinese mulberry paper. A prosperous beginning, and the more so as it ended with a "Come again tomorrow."

That evening when the late dusk fell I climbed the long stairs to the room of discipline, a little wearied in spirit by the many events of the day, more than a little fearful of the reopening of my meeting with Ormond.

There had been so much in that story impossible to put in words or convey to the understanding of any third person, however learned and wise.

He sat by the table near a window open upon the twilight world, with faint stars half hidden by the black upward sweep of mighty mountains, and was looking out toward them in meditation. As I entered he rose and bowing motioned me to a seat; but from some instinct I remained standing before him, waiting for him to speak.

"You have gone and returned," he said, "and in the mountains have found peace—though not the unchanging Peace. And you have stood face to face with love which, discarding circumstances, looks only to the Eternal. What have you brought back?"

The question was unexpected, and I was trying to collect my thoughts that I might answer truly when the memory of Ormond's counsel flashed amongst their disturbance like a light.

"Sir, the man whom I met in the mountains, my true friend, advised me to ask your help in this matter. What I have brought back lies deep in the subconscious, or so I believe, for if I tried to tell you it would be confused and bewildered with so many surface matters of the upper daily life that I could not speak the truth if I would. But my friend said this to me,

'Ask the master to look within and with his own eyes see the disease or health of the dweller in the innermost, and then knowing the strength or weakness that guides you he can point the way.' "

I felt but could not see that the eyes under the hood were intently fixed upon me. Presently he spoke:

"You have faced a great crisis in your life, helped by a man who is higher in evolution than yourself. Where many men would have cursed you, he loved. He did not forgive; he loved. And in the blaze of love's sun the snows of hatred melt into the water of life. Again I ask—what have you brought back?"

"I will be as truthful as I can, but it is hard to understand even the self beneath which is uppermost. Of the deep and hidden self beneath I know little or nothing. I have brought back a great hope, a great love, and the seed from which peace may grow."

I felt the relaxing tension of approval in the voice. Had I ever believed that my impassive master could be glad for me? Never. And that new note added to my courage and strengthened my hope.

"Then you have learned that of all masters of magic Love is master. He is the great Seducer whom the soul must follow through the ocean-deeps or the shadow of death. He is Krishna of the Flute; and what is the world to those who have heard even the echo of the Song Celestial? You have met the Divine face to face on the mountains, for when a man loves he is the Highest. Now because this man gave you life and love—the bread and wine of the Universe—I will give you self-knowledge for now the God within you stirs. Is it your desire?"

With something very like fear running in my veins I answered firmly, "It is my desire."

"Then seat yourself and look out and up into the stars."

I obeyed and their throbbing beauty, so near the earth, so far, held my eyes with a new and astonishing vision. I saw them larger, clearer, brighter than ever before. A million lamps, they illumined the room, and with some sight not mine I saw it and the man beside me, the hood fallen back, face shining with immortal radiance. Stars, stars, some rolling on spheral orbits, some fixed in brooding splendor. The light grew into a glory like the sun, blinded, dazzled, and the mortal could endure no more. In light unbearable my senses swooned into nothingness.

CHAPTER XVI

I AWAKED IN AN ANCIENT GARDEN GIRT FAST WITH four walls of peace. Not a bird-note, not a sound disturbed the profound silence. I lay on the grass dreaming myself back into childhood, the hunter of butterflies, the companion of water-rats, rabbits, and all the secret shy creatures haunting the deep green silence of English woods and waters. I knew where the yellow water-lilies raised golden heads above the ripple and the white water-lily floated, an embodied prayer with pure chalice and golden heart. I knew where crowding cowslips charmed the meadow grass with their breath of cottage fairies, and where primroses long-stemmed and with thick leaves larger than rabbits' ears starred the moss with pale beauty. Of all those things I was dreaming in bliss indescribable for the child's heart is one with nature. He knows the good Earth Goddess who shines for him, rains for him, sends the passionless eddying fall of white snowflakes for his delight, her child who is at home in her House of Dreams-Come-True.

Bliss warm and nourishing as new milk ran in my veins as I thought, "Tomorrow there will be an egg in the white hen's nest when I search before breakfast, and the new kid will push her broad nose into my hand,

and the red calf breathe his balmy breath in my face, and Michael"—so I confused the times—"will run at my heels and love me. There are two new roses opening in my little garden, one red, one snow-white; and in the field the young pheasants will run beside their mother, and the rabbits hop and lope in the twilight, and all there are mine—no, not to hold and hurt but to love. They are mine because I love them."

And as I said this the most exquisite bliss filled my heart—the child's delight of love which gathers the earth and all its flowers, the sky with all its stars to his bosom to be his toys, his joys, his life.

"What you love is yours," sang a brown-speckled thrush from the apple blossoms in the crooked tree above me. "I am yours, yours, yours."

"But if you fly you leave me," I said drowsily.

"No, for your heart has wings. When I fly into the blue it flies with me."

"But in the night I must sleep and forget."

"Not a bit of it!" called a late owl, flying in a muffle of feather to his day sleep in the upper barn. "Because at night you leave your body asleep in the bed by the window, but *you* slip out and climb down the honeysuckle on the wall and lie in the grass glittering with dew and moonbeams. And what do you see then? We know, we owls, for we make our magic circles about you all night to keep you from harm."

"I see the wild things in the woods come dancing out into the garden, the rabbits running with the weasels, and white girls with long hair from the great oaks in the outer wood. And I love, I love them."

"And they love you. They live in your heart!" sang

the thrush. "All the world lives there. O child, be a child forever!"

"No," said the voice of the old man who lives in the little house by the deep pool where only the black rushes grow. "There are fears that come in the night when you wake wild with fright and wet with sweat. There are things that live in the wood with awful eyes and slinking feet. Be afraid, pull the dark over your eyes and sleep if you can!"

"Laugh at them and forgive them for they are poor shadows!" sang the thrush. "They have no life. And be glad, glad, glad!"

"No," said the old man from the little house by the pool. "For they all die and you die too, and the black earth covers you and so an end."

"Live and be glad. The warm earth, the kind earth," sang the thrush, "where green things grow and the rabbits live so safely. Ask them. They know."

And a rabbit bounded over my breast, and I felt the warmth of him like a passing air, and such joy besieged me that it surged in my body, which was not big enough to hold it; and I could bear it no more because all their lives were mine and lived in me, and all their joys beat in my breast—and how could I hold it if it brimmed over, unless I broke my shell like a budding acorn and soared into the air a swaying tower of green leaves and branches and birds' nests to warm me, and bright eyes to kindle my dews? Oh, God—beauty, the unendurable beauty!

Did I cry aloud? I woke in the room in bewildering starlight and moonlight with my master beside me.

"You have seen the child's heart!" he said. "Was the memory dear?"

I could not utter a word. I trembled for joy and wonder.

"You have seen your innermost self face to face. The child's heart that shall grow in glory to wisdom and power. A memory, but yourself. All you need is the man's strength to keep the garden clear of weeds, to make the flowers blossom, the birds sing. The white girls will come shining from the woods, and the word of power bring mighty beings to share your bread and drink your cup. Arise, shine, for your light is come!"

There was a lovely silence in the room. I rose from the chair re-created, strong, young, with energy flowing from the fountains of immortality.

"Can I ever thank you?" I said at long last. "I love you for your infinite wisdom and patience. That is my thanks. Will you teach me still?"

"With gladness while you need me."

"I shall need you always. Why are yôu so wise?"

"Because in many years I have learned to know That One who vibrates at a speed the mind can never grasp and is therefore Quiet. The gods cannot reach Him. When He moves the worlds dance before Him. Yet in this uttermost movement He rests. He is the Moving and the Motionless, the Near and the Far, the Within and Without. The child's heart knows Him in His fair forms, He is the One, the Alone, in whom all lives and moves and has its being, as certain also of your own poets have said. Go now and sleep in peace. The joy you have drunk is yours while you will have it."

I was alone. I stood awhile looking out into the beauty of night, loving it, one with it as I had been long, long ago in the Eden of childhood. And no fiery swords guarded the gate. Henceforth I might go in as I would.

That night I slept like a child.

I woke next day in a changed world, but how impossible to convey that change to anyone who has not known it. Certitude that the way lay open before me; joy in its ascending grandeur and glimpses of the mountains guarding the spiritual city—of which those before my window were but the lovely shadows. As I stood looking up to them and thinking of the diviner heights I realized the truth that Heaven is in a man's own soul, for it seemed that my joy might well out in a great river of light to irradiate the world. Surely joy is a mighty cosmic force. If only two hearts could fuse their rapture it would storm the very heavens and bring peace on earth, good will to men the wide world over. But that cannot be until all the bounds of personality are broken down and the I is lost in the All.

So, with this burning joy upon me like the tongues of fire, I considered my future. My work was dearer to me than ever, and the average life of men appeared impossible. To go down into the world where they buy and sell and chaffer, where the white flame burns smoky and the dry almond rod cannot break into blossom! How would that cloudy air load my newly formed wings, and the whirring machinery catch and grind me into powder if I should lose the clarified sunshine of this? Then could I make my home in Kashmir—not too far from Baltar—and there set up my studio in the hope of conveying some glimmer of the beauty I beheld walking naked on the mountain-tops? A man must do something to justify his existence, and the yoga must be his own and not another's. Dunbar, Lady Lucia, Brynhild, worked each on their own law as easily as planets revolve in singing. Brynhild? But if I consulted her, would not the shadow—no, the light—of Ormond fall between us?

And then—could I hope to climb the difficult path of the higher yogas on which Haridas had set my very ignorant feet? Last night I had reentered the heart of a child. Surely it was for me to walk very simply in the ways of the karma-yoga—the yoga of clean action—and wait the appointed moment of the greater revelation without storming its secret places, the more as all my teachers agree that each of the Four Great Yogas leads to the Vision. I rehearsed them now in my mind. There is the yoga of clean and noble deeds: the mind fixed on the Eternal in the lowliest duties. The yoga of pure reason and intellect, cleaving its way like the eagle sweeping past my window to the snowy peaks. The yoga of burning love and devotion, consuming all the world's illusions in its pure flame. And lastly the yoga of high contemplation and ecstasy and powers higher than those of the happy gods. And of these four none is greater or less than another, and all springing from the same root are one though the blossom they bear differs. For myself it seemed better to choose the simplest and nearest and trust to time for developments.

I must see Haridas. Since we had come to the Lamasery of the Manis he seemed to have withdrawn himself even more than at Baltar. Apart from work on the great manuscript he had some engrossing study of his own, and there were many days when no one saw or heard of him except Dunbar. I remembered the charge to the monks before we had left Baltar: "Our brother Haridas" was to sift and bring back true knowledge of the wonder-working powers of the lamas. How if he too were studying with my strange master to whom the secrets of all hearts seemed to lie open? If so, discipline would certainly be stern and vigilant. No room for me.

Thinking these thoughts all the morning I went out in the afternoon, after the abbot had granted me an hour's sitting for the portrait, into hot sunshine and the winding trails which the lamas used in going to and fro on their mysterious errands in the mountains. They were especially busy now in preparing for the Flower Festival, cleaning, sweeping like virtuous ants in the great chapel as I called it, and those who had the skill molding hardened butter into histories of the Buddha's life and not only of his but of the greatest of Tibetan saints, Tsong Kaba.

I took the way and after watching awhile I went from terrace to terrace, climbing down the rough steps to the big storehouse open on one side to a courtyard where the artists sat at work surrounded by hillocks of hardened butter on which they were to exercise their skill. All was in a high state of preparation, but where the admirers were to come from in this country of great solitudes I could not even imagine.

As our time for leaving came nearer, the inner life and discipline of the monastery became much more interesting to me, and I reproached my own indifference. Now I entered into talk with the chief of the work, an old monk with keen narrow eyes behind high cheek-bones and fingers deft as a spider's spinners in dealing with the figures shaping upon the golden backgrounds of butter. Another set of artists would color them when finished. A very queer sight they were and not without a strange archaic beauty.

"A great saint, Tsong Kaba," said the oldest of the artist lamas to me, "and his story should be known. Carry it down to the lower world, lord of the brush, that men may hear and be glad."

"I must know the story before I can tell it either with brush or pen. What is it?"

He laid aside two flat pieces of wood which did the first rough shaping of the figures, and looked out meditatively over the mountains, and it struck me, not for the first time, that their august beauty molded the higher souls among these men into their own image. Surely the whole of nature is for the soul though the soul is not for nature.

The old man resumed very earnestly.

"He resolved very young to give up the world, and his wise mother cut off his long hair and threw it outside the tent, and from it sprang a tree of noble perfume with a sacred character marked on every leaf, and that tree is to be seen today still bearing the symbols of wisdom on every leaf under the silver dome the Emperor of China set above it. And so he went up into the mountains and fell into meditation, subsisting on the simplest foods that would support life."

"That is the history of all the great ones," I said. "They draw apart and lash the body into obedience."

"Certainly. How could it be otherwise? Well, one

day as he sat— Jewel of the Law, your modeling of the holy Tsong Kaba is villainous! Why give him the face of a low-class Chinese?—To return!—a stranger approached. 'I am a lama from the far West,' he said. 'I come from countries unknown to you. Look at my features and see how they differ from those you know.' And Tsong Kaba looked, and the stranger had a great nose like an eagle's beak and thin lips curved into sharp corners and blue eyes and light hair —in short, a man like your nobility. And he taught Tsong Kaba great mysteries and the rites of worship, filling him with mighty knowledge; and having done this he departed, and his disciple mourned him. And then, lit by the lamp of love, he wrote that great book called 'The Progressive Path to Perfection.' Now see—in this relief observe the great stranger with a face like your own. Indeed the Jewel of the Law has had your august features in mind in modeling. Observe the eagle's beak of a nose and the curious lips!"

I observed with curiosity, but could not recognize the likeness though the face was certainly of a European. This belief, which is fixed in Tibet, of a great teacher from the West set me thinking. Could it be possible that there were more highways between East and West in the ancient days than history has recorded, and that some Christian teacher wandered up into the Locked Country and through the mind of Tsong Kaba colored the Buddhist ceremonies there after the manner of his own people? The likeness to the rites and ceremonies of Catholicism is extraordinary. I commended the modeler and asked whether Tsong Kaba had reformed the discipline also.

"Certainly, and he also divided the lamas into four faculties. You may see them in this lamasery. There is the Faculty of Rites and Ceremonies, the Faculty of Medicine, which includes the study of herbs, the Faculty of Prayers, which is the largest, and the Faculty of Mysticism, which is the smallest because that power must be born in a man, having been gained in many lives and through great experiences. Such a man is your master, the Illuminated Pearl."

This caught me at once. "Then he will be head of that faculty?" I asked.

"By no means. That would mean expounding in the courtyard whenever it met, and he is too great for that. And besides, he is only on a visit, and we lesser lamas do not see him."

"Then where does he live?"

"That is not known. Sometimes he appears at one lamasery, sometimes at another, and all do him reverence wherever he goes. But who can tell his movements? It is said, however, that when the Faculty of Prayers assembles today in the inner courtyard he will be there and lead the discourses. And now, Jewel of the Law, observe the way this foreign lord's hair grows upon his forehead and give the like to your figure of the blessed Tsong Kaba's teacher."

"Could I attend that gathering?" I asked, eager to be drawn more and more into the life of the place that I might have the chance of meeting Haridas and perhaps learning more from him of the man who had influenced me so deeply.

"Why not? Has not the abbot announced that you are all free of our community, and have you not the honor of painting his picture, which indeed makes you one of the Faculty of Artists, as I may call the butter-workers? Have you not seen the inner court? Well, when the conchs are blown follow the sound and I think you will be surprised."

He chuckled at his little joke until his eyes shone like black lines above the jutting cheek-bones, and bent over his work again.

No—I had never seen it. I had never penetrated all the intricacies of that vast abode. The strangest place! It was built on all sorts of different levels, accordingly as the buildings nested here and there in the precipice where they could find foothold, and you could descend from terrace to terrace of the town—for so I might really call it—through the queerest narrow alleys, until the last giddily overhung the sheer precipice above the ravine. We lived in the highest, where the abbot's abode also was, and the chapel was almost a part of it. But there were courtyards here and there and everywhere among the lamas' dwellings, some great, some small, but all surrounded by towering walls and windows, a very ants' nest of lamas, who would sally forth uncounted to take part in the ceremonies.

Decidedly the Manis became an interesting place in its own inward discipline directly one ceased to be self-absorbed and began to observe. And as I stood in the sunshine the roar of a great conch-shell startled me, followed by reverberating echoes from walls that tossed it out to the listening mountains and set the echoes flying home again.

I followed the sound and already the lamas were pouring out from their hidden habitations like bees from a swarm, red-capped, with quaint little ear-pieces, red-robed, filling the place with hot color vibrating in the sun. They were hurrying round corners and by alleys black-shadowed by high buildings, and none forbade me to follow. They led the way in their hundreds—I had almost said, thousands—to a most singular courtyard of enormous size, paved and surrounded with a kind of cloister supported on pillars twisted like sticks of barley-sugar and decorated with carvings in wood, I believe, very richly colored and gilded. The roofs of the cloister were beautiful—covered with turquoise-blue tiles weathered into the loveliest sick greens and deepened and faded blues, with what looked like gold dragons springing out into the air as finials. And the cool gloom and velvet shadows in the cloister where sat the richly robed heads of the Faculty of Prayer—the gelungs, hooded and calm—would have made the dream of a Titian. I stepped into a corner and watched the really marvelous sight of the sea of red sweeping in like a rising tide as each man slid into his place according to rank, and facing the heads sat himself upon the pavement.

When the conchs sounded for the third time not a stone could be seen. The courtyard was a sea of red with deep crimsons, faded Indian reds—all according to the different stages of wear and weather, a wonderful sight indeed.

But my master was not there. Haridas sat among the gelungs, bare-headed, yellow-robed, with his serene face. He listened courteously and with the utmost attention to the setting forth of the thesis of the day, and when a loud collected murmur invited him to speak rose and spoke with such beauty of diction, such ample noble gestures that though I could understand scarcely a word I listened as to great music.

But the spectacle held me by its own force and weight, and I ventured to make color notes in hope the lamas would believe I was taking down what I could of the edifying discourses and arguments. Therefore I stayed until another great blast announced the end; and waiting respectfully until the gorgeous gelungs had disappeared the lamas streamed out of the courtyard, speaking eagerly but always in undertones, and were soon lost in the vast intricacies of the lamasery with scarcely a man to be seen.

Haridas came down from the cloister to join me, holding a palm-leaf fan to screen his face from the level rays of the sinking sun—a strangely Indian figure in these very different surroundings. He carried a Tibetan book in one hand, the leaves printed and held together without binding between two thin stiff covers secured with ties. I have forgotten to mention these before, but some of them were beautifully illuminated, and many grotesque and quaint. Dunbar's working table was strewn with them.

"You wish to speak to me. I felt it while I sat there. But before you begin let me tell you that to-night there is a great and very interesting rite here—the night prayers of the lamas in the open air. We have nothing like it in our form of Buddhism. The doctrine differs strangely. Now—shall we walk up the trails?"

We went side by side and he spoke no more until we were free of the buildings and climbing to the small plateau above them by rocky ways helped out with rudely cut steps. When we reached it we walked to and fro, stopping some time to see the dying light change and dim on the hills, for the sun was low and the chorded colors beginning to fade into the monotone of twilight. Sometimes we spoke, sometimes were silent.

"I wanted to consult you for a moment," I said. "Past kindness encourages me."

As briefly as possible I described the events of my meeting with Ormond, for I could speak freely remembering my talk with Haridas on the hills of Baltar. Later I described my experiences of last night.

"And now I ask your advice. We shall be leaving here very soon and going up to Alam Khan's castle, and you to Baltar. This may be my last chance. You put my feet on the way of Raja Yoga leading to powers I feel myself as yet very unworthy to use even if I could ever attain them. Should I persevere along that path still? Am I fit for it? or fit only for much simpler and humbler things with the heart and belief of a child? And what should be my scheme of life? I have given up the world I knew. It never could tempt me again. That is done."

I told him my dream of Kashmir and a studio there. He weighed that also in silence.

"I think," he said at last, "that you should take more time to consider before any decision. You will meet Ormond at Alam Khan's castle. He is a man of your own race and a very remarkable one in many ways—his advice and affection will help you. For my own part, I foresee your decision—"

"Tell me," I entreated. "It will relieve me of doubts and fears."

"That is just why I must not tell you. Those doubts

and fears all help to form character. Every one of them is a mallet and chisel at its work of sculpture. It cannot be missed."

Sculpture. The word was Brynhild. I ventured a question.

"If I could know what Miss Ingmar's decision in life is likely to be that would help me also. There have been times . . ."

"I know. You have thought it possible that your lives and work might blend to a common end. But be honest. Did you ever desire it with a selfless passion for her good? You thought of it only as a means for supporting yourself along a difficult way. Even then you never wished it with the earnestness such a prize deserves. Am I right?"

"Perfectly, painfully right, I see. Shut in the prison of myself I saw her only as one who might turn the Key and free me."

"Exactly. You must learn to understand the beauty in her and in yourself. Not appealing from lower ground and the need of leaning upon her strength, but as equal to equal with your own gifts to offer. That may lead to a friendship which will bless your life. There can never be friendship without balance of one sort or another. That the gifts should all be on one side is beggars' work. But, understand, I promise you nothing. She is a freed soul, and wings carry people far and in very unexpected directions. That is not to say she is free of human error. It is relative!"

We walked and turned in silence before I spoke.

"I see. I will do my best. After all, Ormond was her friend—he is worthy of her."

"He is worthy of the best, but what that best will be I cannot tell you. Be very thankful that you have a place in the hearts of such a man and such a woman."

"I have a place in her heart?" I asked in great astonishment.

"Certainly. She has a sincere liking for you, and deep interest in not only your art but your life. So have the Dunbars. And consider. Was it without meaning that your aimless wandering to Simla brought you to Baltar? Your past must have sown the seed of many hopes which will bear fruit in what is called the present and future."

Most true. I had realized the deep *intention* underlying all these things, but scarcely with the shock of conviction his words brought me.

"I can tell you this," he added. "Much is waiting for you at Alam Khan's castle which will clarify your thoughts and help you to decide upon the setting for your life. You should go there in great hope and joy. You drank deeply last night of that cup. Was not the drink divine?"

"Divine. It has transfigured the world. Now tell me. Shall I continue the discipline you set me in the Raja Yoga? Or shall I shut that window and open one simply on right living and the practice of my work? I can tell you this—at the sitting the abbot gave me today I felt such power, insight, enlightenment, as to the principles of what I was doing that it almost overpowered my hand. Wonderful—I can't describe it."

"The hand will soon adjust itself to the power. It is a good tool for the time being though far from a perfect one. The pictures of the future will be transmitted from one soul to another in speechless delight, and those of the farthest future will be shared in the universal joy of the Creator of which we shall be a part. There you have sure foothold, and I can tell you that power lies in wait for you along that road. Certainly continue all the practices of yoga. I have your master's authority for saying this. He and I have spoken of you. But the way will never be easy."

This I heard in silence. The dusk had deepened so that his face was scarcely visible—he was but a mysterious presence beside me, and a full moon was rising over the peaks with the stars lamping large until they fainted in her glory.

> . . . As when the moon
> Is drifting like a soul aswoon,
> And harping planets sing Love's tune. . . .

"An ecstasy!" said Haridas, drawing a deep breath.

I cannot tell how long we stood absorbed in the wonder, until at last the perfect moment passed, and we went down to the glimmering building, still silent.

But the night was not silent later. Shall I ever forget that astonishing evening with its barbaric beauty? For when the moon was high the great conch-shells roared a summons, and wrapping ourselves warmly against the chill purity of the night air we all went out into the courtyard of meeting. It was changed like the transformation scene of a theater—amazing. Huge colored lanterns were hung everywhere motionless on the still air. They shed wildly bright, contending lights over walls and windows and the empty courtyard. Great poles had been run up to enormous heights from the roofs with lanterns swaying as if breathing lights on the extraordinary sight beneath. For every flat roof, every terrace was thronged far and near with all the thousands of lamas whom never before had we seen gathered together. It was an army. And each and all were in their red robes of ceremony, and the wild colors and strong moonlight drowned them, transmuting them to such masses of color and light and shadow as I shall never see again.

"This is the most wonderful sight I have ever beheld in my life!" said Dunbar, almost whispering, for it took one's breath. And suddenly the great conchs roared, and louder, drowning them, broke forth the enormous prayer chant of the lamas. Not a man but swelled the chorus. It was overpowering. Lady Lucia caught her husband's hand with the tears running down her face. . . . Not beauty, no—but the same overwhelming emotion as the thunder of a stormy sea, the great human unison in the setting of solemn mountains starred and moonlit—hanging above us in the sky.

"What is it for? What does it mean!" Brynhild whispered, pale as death.

"They are prayers for the removal of evil influences," Dunbar whispered back. "Don't speak. Look —listen. You'll never see anything like it again!"

It continued, swelling into thunder, taken up from unseen crowds below and above us, gathering volume until ears could hardly bear the tremendous onrush of sound. It became unbearable and one could do nothing but endure, overwhelmed as if by the sweeping of a great droning ocean.

At last and suddenly it was rent by the three mighty roars from the conchs and thundering of drums—deafening, terrifying—and this done the thousands of lamas shouted together like the crash of a plunging sea.

Dead silence. The lights were swiftly extinguished.

One lonely figure was left, dark and solitary on the terrace above us. My master.

CHAPTER XVII

THE TIME WAS NOW FIXED FOR OUR GOING AND ALL the arrangements made. It would follow the Feast of Flowers and the farewell tea to be given by Dunbar—a function very unlike its ordinary name.

My picture of the abbot was almost finished, and I liked it better than any other bit of work which had ever left my hands. He made an excellent sitter, lending himself to every suggestion and lightening our labors by much good talk, which Shan-tao, who had been requisitioned for the purpose, translated when it got beyond my depth. I learned much from it of the way and discipline of the monastery and the angle from which the scholarly Tibetan Buddhist mind beholds life and death. Many of the lamas were extremely simple, indeed ignorant people, but there were others of very different types and powers, and his statesmanship and kindly wisdom in dealing with his kingdom interested me profoundly.

The lamasery was of course under the spiritual domination of Lhassa—"the Place of Spirits"—but the abbot had large freedom in matters of rule. Many an interesting side-light on Lhassa itself and on the great popedom of the Dalai Lama also came my way as I worked, and all of it was revelation of the many angles of Buddhism.

The day before the Feast of Flowers it was amazing to see crowds coming as it were out of nothingness—for where they lived I cannot think to this day—to the the ravine of the lamasery far below. They came on foot or on ponies and yaks, in parties, alone, and in caravans, until leaning over the precipice one could see the earth below many-colored with their hundreds swarming in and out of the tents they pitched by the river. Quite a little town sprang up mushroom-like in a few hours, and we went down to see the hawkers peddling very simple ware to tempt the queer, innocent, good-natured people with their broad faces and merry grins. Many arrived chanting prayers, and the sound of strange music ascended to the great height from which we watched like birds from their tree-top nests.

And next day at a given signal all ascended the monastery ways like ants climbing trees. They came with song and mirth from the tents, a storming, smiling, singing army to the mighty quadrangle where the Faculty of Prayers had disputed; and there under the cloisters the Flowers—the works in butter—were laid out for reverent admiration.

Since I had seen them, all had been delicately colored and gilded, and there glowed the stories of the Buddha's and the Saint Tsong Kaba's lives in gorgeous imagery. To our surprise and delight Brynhild's image of the Buddha stood forth in a prominent place, but now his drapery flowed in golden folds, and his face and hair were tinted in life-colors. It was labeled: "This divine image was made by the English incarnation of the divine Tara, Mother of Wisdom and Skill."

And as we stood to see the pilgrims turned many eager glances on our group where we waited in the shadow of the towering walls and nodding and whispering pointed to Brynhild as a kind of smiling miracle of heavenly skill. For all these works are supposed to be done under divine inspiration, and indeed there was real art in the modeling of more than one image, human and animal, for animals were often accompanying the holy personages.

What was extraordinary was that the reliefs were framed with highly decorated and as it were magnificently carved and gilded frames, all in butter. There were views in relief also of such famous places as Potala, the palace of the Dalai Lama in Lhassa, and of the famous monastery where the tree stands bearing on every leaf the sacred Tibetan characters. There were many more and in truth the interest to ourselves was almost as great as to the pilgrims who saw the show with devout awe and amazement.

There was even a miniature theater, with empty and expectant stage. A conch sounded, and there entered a procession of miniature lamas each about a foot in height, on their way to prayers. Mechanically moved, they passed into the wings and disappeared, while enthusiasm grew to a roar. And even while this echoed about us the abbot came out gorgeously robed and attended, with lamas going before, unneeded whips in their hands, to clear the way. He wore a magnificent miter, and in his right hand a cross-surmounted staff, while about his shoulders was a silk cope of noble crimson, held on the breast by a heavy clasp. It might have been a ceremony in the place of St. Peter's instead of in the upper world. And as he came a roar of welcome broke out, and the people clasping their hands and bowing their heads—some indeed prostrate—received his blessing as that of a god incarnate.

When he had gone and restraint was removed they gave themselves up to rejoicing, and we left the quadrangle a sea of tossing, shouting, joyous human faces. We had seen what few Europeans have ever seen before us, the Festival of Flowers.

And next day all was over and quiet, except that in the ravine below the multitude of pilgrims were slowly moving off to distant and solitary homes in the vast fastnesses of the great mountains.

We had grown to love the Lamasery of the Manis and to know ourselves a part of its life. There was not one of us who would not feel it a wrench to leave it perhaps forever, though cordial invitations to come again and yet again were showered on us. Even the Mohammedan Kashmiris who had come up with us had good-natured intercourse with these hospitable infidels, and had led such a life of ease and plenty that they were in no hurry to leave such good quarters, especially with the prospect of moving on again over the alarming Shantang Pass to the castle of Alam Khan.

The Kashmiri is not exactly a person in whom all virtues meet, and in spite of contracts and the immense respect in which Dunbar was held all over the country their head man sent up an ultimatum two days before we started to the effect that pay for men and ponies must be doubled, or they would all go down with Haridas and leave us to make our own arrangements in the monastery.

And on this followed a truly astonishing scene. Dunbar and I received them in a lower room set apart for audience, and behind us stood four gray-dressed lamas, that being the uniform of what I may call the proctors or police of the huge community. Each held his whip at the ready.

Viewing them with wary eyes but still with effrontery the Kashmiri spokesman followed by all the men stated his case. They had known that the agreement obliged them to convey us to the Monastery of the Manis, and this they had done with the utmost skill and courage, he said. But there had been no agreement as to Alam Khan's castle, and a fresh one must be made with double pay for the onward journey and the return to Kashmir: otherwise they would return at once to Gunderbal and Srinagar. Furthermore they expected special recompense for the shock their nerves had received from the shrieking and yelling of spirits on the night at Matayan—which had by no means been included in the contract. But for the nobility of their characters they would have left us then and there. Let the Presences now decide. Their last word had been said.

Dunbar was preparing a dignified but firm reply to the wily villains; I was ready to second him, when without a word of warning the lamas rushed upon them, brandishing and cracking their whips with faces in a grin of rage. They fell upon their prey shrieking, howling, and strong right arms rose and fell with the regularity of flails while cracks and shrieks and curses resounded. It was clear that it would not be for the good of their souls to interfere, and the two of us stood unmoved while the lamas worked their will in grim silence. Finally the leader dragged himself from the writhing heap and crawled to Dunbar's feet. A thousand abject entreaties poured from him as he lay there prostrate.

Forgiveness! Forgiveness! Only terror had wrung those lies from him. He knew, all the men knew, that the contract included Alam Khan's castle. Let the mercy of the Merciful be extended to erring children, and so forth. At length the lamas drew back behind us, satiate, and the paper abjuring the Kashmiri heresy was written and signed with thumbs dipped in ink and pressed on the paper, opposite each being written its owner's name—stately, noble-sounding names very unlike the handsome cowards they represented.

"And that's that!" said Dunbar, wiping his brow when the Babel was over and the room cleared. "But we must get a few good Baltis to stiffen these lily-livered wretches. The Baltis are an awfully decent all-round people. I shall send some of the worst of these scoundrels down and let the others take their places."

I met Brynhild on my way to the upper terrace and made her laugh with the news. Under her arm she carried a sketching block full of notes for future work.

"I never lose a minute now," she said. "When I think of leaving this dear place I can hardly bear it. I have learned so much, seen so much that it's like a kind of queer home. I believe I could live here forever and never tire. But Lance is almost done in with work, and the rest and mountains will set him up. Tomorrow is the last day. How can we believe it?"

I took her to see the hidden portrait, which was to be presented in state before we left. In the lamaseries every trade is represented—carpenters, bookmakers, binders of books, and what-not—and under my direction a very creditable carved frame had been made, ornamented with sacred symbols including the famous Buddhist wheel. I would not have it gilded as the maker earnestly wished, but the wood was polished to the height of its own dull beauty, a deep silver-gray, and it set off the glowing splendor of the abbot's dress and surroundings. I felt a satisfaction with the upshot of my work which was new to me, and I watched Brynhild standing before it, noting every detail with her own keenness. When she was in that mood her strange translucent eyes were like darts of light, searching, piercing, examining. They seemed to grip the object before them as though they would never release it again.

Finally she spoke, straight and candid.

"I like that through and through and with all my heart and soul. If I talked all day I could say no more. The modeling of the high cheek-bones, the composure and dignity, the expression—I love it. That's big work. Big."

I felt the blood flush up into my face. I had thought a little of the same because the thing satisfied me so fully, but the outside voice—and an understanding one—is good to hear.

"Suggest. Criticize!" I begged her. "You know. Make me know where I have come short."

"Nowhere. At least as far as my judgment goes. Look at those wrinkled hands—the fingers on the gold rosary. Beautiful. And the jewels in the clasp. Beautiful again. And that curious shaft of light behind the head from the window, almost with the haze of a halo. Very few people would have dared that, and it was risky, but you have brought it off triumphantly. I should like to have that picture. Of course you'll photograph it, but that's not the same thing."

I showed her the photographs, beautiful clear ones. If one knows how to manage the lens, wonderful photographs can be taken up in that pellucid air when one gets used to the differences to which the camera is sensitive.

"I shall do a duplicate. I have all ready."

She clapped her hands with pleasure.

"Of course I've modeled him in plasticine heaps of times when I got a glimpse of him," she said. "He's such a beautiful person. I never saw such attractive ugliness. Personally I like him better than Apollo—such humanity, wise but tired. I have one now that really recalls him, and the caravan came just now bringing up my gift for tomorrow. Oh, I wish we weren't going. Sometimes I wish they would let us build a swallow's nest of our own behind the lamasery on the great plateau higher up. It would be like living among the sky-people, the sun and moon and stars and clouds for company."

"But Ormond will be at Alam Khan's castle," I said, perhaps a little cruelly. The words were out of my mouth before I could stop them.

There was no blush on her cheek as she fixed her steady eyes on mine.

"Yes, and I'm glad. But still there's something

rather alarming in meeting someone you used to know and who'll be so different now."

"Why so different?"

"Because he was only beginning then, but such a—such a sensitive that one knew he would go very far. He must have been through the Looking-Glass many and many a time since. He could do it even then and didn't know a bit what he was doing."

"The Looking-Glass?" I was mystified.

"Yes. Did you never think the world is like a hard, bright looking-glass? One sees oneself in it, the heroine or hero and all the rest grouped round one, but it's all only a reflection. Nothing real. Just a moving shadow-show, looking as real as real can be. And behind it, hidden away, are the real things, and these are only the shadows they cast. But you must go through the looking-glass like Alice before you understand all that. Why shouldn't John Ormond know one of the ways? There are a good many of them."

I saw she could speak of him more freely now—she had adjusted her mind to it. But I thought she had hit on a wonderful illustration.

"I wonder if Carroll held that in his mind when he wrote the book?" I said.

"I dare say—it certainly was there whether he knew it or no, and they tell me that the mathematicians (and he was one) have a way of their own. At all events you could never have painted that picture if you hadn't been a little way through. You know that yourself?"

"Yes."

"One does. When I knew at Tashigong that I had

got through—it was like a blinding flash. Oh yes, this is your yoga."

She paused. So seldom did she speak of herself, and this talk had had such freemasonry in it, that I leaped at the chance.

"Could you tell me how the knowledge of your gift came to you? I'd give a great deal to know that. It might encourage me."

She turned calm eyes on my face.

"Encourage? You don't need that now. You've achieved enough to make you put on full steam ahead. But I can tell you if you wish."

It was friendly, no more, but it made my heart-beat quicken.

"They put me through a very strict discipline up there. I had seen and felt things before on my own, in a curious erratic way, but they did not want that. They thought something could be made of me, and you know the teaching is that you must know the Law and obey it in all things, until you reach a point where law is forgotten and you can trust to perfected intention. So I followed the rules of Raja Yoga steadily and learned to concentrate, sitting in the great woods overhanging the river rushing through the gorges below. Oh, no, I was never afraid. Fear doesn't come into these things at all. I learned to sit so still and in such concentration that the birds and animals came round me in a way—I can't describe it. But those stories of the Christian saints are true.

"Well, one day—but you know words are nothing in things like this and perhaps you may not even believe me—I saw on the other side of the deep gorge, among the rocks, very high up, a most wonderful flower growing. I had never seen one like it then—a flower with three pure white petals and cupped in three green leaves, and lower down the stem three more, so that it was ninefold—a bit of Nature's own magic. As I looked I loved it; I longed to touch it. It was as if something shot out of me to it. And now—will you believe?—as I thought that, suddenly I was on the other side of the terrible gorge with the river foaming below me and I was touching the flower."

She stopped, looking at me with shining, triumphant eyes. Doubt? I could as soon have doubted that light is light. But the thing half stunned me. I could take such things almost as a matter of course when they concerned Haridas or my master. They were men who lived in a sphere very different from ours. They had an hereditary right of understanding in such mysteries. But a girl like this—a girl with the soul of an artist truly, but yet one who walked and talked and dressed like others—that *she* should have attained the power of an Indian *yogin* if even once and once only, filled me with astonishment bordering on fear.

"Were you frightened?" I asked. "Did you pick it? How did you get back?"

"You will laugh when I tell you," she answered with sparkling eyes, bright under long lashes. "No, I didn't pick it—I never pick flowers, nor will you, one of these days—but I touched it and made it mine. And then suddenly I realized what had happened and I was terrified. I shook from head to foot. The gorge was really appalling—about eighty feet across and sheer down to the rocks and boiling maddened water. Do you know what I did? I sat down and cried, and so my master found me when he came out and shouted across the river; and to shorten my tale there was no means of getting me over, and I had to walk two miles down the river to a ford, and there they met me with a pony. Did you ever know such an anticlimax?"

"But what did your master say?"

"He said: 'Fear is the coward's poison. If you had chosen you could have walked back on the air as you went, instead of crying and splashing back through the pools like a whipped dog.' And he put me back six months in my work. Not, he said, that crossing the ravine on air mattered one way or another very much, but 'the heart of the coward is a lion in the road to perfection.' And now . . ."

But as I leaned forward engrossed, the door opened and Dunbar came in.

"All is ready for the tea. Come along. Lucia has sent me for you. I never saw such a *tamáshá* in my life. The lamas are marching in by companies until my knees are shaking under me with terror lest the butter should give out. If only they had kept the butter works of art we might have fallen back on them, but they were all pitched over the precipice last night. For heaven's sake come and see!"

Sight after sight had I seen at the lamasery, but this really filled me with new amazement. The tea-party, as Lady Lucia called it, took place in the huge quadrangle, which was the scene of all the greater social efforts of the lamasery.

Hundreds, thousands of lamas robed with ceremony

sat on the ground in serried ranks. Under the cloister was the abbot with a distinguished attendant on either hand, and a place for the founder of the feast beside him, to which Dunbar was immediately marshaled. The other gelungs sat at the head of each company.

The abbot's presence was the rarest honor which could be bestowed on host and guests alike. We drew up beside Lady Lucia.

Then a hundred of the youngest monks appointed to serve the others set off at a trot for the great kitchens, and came back staggering under the weight of huge-spouted jugs filled with Tibetan tea of the richest and costliest, bricks of tea broken up and boiled with butter and salt, the butter being the last touch of luxury. Every lama had before him a wooden bowl and platter, and as the attendants came along the ranks at full speed, each raised and tendered his bowl, which was filled to the brim with smoking tea. Followed other attendants rushing like whirlwinds in this excitement, bearing big wicker baskets loaded with oatmeal cakes, each with a great dab of butter on the top, and I am bound to own that a murmur of heart-felt joy and admiration suffused—if I may so phrase it—the whole huge assemblage when the lordly magnificence of these preparations was realized. Indeed each lama raised his scarf and fluttered it gaily in the direction of the cloisters where Dunbar sat in state, with the possible scarcity of butter heavy upon his mind.

"But we ordered *yak-loads!*" protested Lady Lucia anxiously. "Do, Mr. Cardonald, make a signal to him that there's ever so much more in the kitchen. I can see how miserable he is."

I rose and opened my arms to their fullest extent and waved them to show the extent of our butter resources, and his tension relaxed. Cargo after cargo of cakes was borne in, and I must report that in lieu of knives the lamas used their fingers to spread the butter. And still the cakes came and still they ate, and when a second distribution of tea followed, the enthusiasm was loud and deep.

At last it was over and every lama full to repletion and polished with butter until the whole assembly shone. And indeed there was something touching in seeing their simple satisfaction, and realizing how hard their daily fare must be when such a simple orgy was hailed as a kind of miracle. The butter had seen them out and all was well, what was left being distributed for private use. Then the abbot rose and in clarion tones made his proclamation.

"This generous feast we owe to our benefactor the great Dunbar Sahib, as he is called in his country of Kashmir. Let his name be remembered in the prayers of the lamas of the Manis as one whose thoughts are Buddha-like in their mercy, and whose good deeds rise like incense before the altar. And to him and his wife and to his friends we say this: Your going is grief to us. Your return will be joy. Always in the Lamasery of the Manis are rooms for you and food of our best, and the fire of our love to warm you. In going, say this: 'We return.' And joy will remain with us even though you go."

As he concluded the conchs blew a mighty blast, and the lamas rising in companies wheeled like soldiers and lining up to the cloisters laid little scarfs of ceremony at Dunbar's feet until they fluttered their bright colors to the winds, and still the heap grew, till the last company had offered and marched away to the lower terrace, and so the ceremony ended.

Next day came our leave-taking, and on that I cannot dwell. It touched something deep in each one of us which could not find voice in words. And our offerings were made and received with true friendly gratitude. To each of us the abbot made a gift. To Lady Lucia and Brynhild were given ancient golden clasps set in rich designs with turquoises and garnets of great value and very beautiful; to Dunbar two medieval daggers, the hilts set with the same stones.

To me was given what I valued more than any jewels—a noble antique Tibetan picture of the reception of glorified souls in the Paradise of the West. They came in strange boats of Chinese design, blown across halcyon seas with a gentle breeze swelling embroidered sails, and divine figures haloed and rayed with gold guided them to the haven where they would be. And on the flower-enameled shores, with mountains and trees about him, stood a long-forgotten Buddha to welcome the spirits coming like homing doves, his divine majesty surrounded with rejoicing saints bathed in eternal sunshine. But no description can do justice to the warm radiance of peace and home-coming that made the picture the eternal summer of the soul. I could say little, but their kind hearts knew I was glad —and that their treasure had fallen into hands which would treasure it.

The abbot himself at the head of his gelungs escorted us to the lowest terrace, and then the conchs broke forth, and drums and pipes united their wild music to honor our going as we slowly began our journey downward to the ravine. There our party separated. Haridas and Shan-tao, with the precious manuscript meticulously packed and loaded on a picked yak, taking the downward way which turning led to Kashmir and Baltar, and we the way leading upward which I myself had followed on my journey to meet Ormond.

I have kept one matter to the last.

The night before leaving I had made my way to the Room of Learning, and there my master met me, hooded and dim in the dusk of the unlit room.

"Go in peace," he said. "And this I say. If you need me at the castle of Alam Khan I shall be there. For in all the world is no bond so strong as that between master and disciple. This was taught thousands of years ago in India, and the truth stands. Therefore, if there is need, if your soul needs me, call and I come."

What could I say in gratitude? It seemed to me that from the day I had first seen Lady Lucia kindness had risen round me like a sunlit sea. I who had been a lonely man was now ranked and guarded by the miraculous goodness of true friends. And it seemed the final touch and reminder of all this that, as we turned up the ravine and the friendly buildings faded from view, the high terrace above was black—or rather red—with eager lamas hanging over the precipice, regardless of the giddy drop beneath, to watch our going until they could see us no more. So the Lamasery of the Manis faded into a dream, and tears stood in Brynhild's eyes as she looked up and waved her hand.

CHAPTER XVIII

I PASS OVER THE JOURNEY WITH ITS DISCOMFORTS AND dangers. The mountains are crowned with terror as well as beauty, and we had our share. Michael in particular took a gallant part, enjoying himself to the full and encouraging us all to see the fun of it when the shoe pinched. The Kashmiris named him the Dog-Sahib and were right, for he was and is undoubtedly a gentleman—let us say one of nature's own—a much misused phrase. I can see him now wildly rejoicing in the snow—golden in the sun, scattering gold-dust with plowing paws as he raced through it, the little friend of all the world, with the exception of marmots, who drove him mad with their insulting antics and then had the ill taste to plunge to safety in a burrow where no self-respecting dog could follow. What he became to me I had better not attempt to say. Those who understand dogs need no telling. Those who don't, no telling can tell. So he made his little place in the world and held it as he should.

There came a day at long last when our company halted on the top of a wide plateau with a wide river crossing our way, shallow and rippling, for the bulk of the melted snows had all been swept down to India by this time. And on the other side was a cliff higher than our own, sloping upward and upward in rocky but cultivated terraces to the lower ranges of a mighty mountain, twenty-six thousand feet, so they told me, from sea-level. On the terraces were crowded one above the other the small, square flat-roofed houses of a little town, and above them, crowning and centering the picture, one of the most romantic-looking castles I have ever seen in my life.

Not that it was Norman with towers and keeps and moat and drawbridges. The wild mountain blasts and snows will stand no such vagaries of architecture. Flat-roofed, little-windowed and many-storied, it watched over the town, almost a part of the buttresses of rock which backed and grounded it. One tower, a little higher than the roof and evidently designed for watching an enemy's movements, was its only variation from the rectangular, and a flagstaff with a huge yellow banner its only decoration. But its loveliness, the wild little kingdom in the heart of the hills with the hurrying river at its feet and the terrific mountains like lions on guard about it, gave the castle a quality I shall not see even in the great English keeps dreaming over their placid meadows and gently waving woods.

"And this is our last lap," said Dunbar, slipping off his pony, "and here is Alam Khan's first welcome."

For there had evidently been watchers across the river, and a big gun rang out with a sharp crack, and its rolling echoes were still flying round the mountains like birds flapping their wings when another cracked out and another to the number of eleven, until the air was dazed with confused sound. Then the yellow flag descended and dipped three times, and behold! the little town was alive like the swarming of bees to meet and do us honor.

"And first," said Dunbar, "we have to get down to the river, which is no treat. Last time we came my wife's pony slipped on the track, and a nearer squeak you never saw. Tazaki saved her. He's a mountain man from the Japanese Alps, you know. Tazaki, look after the *okusama.*"

He was at her bridle in a moment.

I have forgotten to say hitherto what an impression Tazaki had made on the Lamasery of the Manis. Not unlike the people themselves in appearance, evidently from the same Mongolian stock, but infinitely more quick-witted and resourceful, he had dominated the younger lamas from the moment we arrived. His small brown fingers were miracles of skill, and he left them the wiser by all sorts of cunning feats of carpentering and the swift brush-work in which, like many Japanese, he excelled.

But there were two crowning feats which won him the adoring awe of lamas very much above the young ones in rank. The first was his Japanese knowledge of the Chinese written character—a great and high accomplishment in Little Tibet. The lamas could not hide their astonishment when the written word was put before Tazaki and he read with comprehension. The second nearly drove the lamasery wild with excitement. He was a past master in ju-jutsu, the famous Japanese wrestling science, and before long the lower terraces were full of young lamas, gripping, defending, puffing with zeal and excitement, the drollest sight, until they acquired some of Tazaki's skill; and then I too could resist the lure no longer and signed on as a pupil and did not disgrace myself. He had already taught Lady Lucia and Brynhild and both were as graceful and skilful as they could be. It is an art every woman should learn; there is no such steadier of the nerves.

And they needed a steadier just then. That path wound down the precipice, in many places scarcely a foot wide, a wall of sheer rock on the right, on the left the drop to the river. But they laughed and talked without a trace of fear as they rode down, each with a man at her bridle, and we reached the bottom in safety.

"And look—look! Alam Khan!" cried Lady Lucia waving her handkerchief. "Look! he's had a bridge made for us."

And sure enough there was a Kashmiri bridge of twisted rope-twig swaying across the river that we might leave the ponies to their fording and cross in state. That, I own, was an attention which tried me personally more than the descent, as it swayed giddily over the dazzling water, yet I did it, not with the triumph of the others but somehow. And there on the other side was Alam Khan surrounded by his soldiers and courtiers, and a new chapter of experiences was open before me.

The khan welcomed the Dunbars as old friends and with a touch of chivalry to Lady Lucia, which I thought became him very well. A splendid young man, tall and olive-skinned with high-bred features and gallant bearing, he stood half a head taller than any of his tribesmen and looked the ruler he was. His turban was tied with a smart and errant cock—and what man does not look well in a turban?—and his unjeweled sword-hilt was businesslike as a *Gurkha kukri.* I knew he had been at school in England, but was little prepared for the easy English with which he greeted us. I saw his deep, dark eyes sweep Brynhild in her riding-breeches and long coat with a kind of pleased surprise as he saluted, hand to turban, then he turned cordially to me with the hand held out.

"Welcome, sahib, to the mountains. The friend of my friends is mine. And what news from London?"

London! It seemed as far away as Mars. I had forgotten it. Had I ever really sat in the club window, and yawned at the theaters, and played polo at Ranelagh—or was it another man altogether? I could not remember the way that man thought—the angle from which he viewed a dull, dispiriting world. I might not be a better man, I only knew that I was a much more interested and alive one. The world seldom spreads its vast picture-book wholly in vain. . . . But London! I fell in behind as he led the way with the Dunbars, remembering it with a heart grateful for escape, as we climbed from the river-bed and up the almost perpendicular streets—if the narrow ways, stepped here and there, could be so dignified.

"Did you ever see such a beautiful ruler?" whispered Brynhild at my elbow. "Think of the average king! This is an Indian Apollo— No, Krishna! I can see him glittering in massed jewels with his dark conquering beauty and the flute at his lips and the herd-girls all worshiping—worshiping. And Lance says he's like a tamed tiger with all the fire and strength in him under a velvet coat. In London women would have made him a magazine hero of romance—here, he's a real king and a busy one."

Very busy, with tribes hostile to the British Raj to be watched, and a wary eye to be kept on Russia, and the dangerous ways to keep open for communication—a sword in the hand of England, slender but strong. We may be proud of our princes and their guard on the outposts of the empire.

"What is his faith—do you know?" I asked her.

"He was born a Mussulman and must remain so for that's the religion of the state, but Lance says he translates it into perfect freedom of conscience, though he follows it in outward custom. The truth is, you cannot live at Baltar and know the Dunbars without struggling out into the light somehow. He has seen a lot of them."

I looked about me. Anything I had seen hitherto in the towns and villages of the peoples of this upper world suggested medieval times in its easy discomfort. Satshang was alive and interested. The people were clean and warm, and all were well-fed and happy. I would willingly have delayed to see more but that we were winding steadily up to the castle, and in another quarter of an hour we were inside it with rows of salaaming servants on either side.

An amazing place. The khan had evidently returned from England with a passionate resolve to remodel on the European ideal as far as possible.

There was a wide roomy hall with English fireplaces (I could picture them coming up the passes loaded on yaks) and richly embroidered Chinese hangings as portières. There were Oriental divans against the walls mingled with sofas evidently copied by a native craftsman and all brilliantly robed and cushioned in deep colors, which looked very well in the dimness of the place. For Europeanize as you might, the windows must remain small and narrow to front the piercing winter winds.

But I liked the place. I thought that when the fires were lit and curtains drawn and the snow piling the small street high with feathery silence there might be a Christmasy warmth in the well-lit hall like a jewel set in ice. Well-lit, for—will it be believed?—the khan had imported all the necessary electric outfit from Srinagar, and the river did the rest, and when he proudly touched a button we broke into splendor and stood amazed.

"Lord bless me, that's new!" said Dunbar in huge delight. "Well, you *are* a progressive! And what do the dutiful subjects say to it?"

"The dutiful subjects have got it in their own houses too, Dunbar Sahib! What do you say to that? As it had to come up from the river to here it was quite easy. When I have ridden home at night by the cliff you arrived on above the river, Satshang twinkles like a constellation and the tribesmen about call it the home of the peris—fairies, you know. I hope to get the people a little more fairy-like in time. There's a lot I want to do."

So that was a king's yoga—and a fine one! I saw it in his eyes and the way he held his head. The soul molds the body for good or ill as the snail makes its shell. It has different sorts of beauty to bestow, and one may not recognize them at the first glance; but they are there sure enough for those who know the beautiful when they see it.

But the banqueting hall was my delight, for he had made it a cross between a library and an armory, and very well the notion worked out. Wonderful, medieval-looking guns and pikes and swords, magnificent in hilt and blade, glittered on the high dark walls with daggers and such like small deer of the fighting trade in gallant patterns. One side was wholly given up to books, European and Oriental; I promised myself much joy in looking through them. And while we stood exclaiming, and admiring the magnificent rugs which strewed the floor with color, a door opened quietly and John Ormond walked in.

It was as when a stone is thrown into a pool—a silent commotion spread outward. I saw Brynhild flush and pale and Ormond's quiet face break into a glow of gladness, and knew instinctively that change was upon us. It might be for better, for worse—but it was change. A chapter was closed, a new one opened.

On the surface all was simple enough. He turned to Brynhild.

"I am truly glad to see you. Who could have dreamed our next meeting would be here!" That was all, and in a moment the others were round him, and he extricated himself to grasp my hand with the look in his eyes that I never saw in any other man's—a *faithful* look. God knows I had proved and tried it to the uttermost and never found it fail.

"I came a week ago and Alam Khan has given me

a great time. You must all come up with me tomorrow and see the blue poppies on a hill above this—a sight worth all the journey from Baltar and more."

They went on talking and I listened—the magic of the hills in every word he said and upon us all. I never knew and cannot explain now what it is in these desolate countries that excels all the loveliness of Kashmir, Ceylon and the favored lands where flowers and fruit are spilled about in wild profusion. You may say sculpture against painting, but that does not meet the case for both are alike soul-winning. To me the upper country is a vast cathedral where the winds are organ-pipes, and the mightiest mountain ranges of the world its pillars, and the roof the starred sky with the gazing moon for lamp. I loved its sunshine, but when I think into the soul of it, it is always night, and the mountains felt but not seen—vast presences still in darkness. I left them all talking, noting that Brynhild and Ormond had fallen apart from the others, and followed my appointed servant up the steep, narrow stairs to my room, with Michael at my heels.

The castle grew more and more Asiatic as one left the big downstair rooms behind, and became a medley of queer irrelevant little rooms and almost unnegotiable stairs. It might almost have been the Manis, but with a difference for all that. Here and there was a curtain flowered with orange and black figures, a rug to soften a bare ugly floor. Could it be a feminine touch, I wondered, in a house where all the servants were men? We passed on the fourth story one door of heavy wood magnificently carved by some long-dead Kashmiri craftsman, overlaid with beautiful wrought bars and hinges of iron. I wondered to what part of the unknown place that led. And so through many narrow passages we came to my room.

Here Europe had frankly abandoned the struggle after achieving a very comfortable bed and chair. There was a dressing-room with the big earthenware bath-vessel of India—made on the spot, by the way, for Alam Khan had started an excellent pottery—but I was in the heart of foreign things otherwise and liked it, and the quiet was complete. I looked down into a walled garden with a profusion of trees loaded with golden apricots. They ripen marvelously in these arid altitudes, and when dried a roaring trade is done in them. A mountain stream kept the place with its trees—shade-trees also though of no great height—fresh and green as an English orchard. And there were flowers evidently very carefully tended. As I looked almost under the window, by a stiff tree laden with golden balls of apricots I saw a vision, a most beautiful girl, a gold-embroidered sari on her head draping her after the Indian fashion. She sat on golden cushions and turned what seemed to be the leaves of a picture-book upon her knees.

I had not thought of that side of Alam Khan's life, and it had never been mentioned. Romance! Might I look? Must I look away? What is the etiquette when one sees an Indian princess in her own walled garden? I did not know, but I drew back behind a curtain and watched the picture with delight. Her little slippers were braided with gold. Her dark hair tasseled with pearls fell far below her waist. Her mouth was a rose. She was a princess stepping straight out of an old Mogul manuscript with blue borders worked in intricate gold after the Persian manner, a miniature as it were in gems, so pure and bright the colors. I had seen these things in Delhi, done by Mogul artists when their emperors found the Indian women fair, and I knew. And that nothing might be wanting, on a rose-colored cushion at her feet lay the most magnificent cat I had ever seen, a mass of smoky gray-blue fur, lazily blinking moonstone eyes at the beauty.

I would have given more than a little to know more than the gloriously illuminated initial letter of this romance. But in India one asks no questions about any woman from those who know best about her—much less of princesses with gold-embroidered slippers and pearls and a cat like a guardian jinnee off duty. I took my hurried pencil notes, however, and knew that even this infringed a strict copyright.

Presently she stood up, bright in the hot sunshine, and yawned, stretching her arms until the bangles rang and so went slowly away under the apricots. The cat followed daintily, and a little Indian maid in green and silver came running and heaped her arms with the cushions and all was over. But I had seen, and went down the breakneck stair biding my time.

Ormond only was in the big hall, and his Michael at his feet. The pair were one—they could not be imagined apart. We talked dog for a few minutes, a good talk, and then I asked how he had managed to hit us off so well at Satshang.

"Your master sent to me. You know by this time that such men don't wait for the mail."

"I guessed that, and yet," I said, "I think I have no taste for miracles. There's to me a something repellent in seeking after signs and wonders. I had rather you had heard some other way."

He looked up with a smile of pleasure.

"Of course—of course. The Buddha and the Christ both hated the attitude of mind that wants cheap shows. But there's no harm in using the powers when you know the rules. You see there's no supernatural, for that would be breaking the order of the universe. There are only unusual things, and unusual people have the right to use them on certain conditions. Some day all the supermen in the world will use them as matter-of-factly as we telephone now."

"Do you believe that ever can be?"

"Why not? If men can use them now the knowledge will spread. In Asia we find it spreading very quickly except where contact with our Western civilization checks it. But it's there. A Brahman I knew said a true word when something distinctly unusual had happened and his English employer had laughed at the explanation he gave. 'You, an educated man, to believe such rubbish?' he had said. The Brahman looked straight at him, 'Sahib, such things don't happen in your country. They do in ours.' And the reason is plain. The Indian aerials have been up for ages. They're tuned in."

"But yet—"

"But yet one doesn't do silly things. I'm all for the Indian saint who reproached a believer trying for twenty years to gain power to walk on the water. 'Twenty years,' he said, 'trying to do what you could achieve by giving the ferryman a penny!' No, no signs and wonders for their own sake and very sparingly for any other! Did you see any at the Manis? I bet you didn't."

"Not one. Except the opening of my eyes to what was going on around me."

"Ah, that's a different story. Throwing open the window of perception for others is a gift and grace strictly individual and private. That one may always do, and some men and women reach a point where perception radiates from them unconsciously. Did you feel that with your master? I felt that with him always. It was a greater gift than his words."

I reflected, remembering.

"Yes—I did—a kind of luminous certainty while I was with him. I thought it was my own advance. But did he teach you too?"

"I owe him nearly all I know," he answered with a kind of restrained emotion. "The rest to Miss Ingmar. I met her at first very strangely and soon knew she had that rare gift of directing people to things beyond the point she herself has reached. Though she has reached far—for a woman."

"For a woman?" I asked in the utmost astonishment. "Can't a woman reach as far in spiritual things as a man? Are you becoming an Asiatic, Ormond?"

"I'll answer that question like an Asiatic. Don't you remember the Buddhist nuns and their cry: 'How should the woman's nature hinder me?' But all the same with more pain and much less freedom. A man —wise of the wise—once told me he believed that before some enormous spiritual development in a next incarnation the soul must pass through a woman's experiences to perfect what he called 'the art of dancing in fetters.' I think that true. It may be true only relatively and as a symbol, but true."

"Then you think the Asiatic woman as a whole may be fulfilling her destiny better than the Western woman of the present day?"

"Spiritually, possibly much better, for service is perfect freedom; but naturally spirit and intellect must develop together as they do in Miss Ingmar. On the other hand look at Alam Khan's exquisite wife!"

"I saw her just now—the beauty in the garden. Tell me all about her."

"All? I can't tell what I don't know. You don't expect a flamboyant Western romance? He met her father, the Nawab of Mirkote, down in India—the most splendid old Mussulman you ever saw—true and tempered as steel. Naturally he had never seen the daughter—her name is Maryam—but heard that she was young and beautiful and trained in all a royal daughter of the Prophet should know, and so he asked for her and got her, and as is the way in India the romance began after marriage. Safer than before, don't you think?"

"And now?"

"Each is both, as they say down there, and there's a little khanzada—the most beautiful boy you ever beheld—a small Asiatic angel."

"And do you mean to tell me that exquisite creature is to be boxed up until she dies in all the inanities of a zenana—with perhaps a sister-wife or two to poison her some day for spite!"

Ormond laughed aloud in glee.

"Oh, you Westerners! She's his only wife as much as yours will be yours some day. She was educated by an Englishwoman and reads and speaks perfectly, and with all the zest of her family in everything. Indeed she was her father's right hand before she married, and no doubt you know he's the center of big things in India. Ask Lady Lucia what she is if you think I'm beauty-blinded."

"But you never saw her?"

"Didn't I just! Not here—that would hurt the prejudices of his people. But he has taken her to England twice. Her boy was born there, and there I saw her almost daily—the loveliest thing in mind and body, 'A very incarnation of love and loveliness,' as Kalidasa says."

"I envy you."

"You may. If you could paint that girl's picture, old man—ah, well! He had her painted by Lois Sanderson, and the picture has gold filigree doors to shut across it, and only the privileged may see the Pearl of the Faith. But the two ladies will be with her as they please, and he has twice brought her to Baltar."

Strange country where the extremes of bondage and freedom meet! So I thought, not knowing then that extremes do in truth meet and are one. But that mysterious question of the rights of woman—Eastern or Western—was and is beyond my material judgment, although in its aspect transcending experience I may think I guess. I haunted my window for sheer love of beauty but did not see her again in the garden while we were in Satshang. Later—but that must wait.

Perhaps she guessed an uninvited eye, and her beauty must not be brushed by the moth's wing of a glance without her permission.

But when the others came in and our talk was done, it left me wondering as to Ormond's own attitude to the question. He had referred to Brynhild with calm that was almost indifference. His enthusiasm was for the Khanum Maryam. Did mere esthetic delight in the flower growing in another man's garden stir him more than the mysterious friendship between him and Brynhild? I wondered. As I watched his perfect cordiality and candor it seemed to me that I could not detect a hair's breadth of difference between his ways with her and with Lady Lucia. With both it had something of the detached kindness and affection of the best type of Catholic priest—a man so set apart by some secret strength of his own vocation that women are flowers in God's garden, but never in his own—to be beheld with loving wonder and admiration but not for the gathering.

There was a wonderful exploration after dinner, when Lady Lucia and Brynhild went up to the zenana, and we with Alam Khan explored, preceded by two men with lanterns, the oldest part of the castle, left in exactly the same state as when his grandfather, a hawk of the mountains, raided and plundered his neighbors and made himself a sharp thorn in the foot of the British Sirkar. His grandson led the way with a kind of pride in the old villain's exploits delightful to behold considering his own very different ones; but blood is stronger than wine, and the difference was only that though the same fire and energy were there all right they dashed their flaming torrent in very different channels nowadays.

I shall never forget the old khan's rooms, gloomy, with small forbidding windows whence he might peer like a rat from its hole over the vast mountains and valleys and note whether the Kanjuts were creeping down the precipices with the blood-lust on them, so he might prepare the Satshang men to roll down hefty rocks upon them from the higher heights. Or to see whether the Nagars pushed on by their scarlet-bearded elders were on the move down the long ravine to Satshang. If they were he could call his astrologers and raise his own magic of frost and blast to counter them. Charmed bullets too. Alam Khan laughing bid us run our hands through a sack of garnet bullets (big garnets imbedded in lead to economize the scanty metal) which the old man kept stored up for an evil day, each one guaranteed for a British heart if necessary. Satshang had had stirring times, he said, from the beginning of history until now. . . .

"Let me tell you what is in my mind. I have a notion that as flying develops we may have wonderful towns in these hills where people will come up from India for the pure air and scenery. Why, it would be nothing to fly from Srinagar in decent weather!"

"The worst is," said Dunbar, "that indecent weather comes on so uncommonly quickly in these awful heights. I don't seem to see the most intrepid airman effecting an easy landing twenty-seven thousand feet up on Nangar Parbat. Do you?"

Alam Khan shrugged his shoulders.

"Who knows! The mercy of Allah is on the Sahibs and all their works!"

His ardent dark face in the gloom of the big room caught my fancy. Young Asia, standing by the sack of garnet bullets, looking with undaunted eyes to the future of men's wings. I knew in that minute why Ormond found romance among the hill peoples that London and Paris could never match.

"But Russia—Russia!" the Khan added with darkening brows. "The Bear is at work up yonder, and many of the tribesmen drink his vodka and listen to his smooth talk. And then what?"

Dunbar laid a finger on the hilt of his sword.

"That!" he said. The Khan nodded.

CHAPTER XIX

WE HAD RIDDEN UP IN THE MORNING TO A GREAT plateau towering high above the rear of the castle for a picnic among the blue poppies and wild primulas, a place commanding a tremendous view up the magnificent ravine, which was apparently closed at the upper end by a mountain flinging its crest into the skies, looking six miles distant and in reality sixty —a ravine of as difficult traveling as any in the world. But up the winding track to the plateau all was easy, and the flowers at the top a wonderland.

Sky-blue poppies grew everywhere, swaying on a delicate breeze. I remembered as a child how the sudden sight of a mushroom meadow inspired me with a kind of amazement as at something supernatural. They called to mind quaint elfin presences peeping unseen from shy copses to watch human surprise and delight at their handiwork. One was in touch. So also with these blue poppies, as different from their flaming sisters as if they came from the high hills of Paradise and those others from the depths, with the devil's thumb-mark black on their petals. These poppies were sky-creatures, breathing only the blue air of the mountains and so tinting their delicate veins.

I never saw Brynhild so happy. Neither she nor

Lady Lucia would pick so much as a silken bud of them or of the many-colored primulas growing in thick clumps in little boggy dishes of the rocks—mauve and pink and misty lavender and a kind of ocean-blue, which I have never seen before or since. I, more brutal, filled my hands with them the better to enjoy the dim sweetness of their scent, a little recalling the primroses in English woods.

"Once we had an Englishman hunting for their seed," Alam Khan told me as he stood looking on in amusement at our pleasure. "They were his children and pride, and he could talk and think of nothing else. He stayed with me down below for a while, sending seed back to England by runners to Srinagar, and then he heard of a crimson flower with a black instead of a golden center up in the Lambakhi heights—an awful place and the people about it the most savage in the whole country. I thought it only a ruse to draw him on and said what I could, but he would go, and they robbed and murdered him; but the seeds got back all right and they grow in Kew now."

"I expect he wouldn't have thought it too heavy a price to pay. Men never do when the ideal is in question," Dunbar said. "And Ormond has been up among the Lambakhis and come back safe and sound."

Ormond, stooping over a clump of rosy stars, looked up smiling.

"Wonderful people when you know them!" he said smiling. "But you mustn't trip over their little prejudices or you hear of it sooner or later. They're amazing folk—both men and women wonderfully beautiful in a dark aquiline way like Arabs, or the best type of Persian. The most beautiful woman I ever saw in my life was up there, and no one would marry her because they said she was a mountain fairy and such beauty was for the gods."

"What sort of gods?" I asked.

"Nature. Thunder and snow gods, the sun and moon. And it's the odder because the people about are all either Buddhist or Mussulman, different in looks and customs and everything. But I was up with them for six months, going my own way, and they never laid a finger on me. They talked a dialect of the language about here, which they said was the original, so I could understand them all right."

Thus we men sat talking, while in a sunny corner below us the servants prepared food for luncheon we were to eat later on, and the women wandered about among the flowers, Tazaki following Lady Lucia like her shadow, Brynhild scaling the rocks here and there like a mountain-goat and calling delight at some new discovery through hooped hands to Lady Lucia below. I heard her voice clear and small in the distance, and was tempted to climb up after her, but delayed, thinking Ormond had the better right. The whole scene and day were as clear and apparently safe as if we had been among the mountains of the Bernese Oberland and not one of us gave a thought to any kind of danger.

I remember we men started a great political argument on the chances of an Asiatic civilization superseding the white. Ormond and Dunbar declared such a change was not only possible but certain in the revolving of the wheel of time, while Alam Khan, knowing the peoples of Chinese Turkestan and Mongolia, stoutly denied the possibility, and I, the ignorant one, listened, and wondered what my master and Haridas would have to say to such a future. The talk grew swift and animated, and time went by, and we were all so eager and keen that when the servants came up with the news that tiffin was ready it seemed the morning had fled like a dream.

"I'll go and get my wife and Brynhild. Come along, Ormond. We should get through with tiffin if we're to ride up through the Satshang Pass later."

They went off, disappeared among the rocky ways going upward, and I stayed with Alam Khan, picking his brains on the subject of the hill peoples and their queer notions and customs. Twenty minutes, half an hour went by, and no one had returned. Alam Khan scrambled up a rock and shouted. No answer.

"They are going to be very late!" he called from his vantage-point. "Don't you think, Cardonald Sahib, that if you went by that way and I by this we might round them up?"

He leaped down lightly, and went off with his head man after him, a tall, dour fellow with a dark suspicious face. I took the way to the left and the last spot where I had seen Brynhild at her flower-hunting. As I gained the height I looked down and saw Lady Lucia and Tazaki walking quickly along to a spot where they could scramble down to Dunbar and Ormond waiting below. I stood a second to watch and then went on and up. It was always a kind of instinct with Brynhild to reach the highest viewpoint, and I counted on that.

Presently I reached a spot where I could command

a wider view, and there was Alam Khan making his way to the Dunbars. They met and though I could hear nothing I saw the explanations and the evident questions about Brynhild and the pointings here and there which indicated possibilities. Presently Lady Lucia and Tazaki moved on toward the tiffin ground, and Alam Khan with Ormond and Dunbar came up towards my line of search. I thought it better to wait for their report. In about ten minutes they were with me. Dunbar looked disturbed, Alam Khan confident. He called to me:

"Lady Lucia says she left her more than half an hour ago, going up toward the crags. One of the men had told her there was a wonderful slope of poppies up yonder, and she was determined to see them. No—nothing to be frightened of. There isn't the slightest danger on these lower hills! She would have to walk three or four hours upward before getting into any difficulty. Let's shout together. She's sure to hear."

We sent a fine ringing shout up the hills, and the echoes shouted back magnificently, but no human answer. Then Ormond alone gave a wild ringing cry, carrying to immense distances, a sort of yodel of the hill peoples, with which they communicate from crag to crag. He had given her a sample on the way up and hoped she would recognize it. Again no answer. Dunbar spoke anxiously:

"It's always on the cards that she may have fallen and hurt herself. Sprained her ankle or worse. Let's divide and quarter the ground for two miles. It's impossible she could have got any farther than that. Alam Khan, will you call your men?"

The khan pulled a great golden whistle out of his

breast, and a minute after three shrill blasts had pierced the air twelve men were running steadily upward in a loping trot, as easily as if it were down-hill instead of breasting a steep incline. Each of us took three of them, and off we went in spreading circles, the men stooping low over the ground to examine for traces we Europeans never see. No need to dwell on this. I take up the story where an hour later the parties met at the point agreed. Failure—nothing else. She had disappeared. No answer. No sign had rewarded us.

Alam Khan was the most openly concerned. His pride and honor were outraged in every fiber, and I saw the man in a rage royal, white under his golden skin, black eyes darting flames of anger, teeth clenched and hand on the hilt of the short sword that never left him. What? An English girl, his guest, to disappear in his territory, under the shadow of his protection? I saw the veneer of Eton and Oxford disappear into a kind of cold inflexible cruelty before which his men cowered. That was his father come back, and their own fathers, not to mention the elders among themselves, had felt the weight of his merciless hand when things went wrong. They stood about him, trembling, with eyes fixed on him like dogs' on their master, entreating forgiveness and commands.

"Call up every able-bodied man from the castle and town, and let not so much as an inch be left unsearched. Down with you now, Faiz-Ullah, and be back with them as quick as a bird flies, or by the Prophet of God and his Twelve Imaums I'll know the reason."

A man launched himself against the wind running like a greyhound, his feet almost invisible for speed;

he fled down the steep slopes and vanished. The others stood about the khan dismayed and humble.

"Spread far and wide in a three-mile circle. Search every ledge and precipice. Take the ropes of the ponies in case she has slipped down a hole. And the man who brings back the lady shall have a *jagir* (a grant of land) to him and his heirs forever!"

"And a gift of money to make his heart swell!" Dunbar put in eagerly. "Search, men, search, for the wrath of the khan is on one side and wealth and honor on the other. My God, Alam Khan! What do you think has happened?"

For the men had scattered right and left and we could speak unheard.

Ormond looked the khan steadily in the face.

"I think she has been carried off."

"There are no bears—nothing up here," the khan said furiously. "What should carry her off? I tell you she has fallen and is lying hurt—perhaps fainting somewhere. We shall find her with all these men. They know what they must face if they fail!"

Dunbar was staring anxiously at Ormond. "Have you any reason for that notion?"

"Partly instinct. I shall know more soon. But if she were alive she would have dragged herself along somehow to where she could get in touch. She would think of our anxiety."

That was true. I knew it. Terrible indeed would be the accident that would break her courage and resource. A kind of unknown horror chilled my body.

"But if she were dead?" I said almost under my breath.

"I should know that. So would you," he answered with stern brevity. "How long is it, Alam Khan, since the Lambakhis raided your upper territory?"

"Last in my father's lifetime! And by the life of the Prophet I swear that such a thing is impossible. The children of hill-devils would no more dare attack a woman under my shadow than they would pitch themselves over yonder." He swung a hand to the awful precipice on the other side of the river. "And my guards are miles up in the two forts called Hassan and Hussein, where they can sweep the only trail possible from Kotchak to Zilbor. Talk sense, Ormond Sahib, in this danger and not fairy-tales of the bad old days!"

Ormond passed over the anger—it was easy to allow for that in the young ruler's position.

"Right, Alam Khan," he said cheerfully. "But the wise man overlooks no possibility, and the Lambakhis are rather alarming folk in their way, though I got on well enough with them. Now let's disperse and search again."

I attached myself to him, and not long after we had taken our route saw the advance guard of the men of Satshang pouring up like swarming ants over the lip of the plateau from below. It seemed incredible it could have been done in the time, and nothing but news of the khan's wrath could have so winged their feet. The plateau would be quartered to some purpose now, and now I could speak.

"Ormond," I said earnestly, catching at his sleeve, "had you anything beyond a guess for that suggestion? You have ways of knowing things that are beyond me. Was it that?"

He faced me, half turning.

"It was an intuition, and God knows I have had reason to trust them. I am as sure as that we stand here that that is what has happened. As to who's guilty, I have not seen, but in the first moment of quiet I'll set myself to see."

"Can you guess, humanly speaking?"

"There is more than one tribe about here who might hold her to ransom, and the Lambakhis are capable of anything. No, I can't guess, but I shall soon see. Meanwhile we must omit nothing. Fork round this ridge and meet me at the other end. Good luck!"

For two hours the keenest runners and trackers of Satshang searched the plateau, which after all was only about three miles wide by two deep before it became a mere jumble of wildly spilled rocks leading up into the mountain. It was out of the question to suppose she would have ventured up there unhelped and alone. The track from the plateau to Kotchak, the stronghold of the Lambakhi tribe, was scanned by men crawling on their stomachs for the length of the level stretch until it ended on a glacier which no woman would have dared alone; and when we met in the falling dusk above the descent to the castle there was no more to be said of the plateau. A gathering of eight hundred men had assembled to report failure and take their chief's further orders.

A wonderful sight, for some had lit rough torches, and the tossing light streamed over wild dark faces half hidden by turbans falling over glittering eyes as they looked up eagerly to where Alam Khan stood on a rock, in his European uniform with the stately turbaned head above it.

"Men of Satshang, you have nothing but failure to report!" he shouted above them. "Is it a fitting end to such a story? Is a woman, my guest, to disappear like a lamb lost in the mountains until the eagles have picked its eyes out? And you call yourselves men? Bring your torches and hunt up the ravine. I will lead you, and may the blessing of Allah follow the life and enlighten the tomb of him who finds her."

He turned to us.

"None but mountain men can risk the ravine after dark. Courage will not do it; it means skill, and we must not have a hurt man on our hands. Go down, gentlemen, and eat and sleep. We will come back when we have cleared up the ravine as far as human feet could have carried her."

He was at the head. Nothing but obedience was possible. I have said little of what I felt during that dreadful afternoon, and it would be impossible, for I was too ignorant of the country to gage either hopes or fears. Ormond's words weighed with me most, yet still I believed she might be lying senseless in some hole or shaft of the terrible scattered rocks. The day that began so happily had ended in cruel grief and suspense, and when we got down the winding trail and into the castle, night had fallen on the frightful solitudes about the little town, bringing the added misery of certainty that Brynhild was lost in the darkness, uncomforted and alone.

Lady Lucia was in the hall pale to the lips, but perfectly self-controlled, and beside her a slight figure veiled from head to foot, and two veiled women in the background, silent as statues.

"It is the khanum," she said, as we came in, "and she has done her best to comfort me. She tells me of a woman who broke her ankle and was lost for two days on the plateau, and they found her safe and well at last."

"It is true," said a low voice from under the veil. "But yet my heart is sore for my sweet sister. It is in my mind that perhaps— What has his Highness said?"

"He is searching the ravine, Highness," said Dunbar, hat in hand. "He still hopes as you do. But what else do you think possible?"

I felt her hidden eyes turn toward Ormond.

"There was also a woman two years since who was carried off to Kotchak and held to ransom. The daughter of one of our *tahsildárs*." She hesitated and was silent.

"Highness, what happened? We must know," Ormond said urgently, pushing forward from behind Dunbar. "We are not children but men, and what there is to hear we can hear."

"It is true," answered the sweet voice from under the veil. "Then hear. My husband, the khan, was down in Kashmir and I with him, and though the people in the town made up what money they could it was not enough—and they killed her. They dare not do this to an Englishwoman, for they fear the British Sirkar and the khan's heavy hand, but they would sell their honor for money and count it nothing."

"That is my thought also," said Ormond, and fell back again behind Dunbar. Looking at his face I saw him lost in thought, unconscious of the storm of talk and argument which followed. Presently he slipped away and up the winding stair to his room. I understood his purpose very well.

It was late in the night when the khan returned with his men, wearied and fordone, but still with the set of a steel spring coiled to break loose in destruction of all in its way. His wife, still veiled, sat by Lady Lucia, holding her hand as though to strengthen her in the danger. Sometimes they had spoken together in Hindustani—soft unknown words—the only sound to break the silence of suspense. They both rose as he swung in, and she salaamed, something in her attitude expressing the perfect faith and adoring love of the Oriental wife. His look swept over her and caught Dunbar and me standing behind them.

"This is work for men, not women!" he said curtly. "Though I am glad the khanum should be in her place to give comfort to those who need it. For myself, Dunbar Sahib, I unsay my words. I, together with the elders of my men, believe the unbelievable has happened and that the Lambakhis have carried her off. It is like the work of jinn if it be so for we can find no track at all. But tomorrow my men and I will go up to Kotchak, and I swear on the soul of my father and the mercy of the Compassionate that they shall pay in blood for every hair of the woman's head. Go now and take what sleep you can that we may be ready. For myself, I have work to do."

He turned to his men, and though I could not understand a word it was easy to see that directions, orders, consultation were passing from mouth to mouth of the furious men who crowded about him. There was the Orient in all its pride and anger. It was not Brynhild nor pity—it was the fury of men deprived of the woman in their guard and therefore a symbol of their power. Alam Khan was an Oriental again—his English training shed from him as men shed a worthless garment.

The khanum put a gentle arm about Lady Lucia and led her from the room followed by the two silent women. No place for them when men were on the war-path! Even at that moment I saw that there is something amazingly touching in that soft submissiveness of the Oriental wife with her pliability to the law of her own being as the perfect complement of man. Dunbar soon followed, seeing the khan's wish to be alone with his people, and I with him.

How soon had the gay surface fraternity of East and West which made the charm of Satshang broken asunder, revealing abysses of unbridgeable differences beneath.

For myself I could not sleep. I sat in my window watching the great constellations rolling in solemn procession about the mountains, my mind tossed like the torn peaks with fear and grief. Gradually the great calm of the night dominated by a moon of serenest majesty calmed me a little, and from the delirium of fear and helpless misery—for what is it ever but delirium?—I sank into a kind of quiet that enabled me to look into my own heart as I had never looked before.

Is it that the fear and grief we are rightly taught to despise in themselves tear asunder the veiling curtains, break down the bars and open the way from the prison of selfhood to the Reality outside? How can I tell? But I know this—I had in that moment what I can only describe as a marvelous flash of knowledge. I saw the world and all that is in it only as the attempt at manifestation of some great Idea sitting enthroned above us—I saw myself, saw the woman I loved (for I knew in that moment that I loved her with all my heart and soul) as partial manifestation of the Ideal which was eternally her and myself, one and yet diverse as are differing parts of the same body, and I knew that whether in Heaven or Hell or the eternities neither one of us could in truth suffer any hurt or shame or pain. That, if she did not love me as the world understands the love of man and woman, still in the highest she must love me through life and death and eternity with the only love that is immortal. I might and would fall short of the ideal that was truly me. I might work it out like a very unskilled Pygmalion from the rough marble in which my psyche slept like a beautiful and hidden Galatea, but none the less it was there, and mine the only hand that could release it to the sunlight. To labor at this and extricate it, so that it might be some sort of offering to lay at Brynhild's feet whether she lived or died, became from that moment one of my unchangeable stars of direction, and that not because she was Brynhild but was a spoken word of revelation to me.

This brought a great peace with it. Far below I heard the river running in hoarse music broken by the torture of the rocks to its home in the mighty Indus and beyond that in the ocean. And it became the voice of my own life, flowing through obscuring mountains and gorges to the infinite beyond.

I sat until I could endure the weight of comprehension no longer, then, lying down dressed and ready for the earliest call to arms, I slept without dream or ruffle until a great sun struck the eastern windows with a clarion cry of light. And it was day.

CHAPTER XX

We Englishmen marched with the khan's troops next morning, leaving a guard for the town of Satshang and the castle, and Lady Lucia in the khanum's care. Perhaps it would be truer to say the khanum was in her care for her perfect self-possession was an armed guard wherever she went. It was a part of her yoga that people turned naturally to her in trouble, leaned upon her and took her strength for theirs. I remember Ormond saying one day that she made everyone about her feel greater; any effort seemed possible in the truth and courage of her eyes. Afterwards when I knew her story I understood this better. She had been in deep waters and had brought the Pearl from the depths.

So we marched up the plateau of yesterday—ourselves with Tazaki and the khan's officers on mountain ponies, the men on foot. Their arms were a little mixed in date—ranging from swords and brass-studded hide shields to all that is most modern in the way of rifles, and four Gatling guns, the pride of the khan's heart, followed dragged by ponies. Before us went tom-toms beaten not only with the usual stroke but also in a strange rolling fashion after the manner of drums. The rear was brought up by ponies loaded with food and ammunition.

There could be no secrecy about the attack, for it was certain that every upper crag would hide the glittering, roving eyes of a Lambakhi scout. The khan with Dunbar (whose military knowledge had been trained in the Great War) sifted Ormond for every scrap of information which could be turned to account concerning the Lambakhis and their defenses. The most important appeared to be a great clay fort commanding the track upward from the Satshang Valley to Kotchak.

Very little was said even among ourselves as we trekked on and up. All our hopes and conjectures were long since exhausted, and nothing remained but action. I would willingly have ridden with Ormond, but he kept himself to himself, lost in thought as his pony climbed the steepening way. Once I pulled my pony up with his and asked a question.

"Ormond, have you seen or heard anything to give us hope?"

"I have seen and heard some things, but I must wait like others. And it is not hope but certainty that one feels about her. What can go wrong with her? You know as well as I that she is safe."

I fell back. That was true, but yet the mortal in us shrinks from the desecrations of fear and pain. It was then that for the first time in this grief my heart shot back to my master and the quiet room in the Lamasery of the Manis. I saw it in its wide bareness, with windows open to the glory of the mountains, the sun pouring in a torrent of running gold down their snowy slopes. He stood there looking out and up.

I could be sure of that though only a bit of his profile was visible, and it was as if he were loosing thoughts like birds to fly to hidden dove-cotes in the summits. I suppose it was only memory and my certainty of what he would be doing that brought him so vividly before me, for indeed it was as if I saw through and over many leagues of the wildest mountains in the world's deserted places into the room I knew so well.

What would he say? What feel in such an emergency as ours? Amazing to tell, as the thought crossed my mind, I seemed through the dull drumming of the tom-tom to hear him speak. But was it hearing or only the suggestion, articulate in my own mind? At all events I believed I heard the strong monotone of his voice as I had heard it so often.

"When a man has learned a truth how can he know he holds it with anything deeper than the brain unless he tests it? And what is the reasoning brain? A creature of dust. If your whole soul has assented to my teaching do now what reason tells you you cannot do. Give it the lie. Call me across the mountains and force me to obedience. For we are one in the One."

The men, including myself, were trudging up a track so steep that I knew I must dismount within the next minute or two to ease the pony. That was the surface thought in my mind—that and the antlike appearance of the men streaming out a little on either side to attack the hill sideways as they climbed. Now, will it be believed—but it is true—that, shattering all those thoughts and impressions, came to me a conviction terrible in its magnitude? It was that of power. I felt like a man with his hand on the wheel of some enormous machine capable of devastating the universe if he loosed it without guidance. This resolved itself into one word—"Come"—almost breaking the vessel of my heart with its expansion as it passed through me. And immediately, dropping the reins on my pony's neck and lifting my eyes, I saw that on a rock above me there stood the Man of the Monastery of the Manis.

Now let it be remembered that we were many days' march from the Manis by a way of terror unless with guides and favorable weather— But why should I protest? I knew in my soul what had happened and needed no witness of reason. Power had come to me unworthy, and I had used it as a child does to grasp at the nearest strength for protection. That is what power in man must always mean until he has reached the highest. Then he will take the last step and learn that he himself is the Eternal Strength and invoke that and that only.

He leaned against a jut of rock as I had seen him lean against the window, a little only of his face visible, the breeze ruffling the robe about his feet. And now I was conscious of the men climbing past him, some so near that they could have touched him as they went. I was conscious also that they neither saw nor heard him. Only—and this is strange—as Ormond rode past, he halted his pony for the tenth of a second and looking upward smiled and rode on. The vision was mine to me otherwise.

As I passed, my pony swayed sideways against the rock and halted. The men climbed on without looking at me, trudging monotonously by. The figure bent a little downward as if to speak in my ear, but again no one noticed. The next two men looked listlessly at me and trudged past.

"Get rid of the body idea," he said. "The body can fetter only its devotees. I am here, but the cast sheath lies in the Monastery of the Manis."

One thought and one only passed me at the moment.

"Can you go to her? Can you strengthen her? Where is she?"

I saw a motion in the cloth that hung over his face as though he laughed.

"She has her own strength. She undergoes her discipline and will not fail. Think yourself to her if you have the strength, and see."

I looked up hoping to meet his eyes, and there was nothing. The empty rock stood there, and the men were climbing monotonously past it, and I had dropped out of line and must hurry up.

Strength? I could call for help but could not possess it. I tried to push on abreast of Ormond and after a while succeeded.

"You saw?" I said breathlessly.

"I saw. And the message?"

"She undergoes her discipline. She will not fail."

"It needed no message to tell me that. The gates of life and death are both open for a soul like hers."

"And have you no fear for her?"

"None. But I have a very great desire to teach the Lambakhis the lesson they need. For their sakes as well as ours that particular sort of mischief can't be allowed."

I fell back.

It is no necessity to my story to describe that heavy march with the unbearable delay for the night at the Fort of Hassan, as bitter to Alam Khan as to Ormond, Dunbar and myself. A white blaze of anger consumed that man until his guest should be safe once more under the shadow of his sword, and his men shared it. To them too it was black insult and dishonor that she should have been dragged away from them like a stray sheep, and they fretted and fumed even over the boiling caldrons of mutton, the camp-fires and stories. For who can bridle a mountain man's tongue when the wild lights flicker and flame on the dark?

Next day they swaggered on, full of boasts and threats against the Lambakhis, and it was a strange sight to watch them crossing a mountain torrent on a bamboo bridge flung over it. Here the ponies were left, for it was impossible for them to cross, and the column went on, on its feet.

We passed several blockhouses at intervals which the khan had put upon the higher part of his country and occupied with small guards. Nothing more desolate can be imagined, but they were an immense help to the advance, for grain and provisions of the roughest sort had been stored there for eventualities. It was here we met a Kashmiri Mohammedan fakir on his way down from the Lambakhi country, who, having the reputation of a holy man, could come and go in safety among all the hill tribes, be their religion what it might. Alam Khan had him brought in for question, and we Englishmen were invited to hear.

He stood up before us all, gaunt, with a weather-stained, tattered robe girt up about his knees, a turban of many convolutions surmounting black eyes and splendid aquiline features, majestic as an old Hebrew patriarch's, with snowy beard and sweeping mustaches.

The khan, also a man trained in Islam, saluted him with deference, and put the story of our advance before him in a few words.

"And if your holiness has seen the English lady or can tell us anything of these sons of stoned hill devils it will be well."

Before and when he spoke I noticed the princely manners of this miserably dressed old wanderer. That is a point on which we might learn much from the East before our hail-fellow-well-met civilization destroys the grace and dignity of its intercourse. It was the same everywhere. Servants, pandits, whoever it might be, they spoke with dignity and stately absence of emotion (unless indeed money were in question with the Kashmiris) which made one feel a bit cheap and second-rate in one's hurry. This man answered as prince to prince:

"Highness, I am come from Kotchak where the Lambakhis gave me food and shelter and sent me on my journey in peace. None the less they are a low people, brutal, cruel, and their women each live with many men in a marriage stinking in the nostrils of Allah and his saints. I have seen the Englishwoman. She walks among them high of heart like a being of the Paradise, and when a man great among them dared to approach too near her presence she took him by the arms and flung him over her shoulder like a child, and he lay there ashamed, and the people laughed in his face."

That was the Japanese ju-jutsu! Tazaki, standing at his master's shoulder, kindled with pride. Unless against guns or surrounded, a woman armed with that weapon could give a good account of herself.

"And is she well treated?" asked Alam Khan, his face kindling also, for courage will touch the Oriental as nothing else but holiness can.

"She has a hut and a woman to attend her, and they offered goat's and sheep's flesh; but this she refused, eating only bread and dried apricots. And they let her alone for time to tame, and even now their scouts come to meet you demanding a ransom."

"Does your Holiness know how they captured her?"

"She gathered flowers among the rocks above the plateau, and two Lambakhi men watched, because word was sent up the hills that two most beautiful Englishwomen were come to Satshang from the Manis, and their greed considered a ransom. The other woman they could not take for a man of a strange race but resembling a Gurkha was always on guard at her shoulder. But their chief, the son of a stoned dog, says openly that the day will come when he will have the wife of the khan to be his bondslave and the strings of her pajamas his."

Even through my absorption in Ormond's interpretation of the words and my pride in Brynhild, I was compelled to see the fury of the khan's face. Pale under his olive skin, the blue veins knotted on his forehead, retracted lips showing a line of teeth, he could not command his voice for a moment, but stood with a hand clenched on the hilt of his sword, the knuckles white as parchment. I looked for a furious torrent of rage. He mastered himself, and when he spoke his voice was dry and small but all the more terrible.

"Holiness, eat and sleep under the shadow of our protection and take this chit with you to Satshang that they may receive you with honor. We start now this instant; yet before we go is there any word you would say of their defenses and the best road of attack?"

The fakir made a deprecating gesture with his hands, looking the khan calmly in the face.

"Highness, I have eaten their bread and salt. Of this I cannot speak. But I will say that the Englishwoman is worth a king's ransom, for she moved like a warrior among them. And this also I will say, for it is a thing to be remembered. At her shoulder where she went, went a man with a hidden face, and none saw him but myself, for these low people have eyes that see not the great spirits. But her guard is strong whether for life or death; and how can these idolaters touch a daughter of the Book?"

For so the Moslems call the Christians and Jews who share the Scriptures and the prophets with them. I caught Ormond's look, mingled joy and wonder. A sense of great spiritual events was upon me, of admission to wonders beyond my deserts. Just as my feet walked in the mountains and my eyes beheld splendor among them, so it seemed I walked in the high spiritual countries among austerities and majesties unknown to me until now.

Where was the man who had loitered and laughed with the Mainguys at Simla, who had begun and ended each day yawning with weariness at the limits of his petty world but expecting nothing further? Gone, lost, buried in a man who beholds the infinite horizon from the ascent of the mountains where his way lies onward.

Said Alam Khan: "If they touch a hair of her head—" and bridled himself instantly.

The fakir salaamed. "Highness, this they dare not, unless indeed in desperation they kill her. See the Lambakhi envoys. And now I depart."

"Take this chit to the khanum. I give orders that they guard you as a king's deposit. The peace go with you."

"May the peace be upon you and upon you the peace," replied the fakir, and taking a gift of food departed on his downward way.

Before he was out of sight we were marching upward steadily.

"Does she see him herself? Does she know he is there?" I asked Ormond under my breath. He made no reply, seeming not to hear. Dunbar at my shoulder answered for him.

"What there is to see she sees. I don't doubt that. But don't let us deceive ourselves. Spiritual help is for spiritual needs. It doesn't follow that he can save her body because he can strengthen her soul."

I saw his point. We went on our way with what speed we might. We had marched perhaps a mile when the advance guard notified us that the Lambakhi envoys, if one can so call the bloodthirsty scoundrels, were in sight making gestures for parley.

Alam Khan, splendid among his officers, icy-silent, haughty and aloof as a mountain eagle, halted and waited for their approach, and we at his shoulder waited also. I can see Ormond now, tranquil among the turbulent, assured, prepared. There were many moments when I steadied myself on him, for no vision had come to me since the reflections in the mirror of the passing show had caught my eyes with their glitter and dimmed the reality behind them.

"Let them stand far off, Safdar Ali," said the khan sternly. "What have we to do with murderers, robbers of women, sons of hill-bitches spawned to unknown fathers? The air round them is filthy."

The scowling men stared at him with eyes filled with hate.

"Speak less haughtily, Mussulman dog, for the woman is ours to use, to torture or defile as we will. Hear the terms of the *thoom* our master. He demands in English money ten thousand pounds, a hundred sheep and a ram of the stock you had from Kashmir. And four necklaces of red, blue, white and green jewels and two *peyraks* of turquoise, no stone less in size than an orange pip, for the wives of the thoom. If these things are put in our hands within a week the woman shall come back as she went, and no word more said. And further, Ramghat will give his promise that for a year and a day there shall be no raiding, insomuch that if you left a ram collared with turquoise on the hills, he should come and go in safety."

I saw the khan's eyes flash lightning and the fierce refusal in his look, but Dunbar intervened, speaking in English, with all the circle of eager, uncomprehending eyes fixed on him.

"Highness, we must not risk her life. We must consider. What is money? I will give it gladly, but we must discuss and gain time."

"We must discuss and gain time," repeated the khan with a look I could not interpret. "It is needful; for who can trust these and their like?" He turned to them with a gesture of proud repulsion.

"Come here again in two days' time for my answer. Little as thieves deserve it you shall go and come in the peace of Allah. But if a finger is laid on the woman—"

"That shall be as the thoom pleases. But he does not please," answered the other indifferently. "Have your money ready, for the Lambakhis do not delay on their bargains, and the woman is no more to us than a stray sheep. And take this for truth. If you attack, we will cut her throat."

"And bring the whole British Raj on you? You will do well! Take these murderers of women out through the camp," Alam Khan said to the aide-de-camp at his shoulder.

They were gone and discussion raged fast and furious, the khan declaring that they would never dare to carry out their threat and that it was safer to rush their fort instantly than to trust to their promises. They were capable of taking the money and restoring their prisoner so poisoned that she would die in a week. Had not their chief murdered his own father by sending him a robe of honor in which a man had died of confluent smallpox, and so opening his own way to power? No. Let but the British sahibs agree, and before the two days were out the Lambakhi stronghold should be in their hands and the hive of wild bees which had stung all the countryside smoked out. The bloodthirsty brutes had not a friend far or near. Would Ormond Sahib repeat his story of their defenses?

Ormond rose, requesting that all might be dismissed excepting the khan's chief soldier and counselor, Mohammed Shah. This was done and those left sat in silence to hear. His voice followed the anger of the khan like the lull after a storm.

In a few words he described Kotchak, saying he had good reason for belief that the Lambakhis had mined their approaches with gunpowder made by themselves after the manner of the tribes. But in view of the threat and other matters which had come to his knowledge he was in favor of waiting two days for developments and of not attacking until all other means were exhausted. He fully agreed with the khan that there might be gross treachery in the manner of her return after a ransom. He then added:

"Highness, the Miss Sahib stands in great danger, but remember the words of the fakir—that a man goes at her shoulder who is her guard."

That could not appeal to the English-trained Mohammedanism of the khan.

"If he goes at her shoulder let him guard her while we attack. What is this child's talk for men? If he is there it is a reason the more for our attack."

Ormond continued as calmly as if he had heard nothing:

"My counsel is that we do not move until two days are done. Then, if it is so decided, we can give a *hoondi* for the money to the thoom's men, and if not, we can attack. Between this and then, knowledge and counsel will be given us. Wait two days. Our way will be made clear."

The decision was a terrible one to make, either for attack or delay. Even Dunbar looked doubtful.

"Attack seems out of the question," he said. "Should we not instantly provide the ransom? Cardonald, what do you say?"

I tried to steady myself on Ormond and the knowledge I had gained. What could it be worth to her if like a hasty child I snatched at the feeble war or money weapon, at which the Lambakhis could beat us any day with Brynhild for a hostage, instead of defending her with the spear and sword of the higher knowledge and wisdom?

"I agree with Ormond Sahib," I said. "Let us wait two days. The money can be held ready, but help will come before."

Let the Divine have its way with us. Give it time. That was Ormond's thought, and I knew he was right. I was followed by the man who stood behind the khan, Mohammed Shah, a man no longer young and the very embodiment of reserve and fanaticisms which might in a crisis take the most unexpected directions.

"Highness, I have heard the fakir and the two sahibs, and I say there is more in this than a man can quickly understand, and if great things are at work mortal man must make room. Wait, if it were only twenty-four hours. These men have seen what we have not. They testify of the unknown. Moreover, the dogs will most certainly cut her throat if we attack, and make off to the heights; and how shall we crush them? Let the money be procured. And if in twenty-four hours the Unknown has not acted let us go forward as to a *jehad* [religious war] and fight in the very spirit of Islam."

So it came to a compromise, for Dunbar also came in on our side with all his weight. The khan, chafing like a bound lion, agreed to twenty-four hours before making a move. The money arrangements were put in train. Ormond and I went out into the glittering night for the stars shone over the mountains in glory, the moon still hidden in the caves where according to the Greeks she sits "weaving delicate thoughts." I stood to re-collect my thoughts in the immense tranquillity.

"Twenty-four hours," said Ormond, speaking in a voice which seemed a part of the quiet. "Now let us see. Have you ever guessed who your master is, Cardonald?"

I shook my head. If I had wondered at first who he might be, I had soon lost the outward circumstance of the man in what he was in the essential. "A great man. A wise man. But what does it matter?"

"It matters. It is in my mind that he and he only can at this point help us, and through you. Did you hear down at Baltar talk of a monk who had known the great Chinese pilgrim Hiuen Tsang nearly fourteen hundred years ago, who had then disappeared into Tibet and of whom they tell the story that to this day he is manifested when there is need for his presence?"

My senses could not pierce the meaning of his words. I stared at him with feelings indescribable. There are things so far beyond reason and belief that only intuition—the highest quality in man, that by which he springs to his union with the divine—can meet them at any point of contact, and intention in me was clouded for the moment by the clash of argument and fear.

"You cannot mean it—impossible! Impossible," I said. "This is sheer madness."

"What is impossible? And who is the judge of it? What do we know of the springs of life and death? Because we have always seen and believed certain things is there to be nothing beyond them and the witness of our five senses? I say no more. Consider what you have learned, and realize what you yourself are, if no more."

He turned in the shadows and was gone. Following the khan's orders the camp was now quiet as death, but what chance had I of sleep? I climbed a little bluff of rock beside me and finding a nook that looked out and over the vastness of the mighty ghosts of mountains dim in starlight I set myself to the crisis—the true battlefield of my soul.

And first it seemed that if it were true such a revelation as Ormond's must have come in thunder and lightning and some annihilating outburst of power, and not in a few quiet words spoken in the starlight quiet of night. How could I be expected to believe? And what was the sense of it? Why should an unknown Buddhist monk have been permitted to survive, a monument and a marvel when the greater Hiuen Tsang had trodden the way to the silence like all the rest of the bewildered world? I pass over the unwavering human certainty that nothing exists or is credible but what is within its own comprehension. That is so well known to one and all that no words need be wasted on it. But, in that majestic solitude, realization of my own inexpressible littleness gradually permeated my pride like the soaking and filtering of water into arid sand.

How could I limit the powers or guess the vast designs of the love that guides the world and the other stars? To recognize and obey was my part. But if it were true—if the wisdom poured out at my feet came from a source so supernormal, so astounding, what could I do to be worthy of the least word of it? That wave swept me upward—then came the ebbing reaction. How easily Ormond might be mistaken, superstition, reason loosened by the solitude and overpowering majesty of the country where he had buried himself for so long. That lasted awhile and passing left me face to face with myself bound in the prison of my own selfhood, darkening even the light which had been vouchsafed to me—a puny midget industriously building out light and air from his dungeon, content with the underworld. Oh, the eons of experience and wisdom needed to free and lift me into the clear spaces where Ormond walked with his face set to the dawning east!

Then with a sweep of her besom that drove the cobwebs from my brain, reason confronted me with the cold beauty of Pallas Athene. Did I not know that the mathematicians with their white light shining on the only certainty in human knowledge are even now finding their way through the bewildering reflections of this world's knowledge to the truth taught by the Buddha long since, that interpenetrating and permeating this world of ours (which is merely the product and summing up of our fallible senses) is the true universe, the one reality, to be perceived only by those illuminated and in flashes of the higher consciousness—the world where nothing is as we know it here, the country whence the shadows fall which we in our ignorance protest are the only infallible originals? What do they mean by their theory which reverses all our reason built on the tripod of length, breadth and height, by presenting a fourth dimension, a spatial consciousness which sees us face to face with the impossible in physics and logic as the truth concealed behind all the scriptures, myths and legends of all the faiths? What if that were the only truth and those people, my friends, had found their way to it—not by the toilsome road of mathematical science but the winged flight of spiritual intuition and the road prescribed by the yogins of ancient India in which I myself had set a few faltering steps?

I condense my thoughts—a tumult of fears and doubts and hopes—into the moment when I resolved to trust to the intuitions and knowledge of those about me, uniting them with my own glimpses of knowledge and experience, and to advance into darkness trusting to a light burning behind the many veils. And if it seem strange that I had so often glimpsed, so often fallen again into materialism, I can only offer as an explanation that the swift vibration of understanding seems to be almost invariably followed by the slow reaction of materialism, as if the expiring strength of the body exerted itself to recapture the winged psyche escaping from the chrysalis.

After a while, still sitting there watching the dim light invading the sky which soon would be the moon's orbed glory, the true self in me broke through into communion with power, and with power came sight. I saw that the only help I could give her came from that source—that only. The body is a hindrance and weakness. It is only the soul—the One—to which obstacles are nothing. And I felt in myself a tide of power rising like the sweep of a great billow. I began to believe in myself—not in the little ego of every day but the true underlying self which is a part of the One. I remembered an ancient story told me by my mysterious master in the Monastery of the Manis.

Two birds sat on the same bough. The lower bird ate the acrid fruit of the tree of earthly knowledge and experience. Suddenly aroused by its bitterness he looked up and saw the other motionless, submerged in the contemplation of his own glory. And the bird of earth crept upward upon the bough until the ray fell on him also and lo! he was resumed into the bird of heaven. His supposed individuality had been but a shadow, a reflection of the other, cast among the lower branches, and only the rayed bird of heaven remained.

Great flashes of light dazzled my eyes, whether within or without I cannot tell. They came and went, sweeping and orbing into a steady splendor like a rising sun. Was it daylight? What was it? I saw myself transfigured, caught up— That was the truth—the truth! Then I too was the divine, the deathless—and like a cry in my soul came these words.

"I am neither man nor angel. I am boundless and sexless. I am Knowledge. I am THAT. I have neither anger nor hatred, nor pain nor pleasure. I am birthless and deathless. I am Absolute Bliss. I am He, my soul, I am He."

Now how can I say what followed and the amazing sense of freedom—the slave enfranchised laughing at his broken bonds—which possessed me? It is impossible—there are no words, no thoughts, which can convey the knowledge beyond all wisdom which sweeps in conquering and to conquer. I assert the incredible and am silent.

But this is the simple truth. I sat all night in ecstasy, pouring floods of strength to Brynhild that left me the stronger, transcending all limits of personal consciousness and flowing into hers, the false ego relinquished as one disinhabits the worn-out body when Death the Enfranchiser stands like the Angel at the Gate. I was with her. I held her hand. We walked together in a great darkness—but together. All night I sat and did not know it. For me time was no more. When the dark was thinning like water I heard feet brushing the grass, and starting up saw a woman winding between the rocks from the east—the coming of light already on her face. Far off she stood and beckoned. No sentry heard or challenged, and in the dusk of dawn I clambered down the rock and went as if in a dream to meet her. It was Brynhild and by her side stood my master.

CHAPTER XXI

THEY WERE SIDE BY SIDE—SHE PALE AS FROM THE passage of the storm of some bitter experience. She stood with fixed eyes looking into the sky above and beyond me as if in a dream not wholly sad but very strange and painful.

My master spoke:

"You took her by the hand and led her out and all slept and none stood in the way. And a light of her presence is left behind to be the beginning of an illumination in the heart of these people, for in them also sits divinity waiting its day. And for me, disciple, my work with you is done. It was completed this night when a great light shined for you, and you knew it and were glad. . . . If clouds darken do not fear. Walk always dawnward, and when you see me no more remember how you put out strength and with this saved this woman whom you love. What has been done may be done again."

I stood trembling from head to foot. Speechless, yet something urged me past all resistance. I caught his hand—which I had never touched before and he did not draw it from me. I knew that the hidden eyes dwelt on me with kindness and it gave me strength to plead my gratitude. But before I could say a word he spoke again.

"Disciple, I am Ananda, the beloved disciple of the Perfect One, the Buddha; and to me, because I delayed to enter the Final Knowledge and have known in myself the feebleness of human vision and the perfection of the beauty of human love raised into the divine, it is given to walk on earth aiding and uplifting until He returns again in His incarnation of Love. Where man needs me there am I, coming and going throughout the world forever in bliss and wisdom, known by many names and in many faiths. Sometimes I am the Diamond Scepter, sometimes the Illuminated Pearl, but always the jewel in the hand of the Perfect One, Son of the World-Honored. In a former life you sat at His feet and fell from wisdom. Raise your head now and learn through love."

He threw back his hood and looked at me with eyes like sunlight on an unfathomable ocean. Before me was the face, unsearchable in beauty, of the beloved disciple who guarded the Buddha in life and death, —wonderful, beautiful, high, remote—yet most near, most near. And at such feet I had sat and had not known, had learned and had not guessed! My hands dropped, but my soul held him. Already it seemed his form was thinning, receding, but I would not let him go. His eyes had beheld the divinest life ever lived on earth, had drunk in its unsearchable wisdom and Godhead, his feet had faltered, held back by the weakness of human love from following his Master, until, released into perfect self-knowledge and control, leaving all frailty behind, he had followed into the Way of Peace.

"Son of the Perfect One, yourself divine in knowledge and power, open your eyes to your strength and close them on your weakness. I bless you to all the uses of life and the beatitudes of death and the Beyond."

There was a long silence, and while it lasted the world wavered before me like a thing seen through the rippling of water. When I could see clearly nothing was there. Nothing but the world, divine in the realization of its own Godhead and in the east the miracle of dawn. By what does the life we call human subsist but by drawing energy from the sun through the medium of food? And to those who *know* are there not finer ways of partaking of the universal energy through the mind and spirit and so transcending the grosser corporeal needs, transfiguring the body itself into the perfect vehicle of will? To such, human life and death have the same meaning, and both are only transitory ideas, little passing bubbles on the surface of Real Existence.

Stunned, transfigured, beaten down yet raised to knowledge incredible, the song of freedom in my soul like the shouting of the sons of God, the song of the morning star, I turned to Brynhild. She still stood with her hands dropped beside her and the fixed look of pain on her face. For the first time I knew myself the stronger and had no fear in approaching her. She wavered as she stood like one who breaks under the burden of a long strain. I put my arm about her for support, and she turned and looked at me doubtfully as if near the waking point of a painful dream. It seemed that she was scarcely conscious of who I was. She spoke uncertainly and haltingly:

"I came away. I must have walked in my sleep. It was night and now it is day."

I could not speak. Her weakness was like the clinging self-pity of a lost child.

We stood a long while, I supporting her, while consciousness came slowly back, fluttering palely about her lips and cheeks, not yet touching her eyes. She swayed toward me, leaning against my shoulders. Presently:

"I can see more clearly now. It was you that came in my sleep. Wonderful. You took my hand and led me out and down through the rocks. In the night —in the dark. Nothing could keep you back. You came."

How could I deny it? It might be. What cannot love do? I moved in the midst of truth of the utmost simplicity yet seen by me as a marvel.

"You came," she repeated with wearied insistence.

A new Brynhild. I had never known her. We stood, she leaning against me as the sun's rim gleamed above the horizon. The miracle was accomplished; he had risen flooding the world with light.

Then, loosing herself from my arm she turned and looked at me, golden in the fire of the dawn. How can I tell what followed?

India has spoken for me so often that she may well speak in that great moment of my life.

"Four eyes met. There were changes in two souls. And now I cannot tell whether he is a man and I a woman, or he a woman and I a man. This only I remember: Two souls were. Love came; there was One."

The camp was alive with the sun. After a few

moments, she leading the way, we went down to it and I heard a great shout of welcome.

An hour later Mohammed Shah came to me as I stood alone:

"Cardonald Sahib, it was the man who went at her shoulder, was it not? The Miss Sahib says she walked in her sleep, but surely in sleep the power of the saints is made known. We have seen a great thing, but men will not know it."

"We have seen a great thing," I repeated, "but men will not know."

CHAPTER XXII

Little summing up is necessary. Marriage in the thought of India is a specialized service, as true monasticism is a universal one. The last was Ormond's. The first was ours. Yet marriage itself when its special ends are accomplished tends in India to be merged in higher aspects of mutual service undisturbed by implications of sex, and writing now I see that development latent in our happy present. Latent also in the artist's yoga which has fallen to my wife and me as of witness-bearers to the beauty of form and color representing their facet of the Eternal Ideal.

Before us lay the ascending degrees of yoga, or concentration, through which we must ascend to higher and higher planes of consciousness, and there would now be little let or hindrance in the way. Since we had learned that all life is mind, all development differing degrees of concentration, I had no cravings for signs and wonders, nor had Brynhild. Such as had fallen in our way appeared to us only as the differing points of view necessarily gained in ascending a mountain, not as a veritably changed world. Familiar objects change their places; others glide into the foreground; the landscape from which one has climbed becomes a map spread out, the ways clearly marked and understood now that they are left forever.

My experiences remain in my mind not as miracles but as the manifestation of laws of which I understand the beginning, to be classified later, and more accurately than I can now hope to achieve it, by exact science guided by spiritual vision. Such things will be the daily happenings of a world permeated by the higher consciousness, and will enormously enlarge the scope of human vision. Thus we shall turn the illuminated pages of the book of Nature, recognizing her as the manifestation of the Divine, no longer as His painted veil.

From our own fastness in the Himalayan hills of Kashmir, with the beneficent powers of the Dunbars working beside us and Ormond coming and going like a star upon his orbit of light-giving, I watch with delight the increasing insight and spirituality of science, untroubled as it is by sentiment and emotion, and the more surely guiding East and West to the knowledge of the marvels amongst which we move unseeing. Yoga is undoubtedly the science of religion, taking us beyond the boundary of the senses into the world which mathematical science begins to apprehend as a dim presence transcending and disusing all the old maxims of geometry—the world of marvels come true, and yet itself only a step to the threshold of a higher consciousness above and beyond it.

I have learned also that no man must have a fixed ideal enthroned in the sculptured beauty of dead marble. That is death. The ideal must change and become transfigured with each rising step of consciousness, and none must fear to deny his former convictions or to follow where the new lead him. That they may lead him into strange and difficult places I do not deny, but he will walk in the midst of fire unharmed and rejoicing. I have learned many things since I wrote this story, but it is better left in all its stammering, ignorant record of experiences because this is a way by which others may climb. Some day I may record what I have gained since, if there are any who care to hear.

A part of this being read to Ormond, he objected that in my recording these events I had made it appear that the way is for the treading only of people of high and intellectual power or the deep and searching insight given by many-lived experiences of the upward climb. Unless I have indicated this in my horror of sentimentality and emotion and the pursuit of metaphysical pleasures in religion I scarcely see how I have suggested such a false idea, but in case it has been possible let me end with what is perhaps one of the most passionately beautiful idealizations in ancient Buddhist literature of those "poor in spirit" who seek the kingdom and its splendors in all humility. It speaks for itself better than I can speak for it.

> The Blessed One passed by my house—
> *My* house, the Barber's!
> I ran, and He turned and awaited me.
> *Me,* the Barber.
> I said, "May I speak, O Lord, with thee?"
> And He said, "Yes!"
> Yes. To *me,* the Barber!
> And I said, "Is the Peace for such as I?"
> And He said, "Yes."
> Even for *me,* the Barber!
> And I said, "May I follow after Thee?"

And He said, "Yes."
Even I, the Barber!
And I said, "May I stay, O Lord, near Thee?"
And He said, "Thou mayest."
Even to *me*—the poor Barber.

Such is the song of the outcast Barber, later the writer of a great Buddhist scripture. With that I close. The way is open to all, and all must eventually walk in it. But sooner—sooner than later, I pray for myself and for all the world.

THE END